THE BROAD IN THE KIMONO

Paddy Kelly

THE BROAD IN THE KIMONO

FICTION4ALL

ISBN 978 1 78695 307 0

Cover Design by Paddy Kelly
Graphics by Pedro Sperando

This edition published by
Fiction4All
Tadworth, England

Edited by
Katherine Mary Kennedy, B.A.

British Library Cataloguing & Publication Data available.

Paddy Kelly

**This work is
Dedicated to:**

**The most important two little broads in my
life:**

Katherine Mary & Erin Elizabeth

Paddy Kelly

INTRODUCTION

The political turmoil which now permeates The United States is by no means new. As embattled as the two political parties are, the divisiveness, lies and dirty politics we now witness daily has happened before in The Swamp called Washington D.C.

In the immediate aftermath of the Allies' victory of WWII many saw their opportunity to cash in on the 'big win', not least of which were the politicians and members of organized crime.

The exuberation of the 1930's New Deal spawned a new transition to a wartime production economy and the resultant production mentality required to win the war quickly transitioned the national zeitgeist into an unbridled, all out production-based Capitalism virtually overnight.

However, the exuberant ether of forced optimism brought on by FDR's tackling of the Great Depression and WWII was followed by a late1940's, post war let-down of the crushed social revolution the much needed economic reforms of the New Deal had spawned.

As one 1940's movie character in a scene set in a bar espoused: "Yesterday it was kill Japs. Today it's sell cars!"

Coupled with a post-war disillusionment the U.S. public, for the first time, began to seriously question the institutions they had previously taken for granted - institutions such as government,

Hollywood, the popular press and higher education. Four spheres of influence which quickly realized they had unintentionally been handed unprecedented power to influence the population of the most powerful country in the world.

While the Ivy League universities crept towards neo-Marxism and the senate went off on safari with the communist witch hunts the half dozen major Hollywood studios sought to influence America with the introspective, politically critical Noir genre as well as the movies which have become to be called the 'social justice' films of the Thirties and Forties.

This era, punctuated by political irony, government backed censorship, bolstered at times, by outright lunacy, lasted well into the Sixties. Fear borne, of ignorance, leading to wide-spread political paranoia was heavily influenced by film and vice versa. It is no coincidence that this time period, 1941-1957, is the widely accepted life span of what has become known as *Film Noir*.

Starting with *The Maltese Falcon* in 1941 and ending in 1958 with *A Touch of Evil*, (with Marlene Dietrich and Charlton Heston playing Mexicans), what came to be known as Film Noir mixed with the 'social message' movies of the immediate pre and post war era to contribute to the turmoil of the contemporary American socio-political landscape.

We now have social media to play that role.

In 2003, in Kyoto, a leading environmentalist was asked by a reporter how scientists could hammer home the global warming crisis to politicians. The doctor's answer was, 'Get Spielberg to make a movie.' A year later work began on *The Day After Tomorrow*, a disaster film which espoused the knock-on effects of continued global warming, whose producers, in a fine display of marketplace symbiosis, lost no time in borrowing heavily on Bush's denouncement of the Paris Climate Agreement to hype the film.

Pre-release hype alone practically guaranteed ticket sales of the project and not only helped Centropolis Entertainment et al break even, but in reality the film quadrupled the box office take of its allotted budget and in turn helped to launch the current wave of climate hysteria which in some quarters has achieved cult status.

Ergo the socio-economic power of film.

Of the plethora of significant historical episodes in the chronicle of my series *Building of The American Empire*, one of the least well known is the on-going 1940's struggle between a nearly all WASP congress and a nearly all Jewish Hollywood, led by a near single-mindedly determined studio head, for the control of film content and his quest for industry domination.

On the other hand historical records testify to the fact that radical elements in the United States Senate have, in terms of film content, relentlessly fought to wrest control of cinema from the Hollywood studio moguls like Jack Warner, as far back as the Twenties. However, the crescendo of the battle reached its zenith in the late Forties, just after WWII. And the way out for Washington was to find someone on which to pin the blame.

Before J. Parnell Thomas, before John E. Rankin and before Richard M. Nixon and the other misguided senators who employed the terrorization of writers, artists and actors to establish and maintain their careers, there were a tiny group of men in sunny, Southern California who, who with the compliant aid of the popular press, wielded more power and influence over the American Public than the entire United States House and Senate combined.

However, as much damage as the 'Onorable Gentlemen' from Washington and their cronies in the popular press perpetrated against the U.S. Constitution, they were not behind the genesis of the worst period in America's most overt battle for free speech until modern times and the failed P.C. movement of the last decade.

These men were William R. Wilkinson, J. Parnell Thomas and Eric Allen Johnston: creators of the Hollywood Blacklist.

Wilkinson not only single-handedly ignited Thomas and Johnston's 'Hollywood Blacklist', but inadvertently helped finance his new business acquaintances from New York City; Charlie "Lucky" Luciano", Meyer "The Accountant" Lansky & Benny "Bugsy" Siegel, to usher in the most diabolical curse ever to invade the shores of America – The International Drug Cartel.

So just as Americans today struggle daily with dirty Washington politics, You Tube and Google censoring free speech and raise questions about film content, so too back in 1947 did Americans grapple with dirty politicians who continually skirted the law, out of touch with reality Hollywood elitism and a bias unethical press, we currently call the main stream media.

The circle of life continues.

PROLOGUE

In December of 1942 Charlie' Lucky' Luciano, the then defacto head of the New York crime families, was serving a 30-50 year sentence for a crime he may or may not have committed which, for anyone else would have carried a ten year sentence.

The politically ambitious New York D.A., Thomas E. Dewey, realized that the keys to the White House lay not in the ballot box but under the headlines of the nation's newspapers and like dozens of politicians before him, promised America to eliminate organized crime. A promise he well knew he could never keep, particularly with the head of the F.B.I. consistently denying the existence of organized crime in the U.S.A. while on the hand accepting bribes from the organized crime leaders.

From an extremely impoverished Sicilian family who immigrated when he was nine years old Luciano persevered to rise and achieve two of the most significant contributions to organized crime.

First, he temporarily eliminated the random murder-revenge cycle instituted by his predecessors such as Alfonse Capone, Johnny Torrio, Dean O'Banion and Bugs Moran.

Then by banding the crime member heads as one and instituting the Commission, in front of which grievances could be aired and settled and all killing had to be approved, control was instituted and more energy devoted to ever expanding criminal activities with diminished public awareness thereby reducing police and political interference.

Luciano's eventual plan, known to virtually no one save Meyer Lansky, until the end of the war, was to bring the most profitable commodity, heroin, to the most profit ridden land, America, together in a mega operation of such magnitude that even he failed to fully realize the eventual global impact it would have.

The testimony to that statement can be seen in the fact that today there is not a single village, town or city in the U.S without a significant drug problem.

Luciano's big chance came in 1942 with the sinking of the *T.L.S. Normandy* in New York Harbor on the 9th of February and the institution of **Operation Underworld**.

At the onset of America's entry into WWII *Operation Underworld* was a plan to recruit Mafiosi into the ranks of the sparsely staffed, poorly funded Office of Naval Intelligence in New York City to guard the waterfront.

Although *Operation Mincemeat*, the secret mission setting up the Allied invasion of Sicily two years later upon which the second book in this trilogy ***The Wolves of Calabria*** revolves around, was a British SOE operation and unrelated to *Underworld*, which was an Office of Strategic Services operation by the Americans, they did cross paths through *Operation Husky* the actual invasion of Sicily in July of 1943.

All three were unwittingly instrumental in leading to a joint Sicilian Mafia/New York based Syndicate operation to import massive quantities of drugs into America.

By July of 1943 the Allies were able to launch *Operation Husky*, the successful invasion and capture of the island of Sicily. It was here that the government met with the Mafia outside of New York on their own home turf.

In the interim year American movies had virtually vanished from most of the rest of the world.

When, in 1945, the end of the war seemed inevitable and the sea lanes were opening back up, Charlie 'Lucky' Luciano, Meyer Lansky in cooperation with Don Carlo The Bullfrog' Vizzini had already begun to set up trade routes and U.S. based distribution centers for their outrageously profitable international drug business. They did this via many means to include setting up phony tomato caning operations and smuggling the heroin in as food shipments.

By 1947 some of the political elite in Washington realized they could garner much political capital by continually focusing paranoia on the unknown but still dangerous Charlie 'Lucky' Luciano.

A political ATM from which politicians like Anslinger continued to make withdrawals well into 1962 when Luciano eventually died.

During the organized crime revelations, ensuing head hunts for crime leaders by the CIA, FBI & the

FBN, Hollywood, while fighting off accusations of communism, were led by men like Jack Warner of Warner Brothers and Eric Johnston of the MPPA who struggled to keep their heads down and conceal their organized crime connections with individuals like Benjamin 'Bugsy' Siegel and others.

This chapter of the story is told in ***The Broad in the Kimono***, the last of the Operation Underworld Trilogy, the story relating some of the elements which have given rise to the circumstances modern Americans now find themselves brawling with.

gave rise to what is now known as . . . the International Drug Cartel.

CHAPTER I

34th Floor, the Artic Building
3rd Avenue and 24th Street
Manhattan, New York City
10:30, Thursday, May 8th, 1947

I impeccably dressed in a grey flannel suit the heavy-set body, seemed to briefly float in mid-air before the falling motion set in.

His blue silk necktie fluttered upwards as he fell face-
First, floor after floor blurring past his descending form.

Thirty-four stories below, at street level the blue-grey haired Mrs. Epstein looked behind her as she backed her brand new, beige '47 Chrysler convertible into the parking space and eased out of the busy Downtown traffic on 3rd Avenue.

She shut down the engine, adjusted her arm load of shopping bags and climbed out of the car.

The screams of the passers-by around her suddenly arrested her attention as she fed several nickels into the parking meter. She turned just in time to see the body of the man impact the pavement a few yards behind her with a sickening thud.

Despite the mangled posture of the body, which appeared as though the man had been flailing on the way down, she recognized the blue tie she had selected just that morning for him to wear.

16

It was her husband, Mr. Epstein.

Earlier that morning Anthony Saul Epstein, who usually entered the well-appointed lobby in Lower Manhattan with a smile, instead just grunted to Larry the doorman when he came through the brass-plated revolving door before crossing the lobby's spacious, marble floor and heading straight for the elevators.

Once upstairs he brushed past the janitor and entered his office, hung his hat and coat on the King Edward rack beside the door and went straight to his desk.

Twenty minutes later, as pandemonium ensued at street level, back up on the 34th floor the day maid knocked then let herself into Epstein's outer office and began cleaning.

Hearing no answer when she knocked on the inner office door she let herself in and, as she reached for the wastebasket next to the desk, she spotted the open window then the note sticking up from the Capitol typing machine on his desk which slowly fluttered in the breeze from the open window.

My only hope in life was to improve the condition of an unfair economic system that held no promise to those without wealth to gain even a decent chance for the citizens of this civilization to survive, let alone live.

Although Epstein was a successful Mid-town businessman, on the strength of the cleaner's testimony and that there was a suicide note, all pressured by the fact that there were over a half dozen bodies a day arriving at the city morgue, a cursory autopsy was all that was deemed necessary.

The Coroner stamped 'Suicide' on the outer folder and filed it under 'E'.

Stevens Hotel
Michigan Avenue, Chicago
11:30, Friday, 16 May

Right about the time Anthony Epstein was achieving terminal velocity between floors 18 and 16 of the Artic Building above Manhattan, a small army of wait staff was preparing the Grand Ballroom on the ground floor of the Stevens Hotel, what was to become the Conrad Hilton, on Michigan Avenue.

The hall was designed to seat 1,800 but tonight, with no dinner scheduled, over 3,000 would be stuffed in across the oak parquet dance floor.

It was the 3rd Anniversary celebration of the Sons of Liberty, Chicago main branch.

Paddy Kelly

Established by a group of successful businessmen two years after America entered the war, The Sons were chaired by Joshua 'Jake' Steadman, sole owner of United Engineering and Construction.

At six foot two and weighing in at two hundred fifty pounds and no matter how much he primped, combed and dressed Steadman always looked as if he just stepped off the construction site.

Jake made his money in the late Thirties and early Forties and though most thought it to be in design and reconstruction of many of the Midwest's factories in '41 when the government was gearing up and retooling to get serious about the war effort and required massive amounts of manufactured goods in record time, it was actually in contract negotiations.

With a small nest egg accumulated during the Great Depression, he also had the where-with-all to bargain hard with the D.C. negotiators sent up from Washington to recruit industrial entrepreneurs, Jake wasn't the kind of guy to let a little thing like a world war get in the way of making a quick few million bucks. Patriotism was okay for the other guy but it was at the altar of capitalism and profit that Steadman worshiped.

The mid-morning meet with his accountant to go over the second quarter take from his half dozen business ventures, told him he would likely break the 50 million mark by year's end. Just the kind of ammo he needed to flaunt at the big gala tonight.

The S.O.L., now boasted over 5,000 full members backed by a couple of thousand auxiliary or associate members with a couple dozen volunteers constantly hovering around the periphery.

The Sons' ethnocentric charter was unambiguous and unapologetic about their mandate. Among their alternative choices for titles was America for Americans, The Sons of Freedom and, a personal favorite of Jake Steadman's, the United Sons of America. They had all the bases covered. All that was missing were the white hoods.

That Friday night's function was strictly an after dinner affair, no reason to waste cash on feeding the masses the S.O.L. board reckoned, so the primary purpose of the get together, as could be deduced by one glance at the guest list, was to serve as the fledgling organization's first real pitch at trying to wedge themselves into the upper echelon of American political society.

After all, if New York City, the financial capital of the nation was considered the backdoor into D.C. politics, Chicago was certainly a backdoor into NYC politics.

Among the invitees was the Mayor of Chicago, Martin Kennelly, Deputy Mayor Coughlin, Superintendent of the Chicago P.D., a cursory collection of judges and the primary target for the evening, the Seventh Congressional District Senator, Charles H. Pickham.

It was about an hour into the festivities when someone manned the mike and called on Steadman to address the troops. Situated right next to the stage Jake was Johnny-on-the-spot and as the applause died down he stepped up to the mike and following a few cursory greetings he launched straight into his spiel.

"Thank you. Thank you all for coming. Now, I don't want to get too melodramatic, there's still too much dinking time left in the evening." Appreciable laughter rippled through the crowd. "We, Americans, foreign or natural born, bear an awesome responsibility to the rest of civilization in regards to the safe guarding of the freedoms and morals of western democracy." A moderate round of applause interrupted. "As currently is being witnessed across the seas in Europe there are forces at work as well as all around the modern world that seek to make it clear that it is their expressed intent to usurp our efforts. And the efforts of others like us.

They will, they do, seek to do this through various not so surreptitious means. Control of the international market. Industrial infiltration of other countries. And worse and most damaging of all . . . by flooding our shores with foreign, immigrant labor!" His words were bolstered by the occasional here, here!

"We didn't start that war-"

"NO! BUT WE DAMN WELL FINISHED IT!" Someone yelled out which prompted a general mix of laughter sprinkled with applause.

"That we did, that we did!" Steadman agreed. "We didn't start that war, but we stood together to finish it.

Sometimes people's ability to look ahead is obscured by the events of the moment. We, as good moral Americans have a responsibility, no a **duty**, to look ahead to build a better America. An America for all Americans.

And now we must stand together again. Together to stand against them! The forces that seek to transform our country into what the free world spent the last ten years fighting against. Indeed it is the very reason that myself, Frank Smith, James Fry and others founded the Sons of Liberty and the very reason we intend to take the organization national by the end of next year!"

More applause followed at the already well known news. Steadman's future political ambitions were no secret but intended tonight to serve as an official public declaration.

"When do we put forth a candidate Jake?" A crowd member yelled out. The surprise announcement bolstered by the benign heckle garnered loud applause.

Steadman's impulse was to yell back 'I'm ready any time', but instead he just waved and casually walked off stage.

Better to leave them wanting more! His internal dialogue shouted.

Stepping down from the stage, in-between handshakes and congrats, Steadman made his way over to the packed bar and elbowed a space in the corner next to the man he had quietly staked out earlier in the evening. Not so coincidently the spot was right next to Congressman Pickham.

"Glad you could make it Senator." He signaled to one of the barmen to bring another round for himself and the senator. "What'd ya think of the speech?"

"You'll make a fine politician Jake."

"Whoa, let's not put the cart before the horse I didn't say I was gonna run fer nothing!"

"Yeah Jake, this is my first rodeo!"

"I didn't say that either!" The congressman adjusted his position and smirked. "But, since you mentioned it, I am interested in where you stand." Steadman pushed.

"On what, exactly, Jake?" Pickham reached for his drink but refused the cigar Steadman offered.

"On the state of the country. More specifically on the immigrant situation."

"Well, we're all immigrants, to one degree or another. Some of us got here before the others but that doesn't make us-"

"I'm talking real specific like." Steadman queried. The senator leaned in and lowered his voice.

"Like how specific?"

"Well, there's quite a few folks of a certain . . . ethnic persuasion shall we say that, it's come to light control quite a bit of the financial dealings in this country." Jake took the senator's bait and leaned in even closer speaking in a hushed tone.

"Especially out in Hollywierd, if you know what I mean."

"Like who for instance?"

"Well, without being too specific, the Jews." Steadman specified.

"You talking about Hollywood?"

"Not just. Ya got Benny Siegel, Meyer Lansky Arni Rothstein, the guy that started it all."

"Started what, exactly?"

"You know, organized crime!"

"Let me ask you something Steadman. Guns on the table." The big builder leaned back on the bar and smiled.

"Okay, guns on the table Senator Pickham."

Finally, it was pitch time.

"How is it of all the potential candidates for union president your man Morelli entered at the last minute, was the least known, the least financed and yet got elected by a 'landslide'?"

Steadman shifted the thick Cubana cigar between his teeth and smiled.

"The construction game, Your Honor, is a lot like the political game."

"Do tell?"

"Absolutely! In this game there are basically three kinds of people. Those who own the whores, those who pay the whores and those that are the whores. And, as you well know, Your Honor, it's not about who ya now." He stood straight and tossed a few tens on the bar. "It's who ya blow! Drinks are on me. Look forward to our next meeting." Steadman walked away.

Pickham shook his head/

"It's Congressman! I'm not in the senate and damn sure no judge!" He finished his drink. "You fucking Neanderthal!" The congressman mumbled as he turned to leave.

Lincoln Park
Corner of Duncan Ave. and Route 440
Jersey City, New Jersey
17:10, Monday, 26 May

The sun was still bright and he'd have to wait another three or four hours until dark before he could make his move but he had to be reasonably sure the place was empty.

Doc McKeowen, draped in his brown leather bomber jacket and Negro League baseball cap, casually peered up and over the newspaper he held open as he sat on the park bench. The wide intersection of Route 440 and Duncan Avenue afforded a clear view of the entire exterior of the corner premises.

He watched as one by one the half dozen late model cars sporadically pulled out of the open parking lot catty cornered from where he sat in Lincoln Park.

Doc smirked as he glanced up and to his left as he saw the tall towers of the super structure of the Pulaski Skyway spanning the Hackensack River less than half a mile away. The Pulaski where a year ago he trapped and fought the crooked State Department agent Benson.

He glanced over to the side of the rectangular building as the sign painters began to break down their paints, rollers and two tiers of scaffolding stowing the gear in the back of their Dodge van. The wall sign was a little over half finished.

At just over six foot tall with dark hair, hazel eyes and a medium build, Mike 'Doc' McKeowen had been a swimmer in his youth, never ate or drank to excess, (well didn't eat to excess anyway), even during the holidays and so was in as reasonable a shape as a forty year old bachelor could be. His idea of good fashion sense was to keep the dark fur collar of his brown, leather bomber jacket clean and to always have his N. L. baseball cap cocked back at just the correct angle.

A native New Yorker by birth, save for a couple of years on the NYPD following a 4F rejection by the Navy for a punctured ear drum, Doc's life had been pretty mundane.

Following his divorce he founded his small P.I. firm and met his current girlfriend, Nikki Cole while on a case.

He glanced again over at the employee/customer parking lot of the property fronting the main warehouse building but he couldn't see the back where he knew the executive parking area to be. He knew this from the previous day's recon.

M&M Investigations had been hired by the head of security of an accounting firm, Steinberg

26

Accounting, which also insured several clients who utilized Hudson & Delaware, a privately owned, bonded shipping firm, to ship their goods nationwide. Since the war's end, H&D had expanded into overseas trade as well.

The accounting firm expected and budgeted for an increase in rates for overseas shipping at the end of the war but a month or so into the contract one of Steinberg's bean counters noticed a disproportionate increase in domestic shipping rates after a number of clients started to complain about an unexplained rise in their shipping charges.

When H&D were approached about it they said they'd look into it. After six weeks with no response, H&D's people began to dodge phone calls from Steinberg's accounting department. That's when Steinberg's internal security people were notified. To avoid a conflict of interest claim if they initiated an investigation themselves, they called M&M Investigations to look into it. Doc took the case.

Weights of goods to be shipped were required to be stamped on the manifests which were usually taken off the federal weight certificates prior to shipping. A few pounds discrepancy more or less is no big deal on a truck or a ship, but on an aeroplane accurate weight comes down to the ounce. Doc immediately realized that the air shipment manifests were his best bet to start his investigation. Shipment manifests which were presumably kept in the front office.

H&D Shipping were headquartered on Duncan Avenue in Jersey City across the Hudson River from M&M's Manhattan office. Doc made the trip over by ferry earlier that afternoon and had come to form an attack plan.

He checked his watch, grabbed his Army issue messenger's shoulder bag and went up the block into a local bar. He ordered a drink and ducked into the men's room.

Now dressed in casual but upscale khaki slacks and a light blue dress shirt with a dark blue neck tie, Doc pushed through the front door of the office in the front of the massive warehouse and storage facility and up to the room length service counter.

A thirty-something brunette sat off to one side squeezed into the far corner, at a small desk behind the long counter.

"Can I help you?" Head down, she kept working.

"Hi, good afternoon." Doc removed his hat and brushed back the lick of hair that escaped the thick layer of Brylcream. "Is this Hudson & Delaware Shipping?"

"Yes."

"Who do I talk to about shipping some freight to Italy?" Doc inquired.

"I can help you with that sir." The brunette answered still not looking up from her tiny desk. She finished up what she was doing and stood to help Doc.

"Sorry we're having the sign redone. More paper work. What is it exactly you'd like to ship Mr.-?"

"Fiorelli, Giancomo Fiorelli. Olive oil. My family is in olive oil. We get the olives shipped in from a company in Sicily but they're not yet licensed to ship processed goods back into this country."

"Well Mr. Fiorelli, we can certainly help you there."

She tore a page from a carbonated pad and slid it over to McKeowen. "If you'll just fill out this form for us, we'll have an agent get in touch with you in a couple of days with our shipping requirements and standard rates."

"Super!" Doc donned a pair of horn rimmed glasses and took the pen and began to write. The receptionist stepped back over to her desk and Doc glanced up and behind the long service counter as he slowly wrote.

The cinder block wall separating the customer service area and the warehouse behind only rose about four feet from the wooden floor, from there up the rear wall was glass. He had an unobstructed view of the expansive warehouse behind reception. There was a small office to the side of where the secretary sat.

All manner of freight was stacked across the floor and he watched as a handful of workers shifted crates, barrels and cardboard boxes. He noticed the double sized rolling door in the far rear of the dock area.

"You doin' okay?" She asked. Doc snapped back to the paper.

"It has a box here for estimated weight. I'm not exactly sure what to put. I don't know how much my father wants to send in the first shipment."

"Don't worry about that. We'll weigh it and price it for you."

"Oh, that's very thoughtful. What else do you need?" She stepped back up to Doc and perused the order sheet.

"This your company's main number, Murray Hill 5-5121?"

"Yes, you can leave word with the secretary and we'll get right back to you."

"That'll about do it then! Thank you Mr. Fiorelli, one of our agents will give you a call before the weekend."

"Thank you Miss - ."

"Mornay, Betty Mornay."

"Thank you Betty."

With a few hours to spare Doc decided to grab a beer and a sandwich at the place up the road where he changed but first he ambled around the side of the building which fronted the four lane State Route 440. Being certain no one noticed him he took a good look at the rear, fenced in area of the structure. A small fork lift scurried around the yard, some building material was thrown off to the side of the rear fence and there was a dog house tucked away in the far corner of the yard.

With no one around he rattled the chain link fence hard and watched as, from somewhere, a pair of Dobermans darted out into the yard barking loudly.

"SHIT!" Doc cursed as he turned away from the fence and started to head off down along the shoulder of Route 440.

"SHIT, SHIT!" He had stepped in a big pile of dog shit.

†

Approaching from the rear along the ten foot tall chain link fence it was just past ten thirty that night when McKeowen casually strolled back up to the rear of the H&D building.

The front of the building was far too well lit to attempt entry there.

Aside from the two marked parking spots, apparently for executive parking, the other side of the fence at the rear of the building was cleared away, probably for maneuverability of the forklift currently parked off to the far side of the yard.

With no lamp post in the corner where the building met the fence, light was sparse and so presented no problem. Doc scaled the chain link and quietly dropped down into the yard.

After only two steps McKeowen met his first two obstacles, Butch and Demon, the drooling, growing Dobermans.

He froze in place but moved slowly as he eased the small messenger's shoulder bag to his back and removed a wax paper package from inside his bomber jacket. The low growling transitioned to sniffing as he removed the two pound and half Porterhouse steaks and brandished them to the dogs.

The dogs sat back in place and let off one bark each.

"Well trained little bastards, aren't ya?" He tossed the steaks across the yard away from the rear door and the dogs bounded away. Doc bounded to the door.

The double dead bolt lock on the personnel door was no problem and Doc didn't see any alarm tape on the doors' glass panels. He was inside the warehouse in under a minute quietly closing the door behind him.

Quickly moving up between the stacks of freight to the front office he found the door from the freight area into the customer service area was dead bolted from the inside so he merely had to undo the bolt and the office door was unlocked.

Once inside the director's office aside the secretary's mini-desk he went to the four draw filing cabinet also unlocked and so had unfettered access to all the company's files.

"If I didn't know any better I'd swear they wanted me to break into this place!"

Having previously researched the names of three of Steinberg's clients who had filed price hike complaints, he quickly located those files, double checked that the federal weight slips as well as the H&D weight records were in each and quickly laid them open out on the desk pulling out a small Land camera and snapping several pictures of each.

He then removed the film roll, pocketed it and stuffed the records into the small Army issue shoulder bag and prepared to head out.

Closing the door over behind himself he carefully started back out behind the counter towards the warehouse area when he was forced to duck down.

"Huh! Old Chinese proverb; if something's too good to be true . . ."

The glare of headlights of a pick-up truck blared through the front window as it pulled into the parking lot outside the building. Doc crouched down, froze and waited. He didn't have to wait long. He heard the slam of the truck's door as the head lamps backlit a figure getting out of the truck. Seconds later a flashlight illuminated the customer service area through the picture window and drifted across the space.

SHIT! Doc cursed to himself. He noticed he had left the door between the customer service area back out to the freight dock open.

Maybe they won't see it from there!

"HEY FRANKIE, SUMTHIN' AIN'T RIGHT!" The fat security guard outside called back to the truck.

They saw it!

A second watchman got out of the truck as the first went to the front door and used his pass key. Doc did the only logical thing he could. He ran for it.

Quietly closing over the warehouse door and bolting it behind him he realized it would not look good, for himself or Steinberg if he were caught with the goods, especially off premises where he could be charged with robery. As soon as the door was bolted he unslung the shoulder strap around the bag and tossed it up into the ceiling rafters of the reception area above the door and ran like hell.

The two security guys were coming through the reception area door onto the freight dock just as McKeowen was carefully slipping out the back door into the back parking area.

The two Dobermans were roused from their dog shelter where they were fighting over the wax paper remnants and were nipping at Doc's heels seconds later as he scrambled back up the fence.

"Fucking fair weather friends!"

He was able to make it down the outside of the chain link fence and out onto Route 440 as the two guards were running down through the freight dock and out onto the loading dock to the back parking area.

The two Dobermans chased them back into the warehouse but not before Doc overhead one of them yell.

"Go back around get the truck!"

McKeowen dodged the few cars and trucks racing up and down the state route and crossed over to the Duncan Avenue side of the road as he saw the Dodge pick-up flinging gravel from the front of the building and skidding out onto the frontage road outside the H&D building.

Apparently they hadn't spotted him because the truck stopped at the intersection, unsure of which way to turn. McKeowen was also undecided about what to do next.

An open bed tractor trailer slowing to make the turn off 440 and up Duncan Avenue made the decision for him.

As it swung wide to turn left he ran alongside it for concealment and grabbed onto the rear access ladder between the tractor and the rig and pulled himself up and into the space between the two.

The patrol van turned right at the intersection and drove up into the park.

A mile up Duncan Avenue Doc prepared to jump from the truck at the next red light but realized the tractor had New York plates. He leaned out and red the hand lettering on the passenger's side door.

Broderick's Fresh Seafood
Fulton Street Market
N.Y.C., N.Y.

"When one truck closes, another one opens!" Doc mumbled. He decided he could hang on for another fifteen minutes or so.

By the time the truck was through the Holland Tunnel and was in Manhattan he jumped off at the top of the exit ramp when the driver stopped for the red light on Canal Street.

Knowing his on again-off again girlfriend Nikki would be waiting for him he decided to find a phone booth and call her.

Nikki Cole and her young daughter Kate met Doc back in '42 when she was working as a receptionist for Naval Intelligence Downtown in the Woolworth Building. McKeowen was looking into a fidelity case, which led him Downtown, they met and the rest is not yet history.

As a bonus prize Doc wound up with Nikki's then work mate Shirley who he hired-on partly to make inroads with Nikki.

"You know what time it is? What are you up to? Nikki tentatively asked.

"Oh, not much. I couldn't sleep, so I just rode around town a little." He mumbled into the receiver.

You're full of it McKeowen. Cole had an aversion to profanity and so never used it.

"Yes, I am." He confessed.

You want to come over?

"I'd like that. I'm gonna stop by a diner first and get some grub. See you in about an hour. You need me to bring anything in?"

Just your body handsome.

"Deal!"

And maybe some crullers! The powdered kind.

"Crullers, the powdered kind, check!"

Glancing at his watch he saw it was just after one in the morning and headed off to get breakfast and consider what he had read of the H&D records. Ten minutes later he was at Manny's Diner on Canal, ate then walked back to his office in Greenwich Village to develop the photos.

✝

36

Paddy Kelly

M&M Investigations
Christopher St., Greenwich Village
New York City, N. Y.

The six story former tenement building had been converted to offices just after the First War and the news stand on the ground floor was owned by an army vet, Harry Balducci who lost a leg in the Ardennes during the First War.

Harry's Front Page News was a cramped, pre-World War II corner news stand which occupied the ground floor of 1929 Christopher Street specializing in warm sodas, cold coffee, cheap cigars and stale chocolate bars.

It was with a load of cash, of suspicious origins he bought the space outright. Harry became good friends with Doc when McKeowen began slipping him twenty bucks a week to keep an eye on the lobby which was directly adjacent to Harry's news stand.

Although there was a separate entrance into the building, Doc frequently skirted through Harry's place on his way up to the office to glance the headlines on the papers and check in with Harry who acted as an ersatz message service.

Upstairs in the office Shirley, the receptionist was typing away when he entered.

"Morning Shirley, how you doin' today, lovely lady?"

"You cheatin' on Nikki?" The attractive black girl challenged.

"What do you mean?"

"I mean you smilin' like the cat that ate the canary. It ain't like you."

"Can't a guy just be happy to be working in his own Manhattan office with the prettiest Harlem-born secretary on a fine summer's day?" Shirley leaned back in her chair and raised her feet up off the floor.

"What the hell you doin?" Doc asked.

"Getting' kind'a deep in here. Don't wanna get my shoes musted up."

"Shirley! Are you intimating that I'm being less than veracious with you?"

"If that mean what I think it mean, yeah."

"I'm hurt!" Doc unlocked the door and went into his office. Shirley called after him.

"By the way, not all negroes come from Harlem ya know!"

Doc poked his head back out of his office door and called over to her desk.

"All the important ones in my life do!" He said.

"Redbone come from the Bayou!" She called back through his office door.

He buzzed back out to her via the intercom. *Like I said, all the important ones do!*

Now past the Big Three-O Shirley solidly considered herself approaching old maid status. Through a short series of bad relationships, primarily with unreliable men, and though strikingly beautiful, her modesty and lack of world experience continually obscured her primary goal in life – marriage and family.

Almost immediately Shirley's intercom buzzed again. Rather than answer it she yelled across to McKeowen's office.

"WHAT?! YOU JUST GOT HERE!"

Doc continued to respond through the intercom.

Shirl, place a call to Steinberg Accounting, the head of security. Tell them we've got news on the H&D Shipping case. Thanks gorgeous.

"OKAY." She yelled back. "Somethin's definitely wrong with that man today!" Shirley quietly quipped as she dialled.

"Hello, this is a call from Mr. McKeowen of M&M Investigations calling for a Mr. Kowalski."

Hold please.

"Thank you. DOC YOUR CALL IS GOIN' THROUGH."

Shirley, we have an intercom! Doc said through the intercom.

Jan Kowalski here. The other party answered over the phone.

"Please hold for Mr. McKeowen. DOC! YOUR CALL IS THROUGH."

Doc again rang through on Shirley's intercom line.

Thank you Shirley!

You welcome Doc. She sent back.

The light flashed on the base of his phone and Doc picked up the line.

"McKeowen here, Jhan, can you make it over to Jersey City today?"

What for?

"To meet me at the H&D warehouse, at the reception desk this afternoon at around two?"

You got something for me?

"Yes and Jhan, bring someone from legal."

This better be good McKeowen!

"Kowalski, I'm always good! Don't forget my check! Cash would be better."

Louie Mancino's short stout form strolled through the door just as Doc hung up.

Doc and Louie had a short but unusual history. Back in the late Thirties when Doc was a foot patrolman with the NYPD, he was directing traffic around a road accident on Second Avenue when Louie the garbage man, almost killed him with his seven ton garbage truck. Mancino was in the truck.

They've been working together ever since.

"Hey Shirl." Mancino greeted.

"Hey Louie."

"Doc in?" Shirley kept typing but nodded over to Doc's office and Louie let himself in.

"Hey Doc, just checking in. What was that all about?"

"The Steinberg account."

"You find something on it?"

"Only that they've been boosting the air mail charge for a 16 ounce parcel from $0.54 to $1.10." Doc slid the photos over to Louie who briefly perused them.

"That's a hefty profit!"

"Even more hefty when you times it by seven to eight thousand pounds shipped per month!"

"How'a they doin' that and getting it by the Feds?"

"Probably weighing the mail bags with the locks on, using entire bags for small parcels stuff like that. But that's not our job. We were hired to find evidence of fraudulent billing and now, its money time!" Doc smiled up at Louie.

"Guess they got'a make up for them lost war profits somewhere!" Mancino quipped.

"How's Doris?" Doc casually asked as he continued penning his report.

"She's Doris."

"That good huh?"

"How's Nikki and Kate?"

"Nikki's Nikki and Kate are off until end of August so she's spending the next few weeks Upstate with Nikki's mom until it's time to head back to school."

"I see there's a new guy down in the *Front Page*. Harry doing okay?" Louie pointed out.

"Yeah, he had to go in for some tests on his stump. They found a growth."

"You mean like a new leg growing back?"

"A new leg growing back? He's not a lizard. You ever go to school, stupid?"

"Yeah! And I come out the same way! What about it?"

"What are you doing today?" He quizzed Mancino.

"Got'a file some papers over at City Hall, then off to set up a stake out uptown."

"Any progress on our movie star?"

"Yeah. Got an iron clad confirm that he's defiantly seeing someone else, and said lover is due in to his fav little love nest up at the Gramercy Apartments this afternoon or tomorrow." Louie poked his head out through the door. "Shirl, could you get me the number to the City Clerk's office?"

"Sure thing, Mr. Mancino."

"Shirl! Call me Louie!"

"Yes Mr. Louie!" She sarcastically shot back.

"Keep me posted." Doc instructed.

"Will do Doc. What'a you up to?"

"I'll finish up over in Jersey around three or four then I'm gonna surprise Nikki. Taking her out for dinner and a movie."

As both men prepared to leave. Doc stepped out to Shirley's desk.

"Shirley, I'll be uptown until twelve then over in Jersey from about two on. I'll check in with you at around three or four."

"Okay Doc."

"Shirley?"

"Yes Doc?"

"How many times have I asked you to call me Mr. McKeowen when we're in the office?"

"Prob'ly a bunch."

"You heard from Nikki?" Doc asked.

"No Mr. McKeowen. Would you like me to call her, Mr. McKeowen?"

"No. Thank you Shirley."

"Will there be anything else Mr. McKeowen?"

"No Shirley, thank you." Doc and Louie left together with Shirley calling after them.

"MR. MCKEOWEN! MR. MCKEOWEN!"

Doc ducked back in the door.

"Yeah Shirley?"

"Mr. McKeowen, could I have the rest'a the day off?"

"Uh, let me think about it. I'll get back to you tomorrow." He left.

"Very funny, DOC!"

The attractive brunette behind the service counter craned her neck for a better look at who was getting out of the immaculately polished 1947, black Lincoln Zephyr which had just pulled into the client's parking area in front of the Hudson & Delaware building on Duncan Avenue.

The chauffeur hopped out, scurried around to the side and opened the door for the slight gentlemen with the stylish fedora, Armani suit and leather briefcase. The other back seat occupant, a big burly, dark haired guy with a runaway moustache, climbed out the other side unassisted.

The chauffeur hurried ahead to open the front door before the other two reached it. Once inside the brunette watched as the small guy perused the reception area.

"Kowalski where's your man?" The Armani asked the big guy.

"Excuse me ma'am-" Kowalski asked the brunette. "Has anyone else come in here this afternoon?"

"Just the electrician." She nodded to the pair of legs on the step ladder behind her halfway in the doorway to the warehouse.

Doc, dressed in electrician's coveralls, climbed down the six foot ladder and smiled at Kowalski and the big guy.

"Hey Jhan! Glad you made it!"

"What'a you moonlighting McKeowen? I better be glad we came out here! What's the story? What'a ya got?"

A puzzled Miss Mornay looked on.

"Jhan Kowalski meet Betty Mornay, executive secretary, receptionist and all-round helpful gal Friday! Betty this is Jhan, he works for a company your company deals with. The little guy here will introduce himself. In the meantime, I think we found your problem Betty. It was right up there all along." He nodded to the rafters above the door.

Doc smiled as he opened the messenger's bag he held and handed the three folders over to Kowalski who passed them to the big guy, a legal rep from Steinberg Accounting, Inc. He flipped one open and perused the contents.

Betty was not amused by all the mystery

"Hey! Those are company property! What the hell's goin' on here? You said you was an electrician?!"

"No, I said I was here to fix something!" Doc smiled.

The small guy in the suit nodded and mumbled to himself several times as he flipped through the files and the other three looked on. Doc smiled at the brunette. She didn't smile back.

"What the hell's going on here Mack?!" She again demanded.

"Kowalski, fine work! I see a bonus in your future!" The Armani complimented.

"Thank you Mr. Clemens!" The legal rep opened his brief case, removed a sealed manila envelope and handed it to Betty.

"What's this?

"Young lady, this is an interstate subpoena issued this morning by the Third Circuit Court ordering the owner or owners of Hudson and Delaware Shipping and Storage Incorporated to appear before the circuit court judge no later than –"

"Wait a minute Buster! I ain't no-"

"No later than Monday, June the ninth with all pertinent records. Failure to do so will result in a cease and desist order at which time confiscation of assets will commence." Betty looked over at Doc who pulled a dopey smile and shrugged.

"Why you crummy piece of-" Doc cut her off with a finger to his lips.

"Kowalski pay the man."

"Yeah Kowalski, pay the man!" Doc echoed as he held out his hand.

"You do good work Mr. McKeowen. We shall be in touch in future." The chauffer was at the door as the legal rep exited. Kowalski handed Doc a check. Doc read it and nodded. Kowalski took his leave.

"Thank you Mr. Kowalski. I shall look forward to-"

"Can it McKeowen!" Kowalski was already out the door and halfway to the car.

"Thank you Miss Mornay! I see a bonus in my future!" Doc quipped as he smelled the check and gathered his things. "Any chance you could call me a cab?"

"DROP DEAD, YA BASTARD! WALK!" Betty yelled as she stormed off still into the office holding the subpoena.

"AND I HOPE YA GET RUN OVER!"

"Some people. No sense of humor." Doc mumbled.

CHAPTER II

525 East 20th Street
Gramercy Park, New York City

A pair of military issue binoculars peeked out from between the worn tan curtains draped across the bay window of the well groomed, six story walk-up. There was a small sign to the left of the outside entrance.

ROOMS TO RENT
Monthly/Weekly Rates
(No Gypsies, Musicians or Salesmen!)

The binos focused across the street and in on the burley, uniformed doorman as he held open the door to the upscale Avignon Apartments. An elderly fur draped lady and the poodle at the end of the leash scurrying in front of her nodded as they passed through the double, brass plated doors.

Inside the ground floor apartment Louie broke from his surveillance and spun around when he heard the staccato clicking of high heels on the bare wooden floor then turned back to the window.

"What the hell you doing here?" He blurted out. The small woman set a pair of shopping bags on the floor to his right as she answered.

"Evening Doris. Evening Louie. Nice to see you Doris. Nice to see you too Louie. Gee Doris, nice of you to come all the way Uptown to bring me dinner. That's okay Louie, that's what wives do fer their husbands. Even when they act like total gavones and don't give no respect in return!"

Two years Louie's junior, Doris Mancino was a good looking, petite, brunette with green eyes. Formally Doris Hunsacker she had been married to Louie for the past nine years. They met in high school dated and fell in love. Being dyed in the wool romantics and harboring deeply traditional perceptions concerning relationships, they tied the knot when he was twenty-one, she was eighteen.

Louie's cousin Nunzio sponsored the wedding at the local St. Sebastian's Church hall, his cousin Giuseppe did the catering and Guido provided the booze from his distribution business. Last year at a christening Doris remarked that in the last eight years she had met a new Mancino every three or four months since the wedding.

Louie took a job with his cousin Vinnie's garbage company, Doris worked part time in a Downtown beauty salon and they moved into a one bedroom on West 8th near Lexington.

Due to paying more attention to a young skirt sashaying down the avenue then to the road, the garbage truck Louie was riding on nearly killed a traffic cop. The driver was arrested, Louie was assigned to ride a new garbage truck and the traffic cop turned out to be Doc McKeowen. Six months later when Louie went looking for Doc to apologize for his cousin Gino, Doc had quit the force and went into the P.I. game with another guy. On his off time

Louie started hanging around the one room office and eventually became the go-fer.

The highly publicized Treasury Fraud case just over four years ago earned Mancino his P.I. license and cemented Louie's position in what was now called 'McKeowen and Mancino Private Investigations' alias 'The Firm'.

The banter between Louie and Doris started in around the fourth year of the marriage but the original stars-in-the-eyes, love struck bedrock of the relationship had never wavered.

Unfazed by Doris' haranguing Louie continued to watch the revolving brass door to the entrance of the upscale apartment building across the street. Doris plopped a dish towel-wrapped container down on the window sill in front of Louie.

"Thanks." He mumbled.

"It is my most esteemed pleasure Lou . . ."

"WILL YOU CAN IT? In case you ain't noticed, I'm on stakeout here!" Doris was unfazed by the outburst.

"Is that what you're doin? I thought maybe you developed a thing for middle-aged guys in grey uniforms and funny hats."

Louie paused then casually glanced over his shoulder. "So what'a we got ta eat?" Then he spotted the dish towel draped, twelve inch long, plastic box. "What the hell is that?" He grunted.

Like a T.V. model Doris retrieved then methodically unwrapped then fondled the translucent blue container with the bright orange top, sales girl styled. Louie turned away from the window.

"It's the latest scientific discovery, Tupperware!" She ecstatically declared.

"What the hell is Supper-ware"

"Tupperware, Tupper-ware! A revolutionary new product that allows for the preparation, storage, containment and serving of meals for hours!" Doris spoke with the uncontained pride of Earl Tupper himself. "It keeps food fresh fer days!"

"Who the hell wants ta eat food that's days old?" Louie snapped. Doris looked dejected. Louie eased off. "Where'd ya get it?"

"Macy's!" Doris attempted to hide her irritation.

"Great, now we're shopping at Macys! What next? Shoes from Bloomingdales?!" Doris replaced the container, crossed her arms and pursed her lips. Louie returned to his surveillance of the apartment building. There was a strained silence. "What's in the Tupp-o-ware? Lasagna?"

"Yeah, hold on to that dream Pal! Like I would bend over backwards and spend the day making lasagna for you!" Louie smirked to himself.

"I like it when you bend over."

"It's cannelloni."

"Meat or cheese?" He probed.

"You got some nerve, you know that?! 'Meat or cheese?'" Doris smirked. Louie kept his eyes on the apartment house. "Half and half." She replied.

"What's ta drink?"

"Chianti. You want?" She started to pour some into one of the dozen empty paper coffee cups neatly stacked in a pyramid on top of the three pizza boxes on the floor next to Louie's chair.

"Yeah." He grunted. She cocked her head to one side and stared.

"'Yeah'?!" She blurted. Louie heard the pouring stop.

"Yeah please." The pouring resumed. "Thank you Doris."

"You're welcome Louis." Christened Louigi Frances Garibaldi, the only person with permission to call Mancino by his birth name was Mama Mancino. But Doris had permission to use 'Louis'. On occasion.

Doris set the partially filled cup back on the floor next to him as Louie briefly peered back through the small binos. Doris finished unwrapping the container, took a knife and fork wrapped in a cloth napkin from her coat pocket and handed them to Louie then moved over to the window and rested her chin on Louie's shoulder.

"So, what'a we got? Murder? Extortion? International espionage?"

"Screwin' around."

"A divorce case?! Is that what tree days of surf-ailance is for?!" Louie continued to peer through the binos and jot down notes.

"Doris, ja remember ta pay the rent last week?"

"Yeah, you know I did!"

"Jeet last week?"

"Yeah, I ate last week!" Doris narrowed her eyes. "Okay, point taken." Doris glanced at Louie, gave him a peck on the cheek and fought back a

51

smile. "Thank you for providing for us, Louie. You're a good husband." Louie smiled as he dug into the still warm cannelloni. "No matter what my mother says." She added.

"Please, I'm eatin' over here! Don't bring up ya mother!"

"You seen Doc lately?"

"What'a you care if I seen Doc or not? Course I seen Doc! Seen him at the office." Louie looked over at her. "What'a you care?"

"Why you always got'a read sumthin' into somethin'?!"

"I ain't readin' nuthin' in ta nuthin'! All I did was ask what'a you care?!" He defended.

There was a second awkward pause.

"So?" She pushed.

"So what?"

"Ja see him?"

"What'a you care?!"

"I just think he'd be happier if he spent more time at home. You know, with Nikki." She defended. Louie maintained surveillance as he responded.

"So he and Nicky could have a kid so you could find a million excuses ta baby-sit and therefore you could be happier! Right?" She broke away from the embrace.

"Well excuuuusssee meee if I worry about our friends and their home life!"

"Guy's got a right to god-damned life, ya know? You wanna worry about sumthin'? Worry about all these poor bastard G. I.'s can't find no work. You know what's gonna happen to this economy Uncle

Sam don't get off his ass and find these guys some work?"

"Gimme!" Doris ordered as she grabbed the binos. "Eat your cannelloni! I'll watch." Doris fumbled to untangle the strap from Louie's neck. "What'a we lookin' for?"

"Anything suspicious." Louie said through a mouth full of pasta.

"That's a big help! I can't see nuthin' through these things!"

"Turn them around."

"Oh. Okay, now I can see."

"The little dial on top is the focus. We're lookin' fer anybody that don't belong."

"I'm worried Louie because on account'a after Doc promised Nikki to cut down on the P.I. work he don't know what ta do with himself! Ya know?! And I got a pretty strong feelin' he ain't too happy, and that means Nikki ain't happy!"

"So why ya worried?" He consciously allowed a measure of empathy to infiltrate his question.

"You think that's a good thing somebody ain't happy Mr. Sensitive?" She pushed. Louie let out a sigh.

"Wonderful! *I'm on stakeout with Ann Landers over here!"

"What in God's name . . . ?" Doris' mouth dropped open. "Louie . . . what is that?" Louie glanced between the curtains and across the street. He set his food down and took the binos.

"Jesus! That thing's got more chrome than the Chrysler Building!" He declared as they stared at the mile long limo pulling up to the curb outside the apartment building.

"Get a load of them Dagmars!"

"Language asshole!" His wife corrected.

Gleaming in the late afternoon sun was a chauffeur driven, fire engine red, rag top, 1946 Lincoln Continental.

"That Sweetheart is exactly what I'm gonna buy us as soon as I crack the big case!" Louie slowly raised the binos back to his eyes.

"Which case would that be, Louie? The case of the Missing Hotel Brass Doors, or the case of the pudgy guy in the grey doorman's suit?"

"Shut it!" He adjusted the binos and focused.

The immaculately uniformed chauffer came around and opened the rear, curb side door. A well groomed, middle-aged man stepped out and pulled the white fur collar of his beige, cashmere overcoat higher up on his shoulders.

"That's . . ." Doris yelped as Louie's neck and head jerked to the side when she ripped the binos from his hands ignoring the neck strap still around his neck. "That's James Alexander!" She declared as Louie disentangled himself to make a note in his notebook. "Louie, this is the first time I ever seen a movie star close up!"

"Doris, two hundred feet across the street peepin' out a ground floor window between curtains ain't exactly 'close up'!"

"Louie, that's the guy that starred in *The Hitman Isn't As Hard As I Am*! That's an Academy Award win'n movie star over there! I mean that's the guy who starred with Giselle Maguire in *I Was A Pregnant Nazi Spy*!"

"And that's the guy who is our mark!" Louie quietly informed Doris as he wrote.

"Is there anybody else in the car?" Doris asked with the anticipation of a kid shaking a Christmas present. Louie resumed control of the binoculars. The chauffer offered his hand to a second passenger in the rear seat.

"Looks like there is. Gimme the camera, gimme the camera! Over there!" Doris retrieved the box Kodak and handed it to Louie. He started to snap away in time with the passenger climbing out of the rear of the limo.

"Is that the flusey with him?" Doris hung on to Louie with both hands.

"Probably. They were spotted at the Stork Club last week by a friend of the client's. That's when she came to us."

The second passenger out of the car was a younger version of a Howard Hughes look-alike and both men gave an embracing, mouth-on-mouth kiss before proceeding into the building.

"Yep! I'd say he's light in the feet, alright." Louie quietly announced as Doris withdrew in revolution. She stared blankly, mouth opened at Louie.

"HE'S . . . HE'S A . . ."

"Yes he is Doris."

"THAT'S DISGUSTIN'!" As if driving by a particularly gruesome car accident she couldn't look away. "I thought he was happily married fer Christ's sake! Wit kids no less!"

"Married yes, kids yes. Happily no. It's a front."

"The kids?!"

"Hers from a previous relationship. The marriage is a front to keep him in the game. This is why he flies out here from L.A. a couple times a month. Always arranges something for the wife to be doing for a couple of days while he takes a powder." Louie continued to snap away until the two men disappeared into the building. "The kid's a wanna-be, apparently working his way up on the casting couch. The wife got suspicious, thought he was seeing another dame, so she hired us."

"Two guys?! Together, doin'. . . that's . . . that's disgustin'!"

"No Sweetheart, that's a hundred and fifty a day plus expenses. Which to date is $750 plus!" Doris was speechless at the figure. Louie smiled and basked in her shock. "Buy a helluva lot'a Tupp-a-ware, huh?" Louie smirked as he elbowed his wife. The flabbergasted Doris fell back on her knees beside Louie's chair.

"What a shame! And he's such a good singer too!"

Mancino put the camera down and made some more notes.

"Louie?"

"Yeah?"

"If she's payin' you that much ta watch him, how much would **he** pay you for those photographs?" Louie kept writing.

"Technically, she ain't payin' us. It's his money she's spending. But to answer your question, about ten times that much. There's just one problem." He said as he looked up from his writing.

"What's that?!"

"We're P.I.'s, not lawyers. We got morals." Louie pointed out. Doris pouted. "Anything else you wanna ask me?" He asked, head down still writing.

"Yeah, one thing."

"What?"

"How would you say if I told you I was pregnant?" Mancino stopped writing and slowly turned towards Doris.

Fifteen minutes later Louie wrapped up his surveillance, Doris wrapped up the have eaten Tupperware meal and they headed home.

Doris and Louie made love so long and hard that night the neighbors banged on the wall three times and threatened to call the cops.

The Cobalt Room
Ambassador Hotel
Midtown, Manhattan
19:45 Saturday, June 7th

Benny tried not to squirm too much as he sat wedged in between the pair of seven foot tall areca palms grandly gesturing out into the elegantly appointed dining room. The rattling of Lenox china and Revere silverware suddenly seemed louder as he impatiently waited.

If you looked in the encyclopaedia under 'bookworm', you'd likely see a picture of Saul Benjamin Joules. Short, slightly built frame topped off with dark curly hair held back away from his eyes by a pair of horn-rimmed glasses.

Thanks to asthma, bad eyesight and flat feet, he was classified 4F the day after Pearl Harbor. From that point on, for Benny at least, the next four years became a never ending series of military victories, defeats and atrocities lived through broadcasts from the distant planet of Europe and listened to over his family's floor model, RCA Victor.

Saul Joules had a sour ring to it so he began writing under the name Benny Joules back during his third year at Columbia. After all, wasn't college supposed to help you reinvent yourself?

Following graduation he shunned law school, and took up a small apartment just off 9th Street, cashed in his bar mitzvah bonds, bought a brand new Smith-Corona and started banging away.

That was two years, three short stories and one and half novels ago and it still didn't sit well with his Brooklyn based, middle class parents.

That is until about three months ago when his California agent sent him a wire that Warner Brothers were interested in the third draft of his very first script.

Paddy Kelly

Since then, when ever anybody spoke his name he pictured a dark, crowded cinema with credits rolling on the big screen:

"The Formula"
Screenplay by
Benny Joules

As a second generation German-American Jew, Nina Twissleman had no qualms with her heritage but was put off by her family's Draconian adherence to their cultural dogma.

At five foot seven with silken blond hair set off by emerald green eyes Twissleman was never alone on a Saturday night. Or any other night she chose.

Her last year at Columbia University was becoming a bit of drag but a practical necessity and now that she had a part time job and an income to look forward to she was eternally grateful that her parents sprang for the bread for her tuition.

Life had begun to assume the irritating metronomic tic-toc of school, work home, work home, school work home and had begun to take its toll. That is until about six months ago when she met this slightly off-beat writer at a literary reading on Bleeker Street. Two days later she was head-over-heels for Benny Joules.

And no longer a virgin.

Predictably her love affair with Benny didn't sit well with her Manhattan based, upper-middle class parents.

Suddenly Benny's heart leaped when he glanced over at the door to where the maître'd was pointing Nina to Benny's corner table. But he actually had to catch his breath when she began to glide across the room in her turquoise-green, knee-length, chiffon dress, her blond hair piled high on her head.

He rose to pull out her chair.

"Jesus woman! Now I know why we won the damn war!"

"Thank you, Mr. Joules. Your verbal considerations may or may not go unrewarded." They traded a quick kiss.

"Good for me, I think." He retorted as he adjusted her chair for her.

"Okay, what's so important that you make me –"

"Hold on!" He held up a hand while he perused the room and spotted a waiter over by the bar. "WAITER!" He shouted.

The room full of well-dressed swells froze and zeroed in on the crass S.O.B. dining at a place like the Cobalt Room and yelling across the floor for a waiter as if he thought he was in Katz's Deli.

The little waiter scurried over.

"Is everything alright sir?!" He asked staring at all that was visible of Nina. Royally embarrassed, she was bent over nearly hiding under the table pretending to look for something she dropped.

"Two glasses of your finest bubbly, Garson!" Benny ordered. The waiter scurried back across the room and Benny ducked under the table to look at Nina face-to-face. "Shall we move back up to the penthouse?" Red faced she sat back upright.

"You know Joules there are times when I'm tempted to introduce you to my parents just for punishment!"

"Have a little faith oh goddess of all schicksas! Have a little faith!" He fished something out of his inside breast pocket. Her eyes widened and she sat bolt upright but was only able to breathe again when she saw it was a Western Union envelope. He removed and handed her the telegram.

She fought back the heart palpitations as she glanced down and read the wire. It was from the only other person who held unwavering faith in Benny, his agent.

Benny we did it STOP
WB authorized option pay't of $10K STOP
Will be in touch STOP
JR

Still clutching the telegram Nina was speechless. In an instant she realized the animosity and eventual hatred her love for Benny would breed in her parents was swept away and all the hopes and dreams for their future she had been nurturing were vindicated. He stared blankly trying to gauge her reaction.

"Well say something for cryin' out loud!!"

"Is this for real?!"

"No, no. I got it at the joke shop over on Broadway! OF COURSE IT'S REAL you schmuck!" He leaned over grabbed both her cheeks with his hands and kissed her hard. Again heads turned but this time Nina didn't mind.

The waiter brought the champagne and, without words, they toasted.

†

U.S. Capitol Building
Office of Congressman J. Parnell Thomas
Monday, June 9th

"Helen you got those papers from the District Court I need to sign?"

"Yes congressman, right here." The forty-something secretary passed the hefty senator a sealed folder across her desk in the small reception vestibule, smiling at him affectionately as she did so.

A brown-eyed, short, stocky man with a balding head some described Thomas as pugnacious.

As he reached over to retrieve them the senator glanced down and spotted a folded over tabloid on her desk. He reached for it and waved it at the embarrassed civil service worker.

"Helen, how many times have I told you these things will rot your brain?"

"I'm sorry J. P. I like to read the gossip pages. It helps me think my life's not so bad."

"Uh huh." He mumbled as he perused the column on page three. "*Tradeviews*! What kind'a name is that for a column? This is nothing but a gossip rag!"

Parnell, who was seeking to reignite the failed communist scare of 1940 in the Congress, was suddenly attracted by a story on communist sympathizers in Hollywood.

John Parnell Thomas was born John Patrick Feeney Jr. in one of the toughest, gang ridden districts on the Eastern Seaboard, Jersey City, New Jersey.

Due to the fact that at the time Mr. Feeney, AKA Thomas was growing up, the turn of the last century, Irish more or less had two choices for good advancement in America; organized crime or politics. There was a simple solution if you wanted to walk the Straight and Narrow: change your name. So John became 'J' and Patrick became Parnell while 'Feeney' became a nice respectable 'Thomas'. Problem solved. No one was the wiser. For now.

Language is a wonderful thing. A fact that accomplished journalists like Willy Wilkinson, Editor-in-Chief of *The Hollywood Reporter*, and weekly author of the *Tradeviews* column, were fully cognizant of.

Thomas read on.

This is not an issue that concerns merely a few hundred writers. It concerns millions of readers who depend on the free trade of ideas. It concerns still more millions of children who can't yet read but were born with the right hope of a free world.

"We still gonna meet up later tonight?" The secretary cooed.

"What?" Parnell spat.

"Tonight! Are we still meeting?!"

"No, sorry, can't. Gotta take the wife out." He absentmindedly answered. She pursed her lips. "Can I borrow this?" He asked brandishing the tabloid halfway through the door to his office.

"Be my guest!" She turned and banged away at her typewriter.

The phrase 'communist sympathizer' in the article is the phrase that caught Thomas' attention.

'Communist sympathizer' was considered the exact equivalent of 'actual' communist. Only the verb 'sympathizer' provided those flinging the charges a legal shield to hide behind by requiring no proof of one's accusation. It was like the statement 'he stands accused of rape'. He might as well have done it.

'Communist sympathizers' were the exact words William R. Wilkinson used to brand eleven studio writers on the front page of that week's *The Hollywood Reporter* in his widely read *Tradeviews* column entitled ' Vote for Joe Stalin'.

Largely considered a revenge move against the studio heads who froze him out a decade ago when he wanted to break into 'The Biz' as a producer, he decided to go after their bread and butter; the talent.

Thomas sat behind his desk pondering that headline but was interrupted when the intercom rang.

"Congressman Thomas, Mr. Jack Warner of Warner Studios on line one for you."

"Thank you. I'll take it Helen."

CHAPTER III

Office of *The Hollywood Reporter*
1500 Wilshire Boulevard
Hollywood, California

Stout but not short, with a full head of salt and pepper hair, balanced by a well-trimmed moustache, L.A. resident and man about town, showman, entrepreneur, club owner, publisher and movie producer wanna-be William R. Wilkinson was a man of many talents. But most of all Billy wanted to be a movie studio owner.

In reality, Wilkinson was a gambler. A hard core risk taker born to games of chance.

Not your once-a-year games of chance like the upcoming Baseball World Series or your spend-a-Saturday-at-the-pony track kind of gambler, but your dyed-in-the-wool, come-on-baby, Daddy needs new shoes, this one's gonna hit-pay dirt, bet it all on black kind of gambler.

Back in the late Twenties Wilkinson worked for a long time accumulating assets and money then betting everything he had on establishing an independent film studio. Unfortunaty he picked the worst place possible to do it – Hollywood.

With no New York bank backing, no significant L.A. connections and no Jewish blood in the family he'd had a better chance of selling ham sandwiches on a Saturday morning outside a synagogue.

So, in the early Thirties, he turned to the growing magazine game.

Initially he paid the bills with the profits on his tabloid, *The Hollywood Reporter*, a gossip rag he gave birth to, some claimed, to get back at Warner and the studio heads for freezing him out then killing his studio dreams.

In keeping with his philosophy to always think big, Billy covered only the 'Big Stories'. Stories such as who was sleeping with whom, which studios were rowing with which big name stars or starlets and which personalities were in trouble with the law. In between the gossip he squeezed in some movie reviews.

By printing dirt about the Hollywood actors he could hurt the talent pool and producer's stables thereby potentially damaging B.O. sales. But sabotaging box office sales was only a part time interest.

Starting back in 1930 Billy had been careful to make all the right connections required to build and maintain his alternative businesses that is his publishing interests along with his partnerships in night clubs on the L.A. Strip along with several other small operations.

When the studio heads banded together to boycott his paper and banned his reporters from all the film lots due to the damaging gossip he was churning out, he ordered his guys to climb over the walls and fences, hide in alleyways etc. to get candid photos and to dig through the garbage cans of studio execs homes and offices to uncover dirt he could use against them and thus increase circulation.

Never knowing when to say enough is enough, and after the studios were scandalized into submission, Wilkinson set his sights ever higher.

It was during this period that it was rumored he began to harbor ambitions of owning the ultimate night club. A gambler's haven for the hard core junkie gambler where there was always subdued lighting, no open windows to the outside world, no clocks, comfortable seats at the tables and most importantly free drinks for the gamblers served by sexy ladies. A 'who needs a wife?' type of atmosphere where there was no reason to leave until you were flat broke and had to be thrown out.

Billy saw *The Hollywood Reporter* as his ticket to that paradise.

If William R. Hearst is the Father of Yellow Journalism, William R. Wilkinson can be considered the Father of American tabloid journalism.

It remains a toss-up which one did more damage to America and American journalism.

So with the depth and breadth of this street network now established it was no great coincidence that a friend of his, a guy named Rothman, while driving through Nevada on his way back out to L.A., happened to cruise by a site which lie dormant in the 105 degree heat of the Nevada desert. He noticed a 'for sale' sign on that plot of land which was several miles outside of the small town of Las Vegas.

Rothman, well aware of Billy's ambitions, was also well aware that if Wilkinson was ever to realize his fantasy casino it would have to be outside the confines of the increasingly regulation prone L.A. area where the much publicized LAPD-Mafia war was heating up. A social phenomena *The Hollywood Reporter* also paid more than adequate attention to.

Rothman told Billy and Billy, confident he had the liquid assets required to dive right in, which he didn't, and after driving out to see the property, wasted no time in drawing up a plan.

Until about an hour ago when he got another wire from his L.A. agent, Benny Joules was on top of the world. Now tucked in his top pocket, burning a hole in his chest as he descended the stairs down onto the Bronx-Manhattan line subway platform, he could hardly focus.

WB Producer backed out STOP
No reason given. Project now on back burner
STOP
Will be in touch STOP
JR

Two years to realize the dream, two minutes for some know-nothing, pencil neck suit to shoot it in the back.

Some money-hungry prick he'd never even have the displeasure of meeting so he could hate face-to-face.

The smell of ozone permeated the air and the screeching of steel wheels ground in his ears as the breeze from the tunnels blew across the platforms. The crowd undulated towards the edge of the platform as the train approached.

He thought about how it would be if he ended it right now. Just one step off the platform and it would all be over.

Ten inches into the eternal abyss.

"Writer's Life Tragically Cut Short"

Presumptuous to think *The Times* would give front page coverage. Who the hell would? *The Daily News* maybe? Probably run it for days!

"Drama Writer's Dreams Derailed Downtown!"

"Hey Pal, you gettin' on or what?" The pugnacious guy in the woollen Ike jacket pushed past him onto the train.

"Sorry . . . yeah, yeah I'm going." He shuffled into the crowded car, grabbed a strap and stared aimlessly as the doors slid shut.

The girl he was going to meet was just then crossing Washington Square Park and coming out on MacDougal Street.

By the time Nina reached the near empty French styled cafe on the West Side Benny was already there, brooding in a dark corner. She glanced at the empty table top before she sat.

"This seat taken?" By way of an answer he slid the Western union across the table. She read as she took a seat.

"WHAT THE HELL. . ." She caught herself. "What the hell is this?!"

"I . . . I don't know! I'm no dissident. I tried to sign up, but they wouldn't let me. I've never been a Communist." She looked at him.

"Did you call him?!"

"Of course! He says there's an investigation."

"I know you were never a Communist. Maybe they got the wrong Joules?"

"Two years! Two freakin' years playing around with that script! I finally get it done, get it on someone's desk and they say, 'Great kid! Where you been our whole life?' Here's a nice big fat check! And a couple of weeks later they tell me it's on hold 'cause of some investigation!"

"What the hell does that mean anyway?! 'On the back burner!'" She challenged as she quoted the telegram.

"Who the heck knows?"

"Maybe they put it on the back burner means it was a half cooked idea?" She weakly joked.

"Can you be serious? Just for once?" He half mumbled. He took her hands across the table. "I mean, I been giving it a lot of thought and . . ." In her mind Nina began to tense up. "I have a standing offer at the New Yorker. If I take it we could get an apartment together over on the West Side, you could start grad school, and we could. . ."

"Could what? Exactly?"

"You know, talk about getting-"

"Whoa Cowboy! Just because we're sleeping together, sharing each other's tooth brush, personal secrets and talked about maybe tying the knot in couple of years, let's don't be presumptuous, okay?!" She immediately saw the emotional damage in his face.

"Benny!" She squeezed his hands. "You're feeling a bit . . . vulnerable. Kicked around. Dejected. This is not a good time to make life impacting decisions. This, whatever it is, is only temporary."

"Are you saying that you don't want to marry me? That marriage is not in our future?"

"I'm not saying 'not ever', just not now. I haven't decided on grad school yet, that's another year maybe two. You need a steady job. I mean what happens if one of those jerk wad studios decides they want to buy something else you've done? You'll have to-" He shot her a look of consternation. "WE'LL have to move out there."

Benny took the cue to change the subject.

"I went to a Ring Lardner lecture once! Does that mean I'm a communist?!" Nina looked down without answering.

"1500 writers struggling for a couple of dozen jobs out there in Hollyweed, I land one then get labelled a commie!"

"Benny, we don't know that that's what this is about!"

"Out'a nowhere! With all that crap in *The Hollywood Reporter* about commies in Hollywood, what else could it be about?! I mean, I could give a shit about anybody's politics!" Nina shifted to the chair next to him and embraced.

He looked her in the eye. "I'm scared to death, and nobody can tell me it isn't because I'm afraid of being investigated!"

"So what if they investigate? They're not gonna find any evidence of anything?!"

"Evidence? EVIDENCE?! This is the American authorities they don't need any evidence! They'll make evidence, it's what they do!"

He had been straight forward with Nina about his manic depressive mood swings the first night they slept together. He didn't have much choice. She blew so many holes in his defences so fast that there was no time to recover. And it felt pretty good. It was a dynamic he hadn't expected. Now she was keeping her end of the bargain and helping him deal with it.

"Nina, they're putting people in jail! Prison! For what they say or write! Or believe in! This is

America, there's supposed to be an amendment allowing free speech! I mean . . . where's the line?"

"How do mean, the line?"

"How do I mean a line?! THE LINE BETWEEN TRUMAN AND FRANCO! THE LINE BETWEEN SENATOR THOMAS AND BENITO MUSSOLINI! DO YOU KNOW WHO HIRES JAILBIRDS? HUH, DO YA? NOBODY, THAT'S WHO!"

She glanced around the cafe and thankfully there was no one in the immediate vicinity to be alarmed by his shouting.

"Hey, I've got it!" She declared trying to lighten the mood. "Why don't we take a ride up to the park? Walk around a little?" He didn't respond. She leaned in and lifted his chin. "Treat you to a ride on the carousel!" He forced a weak smile. She leaned in closer, looked side to side and whispered, "I got five bucks. What say we go up to the park, get a couple of non-kosher hot dogs, sneak around behind the monkey house and eat 'em? No one will ever know!" He was still sick to his stomach but, looking into her sparkling green eyes he couldn't stay mad. His fears slowly evaporated.

"Alright. Two conditions."

"Name them!"

"Brown mustard and sauerkraut."

"Deal!" A waiter came up to the table and spoke in a heavy French accent.

"May I help you please?"

"Do you have kosher hot dogs?" Nina asked.

"Quoi s'il vous plait?"

"With brown mustard and sauerkraut?" Benny added.

"Zis café is French. We dun make no hot dawgses!" He sarcastically barked.

"Oh!" She said. "Looks like Central Park it is!" They sprang to their feet, grabbed their things and ran off.

The irritated waiter shook his head and went back inside cursing under his breath in French.

✝

"You want more money?" The thirty-something going on forty-something, bleached blond snapped at her son. Sitting at the breakfast table in a robe, her hair in curlers and wearing slippers she sipped from the near empty wine glass, the wine no doubt contributing to what once was a respectable female physique.

The extent and beauty of the expensive kitchen was diminished by the chaos of the dirty dishes in the sink and splayed across the ten seat, mahogany table.

"Yeah!" The husky teen snapped back.

"Then get off your ass and get a job!" Doing up her robe she shuffled to the far cabinet and fished out an open bottle of Cabernet Sauvignon. "You're eighteen years old fer Christ's sake! Ain't you tired of free loadin?!"

"Ain't you tired of drinking at nine o'clock in the morning?" He shot back.

Just then Jake Steadman came down the staircase doing up his tie and came into the kitchen.

"Here!" Steadman barked as he handed the kid a twenty. His wife topped off her glass. The kid snatched the bill but stood with his hand out again. His father relented with another twenty.

Without salutation the boy darted out the front door, ran to the curb and jumped into the black '45 Olds waiting at curbside. The car sped off.

"What time you coming back tonight?" She demanded.

"Dunno. I'll call ya from the office." Steadman gulped down the remnants of coffee and also headed for the door.

"When are you gonna stop pandering to that kid?!" She challenged.

"About the same time you quit drinking at eight o'clock in the morning and dry out!"

"Like father like son! And it's nearly ten o'clock!" She leaned back against the counter top. "You know despite all your money he's gonna come to no good! He's still your kid!"

"How do I know he's my kid?" Steadman let the door slam shut behind hm. His wife watched his new Chrysler New Yorker pull out of the drive then darted for the kitchen phone. The party on the other line picked up on the second ring.

"Leroy, he's gone." She spoke into the phone.

I be over in half a hour Baby. Came the response.

She scurried to the bathroom to clean up.

CHAPTER IV

1929 Christopher Street
Greenwich Village
New, York City, N.Y.
Monday June 30th

Rather than a dishevelled Nina Twissleman it was an emotionally charged, single-minded Nina that pushed through the front door and made her way to the index board on the wall adjacent to the elevator in the small lobby of 1929 Christopher Street.

Decked out in a white shirt, dark blue jacket with a tight, matching skirt and wearing black heels, she didn't notice Harry leaning over the counter leering at her through the show window separating his news stand and the lobby.

She removed the white glove from her hand and using her index finger, scrolled the building index.

Harry, sitting at his station behind the small, crowded counter in his news store, leaned over again and peeked through the side window into the lobby. After a minute he limped over to the side door and cracked it open.

"You looking for Doc young lady?"

"Doc who?"

"Doc McKeowen."

"No! I'm looking for M&M Investigations." She read from a torn piece of paper then returned to perusing the board.

"That board ain't gonna do you no good lady!"

"Why not?" She asked the floor.

"Cause, it ain't been updated since '37"

"Then why is it here?!"

"Fer show. Got'a keep up appearances."

"How conscientious!" The sarcasm wasn't lost on Harry.

"M&M's up on the sixth floor."

"Thank you." She stepped over and rang for the elevator. Harry smiled and re-opened the door.

"Ringing for the elevator ain't gonna do ya no good."

With one hand on hip her head dropped. "Dare I inquire why?" She asked staring at the floor.

"Cause it's busted. Been busted since-"

"Since '37!" She cut him off.

"That's right." He quietly nodded.

"Thank you for all your help."

"You're welcome."

Glad I wore high heels! Nina mumbled to herself as she rounded the first two stair cases to the second floor. By the fourth floor she decided to take her shoes off and finish the climb in her stocking feet.

Twelve flights and fifteen minutes after starting it was a winded Nina which stood outside Doc's office door, both hands on her knees, purse dangling from her wrist and panting like a race horse just run a Derby.

Steadying herself against the doorjamb, Nina was bent over sliding her shoes back on when, without warning, the office door swung open hitting her in the ass and knocking her forward. Louie appeared from behind the door.

"Ohh! SH . . . SHOOT! Sorry!" Mancino declared.

"Hi." She greeted composing herself. "Real classy location you got here!" Nina panted back using Louie's shoulder to steady herself as she perused the circa 1920's hall which was in need of a good coat of paint.

"Thanks! We got lucky on a case few years back and moved up here to-"

"Yeah, yeah, don't care! This M&M?"

"Yeah, yeah! I mean yes it is! Come in please." He held the door open for her. "Shirley can you get this lady some water?"

"Yeah. She okay?" Shirley scurried from behind her desk to the water cooler, filled a Dixie cup and brought it to Nina.

"Sorry ma'am. Elevator's been out since-"

"Don't tell me, since '37?" Nina gulped down the water.

"Yes! How'd you know that?" Shirley asked.

"Lucky guess. I'm here to speak to a...." She consulted the paper again. "Michael McKayhen."

"It's McKeowen and he don't like nobody callin' him by that name."

"McKeowen? If his name is McKeowen-"

"No, that other name." Shirley leaned and lowered her voice. "Michael, he don't like that. It's Doc."

"Is he a Ph.D.?" Nina was shocked. Louie and Shirley had a laugh and Doc's office door opened.

"Somebody declare a day off?" McKeowen growled. "You guys don't have any work to do I can scare some up for you." Louie smiled as he continued to ogle Nina.

"Louie Mancino." He introduced himself. "Can I get you something else? A tea, coffee? More water?" She handed Louie the empty Dixie cup and looked at Doc.

"No thank very much. I'm here to hire a detective."

Louie sprang in front of her and pointed over to his office.

"How fortunate, for you I mean. I'm a detective and I just happen to be between cases!" Doc made eye contact and addressed her.

"Step this way please Miss-"

"Twissleman. Nina Twissleman." Doc ushered her into his office.

"Louie, you scanned through those surveillance reports on the Jensen case yet?" Doc prompted.

"I'm waitin' on Shirley to get them in alphabetical order so I can-"

"They on your desk Mr. Mancino." Shirley said without looking up from her typing. Doc led Nina into his office. Louie leaned down to Shirley as she typed before heading to his office.

"Thanks traitor!" Mancino quietly snapped as he watched Nina disappear into Doc's office.

"You married!" Shirley shot back. Go scan sumthin' else. Like some reports!" Mancino ducked into his office,

Shirley smirked and shook her head.

"How these two get **anything** done is beyond me!" She mumbled.

"How can we be of help Miss Twissleman?" Doc asked as he took his seat behind the mahogany desk.

By way of an answer she reached into her purse, produced a manila envelope and handed it to Doc. He pulled out a half dozen, eight and a half by eleven, black and white glossies of what appeared to be a crime scene and shuffled through them.

From various angles they showed a young man, twenty-ish, clearly dead, hanging from a closet rod in an apartment.

It was Benny.

The backs of the photos were stamped; 'Property of NYPD. DO NOT REMOVE!'

Doc, already a long standing member of the unofficial NYPD 'suspicious persons' list immediately became suspicious.

"These are official police photos! How'd you get them?"

"That's not important Mr. McKeowen. All that matters is those photos are all the evidence I have of my fiancé's death."

"Your fiancé?"

"That's right, Benny. Saul Benjamin Joules is his birth name. His pen name is Benny Joules."

"Do you have any doubt that he might be dead?"

"No. His parents were summoned to the morgue to I.D. the body. He's dead."

"What'a the cops say?"

"Clear case of suicide."

"Was he a depressive? Fool around with drugs? Did he have any reason to commit suicide?"

Nina got quiet and looked away and didn't speak.

"Why would he have wanted to off himself?" Doc pushed.

"A bit crude don't you think?! 'Off himself'!" She snapped.

"So he had a reason?"

"He signed a movie deal with a Hollywood agent who sold a script he wrote to the Warner Brothers. They optioned it and said they would start production this fall. Less than two weeks later they reneged."

"The agent or the studio?"

"No idea. The agent sent a telegram, that's all I know."

"Your fiancé have any skeletons in his closet? Anything the studio might have thought would bring bad P.R. down on them?"

"Please! Benny was a squeaky clean as they come! Didn't drink, didn't smoke and didn't gamble. Attended synagogue until he went off to college! There's no way in hell he 'off'ed' himself!"

"You don't buy it was suicide?"

"No. I don't know. Not in my heart, no."

"So, what are you asking us to do?"

"Find out why!"

"Why what, exactly?"

"Why he may have been murdered."

"If he was murdered."

"Okay, if."

"He have any enemies, anyone who'd want to see him dead? Anybody who might profit from his death?"

"Does this mean you'll take the case?"

"No. Not until I have more information, especially why you think his death is any different from the four to five hundred or so other suicides we see in this city every year."

"It's actually closer to three hundred according to the New York Coroner's Office." She corrected. Doc was impressed.

"As to why is this one different . . ." She continued. "How many of the other three hundred do you think had their whole world ahead of them?" She pushed.

"All of them!" Doc shot back.

"And were engaged to be married, a promising career in writing with a possibility to break into Hollywood movies?"

Doc sat forward in his chair.

"Miss Twissleman, with all due respect to your fiancé, murder cases are for the Homicide Squad. We're not cops. We investigate insurance fraud, extortion, infidelity, arson, you know the normal stuff."

"I read in the papers about how you broke open the husband-wife murder case, the Central Park murderer. I thought-"

"That was an insurance case and I don't discuss other people's cases with clients or people not involved." Doc's mind was made up as he wrestled with how to make her understand. "Nina, these photos are property of the NYPD and are part of an on-going investigation. I could lose my licence just by being in possession of them!" Doc handed her back her photos. "I'm sorry we can't help you Nina."

"But I-" She started and was cut off as Doc stood up. Nina got the hint. "It's **Miss Twissleman**, Mr. McKeowen!" She slid the envelope of photos back into her purse and turned to leave.

Louie, who had been standing by his office door until he heard Doc's door open, darted out feigning to go off to the side to the coffee pot.

Shirley, hearing the knob on Doc's door turnr quickly scurried back to her desk and resumed her typing. Nina made her way across the office and stomped out the front door.

"What the hell you suppose is eatin' her?" Louie ventured.

"Probably just pissed off because somebody dropped a house on her sister." Shirley quipped. Doc emerged behind Twissleman and was immediately confronted by Mancino.

"What happened? What'd you say to her? Did'ja take the case?!" Louie pushed, his eyes glued to

Nina's firm, lithe figure as the door closed behind her.

"No." Doc made his way to Shirley's desk and dropped a pair of files on it. "Mark these as closed, date them and file them please Shirl."

"Yes Mr. McKeowen."

"Oh my God Doc!" Louie followed him around the small office as Doc went to the coffee pot.

"We're not taking the case Louie." Doc said ignoring Mancino as he headed back to his office. Mancino stood shocked then decided to follow him in.

"Doc, I know she's German and all and they did lots of bad shit to the Jews in the war–"

"She's Jewish Louie."

"Well there you go! All the more reason we got'a help her! She was prosecuted during the war!"

Anticipating Mancino's onslaught Doc busied himself at his desk.

"She was nowhere near the war. She's only about to finish university, she's probably never even left Brooklyn!"

"She was probably too scared!" Louie argued.

"When did you become such a champion of ethnicity?" Doc challenged.

"Ethics ain't got nuthin' to do with it Doc! This is about helpin' the little guy. You know, Jews and Italians workin' to help each other. Like during the big linen strike up in Massachusetts back in 1812."

"1912 Einstein."

"Or the partnership between -"

"Luciano and Lansky?"

"That ain't right Doc! I'm talkin' about good Italians helpin' Jews!"

Ever sensitive about being Italian-American when there were near weekly headlines about Italian gangsters in the papers, Louie was put off by Doc's comparison.

"Meyer Lansky's as Jewish as they come besides, you wouldn't be talkin' about Italians helpin' Jews if the Jew in question wasn't a hot little number with blond hair and green eyes now, would ya?" McKeowen challenged.

Louie tried to look insulted. It didn't work. "Forget it Mancino, you're out'a your league. Besides, you're married and you gotta work Saturdays." Doc chuckled.

"That ain't funny Doc. Some people might mistakenly misconscrew that as racist!"

"Yeah, racism in New York. That'd be unusual wouldn't it?"

"Doc, we gotta take this case!"

"Louie, all I gotta do is die, pay taxes and keep Nikki from getting pissed off at me! I don't **gotta** take this case. I don't need it, you don't need it and therefore the firm don't need it! I'm tellin' you straight up, this case is wrong. It smells bad about nine different ways from Sunday and I'm in no mood to get mixed up in some messy shit, especially when things are looking like they're finally going our way! We got a case load to carry us well into summer of next year and this year, for the first time in my life, I plan on a summer vacation for Nikki and me. A proper one with sand, sun and surf someplace other than crammed in between a hundred thousand sweaty bodies on a smelly beach in Coney Island eatin' three week old hot dogs!"

"The kosher ones are usually only two weeks old Doc. Besides-"

"Ferget it!"

Shirley sat quietly feigning paper work as her mind dutifully recorded every word of Doc and Louie's exchange.

"Yeah, maybe you're right Doc." Louie acquiesced. Doc became immediately suspicious. "Just outta curiosity, his wouldn't have nothin' to do with you bein' afraid of Chief Sullivan now, would it?" Mancino challenged.

"Fuck that washed-up, useless piece of shit! Asshole's never cracked a case in his life, probably hasn't made a dent in this one and highly unlikely he ever will!"

"Then think, just for a few seconds, think how beautiful it would be if you cracked it! Do you know when Sullivan would live that down?" Doc peered at Louie. "NEVER! That's when Doc! Never ever!"

Doc made for the door.

"Where you goin'?" Louie demanded.

"It's almost lunch time. I'm going down the corner, to get a couple'a one week old dogs." Doc turned back to Shirley as he headed for the door. "You want anything?"

"Don't look at me, I ain't no rich P.I.! I bring my own lunch!" From under her desk Shirley brandished a Tupperware container. Louie looked over at her.

"Macy's?" He inquired.

"Canal Street. They're half price."

"Figures!" Mancino grumbled back into his office.

✝

Office of *The Hollywood Reporter*
Sunset Boulevard
Tuesday, July 8th 12:45

William Wilkinson's Hollywood office occupied the second floor corner office on Wilshire and Valencia. It was there that he worked as, when he was in town which wasn't too often as of late, the Editor-in-Chief and sole owner of *The Hollywood Reporter*, the oldest Hollywood based weekly devoted to the film industry.

"I'm just sayin' I got guys I know who run in certain circles-" From across the desk Rothman's offer was cut off before it really got started.

"Nothing personal Roth, I know you're a great fixer, but I know the circles you run in and I know the kind'a guys they run with. That kind of money I don't need! Thanks, but no thanks."

"Your funeral brother." The small man shrugged and stubbed out the remaining half inch of cigarette in the aluminum desk ash tray. "But I get the

88

distinct impression you're in over your head on this one." He surmised.

"Don't take it personal, it's just that if I fall in with those guys sooner or later they'll own my ass and I'm not looking for a lifetime of indentured servitude, I just need a loan to get me through this rough patch."

"Okay." Rothman stood to leave. "Lemme know if you change your mind."

"I'll see ya later at the club."

"I'll be there around eight or nine."

"And Abe . . . thanks."

"What'a friends for?" Rothman left.

The fact that Wilkinson was only able to keep his head above water by robbing Peter to pay Paul despite his multiple investments in and around the L.A. area, was no secret. What was not as obvious, although it was bubbling to the surface, was his constant frustration at not being able to make the giant leap towards, the one big break that would allow his fortunes to turn a corner and launch him into the 'Big Time'. A place Wilkinson firmly believed he had earned the right to be.

Now driven to spread his wings beyond the magazine trade and the partial ownership of a few clubs, Wilkinson called in the 'cash ringer' he had been sitting on.

He manned the intercom on his desk.

"Jackie, put a call in to Bill Bellows at the Wells Fargo Bank and buzz me when it's through will ya?"

Will do Mr. Wilkinson.

89

Billy had tapped $200,000 from his friend the industrialist Howard Hughes and was calling his banker to check that the wire transfer had cleared.

Mr. Wilkinson, Mr. Bellows on line one.

"Thank you Jackie." He picked up. "Bill! Billy here!"

Never gets old William. The banker flatly responded. *What can I do for you?*

"I'm expecting a wire transfer from the Hughes Corporation into my private account?"

Is it coming in from in state or out of state?

"Out of state I think."

I'll have to go over to the transfer desk to check the logs. Do you want to hold or will I call you back?

"I'll hold."

Okay, wait one.

Minutes later Bellows returned and informed Wilkinson the cash had been deposited in his account and was available. Wilkinson at least had the good sense to realize that 200K was not going to transform his dream casino from fantasy to reality so he wasted no time putting the second phase of his plan into action.

Later that afternoon Wilkinson pushed through the double doors of the Grand Casino in the town of Pacheco, up north in Contra Costa County, far enough away from L.A. that he wouldn't be recognized

The smell of cigarette smoke and cheap perfume coupled with the bright rainbow flash of neon permeating his senses as he entered the room made him feel all warm and fuzzy inside.

Melded with the delightful mechanical clatter of the slot machines set against the chatter of the crowds swarming the main floor as he walked through the casino and his spirits were lifted.

The casino manager was called over by the teller when Wilkinson slapped two stacks of cash on the counter and asked for 100 thou in chips. The manager approved the transaction, Billy staked out a seat, ordered a couple of drinks and went to work at a blackjack table.

After a very short hour Wilkinson was down by $150,000 at the craps table but knew his luck was due. He had been in this situation many times before.

A pair of wins with the right amount would put him back up again. Three wins would put him ahead and possibly back on track to hit his required goal; walking out of the casino with $500,000, enough to get his stalled project up and running again.

Thirty minutes later he was back up another 100 grand.

He briefly considered quitting when his chips reached the 375,000 mark. But only briefly.

By his third hour at the table he began to sober up, by then he was back down to 25,000.

He bet the first half and lost.

There was only one person at that table who realized the next hand might seal William 'Billy' Wilkinson's fate.

Finally the Indian dealer turned to Wilkinson.

"It's your bet sir." She informed.

His up card was six of hearts. He sneaked a peak at his down card. With no hesitation he bet his last $500 in chips.

"Call." She said.

He turned his down card up. A three of hearts. Nine total, same suit, that was a good sign. Low numbers, that was a bad sign.

He signaled for a hit.

She dealt a six of spades. Fifteen showing. No choice.

He signaled again. She dealt.

That it was the Queen of Spades probably should have been an omen to William Wilkinson regarding his future. But addictions always blind to the truth.

Billy left the casino and walked across the road to his run down motel $200K down and with nothing on him but an encroaching hangover.

One hour and a half dozen drinks later, riddled with Catholic guilt and shame tempered by anger, Wilkinson picked up the phone in his room and asked the operator to place a call to his close friend back in L.A., Abe Rothman.

"Your offer to introduce me to your friends still stand?" He probed when Rothman answered. Fantasizing how big his piece of the fantasy casino pie Wilkinson planned to build might be, Rothman was only too happy to talk.

"Absolutely Wilki boy! What'a friends for?"

✝

Formosa Restaurant
West Hollywood

Less than a week after his offer from Rothman Wilkinson contacted his lawyer, Greg Bautzer and they were sharing a power lunch at the Formosa Restaurant just off Santa Monica Boulevard in West Hollywood.

The long, neon festooned bar to the right of the entrance highlighted the large dining room and was in turn itself highlighted by the countless numbers of B&W stock shots of Bogey, The Duke and Rita Hayworth mounted overhead around the entire circumference of the room. To the left tables and booths filled the floor.

In classic secret agent fashion Wilkinson had arrived a half hour early, took a seat in a back booth facing the door and primed himself with a couple of house specials, Mai Tais. From his surreptitiously selected secret seat he watched as Bautzer entered the place.

The waitress met him at the table.

"Another one of these and a scotch rocks for the gentleman." Billy informed her. Bautzer dropped his briefcase on the seat between them and they greeted.

"You sure you want to go in this direction?" Bautzer instantly probed.

"Yes! Now, I thought about this and I need you to buy the property in your name. I got a rep in this town and if word gets around it's me buying the land the price'll go through the roof. Plus people will start snooping around."

In reality no one would be likely to snoop around, they would just write it off to one of Billy's many get-rich-quick schemes, Bautzer mused to himself.

"You're probably right, that makes sense. What else?" The lawyer pushed.

"What is she asking for it?"

"She's got it up for a hundred thou, but I think if we wave cash in her face she'll knock ten maybe twelve points off that."

'It' was a plot of land, 40 acres in total, a mile east of U.S. 91, one mile south of the Hotel Last Frontier, the oldest, fulltime operating casino in the otherwise desolate area ironically known as Paradise.

"Ninety K's still a little too high but if you can get her down to eighty-five, buy it. And don't record the deed until I give the go ahead, got it? Just sit on it."

"You're payin' the bills." The lawyer agreed.

"Good."

"What about contractors, architects all that kind of stuff?" Greg asked. Billy smiled and sat back as the waitress brought the drinks.

"Can I tell you about our specials today, gentlemen?" She asked. Bautzer started to say something but Wilkinson cut him off.

"No thanks Doll. We're not gonna be eating. Here . . ." He passed her a twenty. "Keep the change."

That was his secret code for; 'Go away and don't come back until we call you'.

When she was out of earshot Wilkinson resumed.

"Plans are drawn up, materials are estimated and crews are being lined up."

"What about a title search?" Bautzer.

"If she's got it up for sale she must have clear title. Word has it she bought it from one of the original settlers. Hell, fucking Arizona is barely seventy years old fer cryin' out loud, it's the least populated state in the Union!"

"Billy, I got'a ask. Money? This is not a neighborhood fruit stand you're looking to open here and this isn't The Strip, The Trocadero or Ciro's. What you're talking about is twice as big as both of those . . . combined." Bautzer pointed out. Billy was not fazed.

"I got a ringer. Guaranteed loan, plenty of dough to cover the whole pie." Greg fought hard to conceal his amazement but didn't do a very good job of it.

"What about legal regulations on gambling?"

"Done. Already did the research two years ago. Ten times easier than here. The town of Paradise is not incorporated! Why do think I been looking at Nevada for the last five years?"

"Which also means they can raise taxes whenever they want and under no obligation to increase or upgrade essential services!" His lawyer reminded him.

"Once this project gets off the ground and they realize how much revenue it's gonna bring in, trust me the town fathers are gonna be bending over backwards to keep me happy!"

"Sounds like you got it all figured out."

"I always do Gregy Boy! I always do!"

Billy signaled and the waitress served more drinks then disappeared.

CHAPTER V

That afternoon Louie returned to the office to find Nikki doing something he'd never seen her do before, typing a report, filling in for Shirley.

Nikki and Doc met back in '42 when he was investigating a counterfeiting case which led him to the Woolworth Building downtown where she was a receptionist. Fresh off a nasty divorce the last thing McKeowen was looking for was romance but Nikki Cole's blue eyes and auburn hair instantly gobsmacked him. The fact that she was always impeccably dressed and mentally sharp as a tack seriously breached his defences.

At thirty-two and with a daughter from her first marriage, her high school sweetheart-come-husband, was killed in the war. Nikki now with Doc these past five years, felt a void had been filled.

"Hey Nikki!"

"Hey Louie, how's it hanging?" She continued flipping
through the Rolodex on Shirley's desk.

"Low and to the left Sweetheart. What'a you doin' at the desk? Where's Shirl?" Louie moved to the coffee pot.

"Doc gave her the afternoon off. Dentist."

"Dentist?! That woman's got the most perfect teeth I've ever seen in my life!"

Nikki gestured Louie in closer and whispered to him.

"Don't tell Doc, but 'Dentist' is Shirley's code word for meeting her boyfriend."

"So she's not just **her teeth** getting drilled?"

"Louie! You kiss your mother with that mouth?"

"Shit Nik, my mother's Sicilian, she taught me to talk like that." Louie finished fixing his coffee with six sugars then started sifting through the mail on the desk. "So, why you here?"

"Eight years in the New York Public Library and six years at Naval Intel downtown and now not working anymore, I'm getting a bit antsy. Not used to dust gathering on my brain I guess."

"What's Doc think about that?"

"Oh I'm sure he'll support me."

"In other words, he doesn't have an opinion because he doesn't know."

"And I would appreciate you waiting until I tell him before you say anything!"

"What's it worth to ya?"

"Let me think about it. How about you don't let on to Doc that I want to do some work around here, and I won't tell Doris you drool like a Doberman looking at a sirloin every time a pretty blond comes in here? Deal?"

"In Sicilian we have a word for people like you!"

"So we have a deal. Good! I always liked you Louie from the first time you showed up here."

"You and Doc weren't together when I first showed up here!"

"Well, whenever I first met you."

"Anything else, Don Vito Cole?" Nikki smiled at Mancino's sarcasm.

"I got a message for ya." Nikki passed a message chit to Louie. A single phone number was scrawled across the small

yellow paper.

"Huh? Lower Manhattan exchange number." He noted.

"Yeah, down near the Battery." Just then the phone rang. Nikki picked it up on the second ring.

"M&M Investigations. How may I help you?" Nikki cringed and pulled the receiver away from her ear. Louie shrugged at her and she held out the receiver so he could hear. There was a loudly crying woman on the other end.

I need to speak with . . . a Mr. Mancino! The detective! The caller eked out between emotionally racked sobs.

"It's for you." She passed the phone to Louie.

"Hello?"

This . . . this is the . . . fourth time! Ya hear me?! The fourth time! The near hysterical female shouted from the other end.

Louie covered the receiver and turned to Nikki.

This broad call here four times?

"I don't even know who the heck it is!" Cole whispered back.

"The fourth time for what?" Louie challenged the caller.

Forth time he promised . . . he'd quit messing around and the fourth time I . . . I caught him

99

messin' around! She sputtered out in a heavy Brooklyn dialect.

"So what can we do for you Mrs . . . ?"

Abernathy. Emily Abernathy!

"So what can we do for you Mrs. Abernathy?"

I want a DIVORCE! She shouted before breaking into another sobbing fit. *He has lots'a dough and I want a settlement! After thirteen years'a marriage I'm entitled!*

"Exactly how much dough does this guy have?" Louie felt the punch to his thigh as he finished the question.

TONS! She shouted. *You know that new harbor facility down on the Battery?* Cash register bells rang in Louie's brain. *And that proposed refurb of Pier 42 over on Luxury Liner Row?*

"What about them?!"

He's got all the contracts and I want my cut!!

"You got proof of what he did?"

I got pik-cha's!! Lots'a pik-cha's!

"Hold on." Louie handed the receiver back to Nikki. "Put this on line two, I'll take it my office." He said, handing her the receiver and moved to his office.

"YOU GOT IT?" Nikki shouted into Louie's office.

"YEAH, YOU CAN HANG UP." Shirley wasn't the only one not accustomed to the new intercom.

"OKAY!" Nikki shouted back but didn't hang up. Listening carefully for Louie to pick up the phone she timed it to coincide with a convincing 'click' sound fooling Louie into believing she hung

100

up before she covered the mouth piece with her hand.

"Can you make it Downtown?" Louie asked. "We can meet at the Mayfair on 15th Street. In the bar room." Louie always gleaned a higher sense of purpose when meeting in swank hotel bars or lobbies.

No, that's your stomping grounds. Uptown you're less likely to be recognized. She reasoned. *Make it the Rose Room at the Gramercy on Lexington. Make sure no one else comes! I don't wanna chance him getting wind of what I'm up to!* She sniffled.

"No problem! Standard procedure in these cases ma'am. See you at the hotel in about an hour Miss . . . Miss?"

Abernathy. One hour. I'll be wearing a red scarf. She said and hung up.

Nikki carefully waited until Mancino hung up then quickly followed suit. As he came back into the reception area Nikki feigned typing.

"Who was she?"

"A client! Just a client. A new client. A client you don't know."

"So I'm guessing she's a client? You want me to start a file?"

"Nah! Not necessary til after I talk to her."

"So when's she coming in?"

"Well, she's kind of upset, I thought it best we meet outside the office first."

"Good thinking." Nikki smirked as he left the office then mumbled and turned back to her typewriter.

"This is not going to end well!"

With visions of his and Doris' next six month's rent being paid off, possibly even a new car in their future, Louie danced down the hall before twirling onto the staircase.

✝

Steadman Building & Engineering
Westside Warehouse
Forest Park, Chicago

Jake Steadman had grown his company from a small three man construction crew before the war to a twenty man operation with half a dozen vehicles working out of a South Side warehouse by early '44.

As the end of the war crept ever closer he rolled the dice on the expected post war boom and applied for a one million dollar loan to sink into his now forty man operation and to build a third warehouse for materials storage and to allow him to buy wholesale in bulk.

The loan was approved, the building built and Steadman was in a position to break into the big time.

By the time the ERP, the European Recovery Program, alias *The Marshall Plan*, had made it through Congress, Steadman's was one of the 250 construction businesses nation-wide which was approached by the Army Corps of Engineers to participate in the fabrication and shipping of building materials for the reconstruction of what was left of the European continent. The contracts were lucrative but for a three year cycle only and would require re-bids and renewals. That time was approaching.

Joshua 'Jake' Steadman was in the Big Time.

That Thursday afternoon Jake was in the middle of daily business, working at his desk in his downtown office when he got a phone call. The caller was brief and to the point.

"They'll be a drop in two days." Was the entire message.

"Send it to warehouse three." He responded and hung up.

Two days later, at precisely noon, as usual, a dark green Ford, half ton pick-up with its cargo draped in a canvas tarpaulin, pulled up to the middle bay of the three bay dock in the rear of the warehouse. Two rough looking Italians climbed out and went to work unlacing the hemp rope holding the tarp down over the dozen small sacks marked 'Industrial Adhesive'.

"Antonino." Steadman greeted.

"Hey Jake! Where d'ja want 'em?" The big fella asked. Steadman motioned for the men, a small sack under each of their arms, to follow him. He led them inside then off to the right side of the warehouse and into a back corner.

They made their way over to a small office partitioned out of the rear corner of the building.

"I had this installed last week." He boasted as he swung open the hefty door to a small walk-in safe. "The guys think it's for explosives." The big guy with Antonino stopped halfway to the safe which was embedded into the rear wall.

"You got dynamite in there?!" Antonino's friend challenged.

"No! That'd be illegal." He laughed at his own joke. "I can store two maybe three truckloads at a push in here if you get backed up for some reason. But I prefer to keep it moving. I don't wanna get caught with a twenty-five pound bags of cocaine on my premises."

"Oh, no danger of that Mr. Steadman!" The big guy blurted.

"Why not?"

"This ain't cocaine. It's heroin!"

"What?!" Steadman was amenable to getting into the dirty water but was smart enough to always be cautious of the depth. Initially agreeing to hide weapons and the occasional bit of recorded evidence for the Chicago mob was okay and last month he even agreed on the odd shipment of coke. This was the first he'd heard of heroin.

"The bosses found a new way of getting' their stuff into the country and dropping it off at the distribution points. So, they's decided on shifting the commodity, you know to boost profits."

"Yeah? Well I got no problem with boostin' profits, so long as I don't get boosted by the CPD!

Just one question, when were you Jamokes gonna tell me about this little switch-a-roo?!" Antonino smirked at his partner and nodded back at Steadman.

"I thought you might have some questions about that." He reached into the back pocket of his blue jeans and tossed an envelope over to Jake. "There's an extra ten Large in there." Jake thumbed through the notes packed into the envelope. "We copasetic?" Antonino asked.

"Yeah, we're copasetic! Just keep it kosher from now on! Make sure your guys understand no dead bodies! This isn't a union hall. It's my place of business."

"Yeah, yeah, sure thing Jake." Antonino took a few steps back closer to Steadman. "Could I axe you a question?"

"Sure Anto." He made eye contact as he responded.

"Maxi, grab the rest'a the sacks!" He called over his shoulder. Maxi headed back out to the truck. Once he was out of ear shot Anto continued.

"How come a guy like you, wit everything you got, decides to get int'a this bizness? I mean we didn't come to you, you came to us!"

"You hinting that Mr. Black is not satisfied with my services?"

"No, no, I ain't sayin' that at all! It's just that you ain't got no record, you ain't connected and you seem to be pretty well off, so I know it ain't the money. You lookin' to get a foothold in the organization? Lookin' fer a favor maybe?"

Steadman smiled, crossed his arms and leaned into the wall.

"Fair question Anto. Now let me ask you something. Are you a commie?"

"What?!" Anto was stunned.

"Are you a commie? I mean, they're uncovering commies every day in this country. California out in Hollywood, down in Louisiana. I even read in the papers were there's talk of some commies over in Washington. I just thought there might be a chance you might be one."

"**FUCK YOU**!" Anto yelled just as Jake's secretary, with an arm full of folders, appeared across the floor.

"Mr. Steadman are you alright?" She asked.

"Yes Janeanne, everything' okay."

Giving Anto a dirty look she moved on.

"We're at war and few people realize it!" Steadman pressed on.

"What the hell you talkin' about? The war's been over two years now!" Anto protested.

"You ever hear the saying that the greatest trick the Devil ever pulled off is convincing people he doesn't exist?" Anto answered with a blank stare. "The war didn't end with the Japs givin' up Anto. It merely shifted to another theater of operations. We're in the dawn of new war. A war where there aren't any outside threats anymore. It's much worse!"

Although Antonino Carlucci had yet to make his bones, he had participated in two armed robberies, drove getaway for several hits, and assisted in disposals of bodies. Consequently he was rated as fearless by the crew bosses he had worked under. However the gleam and intensity with which Jake Steadman now spoke about things Anto didn't quite understand, scared the living shit out of him.

"The new threat is from within, Anto. Internal from deluded politicians. Politicians who have crossed over to the other side and have sold their souls to the Devil for fame and power!" Steadman made direct eye contact. "People of that ilk will stop at nothing to gain power and when they do, gain more power, they want even more power. They'll take anybody down, even the president to get what they want. It's an addiction!"

His mind still snagged on what the word 'ilk' meant, Anto missed the underlying anger, fueled by extreme fear that America could go back to the way it was before the war and that he would lose everything he'd built up over the years.

Anto certainly had no possible way to sense that Steadman had already crossed the line from caution to fear where it was only one tiny step to paranoia.

He suddenly sensed the aversion in Antonino's body language and backed off by taking a break and offering the big man a cigarette.

"Anto, the bottom line is . . ." He lit both their cigarettes. "Uncle Sam is doling out thirteen billion to rebuild Europe and I'm gonna get my piece of the action! That's all I'm saying. Only one thing can fuck that up."

"What's that?"

"A return to FDR styled Federalism! Tellin' people what they can and can't do with their own businesses, their own money. Their own lives! In other words, Comm – over regulation! I mean, nobody wants the government telling us what we can and can't do with our own businesses, am I right or am I right?"

"Yeah, yeah. That's bad." Maxi came through with two more sacks.

"Exactly!" Jake said.

"Thirteen billion. Sure buy a lotta heroin! Hey Jake?"

"Yeah Anto. Lotta heroin." Steadman locked up the safe as they finished off. "Or a lotta political influence." He added.

Jake stuffed the envelope into his back pocket, stomped out his cigarette and headed back to the office.

Suddenly remembering he didn't smoke, Anto followed suit.

The Rose Room
Gramercy Park Hotel
Lexington Avenue, N.Y.C.

It was just past three when Louie Mancino emerged from the BMT line subway kitchen on the corner of East 59th and 5th Avenue a block from the hotel.

Stopping in front of a Horn & Hardart's, he pulled a crumpled tie, already tied in a loose Windsor, from his back pocket and put it on over his short sleeved yellow and maroon bowling shirt and reset the collar.

Once through the brass plated revolving door and in the expansive lobby he stopped to check his look in the large wall mirror behind the reception desk. Removing the tie he decided the bowling shirt presented the right look and removed then re-stashed the tie. He scanned the area and spotted the red scarf woman across the lobby in the far corner.

Despite the Uptown address and the swank of the hotel the bar area was distinctly lack luster.

The bar ran the length of the back wall and there was a tall, functioning hearth off to the right as he entered straight in off the noisy street.

Dark, always a plus, the entire three walls were lined with plushly upholstered, olive green chairs with a thick mustard yellow stripe running down the center of each. Mancino was ten feet from a table in the corner when the girl in the red scarf turned and looked to the side and he got a good look at her face.

The face belonged to Nina Twissleman, the client Doc had refused.

Louie made straight for her and as he did she stood, dropped the scarf on her chair and made an exaggerated gesture of throwing back her long blond hair and adjusting her tight fitting, strapless, cobalt blue dress.

"Shit!" Mancino mumbled to himself. "Why'd it have to be blue?" She smiled again and waved him over. He approached but refused to shake her hand.

"You know I could get fired just fer talking to you? You know that don't ya?"

"Yeah, yeah. Life's a gamble." Nina gestured to the chair opposite and Louie reluctantly sat. "You want a drink?" She offered.

"No, I'm on duty." He refused. "Okay, maybe a beer." He decided. She signalled the bar man and mouthed 'a beer, then pointed to her half empty Manhattan.

"Okay, so you think my case has merit. Otherwise why would you be here?"

"I think somethin's got merit but I ain't promisin' how long I'm here for."

"Look, I'll lay it out for you, step by step, if you think it's too tough of a case, we'll let bygones be bygones and go our separate ways. I'll even pay for your beer, deal?" She proposed, adjusting her low cut neckline just enough.

"You got five minutes Miss Twissleman."

"Nina, please."

"Okay, Nina Please. You've got five minutes."

As she bent over the low coffee table to place the photos in front of him, Mancino resisted the temptation to glance down her low neck line.

"These are police photos of the scene." She fanned them across the table. "You should know we were together long enough for me to know him well. Very well. In the Biblical sense. Benny was **not** suicidal!"

"Where is this?"

"His place, in the Village."

She again bent forward to point to one of the photos. Louie again fought back the urge to peer at her. He lost the fight. She caught his glance and quietly celebrated her victory.

"I will confess I thought the case had some merit when Doc first told me about it." Louie blurted.

"So you think M&M should have taken the case after all?"

"Yeah, definitely. But-"

"But you didn't want to embarrass Doc in front of everybody?"

"Yeah, exactly!"

"So you let it go?"

"I had to!"

"Why?"

"I don't let it get around but . . . M&M's really my agency."

The bar man brought the drinks to the table and set the check next to them. Mancino nearly chocked when he saw the beer cost $3 the Manhattan $5. Nina noticed and grabbed the check and set it aside.

"I took Doc in a few years back when his wife bailed on him. Felt sorry for him. Turns out he's an okay P.I., but I still need to keep an eye on him." Mancino quickly scanned the area for spies. "I'm actually about to step off on my own." He loudly whispered.

"Really?! But if it's your agency . . ."

"I mean, step off into another office." He fumbled. Nina smiled.

"You helped McKeowen break up that smuggling ring back a couple of years or so, didn't you?"

"Yeah! You read about that huh?"

"I did. Then you must'a been there for that counterfeiting thing with the Treasury agent guy?"

As it dawned on him that Twissleman had done her homework Louie's radar went up.

"Yeah, all I'm sayin' is . . . it's high time I fly solo. I'm a loner by nature. A stand alone kind'a guy. You know, kind'a guy goes his own way regardless of where the crowd manders."

"Manders?" She queried.

"Yeah, you know, wanders without direction."

"Oh, so I take it you'll take my case?"

"No."

"NO?! No as in you won't take the case?!" The little schemer was stunned.

"Definitely! I mean definitely not! And do you know why?"

"I don't give a shit you little butterball! Why the hell did you bother showing up and wasting my time?!"

"Why'd ja think? I wanted to see what kind'a line you'd throw at me."

"You're an asshole!"

"Yeah, but that's besides the point."

Nina stood and stormed away across the lobby and out through the revolving doors of the main entrance.

A business man who had been observing from across the way folded his newspaper, tucked under his arm and strolled past Louie.

"That's the problem with the high priced ones!" He offered. "They're also a bit high strung. But don't sweat it, there's plenty more of the cheaper ones over on 9th Avenue!" He advised as he breezed past Louie.

Mancino got up to leave when the bar man caught sight of him heading for the door.

"Hey Mack!" Louie turned to see the irritated bar man. "This ain't the Salvation Army! That'll be eight bucks!" He yelled over. "For the drinks."

"Fangulo!" Louie quietly cursed. He chugged his beer.

CHAPTER VI

Warner Brothers
Motion Picture Studios
Hollywood, Lot W

The writer's offices at the Warner studios, known as the Writer's Roost, were in reality just a row of partitioned off ten by ten spaces in a converted, wood framed warehouse two stories high and a city block long located just off the back lot.

"Joe! Come here!" Ray Chandler, working as a contract writer, stared out the second story window of the studio office assigned to him and a another writer called Joe Sistrom. Save for the half dozen suits leisurely sashaying up towards the studio commissary, the long narrow street being heated by the bright sun was otherwise abandoned.

"Lem'me alone!" Sistrom called back from where he lay on the over-stuffed couch acting as a serrogate womb.

"Come here will ya! Look at this!" His fellow writer just rolled over and faced into the couch back without responce. Ray threw a book hitting him in the ass.

"What?! I'm working on a good scene here!" Joe protested.

"Get over here and look at this scene!" Reluctantly Sistrom slowly rose and meandered over to the window.

"What?!" He challenged. Chandler nodded down at the strung out group of studio execs heading to lunch. Ray was transfixed with a sinister delight and felt compelled to launch into a commentary.

"Look at them, the big boys strolling over to lunch in the executive dining room. Note the loose groups, the cocky swagger. What'a they look like to you?" Chandler challenged.

"I don't know! A gaggle of execs goin' ta lunch. What are you seenin' that I don't, what'a they look like to you?"

"Like a bunch of topflight Chicago gangsters moving in to read the death sentence on a beaten competitor. I noticed them when they came around the corner. It brought home to me, in an instant, the spiritual kinship between the operations of big money business and the Mob rackets."

"Oh." Joe was unimpressed but smiled despite himself, patted Ray on the shoulder and made back for the couch. Ray stayed glued to the window pane as he quietly narrated into the glass window.

"Same faces, same expressions, same manners. Same way of dressing and the same exaggerated leisure of movement." Sistrom looked over at Chandler and shook his head. "Notice the one in front of the group picking his teeth with a toothpick."

"Congratulations Pal! You're startin' to see the big picture." Sistrom said as he once again surrendered to the couch. Chandler watched until they disappeared around the corner.

Down on the street the mood surrounding the bundle of box office barons was a little more terse.

Harry Warner had come in to town on one of his ever diminishing trips down from his San Fernando valley horse ranch. To everyone's surprise, given the brothers pothole strewn relationship, Jack had actually asked him in.

There was no joy in Mudville that day as the studio writers had just that morning voted overwhelmingly to reject the Warner's company-run labor union and attempt to expand there own fledgling Screen Writer's Guild, pending their own, newly appointed committee's approval.

For years the writers were like the slave labor of the film farms. During the birth of the industry, back when writers didn't even get screen credit, there was no such thing as a scale and they were paid whatever the studio could get away with. Warner's thinking was there was always another idealistic writer waiting to take the place of anyone who he had a problem with. So it had come to the point where the writers, as did the actors a few years before, taken the decision to organize.

Leading the small parade of execs down on the street, were two of the Warner brothers themselves, Jack and Harry.

"Scheming little bastards give me ágata!" Jack complained regarding the writers.

"**YOU'RE** GIVING **ME** ÁGATA WITH YOUR RANTING AND RAVING!" Harry sprang back. It had been a bumpy morning. "How do you expect to enjoy a meal in that frame of mind?" Harry attempted to change the subject.

"Since when do we enjoy commissary food?" Jack answered by shaking his head and picking up the pace just enough to pull ahead of his brother.

Harry got the point, but the tactic was ineffective. Besides, the brothers weren't really having an argument. It was Jack Warner holding court, Harry just happened to be in the vicnity. Harry soldiered on as Jack continued firing.

"It's just the ingratitude that gets up my ass! The ungrateful little bastards never consider what we've done for them!"

The two were certainly no strangers to fighting and several studio employees had once claimed they saw Harry chase Jack through a studio with a lead pipe, shouting, "I'll get you for this, you son of a bitch!", apparently intent on doing him bodily harm.

"It's not the end of the world, is all I'm saying! We been through worse!" Harry counseled.

"No it's not the end of the world. Just the end of the system we spent twenty-five years building! And for what? A bunch of hacks! Half of 'em couldn't write a fucking ransom note, other half couldn't write a post card!" Jack quick-stepped to catch up to his kid brother. "Wasn't for us they'd be rummaging through garbage cans on the Lower East Side looking for a meal!"

The hangers-on slowly but silently drifted back behind the two to give some space..

In 1947 the boys were at the top of their game despite the fact that it was the worse year on record for the industry overall. Even worse than the Depression years.

It was the first boom year for T.V., Americans had less disposable income, and a temporary dip in the post-war economy all contributed to the film industry's headaches. But the Warner's were still top of the Big Five Pack Studio heirachy.

The boys were able to stay ahead of the pack and triumphed by overcoming one problem after another such as getting in on 'Talkies' on the ground floor.

Back in 1925 their younger brother Sam Warner had acquired the radio station KWBC, after which he decided to attempt to synchronize sound to pictures. After several years of refusing to try it Jack finally relented and agreed to experiment with the new technology on shorts only and then only with background music.

By that point Western Bell Electric Laboratories in New York was making significant progress in the recording field and when Harry went out to visit them he was duly impressed. But there was another obstacle.

In America so many Jews had emigrated from Europe before and after the war, anti-Semitism had begun to rear its ugly head, making it uncertain as to how receptive the WASP's at Bell labs were going to be regarding a business partnership with a prominent Jew.

The Warner boys concocted a plan. At a dinner with the higher ups at Bell Labs Sam, the least orthodox of the three, had his wife Lena wear a gold cross necklace as part of her evening ensemble. It worked. The subject of ethnicity never came up.

A couple of days later Harry signed a partnership agreement to use Bell Labs to play around with the sound-on-film process. A couple of years later in 1927 with release of *The Jazz Singer* 'Talkies' were born.

Cleverly opting to produce a broad range of material as opposed to their competitors who rooted around for "The Niche" market, Jack and Harry successfully navigated through the dark years of the Great Depression and emerged the only one of the majors not owned by the Wall Street moguls who controlled the various financial institutions the others had to turn to and go into hock with, most up to their ears.

Jack's tenacious grasp on the studios, which had gradually swollen to a strangle hold behind his brother's back, had secretly formed a syndicate with himself as the head to buy the studio which he then put on the market, for the purpose of gaining sole control. Relatives and friends were of no concern.

It's a toss-up as to whether Jack, later known as much for his bad jokes as his nickname the "Strategic Generalissimo" by his employees, ever really had any 'friends'

Near the end of the war, Jack Warner was drafted by the U.S. armed forces and made a lieutenant colonel. He never actually served on 'active' duty, he produced films for the war effort.

"Mom was right!" Harry muttered as they stepped in out of the sun and entered into the executive dining room.

"Right about what?!" Jack challenged.

"Out of all of us you're the bullheaded one!"

Like something from a Bugs Bunny cartoon, as they came through the front doors the head table suddenly cleared out.

There's an old office quip about not being informed about events in a timely manner;

Around here they treat me like a mushroom. They keep in the dark and feed me shit.

No one at Warner's was a mushroom when the brothers were going at it. Well almost no one.

The table cleared out in record time, except for one mushroom, a junior producer who was absorbed in a script as he ate his tuna casserole.

Unlike the lesser mortals who were required to serve themselves, Jack and Harry sat down across from one another at the other end of the table and waited to be served.

Jack picked up the spat as if they had been going all night. A sentiment Harry woefully shared.

"It's the gratitude angle I'm talking about Harry, ya know what I mean?! Take that ungrateful son-of-bitch Zanuck! We made him! I mean we took him from nothing! Gave him a shot at the big time, the right scripts, top talent. Then when he becomes a name what does he do? He stabs us in back and goes to Fox! Tries to start **his own** studio! We could've saved all the fucking money and headache and fired his ass early on!"

Harry looked around but for some mysterious reason there wasn't a waiter or waitress in sight. Jack continued his rant.

"And don't kid yourself, any one'a these people'd do the same thing if they thought the grass was a little greener!" Jack looked to his left at a now not-so-preoccupied young exec picking at his food.

"YOU!" Jack snapped. The young man jumped. "What's your name?"

"Margold Mr. Warner, Barry Margold. Acquisitions."

"Margold, Acquisitions." He turned back to Harry who feigned a piece of lint on his lapel.

"You see this kid here? Eight maybe ten years he's senior in his department. Then he moves up to Head. Next he transfers to Major productions then gets to the top there. At that point we've spent a cool mil on his education. Does he say, 'Thank you Mr. Warner? Thank you for the education which will build me and my family a good life? Launch me into the elite of American society'? Hell no! He thinks he knows everything and goes off to a competitor and we're stuck holding the bag!" Harry read the kid's mind as he posed a question to his brother.

"What's your point, Jack?"

"My point is we save ourselves the expense, wasted time and headache and fire the ungrateful little bastard now!"

Jack shook his head. Margold's face went pale. "Margold, pack your shit! I want you off the lot by close of business today!" Jack ordered.

A waiter arrived and they ordered.

†

Battery Park, Manhattan

Standing on the riverside path in Battery Park Doc looked up from the busy harbor at the mouth of the Hudson as he noticed something. He elbowed Louie who leaned on the same rail next to him. Doc nodded off to the left of the grounds.

"Looks like we got some action." Doc casually noted as he turned around, leaned back and mounted his elbows on the rail. Louie looked over and watched as a slight but muscular thirty-something dressed in jeans and an Army Air Corp flight jacket sprinted across Battery Park and ducked behind the Clinton Monument.

"Nice bomber jacket!" Louie quipped mocking Doc's jacket which was similar the runner's.

"Not a bomber's jacket. It's a fighter pilot's jacket! That guy must have seen some action" Two men dressed in dark suits had entered the north end of the park just 150 yards behind him and appeared to be in pursuit.

"Mob guys?" Louie inquired of Doc.

"Nah. Feds." Doc confidently answered as they watched the play unfold.

"How can you tell?"

"The shoes. No self-respecting Mobster would be caught wearing Sears shoes. Any self-respecting

Italian would know that." He lightly back handed Louie's shoulder for emphasis.

"Point taken." Louie conceded.

The two suits stopped on Doc and Louie's side of the large circular Clinton monument.

"If they're too dumb to split up he'll circle around and probably head for the bay." Doc predicted.

"Ya think?"

"Stands to reason. The park's wide open, no place to hide here. He came in through the north gate, headed here on purpose. Must'a had a reason."

The Feds didn't split up but both took to the north side of the monument. Doc and Louie watched as the guy in the jeans skirted south around the wall of the monument avoiding them and came into sight. Louie caught his attention and gestured to where the Feds were on the other side of the wall. The guy nodded, waved and headed straight for the Battery retaining fence along the river side 30 yards away.

"You know that guy?" Doc asked Louie.

"No, but if he's dodge'n the Feds he must be okay."

Criminal activity was certainly not a novelty to the Manhattan waterfront but this wasn't exactly an everyday occurrence.

Doc and Louie watched as the two Feds made their way over to them and whipped out their I.D. and badges.

"You two seen a guy in a brown leather jacket and jeans running around here?"

"Why no we haven't officer. But, as good law abiding citizens, if we do see anybody that fits that particular description we'll be sure to let you know." Doc answered.

"You mean that guy?" Louie pointed out across the harbor. Both Doc and Louie smirked as a seventeen foot, mahogany Chris Craft *Runabout* skipped across the water over to the Brooklyn side of the harbor where a single engine De Havilland Beaver sea plane was tied up to a small floating dock moored on the Heights.

"SHIT, SHIT, SHIT!" The one Fed cursed as he looked around frantically then darted off, his partner in tow.

They made it over to the east edge of the Battery where they spotted the tall aerial of the small Coast Guard Station out on Governor's Island.

Doc and Mancino watched as, after discharging its passenger, the *Runabout* turned and sped north up the East River hugging the Brooklyn shoreline then disappeared underneath the Brooklyn Bridge.

Doc and Louie casually watched the show as the plane fired up its engine, did a tight 180 to face New Jersey and sped straight west across the harbor.

A white spray tail fell from the twin pontoons as the plane lifted out of the water just in time to clear Liberty Island but had to bank hard to the right to clear the Statue.

Tourists waved to Jimmy Dugan as he buzzed by overhead.

Back on the Battery the two agents pushed past the few dozen civilians lined up along the entrance to the ticket booth for the next *Circle Line* tour boat and scurried up the gang way. As they did they shoved the ticket taker out of the way knocking him to the deck. It only took seconds before they realized they didn't know their way around the large vessel. One of them ran back over to the ticket taker who was brushing himself off.

"How do we get up to the pilot house?"

"GO FUCK YOUSELF!" The young guy spat.

By the time Jimmy was over Jersey City they made it up onto the quarter deck, identified themselves and got the captain to contact the Coast Guard station.

Back down on the quay Doc and Louie exchanged glances.

"That's one way to avoid traffic!" Doc said.

"Guess so." Louie agreed.

"Let's catch a taxi over to Water Street. There's a great little Chinese place over on the FDR." Doc suggested.

"Who pays?"

"Who always pays?"

"Great, let's go!" Mancino replied.

Jimmy Dugan was an ex-hot shot scout pilot from the Eighth Army Air Corp. He earned the moniker 'Cat Man' after he was shot down for the third time and evaded capture.

The third time may have been a charm, but the fourth time was nothing short of a fluke. When he crash landed behind his own lines they counted Ninety-six holes in what wasn't left of his Curtiss Seagull aircraft. Ninety-nine if you counted the holes in him. He was recommended for the highest honor the Air Corps could offer for chucking hand grenades out the window onto German FLAK positions the fighters couldn't get low enough to hit, thereby helping to save a squadron of very expensive aircraft as well as some lives.

He also got his picture plastered all over the papers back home but his mom, dad and future ex-fiancée would never know his notoriety wasn't due to mad-cap heroics.

The morning of the mission, Jimmy was nailed running contraband out of Messina. Not just trinkets and tinned beef either. Class A drugs. Narcotics. Lots of 'em. Thanks to a tip off he ducked out of the barracks and on to the airfield two steps ahead of the M.P.'s and since his flight plan had already been filed was able to put about ten thousand feet between himself and the Mickey Mouse Patrol in a matter of minutes. He joined up with the squadron a half hour later and since the order for him to return to base was conveniently garbled in transmission, and he wasn't sure what the hell else to do he flew the mission.

While he was airborne it occurred to the slightly over ambitious young man that returning alive meant one of two things. Life in a military stockade at the mercy of merciless goons or a bullet in the head from a bunch of pissed off Sicilians who wouldn't believe the truth. Namely that Army Intel was tipped off about the shipment, plain and simple.

So after getting all shot up and spreading his aircraft over half mile of airfield and being observed by Curtis J. LeMay's personal Aide de Camp, who always made it a point to be in the control tower to "Welcum da boys home!", and who hadn't yet been briefed on Lt. Dugan's impropriety, Jimmy got heself an Air Medal, a way out, some major headlines and a ticket home.

Mysteriously the two cases of morphine, three cases of pharmaceutical grade coke and four cases of chloral hydrate and assorted strength boxes of xylocaine were never found.

By the end of the war, like so many other ex-G.I.'s Jimmy couldn't quite make it on the $27.50 a month handout Uncle Sam was rewarding him with for risking his life to rid the world of Fascism.

After meeting a friend he knew from before the war he was impressed that although his friend only worked part time the friend always had cash in his pocket.

Three beers later the friend gave him a number to call. Jimmy called it and mentioned his friend. After a short meet with a local hood Jimmy Dugan was put to work.

Following a probationary period, to establish his trustworthiness, his U.S. Government acquired skills were put to good use. They even bought him a brand new De Havilland airplane.

Air routes to run the drugs had been planned before the war and well established by 1945 from Greece, Turkey and Yugoslavia, through Sicily into Marseilles and on to Florida, Philadelphia, New York and Chicago.

Down in the safe haven of Cuba Jimmy had lived very well for the last year, however nothing lasts forever.

Having nearly exhausted all his earnings from the previous year, Dugan's long term retirement plan had once again reverted to his pre-retirement situation. That is going back to work to run drugs for The Mob.

From the late 17th Century the Florida archipelago had been used by pirates wanting to avoid Dutch tax collectors to the rum runners of the 20th Century. The islands of the Florida Keys were seen as the perfect docking site for landing illicit cargo and people to be smuggled into The United States.

Two days later Jimmy was on another run for the Mob from Cuba.

As the first island of the Florida Keys crept over the horizon Jimmy downed the last of his flask in relief and prepared to land.

Dugan's De Havilland, an STOL aircraft, short take-off and landing, had been purposely designed to negotiate restricted areas and suited the needs of the New York smugglers perfectly.

The improvised, hard pack runway he now approached was less than one hundred yards from the beach, and the two fishing trawlers anchored in the adjacent shallow lagoon stood ready to be loaded.

As Jimmy taxied up to the hundred foot long, improvised dock a small army of local natives emerged and split into two groups. One group approached the plane from the rear the other readied a motor launch beached off to the side.

Jimmy shut down the engine, climbed out on the pontoon and opened the passenger side door and then the custom made cargo door in the starboard side of the fuselage. The crew went to work immediately unloading the one kilo packages of opium.

From the plane the drugs were loaded into wicker baskets which were carried on the heads of the workers over to waiting fish crates on the beach.

The crates were half the depth of the standard fish crate and slightly smaller in dimension. Once packed with 12 to 14 bricks of the drug these were then topped off with raw fish and dropped into full sized, empty crates which were then topped off with more fish. The fully loaded crates were then loaded into the motor launch and ferried out to the two waiting trawlers.

Dugan wandered over to the packing area but, from a full fifty yards away he was repulsed by a pungent odor.

"Jesus! That shit stinks! What the hell kind'a fish is that?!" Jimmy peered over into one of the crates.

The old, black Cuban slopping the fish peaked out from a wreath of white hair and whiskers.

"Be some Spotted Sea Trout, Snook, maybe cod." The elderly guy informed him.

"Who's gonna eat that stuff?"

"Oh hell no man! Can't eat that fish. Get real bad sick man! Fish too old, two, tree day old. Da bad smell keep customs man from diggin' too deep in da crate!"

"Nice to be working with professionals again." Jimmy nodded.

A neatly dressed, fortyish guy finished his inventory of the cargo, went over to a battered old pick-up and retrieved a black leather briefcase. He passed it off to Jimmy and informed him there would be another run in four to five days.

The Jimmy Dugan airfreight delivery service was back in business.

CHAPTER VII

Private Home of
Hal Halstein
North Hillcrest, L.A.

With several months yet to the kickoff of the official Oscar season producers organized 'parties' aimed to influence, persuade and cajole those with sway in the industry to vote/petition for their particular production.

Billed through the grapevine as 'The Event of the Year', as most Hollywood parties were, this party, was referred to as an 'affair' to the Hollywood crowd, hangers-on and the few privileged press graced with access.

William Wilkinson was definitely not one of those.

Warner rarely attended such functions, but was just as rarely omitted from the guest list.

Tonight's function was staged on a quaint little two and half acres estate out on North Hillcrest about eleven miles south west of downtown L.A.

The estate's owner was actually a Wall Street exec who handled the Lowe's corporate account back in New York and happened to have just returned from Europe trying to reestablish the film industry ties lost during the Nazi reign of terror.

The main house, built on the highest plateau in the foothills, overlooked the flatlands and peered down on the diminutive, distant skyline of the tiny city that was L.A.

Out in the back garden amongst the Tiki torches, evening began to fall. Jack Warner, surrounded by a collection of producer wanna-be's crested by a gaggle of hopeful ingénues, was holding court when an HR exec pushed through the group and signaled him aside.

"What is it?"

"The SWG people voted on whether or not to organize, we just got the results."

"And?"

"You sure you wanna hear it?"

"Why the fuck would I ask you if I didn't wanna hear it?!" Warner barked.

"They've rejected the studios' offer again. They've appointed a chairman, have announced they're gonna elect a board and stage a vote on a new charter."

"Fucking *Wagner Act*! I should have dumped Hellman, Dunne and the rest of those clowns back in the Thirties when they started this shit!"

"I know what you mean Jack! *Wagner* not only allows them to organize but to strike if they don't get what they want! And enough bums in the last ten or twelve years have put it to good use in other industries! Remember what happened with Ford and the other car industries! Nearly ruined -"

"Yeah, yeah I remember!"

There can be little doubt Jack Warner saw a threat to his bottom line if the writers were allowed to organize especially after the court ruling which paved the way for the actors to form their own union, the Screen Actors Guild.

But the sensation of yet more power and control slipping through his fingers with the formation of a writers guild, so hot on the heels of the SAG formation, was seen as a direct challenge to his status as king of the hill not only at his own studio but as the leading figure in the film industry.

Warner dumped his champagne into the bush behind him when he spotted a waiter circulating with a tray of scotch. He traded his empty flute glass for a rocks glass on the tray and threw back the scotch. "Who's this so-called Chairman?"

"No word yet." The HR exec answered.

"Get a hold of Ronnie Reagan, see if he knows anything."

"He's president of the Screen Actors' Guild! What's he got to do with-"

"JUST DO IT GOD DAMN IT!"

"I'm just saying that I'm not sure how that'll work. They've been keeping the actors at arm's length especially since the rumors that Reagan's snooping around for Hoover-"

"Just do it! We don't nip this in the bud next thing they'll be tryin' to coerce the radio and T.V. guys into this little charade!"

"Okay!" The exec disappeared through the crowd.

A small gaggle of guests had gathered out by the pool to enjoy the cool breeze dissipating the heavy humidity which hung in the evening air. A halo of cigarette smoke hovered over their heads.

Now tucked away in a far corner and not in a particularly sociable mood but feeling compelled to 'make an appearance' Warner was casually listening to a triplet of junior producers as they rendered their Oscar opinions.

"It was obvious from the time of release the shoe-in was going to be *Gentlemen's Agreement*!" The one well on his way to a bad morning affirmed.

"How do you figure, what are you, Nostradamus?" The bow tie challenged.

"Please, it's all about Jews! Sam Goldwyn, a Jew. Screen play by a Jew, from a book by a Jew with a story about a guy posing as a Jew to expose prejudice towards Jews! You think *A Wonderful Life*, a story about Christmas which celebrates a guy killed by the Jews is gonna have any chance against that?"

"*The Jolson Story*! That was nominated and that's about a Jew." The third affirmed.

"Yeah, but it's a remake of a picture they did nearly twenty years ago!"

"Come to think of it, a guy named Hobson wrote the book *Gentlemen's Agreement*, and he ain't no Jew!"

"Yeah? Then how come he was booted out of the L.A. Country Club? Wasn't fer not wearin' a tie, I'll tell ya that fer nuthin'"

"Okay, maybe. But ya got'a admit, Zanuck did a helluv'a job on the production!"

Uninvited Warner, now standing nearby, leaned in and offered his two cents.

"Fuck Zanuck!" Jack declared before walking away.

He didn't get very far as he bumped into Billy Frank, a senior producer from 20th Century.

"Evening Jack, how's tricks?"

"Frank, you know people here?"

"Yes and no. My wife's the number two girl over in casting."

"What have you heard about this so-called Writer's Guild thing they're tryin' to organize?" Warner pushed.

"As far as I heard the Writer's Guild got an answer Wednesday or Thursday on their petition to the Labor Board in D.C. They've been granted the right to arbitrate. That means-" Frank started.

"I was born during the day but it wasn't yesterday, god damn it! I know full well what it means!"

"So, I take it they snubbed the Playwright's Guild idea you offered them?" Frank asked,

"Snubbed it? They practically took a shit on it!" He snatched another scotch as a waitress drifted by.

"I'd keep an eye on developments with these writers, Jack. This thing is not gonna go away and if I'm right-"

"Which I suspect you are!" He threw back his scotch.

"This thing is gonna get a helluv'a of a lot nastier before it's all over. You can take that to the bank, brother!"

"Maybe nastier then they know." Warner tried to relax and dispel the anger welling in him. "You intend to go out to this New York thing Eric Johnston is setting up in October?" Warner queried.

"Not sure, I haven't heard any details yet. You going?"

"I haven't spoken to anyone either. What's he hoping to accomplish anyway?" Warner probed.

"The way he sees it, back before the war when senator Dies and that other clown, what's his name, the crooked son-of-a-bitch from New Jersey?"

"Take your pick! You probably mean Thomas." Jack offered.

"Yeah Thomas. Back when Dies and Thomas launched their bid to take control of the industry when they couldn't find any commies in the Boy Scouts-"

"Back in '40-41, yeah. I'm not that senile!"

"Dies was never gonna be a problem. He's just another racist redneck, a Texas hillbilly!"

"True but he's also one of the founders of this HUAC thing." Warner cautioned.

"Point is, in 40-41 we beat them pretty good." Frank continued.

"Did to them what Patton did to the Nazis. Kicked them in the ass is what we did!" Jack affirmed

"Exactly! Which is why they're gonna come back at us this time with everything they got!" Frank warned.

"I can't understand what the hell they want with control of the film industry?! They can't profit by it!" Warner naively asked.

"Maybe not financially but P.R. wise they can. People are not happy with our boys in D.C. Jack! Why do you think the Republicans swept the elections? They sure need to look like they're doing something to earn those big fat pay checks."

"They will do something about it! Probably vote themselves a damn pay raise!" Warner scoffed.

Frank continued.

"Everybody still remembers how Congress dropped the ball on Wall Street regulations after the Depression hit and how it was FDR with his New Deal had to come to the rescue. People are still blaming the politicians." He opined. "Things are still not fully back on track and neither the democrats nor the republicans are looking too good in the public's eye these days.

Thomas, Dies, Rankin and those guys still have no sense of humor about being left with mud on their faces after they made their much publicized racketeering and communist conspiracy charges against us and then were pushed aside because the country needed you, me and the film industry for the war effort! Their big splash of 'communist investigation' turned into a big nothing burger."

"Your point being?!"

"Roosevelt's dead, the New Deal days are over and there's a bunch of new sheriffs in town. The old guard is gone Jack, we got a god damned guy in the White House –"

"The Haberdasher!" Warner cracked.

"Exactly, the Haberdasher! A guy who still asks his mother for advice and will bend to the loudest voices because he's hustling for re-election against Dewey!"

"So?"

"So, what'a **we** do when a picture turns out to be a lemon? A real stinker?"

"Fire the fucking producer!" Warner declared.

"Not just! We do exactly what these schmucks in congress are looking to do! Repackage it and resell it! They couldn't get a foot in the door with the conspiracy laws using *The Sherman Act* and their debacle of anti-American investigations fizzled out big time so that leaves the commie angle! Stands to reason."

"Your might have a point Frank." Warner's conceded.

"Johnston figures now that the congress has got momentum in the press, they're gonna come after us again only this time with the commie angle!"

"Commies?!" Despite being cloaked in an interrogative the wheels were turning. "You think?" Warner asked with sincerity.

"His reasoning is pretty sound to me. I don't see there's any choice. We got'a take a stand, one way or the other. You know as well as I do we don't take matters into our own hands Congress'll be gunning for us next. They'll regulate us out of business inside a year and claims of 'commies in the ranks' is just the spin they're likely to use! We got'a stay ahead of the curve!" He proposed.

"Huh!" Warner began to see things in a new light.

"I think I just might get myself out to Johnson's thing in New York. When is it do you know?"

"October, no day yet but I'm sure he'll put it out through the MPPAA bulletin or call us."

A server from the caterer's came towards him with tray of half full champagne glasses.

"Where's a phone around here I can use?" Warner asked the server.

"There's one in the sun room sir you're welcome to use that one."

"Thanks. Frank, have your girl call my girl, let's have lunch sometime."

"Will do Jack. Great seeing ya again."

Five minutes later Warner had a studio assistant on the line.

"Al, get a hold of Bill Whitcomb at the Pinketon's Agency. Tell them we need a man for a day so. Make an appointment and have him come to my office day after tomorrow, I'll tell him what it's about."

Sure thing Jack.

"Then put a call into Eric Johnston's office. Tell him I'll be at the New York meeting in October." He'll know what it's about."

Yes Mr. Warner.

✝

The 8th Street Playhouse where Doc and Nikki had gone to see a Billy Wilder double feature that evening, was only seven blocks from the office and as it was a pleasant evening they decided to walk back to Christopher Street where Doc had to collect some paper work for a morning court appointment before heading back to Nikki's place for the night.

"Is there such a thing as double indemnity?" Nikki asked as they strolled arm-in-arm up 8th Street towards 6th Avenue.

"Yeah. We, I, had a case back about seven years ago. One of my first cases. Guy fell off a cruise boat in the Hudson on his honeymoon. The guy had some money so Mutual Life hired me to determine if the wife was scamming them."

"Was she?"

"Nah. Coroner ruled it accidental drowning. NYPD found no motive by the wife and I was convinced she was genuinely bereaved."

"What were the circumstances?" She asked prompting Doc to look over at her and smile.

"Why, you thinking of becoming a P.I.?"

"No, no. What makes you say that? Just curious, that's all." She defended.

"Several passengers on the cruise testified he'd been drinking heavily before and during the cruise. She was in her cabin when he fell overboard and there were half a dozen witnesses on deck when he decided to play Johnny Weissmuller."

"So T.O.D. agreed with the fall time?" She casually inquired. Doc stopped and stared at her.

"T.O.D.? You been talking to Mancino?"

"No! Why would you think that?" She looked way, pretending to be distracted as she answered.

"No reason. No reason at all." Doc replied.

140

"Thanks for going to see that movie again. It was really good." Nikki said to change the subject.

"Glad you liked it!" Doc added.

"I never would have seen Fred MacMurray in that role. He really pulled it off. Sorry I didn't see that when it first came out."

"That's why they have these tributes. I think they're a good idea." Doc commented.

"I need some nail polish remover and a few other things. There's a Rexall's over on the corner of Grove and Hudson. I think they're open until nine. Can we stop?"

"Sure, why not?"

Two minutes later they walked past the ten foot high, green and orange wall mural of the 'Rexall Pharmacy, prescriptions, toiletries, gifts' and rounded the corner to the front door. The green canvas awning hadn't yet been drawn in and the red neon window sign still flashed 'OPEN'. They were in luck. Sort of.

The premises had a single door entrance, one way in one way out, and there was a long counter off to the right with a pair of double shelved gondolas between it and the left hand wall.

"It's like when-" Nikki suddenly stopped talking, grabbed Doc's forearm and nodded into the store as he stood halfway in holding the door open for her.

"When what?" Doc made eye contact with her and his demeanor changed noticeably when he looked over in the direction she had nodded, straight ahead, into the all but deserted shop.

From behind the counter the night pharmacist had a revolver pointed at him by a rough looking character standing on his right and who had his hands in the register pulling out the cash. An additional stick up man on the other side of the counter was also armed, albeit with some kind of a Saturday Night Special. He looked over and saw Doc and Nikki frozen in the doorway.

"GET IN HERE! NOW! GOD DAMN IT! RUN AND I PLUG THE OLD MAN!"

Doc took Nikki by the hand and slowly, together they inched into the shop, McKeowen keeping himself between Nikki and the gunman while holding one hand in the air.

"Stay behind me." He directed.

"You got a gun?" She whispered over his shoulder, knowing full well he never carried a gun as a matter of habit. He inched the hem of his bomber jacket up to reveal the hand cord of his black jack dangling from his back pocket. "Nice! Does it shoot bullets?" She nervously quipped. Doc maintained concentration on the one in front of the counter with the pea shooter while noting the thug behind the counter next to the pharmacist had a larger caliber wheel gun.

"That's just petty cash to make change. The day's receipts are in the basement safe. I was about to close-" The elderly pharmacist explained.

"SHUT UP AND QUIT YER BABBLING!" The tough guy glanced over at Doc and Nikki but ignored them. "Why you got a safe in the basement for?" Displaying he would starve if forced to survive on what little education he had, the thief clearly showed why he turned to armed robbery.

"The cash is put in those little plastic cylinders and dropped through that hole over there which deposits them directly into the safe in the basement. Only one with the combination's the owner. Won't be here till morning." The old man spat on the floor hiding any fear he might have harbored.

The idiot's face on the side was covered with a puzzled mask.

"Why you put your money in a hole in the floor?"

"In case there's a hold up?" The old man quipped sarcastically.

"Where'd you keep the chemicals?!" The one with the revolver demanded as the #2 man kept his weapon trained on Doc, watching as the apparent leader counted what little cash had been in the register.

"Don't look like there's a whole helluv'a lot there Frisco, do it?!" Idiot #2 asked.

"Thank you for your observation Bonehead and I'd be real grateful if you'd stop usein' my name!"

"Drugs are in the back. In the wall safe." The pharmacist volunteered.

Doc let go of Nikki's hand.

"Look, take my wallet!" Doc offered as he pulled his wallet from his back pocket and held it out with his left hand. "I just got paid and got almost two hundred and some change in there. At least you'll walk away with something."

As idiot #2 reached for the wallet Doc moved the couple of yards towards him, dropped it and grabbed his wrist pulling the gunman into himself and forcing his left hand, the one worth the weapon in it, up to the one behind the counter.

"NIKKI DOWN!" He yelled as he emptied the pistol in the direction of thug #1.

While thug # was rolling on the floor gasping for breath Doc was able to grab dumb dumb #2 by the wrist and pull him in while back handing him in the right side of the face with his black jack. A follow through to the other cheek, signaled the cracking of bones and sent him to the deck while his small hand gun went sliding across the floor to Nikki's feet.

On cue Nikki fell to her knees and scrambled behind the shelves of an aisle display as she heard several rapid shots fired.

Peeking around the corner she looked up in time to see the man being held by Doc drop to the floor unconscious. His pistol slid over to her knees as he fell.

The several small caliber rounds Doc emptied into Thug #1 didn't kill him but put instantly put him out of action by causing him to grab his chest and fall over backwards in time for the old man to grab the baseball bat he kept under the counter and go to work.

Two rapid fire rounds were fired from the wheel gun when #1 grabbed his chest and went down with one jettisoned just over Nikki's head with the second getting lodged in the ceiling.

Paddy Kelly

Hearing the ruckus out front an unseen thug #3 emerged from the back room and quietly snuck out from where he was snooping around for anything of value.

Armed with the only weapon he had, an Army bayonet, he quietly slipped along the left wall concealing himself between it and the products aisle on his left.

Undetected by him a sitting Nikki held the small gun out stiff-armed with both hands drawing a bead on him as he crept along the wall.

Three rounds caused the row of aerosol deodorant cans on the shelf next to his face to explode and deodorize his eyes until aluminum chloral hydrate coated his entire face which caused his hands to shoot to his eyes stabbing himself in the left cheek then start screaming as he ran in circles and crashing through the shelving.

Nikki in turn screamed, dropped the gun and covered her mouth in shock while Doc made it across the room and neutralized bayonet man with a crack across the back of the scull with his blackjack.

Collecting up the .22 hand gun Doc cleared it and stuffed it in his belt next to the empty Bersa pistol he had collected from Thug #1.

"You okay?" Doc asked he helped Nikki up and dust herself off.

"At least you've not forgotten how to show a girl a good time McKeowen!"

"Your hand's bleeding!" She declared as she examined the gash across his knuckles of the right hand.

"It's nothing."

Nikki grabbed a wad of tissues from her purse and pressed them to Doc's hand.

"You okay Pops?" Doc yelled over to the old man who was on the phone to the police. He turned to Doc just as he finished up the call and shot Doc a thumbs up.

"Doing fine son, just fine. Much obliged by the way."

Doc and Nikki made their way back over to the counter.

"You can take the boy outta the cop but ya can't take the cop outta the boy!" Nikki quipped as she hugged Doc.

"You called the cops?" McKeowen asked,

"They're in route as we speak."

"What about an ambulance?" Doc further probed staring down at #1's mangled legs.

"Hmmm." He mumbled. "Suppose I ought'a." The old man reluctantly spat then redialed the phone.

Doc presented the guns to the night clerk.

"Here ya go old timer. Insurance for the future."

"Thanks!" The old guy snatched the Bersa but left the ,22 on the counter. "I leave that one for the cops. Gotta make sure they get done for armed robbery!"

"Shoot, acetone! I forgot to get polish remover." Nikki declared as they were nearly out the front door. They headed back in and grabbed a bottle off the shelf.

146

Doc reached into his pocket for money but was stopped by the pharmacist.

"It's on the house young man! And you two feel free to come back anytime."

"Huh, a Bersa FCA Armas. Rare in this country." He commented as he assessed the small fire arm they confiscated.

"Looks strange." Nikki commented.

"Some kind of little South American job, Argentinean looks like." He popped a round out of the small magazine and inspected it. "It's a .22 rim fire."

"What's that mean?"

"Means it ricochets off and around the bones when it hits."

"Oh my god! You mean I could'a shot that guy in the head and the bullet would'a bounced around in his scull?"

"Maybe, but only because there was a lot of space in there."

Later, back at the office, Nikki wrestled with the idea of approaching Doc about working in the office, maybe even on some cases.

"Doc?"

"Yeah?" He answered opening the lower left hand drawer to his desk where he emptied the ammo and cleared the action on the pistol before dropping it in, joining the other half dozen guns, several knives and three sets of brass knuckles already there.

"Gonna have to have a garage sale one of these days!" He chuckled.

"Doc?" Nikki strategically poured both of them a drink and handed him a rocks glass of whiskey.

"Yeah babe?"

"Ya know how sometimes when we go out to eat and we're not exactly sure where we want to go, but we talk about it, and we finally agree on someplace? You now, agree together?"

"I don't think I like where this s going."

"Where do you think it's going?" She challenged.

"No idea, but I don't like it."

"Sit here, let me take a look at that." Nikki pressed an alcohol soaked cotton wad hard against his wound which elicited a muffled grunt.

"You were saying?" Doc pushed.

"Okay, we sit down, we eat and then after we leave we decide maybe that wasn't the best choice we ever made."

"Nikki?"

"Yeah?"

"I'm not taking that girl's case."

"Who said anything about-" She was cut off by Doc's stare. "Okay! Why don't you give it to Louie, let him poke around and if he unearths something, you can step in or pull him off it."

"Because Louie will either wind up with a bullet in his back, in jail or wrapped up in a lawsuit, that's why. All three scenarios with which we can do without. By the way Deadeye . . ."

"What?!" Nikki asked.

"Were you really gonna shoot that guy?"

"No! I just wanted to scare him little."

"Well, good job. You sure as hell did that!"

"Please don't change the subject. Louie has a point." McKeowen didn't respond. "I'm just sayin', that girl sounded pretty desperate the other day when she was in here, and –"

"They're all desperate! It's like when they go to the doctor with an ear infection. They finally go when it hurts too much and by then it's usually too late."

"And you, being the kind'a guy who normally helps people, ya know. . . "

"You tryin' to sneak in through the window?"

"I'm tryin' to get you to tackle an interesting case. It's going on six years now since the Treasury case-"

"Five years! It's only been five years."

"I think I know you well enough to know you've been off your spark lately."

"What'a you talkin' about, 'off my spark'? My spark is right on the money!"

"Com'on Doc! Insurance scams? Fraud cases?! That's the kind'a stuff that's okay for Louie but you should be out there bustin' open the big ones!"

"What'a you my manager now?" Nikki was disappointed Doc reverted to sarcasm in his irritation. "Since when do we consult on cases and more importantly why are you so interested in this case?" Doc demanded.

"We don't consult on cases because I never had an interest in what you do, and I used to be too busy working Downtown, but things have changed, our situation has changed."

"Uh huh." He grunted with increased suspicion.

"You said we should always be trying something new. So now we can try something new! Besides, there's always a first time for everything!"

"Oh well that makes perfect sense! I never jumped off a cliff, should I try that for the first time?" Doc regretted the words even before they left his mouth. Having approached the discussion with what she considered a modicum of reason Nikki felt attacked and pursed her lips before letting anger overtake her.

"Maybe you **should** go and jump off a cliff!"

She stormed out of the office intending to slam the door to emphasise her anger but was thwarted by the door check at the top of the door, installed specifically to prevent the door from being slammed. Office door windows, which broke when doors were slammed, were expensive.

"AGGGHHH!" She screamed in frustration, kicked the door and stomped over to the staircase, yelling a final insult. "JUST DO ME A FAVOR AND MAKE SURE IT'S HIGH ENOUGH CLIFF! OR MAYBE A BRIDGE! IN BROOKLYN."

Doc listened as the clip-clop of her high heels faded down the marble stairs before falling back into the chair behind his desk.

"Real smooth asshole!" He opened the lower drawer where he stowed all the guns he had appropriated in the last few years from thugs and mugs and reached in the back to produce the bottle of Jameson's' Whiskey. One of Louie's bowling trophies on the wall shelf next to his desk was the first thing that caught his eye. He reached over, pulled it down and wiped the dust out from the small gold cup and poured some whiskey.

"Best thing's ever happened to you, she tries and connect with ya and what'a you do? You piss all over her! Real smooth asshole!" He threw back his drink then stared at the trophy plate. "Plumber's League Intramurals!"

1st Place
Louie Mancino – High Score 278
September, 1944

"Fucking Mancino! You silly WOP bastard!" McKeowen laughed as he thought of how far Mancino had come in the last five years. Then his mind wandered to the Twisselman case.

"Why the hell is she so interested in this girl's case?" As he often did Doc talked aloud to himself when faced with a problem. After a stiff drink. He found if he spoke things out loud they took on a different complexion then if you just skimmed through them in your mind.

He continued, addressing the framed photo of his dead father in his NYPD uniform.

"She doesn't know this Twisselman dame. They never met, and she's never had a real interest in police work. So where's the connection?" He poured another drink. "Besides, this broad walks in here, slaps classified, NYPD black and whites on my desk and wants me to get involved! All because

151

her hack boyfriend got spanked by his Hollyweird agent! Fishy!"

A half an hour later, having completed his anger arch and now returned to calmness, Doc headed back to the apartment much more relaxed.

"Hey, hey! You awake?" He gently shook Nikki through the covers. "I wanna talk. You awake?"

"I am now!"

"Sorry."

"That's okay, I was sleeping anyway." Nikki reached over and switched on the lamp. "What is it?" Her voice clearly registered residual irritation.

"I been thinking."

"Thinking or drinking?!"

"Some of both but mostly thinking."

"Did it hurt?"

"I'm trying to be serious here!"

"Uh huh." She grunted.

"I get where you're coming from." He conceded. There was a long silence as she pushed up to a sitting position, her back against the head board.

"I'm listening."

"It's not that I don't want you involved in the agency and I get that you're bored. And I'd love to have you around the office. It's just that . . ."

"Yeah?"

"This ain't like working in a library, or for the Navy. This isn't just desk work. There's real danger involved. Half a dozen P.I.'s have been waxed just in Manhattan since I started this operation. Salmon got nailed by the feds and is doing time. We aren't exactly held in high esteem by the cops, the staties or especially the feds! They don't exactly shed a tear when one of us buys the farm. Hell, I should'a been dead three, four times already in the last couple'a years."

"I remember when you got shot on the ferry."

"EXACTLY! How'd you feel when Louie called you and told you they were operating digging bullets out of me?"

"Pretty bad! Especially when they told me it was touch and go after six hours in surgery."

"Exactly what I'm getting at!" Doc blurted.

"I mean, all I could think of was, 'where the hell am I gonna find another boyfriend at my age?" Nikki said straight-faced.

"Oh, we're just on a roll tonight aren't we?"

"Really! At my age and with a daughter!"

"I'm trying to tell you I don't want you working with Louie and I because I can't risk getting you hurt."

"Why? Because you think I can't take care of myself?"

"No Nutjob! It's because if anything happened to you I'd . . . I don't know what I'd do." She put a finger to his lips.

"Shut up and get in bed, ya big lug!"

CHAPTER VIII

The four story, Brownstone Walk-up at 74 MacDougal Street lies just south of West 3rd, about a block and a half away from Washington Square Park, which is exactly where Louie Mancino could be found that evening just before dark.

Your basic residential Greenwich Village pedestrian thoroughfare, MacDougal was lined with higher priced Georgian styled homes which had been converted from three story mansions into three story walk-ups after the Civil War but still maintained an air of respectability.

Benny Joules may have broken with his family tradition by shunning law school and guaranteed financial success but he certainly had not broken with his parent's money.

The place was separated from the corner of West Houston by another apartment house and a one story restaurant. Louie spied the only alley on the block between the restaurant and the last building on the corner.

After casing the place from across the street Louie decided it was dark enough and there was little to no foot traffic so he'd go for it. His cover was to act as if he had business there and, once he determined there were no dogs, neighbors or other obstacles, he would scale the alley's gate and break in from the rear of the building.

This was the address where they found Benny's body and so had been stamped on the NYPD B&W's Nina had shown Doc and later Louie at the hotel. Benny Joules' place was the basement apartment where the rent was cheaper than the above ground flats.

Excited to pursue his first solo homicide case, it was with some trepidation that Mancino had considered going behind Doc's back for the last week before 'sneaking a peek'. But he told himself if things got too sticky he would bail out. Which is how he explained it to Doris. She saw through his excuse immediately and said so.

After flopping over the alley gate and falling on his ass, he got up dusted himself off and listened carefully, then dropped to his knees and sniffed the ground. With no sound of barking and no smell of dog shit, Mancino hated dogs, he crept to the back yard.

Gingerly producing his mail order Acme lock pick tool pouch from is breast pocket, Louie carefully accessed the back door. Working around the two inch wide, yellow police tape stretched across the doorway in a big 'X' it was with the precision of a neurosurgeon he selected a number 2 rake and hook pick and went to work.

After thirty minutes or so he switched to a ball pick.

Then a diamond pick, and finally decided to fiddle with a ball key.

A short hour and fifteen minutes later there was success when Louie smiled broadly in triumph, the knob turned and the door pushed open.

Meanwhile, a shadowy figure who had been watching from an all-night coffee joint across Houston, as Louie first drifted across the street and fell over the fence, made his move. The observer carefully scurried across the street and approached the house and descended the front stairs to the below sidewalk level front door.

His hand moved to the front door knob and entered directly into the below ground apartment.

"FREEZE!" Mancino yelled as he leveled his .38 and blinded Nikki with his flashlight. "WOW! Your eyes are really blue!" He complimented as he lowered his weapon but maintained the light in her eyes.

"Thanks Dick Tracy! NOW GET THAT FRIGGN' LIGHT OUTTA MY FACE!" Nikki yelled using both hands to shield against the glare of Louie's high powered Ever-Ready.

"WHAT THE . . ."

"Be quiet!" She demanded looking around.

"What the hell are you doing here?!"

"What the hell am **I** doing here? What the hell are **you** doing here?! You said you weren't interested in this case!" She counter challenged.

"Well, now I'm interested! Why the hell are you here?! Doc finds out you're tryin' to take a case, **which he will!** He'll have a cow!"

"Who's gonn'a tell him, Mr. Blond oggler?"

"You need to leave so I can finish up and get out of here in hurry!" Louie instructed.

"By 'in a hurry' do you mean like the two hours it took you to get into this place?"

"It was only about an hour and a half . . . how the hell did you get in?"

"The door was open. Didn't you open it?"

"No! Why would I open it? I came in through the back remember?"

"Okay, okay. Did you find anything?" She asked.

"No I just got here."

"An hour and a half ago." She mumbled.

"Let it go Cole! You gonna leave or what?"

"What's the point? I'm here aren't I? Why don't we do this together and we can both get out of here sometime tonight?"

"Awright, awright! You take in here and the kitchen, I'll take the bed room and the bathroom."

"Okay, sounds good." With renewed enthusiasm they split up and started their agreed upon chores. Nikki, brandishing her own smaller flashlight, hesitated then called over her shoulder. "Louie!"

"Yeah?"

"What'a we looking for?"

"Clues, Cole! Clues!"

For the next fifteen, twenty minutes they combed the place turning up absolutely nothing. When . . .

"Shit!" From in the front room Nikki's head snapped up as she cursed.

"What is it?!" Louie's head popped out from behind the bedroom door.

"I heard something outside!" Just as she spoke the front door knob turned.

"Someone's here!" Louie whispered back.

"Ya think?" They ducked behind the couch.

The front door swung open, a hand reached in and the lights flicked on.

Nina Twisselman turned to see Nikki and Louie slowly rising from behind the couch.

"Well, well, well!" She spewed. "Look what the cat dragged in!" Hands on his she stared coldly. "Explain, Mr. and Mrs. We Don't Want Your Case!" Louie stuttered into an explanation.

"I . . ."

"We!" Nikki corrected.

"We, after some thought, we decided that perhaps we-"

"Doc!" Nikki injected.

"Perhaps, after some thought, Mr. McKeowen might have been a little . . . anticipatory . . ." Nikki looked over and gestured him to continue. ". . . in his decision to eject your case in such a hurry." Nikki's head fell as she covered her eyes and shook her head. Nikki dove to the rescue.

"What have you decided to do with your case Miss Twissleman, if I may be so bold as to ask?" Nikki attempted to rescue.

"What'a you think? A bunch of Bozo's tell me to piss off and I'm gonna fold up shop and walk away? Days later you show up at the scene of the crime snooping around Where the hell did you people learn to be detectives? Ringling Brothers and

Barnum and Bailey? I'm gonna get to the bottom of it is what **I** have decided to do with **my** case!"

"Okay, okay, let's all take a deep breath and reset our speedometers!" Nikki suggested. "Miss Twisselman, have you found another agency to take your case?"

"No! After you guys I went to three others. After I gave the story they all turned me away."

"Are the FBI involved? That sometimes gets P.I.'s to shy away." Mancino suggested."

"I went to the FBI. They said there's no point, it's a local matter and besides there's no evidence anybody crossed any state lines."

"No update from the cops?" Louie ventured.

"Please! All I can get out of the cops is they don't rule out suicide and that they wanna paint him as a pinko."

"Was he communist?" Nikki asked.

"Get serious! He was a dedicated writer, that's it. No politics whatsoever! He never even voted."

"Have you come across anything else that might be important?" Louie inquired.

"Why should I tell you guys?"

"If you haven't found anyone else we'd very much would like to take your case." Nikki politely offered. Louie was shocked at her use of the first person plural.

"Miss Twisselman, may I have a moment to consult with my colleague?" Louie requested. Nina shook her head and stepped into the bedroom. Mancino pulled Nikki aside.

"What the hell you doin'?! We can't just sign on a case without Doc's approval! And he ain't gonna approve it!"

"Leave Doc to me." She called Nina back in and offered her hand. Nine peered at her but tentatively shook.

"Okay, deal. What now?" Nina questioned with no attempt to hide her challenging tone.

"Anything else you can tell us?" Louie probed.

"Benny had some friends he made here in the Village. I found out one of them is a dealer who graduated to pusher who sold to Benny once or twice."

"You get to talk to this dealer?"

"Yeah. He says he noticed Benny was real depressed after the rejection notice so he offered Benny some free scag. 'What's the harm in that?' he asks me?"

"Seriously? Heroin?!" Nikki pushed.

"Yeah, what are friends for huh?" Nina sarcastically quipped. "He says Benny was supposed to meet him at Washington Square Park, by The Arch, that afternoon."

"But he didn't show?"

"Oh he showed alright but he told me he didn't wanna give Benny the dope."

"He say why not?" Louie asked.

"Not in so many words but Benny was with some creepy cat who stood off across the path and didn't come with Benny when he went across the park to score. And I mean Frankenstein creepy guys from the doper's description! And when the pusher pointed him out and when he saw them looking at him he bolted across the park and disappeared up 9th Street."

"Would you know him if you saw him?" Nikki asked.

"Yeah sure! There's no other creepy looking guys in lower Manhattan, right?"

"I mean the dealer! Would you recognize the dealer?" Cole asked.

"Sweetheart! Get a clue! I just talked to him a couple'a days ago!"

"You tracked him down? Well done girl."

Outside on the street a car slowly rolled up to the curb with its headlights out. Nikki scurried to the window and peaked through the curtains out the window.

"SHIT! It's the cops!" She declared.

"What did somebody take out a god damned ad in the *Daily News*, 'Everybody meet at Benny's place'?" Louie griped.

"We'd better-" Nikki turned to Louie. They both looked around. The back door was open and Nina was gone.

**Reception Hall
Field Museum of Natural History
1400 Lake Shore Drive, Chicago**

The infamous Democratic Political Machine has dominated Chicago, the largest democratic stronghold in the country, for most of the Twentieth Century.

Democratic loyalties there have dominated along ethnic lines since 1931 when an Austrio-Hungarian Anton Cermak was elected mayor.

Less than two years later he was murdered by an assassin's bullet who was out to kill President Franklin D. Roosevelt while in Miami when a woman, who saw the criminal brandish his pistol used that universal, womanly defense; she whacked him with her purse. The killer got off several shots missing FDR but unintentionally killing Cermak.

In a final irony Cermak's final words were construed as an apology to the President and is carved on his grave stone; 'I'm glad it was me and not you.'

At the Field Museum of Natural History that evening was a Democratic fund raiser where the valet service outside at the base of the sprawling, granite staircase was a hub of activity as donators, supporters and hangers-on arrived and drifted up the stairs into the Museum's sprawling functions hall.

Not having made the political headway he was hoping for with Senator Pickham regarding the Sons of Liberty at the hotel some weeks ago, Steadman changed tactics. He would aim a little lower but up the ante. Among the donators and supporters that night was the newly elected Mayor Martin H. Kennelly.

The guests had by now only half filled the hall and there was a good hour to go before the ceremony and the speeches. Enough time to get at least partially anesthetized beforehand.

"Which one's Kennelly?" Sitting alone at a corner table Steadman spoke to the waitress, an acquaintance from his local tavern, as she set his two double scotches in front of him.

"You live here and you don't know what your mayor looks like?" The thirty-something brunette cracked.

"Look Doll, I don't read the papers, my radio is permanently tuned to the Jack Benny show and I damn sure ain't got one of those new-fangled contraptions everybody's pissin' themselves about just to sit like a lump on a log and stare at black and white moving pictures!"

"You talkin' about televisions? Those things are amazing! I bought one on time last week and they're-"

"Congratulations. You want this or not?" He held up a tenner. She snatched it from his hand.

"That small gaggle of short pudgy, balding guys on the other side of the bar?" She nodded across the room.

"Yeah."

"He's the least bald." She breezed away. With no compunction about interrupting the Mayor and the two councilmen he was with Steadman downed one of the scotches, dumped the residual ice into the full glass and launched off.

"Congrats on your election Mr. Mayor." He barged in taking Kennelly by surprise.

"Have we met?"

"Joshua Steadman! Please call me Jake." He pulled up the empty chair. "We met at last year's function. I volunteered for your campaign!"

"Oh, which district?" Before Kennelly could inquire any further Steadman rambled on.

"Big fan Mr. Mayor, big fan! As is everyone at the lodge."

"What lodge would that be Mr. . . . Steadman?" He cautiously shook Steadman's hand.

"We met at the Kelly function Mr. Mayor."

"Oh yes. Thank you for your support." The Mayor rose to leave and Steadman correctly sensed he was already losing his mark.

"Sir we at the Sons of Liberty couldn't agree more with what you're doing in City Hall! You had our full support throughout the campaign!"

"That's good to know and thank you again for your support."

Steadman pushed hard for the next five minutes and, as Kennelly was about to excuse himself for the second time, finally found the common thread he had been fishing for.

"We are particularly interested in your negro zoning integration efforts sir." This caught Kennelly's attention.

"Oh? How so?" Finally Jake struck pay dirt.

"The propositions and discussions you've had with Councilman Kelly, sir. We at the lodge, myself included of course, feel that the American negro

164

needs all the help he can get. After all, we're all Americans and a strong negro population is a strong U.S. population! That's how we see it anyway."

The mayor pulled back and gave Steadman a more serious look.

"I firmly believe and support Mr. Kelly's integration policies. Of course you probably already know that." Kennelly said as he retook his seat.

Martin H. Kennelly became the father of the non-profit Allied Van Lines when, back in 1928, he formed a consortium of moving companies. A captain in the Army during World War I following his discharge he became the head of the National Red Cross. Altruistic, to a fault some say, he was also a reformer true to his Irish Catholic roots. But he was no dupe. He understood the world of Chicago politics had little interest in pure altruism.

"What exactly is this Sons of Freedom you belong to?"

"Sons of Liberty sir."

"Yes, Liberty."

"Well, Mr. Mayor exactly what I came over to chat with you about! The Sons of Liberty, would very much like to assist in your racial integration efforts!"

"Well that's great news! We are in desperate need of funds at the moment-"

"Oh not financial-wise Mayor. We can do much better than just throwing money at the problem!"

"Oh? What are you proposing then?"

"Organizing demonstrations."

"I see."

"Demonstrations in conjunction with petitions and fund raising of course!" Steadman quickly added.

"That might be useful. How extensive are you capable of reaching?"

"I own a large construction firm, built it up during the war, now with the wide-spread strikes going on across the country I'm one of the only large companies in Chicago with complete control of my work force! I pay my men fifty percent above the national average and so have no interest in striking."

"That's good to know, some of those strikes are getting pretty nasty. If e do business I'll need your absolute guarantee there'll be no violence or rough stuff! Those people have as much of a right to come up here from the south and earn a living as our people did before the Great War."

"Truthfully sir I . . . I don't see the negro the main threat!"

"Really? Who then?"

"The Reds of course!" Steadman was careful to monitor Kennelly's expression when the topic switched to the commies.

"The Communists do appear to becoming an issue!"

"The way I see it Mr. Mayor, it comes down to a handful of key responsible parties in society to protect our Christian values in order to preserve the American way of life."

"I couldn't agree more Mr. Steadman. Tell me, do you allow Negroes in this patriotic organization of yours, this Sons of Liberty?"

"Ours is a young organization Mr. Mayor but we do have the issue up for a vote on our Annual General Meeting." Steadman lied as smooth as a polished Oldsmobile.

"And when is this AGM of yours?" The mayor inquired.

"This November sir."

"I'd like to be kept up to speed on the outcome Mr. Steadman. Maybe come to speak if you like."

"I think we might be able to arrange that Mayor Kennelly."

"Brilliant! If there's anything the Mayor's office can do for you . . ." As Kennelly rose to leave for a third time Steadman stood with him and wound up for the pitch. "We do have one small problem that you perhaps could help s with Mr. Mayor."

Kennelly, no dunce, braced himself as he fully expected to be hit up for some kind of favor but not so soon.

"We need the city's approval to expand our charter beyond 5000 members and apply for state recognition." Steadman explained. Kennelly exhaled a mental breath of relief.

"That shouldn't be too difficult a proposition Mr. Steadman!"

✝

Next morning at his main office Steadman arrived at work quite pleased with the progress of his master plan.

"Mornin' Boss."

"Mornin' Thornton." Steadman greeted his Number Two man.

"How'd it go last night? You get your quota of brown nosing in?!" He mocked as he draped his jacket over a chair.

"Laugh if you want to, but when the S.O.L. goes national and we're poised on the doorstep of becoming a major political party you'll be trippin' over yourself to brag how you were in on the ground floor!"

"Going national?! So you think you finally made some headway?"

"I'm pretty sure I got Kennelly's attention by hooking into his integration initiative with the niggers. Looks like we're gonna get our City Cert!"

"You ain't thinkin' about allowin' nigra's in the S.O.L., are ya?! The board ain't gonna like that!"

"Bobby S. Thornton do I **look** stupid to you?! You ever heard of a public persona? Course I ain't gonna let them in! Ain't you learned nothin' from these FDR democrats? It don't make a shit of difference what you do, it's only what you say that matters!"

"With a city charter we have a recognized base. Membership already extends across the state and once we hit ten thousand members the dues payments will get us to out to Ohio and down to P.A. which guarantees us the remainder of the mid-

West. Then it's only a year until we reach the Eastern Seaboard!"

Steadman reached across his desk and flipped on his intercom.

"Janeane?"

Yes Mr. Steadman?

"Janeane, make out a check for a thousand dollars to the Chicago Democratic Party. Make sure you annotate it as a donation."

Yes Mr. Steadman.

"And then get me the Mayor's office on the phone."

Two minutes later Steadman was on the line with Mayor Kennelly personally informing him that he had just made a thousand dollar donation.

"May you do great things in the future Mr. Mayor!" Steadman blurted.

Mr. Steadman, let me assure you, the Democratic Party is the party which will change the face of America! Kennelly boasted.

The Hotel Del Coronado
19:10, July 14th

In 1888 when it was first opened the Hotel Del, built in the style of American Beach Resort/Victorian architecture, was the largest hotel structure in the world and the second largest wooden structure in the U.S.

The Broad in the Kimono

The Hotel Del Coronado Situated on the main beach of Coronado Island about two hours south of L.A., is the type of structure you'd expect to see in the movies. In fact you probably have. It's been used in several Hollywood productions. It's also the kind of place that reeks of money.

With seven floors, seven restaurants and seven hundred and fifty-seven rooms the $250 per night price tag and $50 per plate, a weekend getaway for two starts at around $600. Of course the only folks who frequent the place are rich tourists after they've seen Hollywood and politicians foolishly attempting to maintain a low profile while trying to impress a groupie with a weekend fling.

It was just past eight that evening when a guy, thirty-ish, came through the front door and into the ribbed, oak beamed Crown Dining Room.

Perhaps because he stopped, stood with hands on hips, slid back his hat and stood staring at the ornate room like someone just seen a two headed dog or maybe it was because everyone else was dressed in suits, tuxedoes and evening gowns while he was decked out in a disheveled two piece suit, brown work shirt and fedora that he looked suspiciously out of place. Who knows?

He was immediately accosted by the tuxedoed maître'd'hôtel with the red cumber bun who stepped from around his polished oak podium to stand in front of the guy and block his path.

"May I help you sir?"

"No, but thanks. I'm meeting someone. For dinner."

"I am sorry monsieur but we require a tie for dinner."

Without flinching the guy produced a rumpled and creased, tan, square cut tie form his back pocket and brandished it in front of the faux Frenchman. It was already knotted in a loose Windsor. After donning the tie, and with the obstruction eliminated, the guy breezed past the mâitre'd, perused the room and made his way over to a table by a beach-side window.

"The Boss sends his apologies that we had to meet so far out'a town." He addressed the tall, lanky fellow at the table.

The man delicately eating lobster was Harry Bridges well-known as the leader of the American Labor Union Party, a left leaning, borderline communist organization and a notorious labor organizer.

During a misguided trip to New York City back in the early Forties Harry made the mistake of arriving in Manhattan to organize the stevedores and dock workers under the communist banner. Joey 'Socks' Lanza, who ran the Fulton Street Fish Market, showed him some Big Apple hospitality.

Lanza, along with some of his boys informed the disillusioned Mr. Bridges that the New York City waterfront already had a functioning union organized by Socks Lanza himself.

Harry was generously assaulted, bundled into the trunk of a sedan and driven to the airport where he was given a one way ticket back to L.A. along with a warning about ever showing up on the East Coast again.

Harry wisely confined all future union activities to the West coast.

"Right, glad you made it." Bridges' speech was tinged with a heavy accent.

"Oh! English, hey?" The tie commented.

"Australian boy-o. English are POHM's, I'm Australian." Oblivious to what was just said to him the tie pushed on.

"Again sorry to keep you waiting."

"Yes this is rather rough here." Harry quipped as he slowly squeezed another lime wedge into to his frosted margarita and glanced out at the flaming sunset igniting the horizon while the gentle crash of the surf broke on the pristine beach. "But I'll manage." He watched a pair of bikini clad young girls run giggling down to the water and splash around in the surf line.

"Yeah I'll bet you will, especially since we're picking up the tab!" The guy, actually a private detective from the Pinkerton Agency out of the San Diego office, mocked.

"So what is it I can do for you detective Hammet?"

"I'm instructed by our client to inquire as to how his firm might go about avoiding any possible union trouble they may run into in the next few months or so."

"And?"

"They are interested to know if you Mr. Bridges can do anything about it?"

"That depends on two things."

"Which are?"

"What's in it for me and exactly how far is your client willing to go?"

Bridges' bluntness took the rent-a-cop off guard.The Pinkerton attempted to explain while maintaining the secrecy he was sworn to.

"Let me explain his, their, situation. This is a big firm that hired us, I mean B-I-G! If his workers don't go for the deal he's offering them there's good reason to believe the entertainment industry in the U.S. could completely collapse as we know it."

"So your client, presumably some big studio exec, Mr. Warner I'm guessing, wants to know if there's anything I can do to stop his people, presumably the writers, from closing down his studio by going on strike? That about it?"

The stunned detective was under strict orders not to reveal the Pinkertons had been hired by Jack Warner but the accuracy of Harry Bridges' descriptions so took him off guard that he nodded like an automaton.

"Ah . . . yes . . . exactly."

"No."

"No?! That's it? Just no?!"

"Yes, that's exactly it. No." Bridges repeated.

"Then why'd you take this meet if you knew what it was about? I'm supposed to be having dinner at my mother-in-law's!"

"How ever did you chose?"

A uniformed waiter appeared at the table and offered a pair of menus.

"May I tell you about our specials tonight? We have-"

"No." Bridges cut him off. "I'll have another one of these and the gentleman will have . . . probably a beer."

"Make it a scotch, rocks. A double."

"In answer to your query," Bridges explained. "I didn't know what it was about when I agreed to the meeting but I have since done my homework. I must say that for a premier private detective agency, some of your affairs are not very private. I read in *The Hollywood Reporter*, Jack Warner who is notorious for mistreating writers, offered them a union, *The Playwrights* something or other. They have recently been granted the right to organize by the Department of Labor, and so have formed their own little club as a writers guild. I predict it won't last. I just read the papers and pay attention to the six o'clock NBC News Hour on the radio. No investigation required. It's only logical, given those developments, he'd try something desperate." He goaded Hammet with an exaggerated smile. "You do realize the IATSE is the largest union in Hollywood and is run by the Mafia?" Bridges queried.

"That ain't nothin' but a rumor!" The tie protested.

"Mr. Hammet, I have met a couple of gentlemen from the Mafia and don't wish to meet them again. I assure you it is not a rumor! More importantly I am in unskilled trade labor organizer, stevedores, truck drivers, factory workers that sort of thing. I have nothing to do with the arts, much less film." The waiter appeared and gingerly set the drinks on the table.

"I have a suggestion that may be of help to your client. But, I repeat, what's in it for me?"

"Name your price." Hammet snapped. Bridges smiled.

"Then your problem is simple! Just find a couple of communists, leak it to the papers and say they're causing, you know . . . whatever."

"But you're a commie!"

"I'm a socialist ya ruddy Yank! And that's why I know what I'm talking about."

"You found out the hard way that's for sure! I read what Lucky's boys did to you in New York!"

"Yeah, yeah let's don't get carried away. Next question, who does the only organizing in Hollywood?"

"The Mob! Capone set it up back in the Thirties."

"You're not as dim as you look! And who do the gangsters hate?"

"They hate commies."

"Oh master of the obvious, who controls the top men in the senate?" He gave the Pinkerton a moment to think as Hammet knit his brow. "Okay Dr. Fermi, don't hurt yourself thinking."

"Who the fuck is Fermi?"

"Not important. The same people who control the Hollywood technicians."

"Okay, but at the end of the day you can't label all the writers commies!" The slow detective argued.

"You don't have to call them **all** commies, just a few of them. The leaders."

"I see."

"You are a detective, aren't you?" Bridges challenged.

"Yeah, why?"

"Didn't that loud mouth hack editor up in Hollywood what's his face . . . Wilbertson?"

"Wilkinson."

"Wilkinson whatever, say in his paper he knew a couple of commie writers? Get their names. Use them." He shrugged as if it was obvious.

Hammet's facial expression clearly indicated the penny had dropped.

"What happens when they deny it, maybe launch a lawsuit? What then?" He argued.

"Lawsuit?" Bridges laughed out loud. "I'll tell you what happens, their precious contracts are cancelled, they're out of work and your client gets to claim they were communists all along, that's what happens."

"What about proof?"

"As far as proof, he doesn't need any proof! It's guilt by accusation! You don't have to commit a crime in this country to be accused of a crime and be dragged into court and convicted. This is America!"

"But bein' a commie ain't a crime in this country."

"Doesn't matter, it will be soon enough, mark my words."

"You think the strike threat dies with Wilkinson?"

"Who cares? Like a dog with a bone once the press latch onto Warner's got the upper hand. Wouldn't be surprised if it gets big enough for the Washington boys to get involved." The Pinkerton leaned back in his chair and nodded as Bridges continued "You remember what happened when the papers reported Nazis infiltrating the New York City waterfront at the start of the war?" Bridges pushed.

"Yeah, I remember, so where's the connect?"

"What was the general reaction?" Bridges asked.

"It was pandemonium is was it was! The agency put us on twelve hour shifts for months thinking the Krauts were gonna hit L.A. harbor, Longbeach , Orange County!"

"And when the dust settled, how many Nazis did the FBI catch infiltrating the waterfront?"

"I dunno. Six, seven that I read about."

"Exactly. Believe me son, if it's one thing I know about, it's how people react when they're told there are communists, Nazis or Martians in New Jersey for that matter, even when there's not!"

✝

CHAPTER IX

Doc breezed into the office that morning flipping through the mail.

"Mr. McKeowen! Mr. McKeowen! I'm glad you here!" Shirley could hardly contain herself as she sprang out from behind her desk to greet Doc even before he hung his jacket on the coat rack.

"Well it's nice to see you too Shirley! It's been what a whole day and a half?"

"You gonna love this!"

"What exciting news have you got for me this morning Shirley?" He handed her the mail and moved to make a cup of coffee.

"Yo' partner in crime has –"

"With Mancino's aversion to his Italian heritage I don't think he'd appreciate you calling him 'my partner in crime.'"

"Well he can appreciate or not appreciate all he want to cause he's a crime partner now!"

"Shirley exactly what are you struggling to tell me in your adorable, down home dialect?" Annoyed, but only slightly by Doc's insult, Shirley assumed hands on hips and launched the assault.

"You know that one phone call you gets when you in jail?"

"Yeah?"

"Well Mr. Mancino used his to call here!"

"SON-OF-A-BITCH!" Doc set his cup of coffee next to her typewriter, dropped both hands to her

178

desk and hung his head. "God damned twelve year old boy in the body of a man!"

"I would'a guessed nine. Ten at most!" She said as she reached over and moved his coffee away from her Underwood.

Ten minutes later Doc was taking the police station granite steps two at a time and pushed through the front doors of the 6th Precinct two blocks away on 10th Street.

McKeowen was greeted by his worst nightmare. Behind the elevated chief's desk, consulting with a beat cop was Police Chief Sullivan. Sullivan was a dominate factor in the precipitation of McKeowen's resignation from the force.

Two years into his NYPD career Doc's father, a twenty year man on the force, was ambushed at a drug bust on the Lower East side.

Although never having actually worked in Sullivan's precinct house in the two years he was a beat cop, Doc had strong reason to believe Sullivan had inside knowledge of the cause of his father's death when he was killed on the drug raid when working with a squad of narcotics detectives back before the war. The concept of a dedicated narcotics squad, the first in NYPD history, was his father's idea and some members of the force were less than enthusiastic about the idea. The fact that no bad guys were at the scene the night of the raid was extremely suspicious.

"Here to bail out the help are ya McKeowen?" Sullivan grunted as Doc approached the desk.

"What's the story?"

"Caught your two Junior G-Men snooping around a private premises over on 9th."

"**Two** Junior G-Men?"

"Yeah. Except one of 'em's a broad. You stooped to hirin' broads now McKeowen? Things that bad huh?"

"The woman's name wouldn't happen to be Nikki Cole, would it?" His anger deteriorated into trepidation.

"So you did stoop to hiring split tails! Pathetic."

"Just show me see the charge sheet!"

Sullivan nodded to the other cop who then rummaged through the desk and passed Doc a thin sheaf of documents which he quickly perused.

"Private premises? Was the guy home?" McKeowen pushed as he scanned the sheets.

"No, cause he's dead! That's why it's a crime scene!"

"Dead? What are they charged with?"

"B&E, trespassing, interfering with an on-going investigation and resisting arrest."

"Resisting arrest?!"

"Yeah, your tough little girl friend gave the arresting officers a lip full when they threw her in the squad car."

"I'll bet that 110 pounds was a real bitch to handle with only two or three big strong cops responding to the scene! Sounds like you stooped to hiring fairies."

"Your partner was none too friendly either!" Sullivan added as if to reinforce the argument.

180

"Yeah, that's why I quit being a cop Sully. Too many people hurling insults all the time. Hurt my feelings."

"You're a barrel of laughs you are McKeowen! Let's see how funny you think it is when your friends go to arraignment!"

"Yeah, yeah, yeah! Bail been set yet?"

"Yeah tough guy, bail's been set. Two hundred and fifty bucks! Each! Cash only!"

Doc dug out $250 and tossed it on the desk.

"That's for the girl. You can keep Mancino."

"You don't want him?"

"There's two hundred and fifty bucks there. Where do I sign?"

Sullivan stamped two copies of the bail papers and tossed them back at McKeowen.

"She'll be down in a few minutes."

A 'few minutes' turned out to be forty-five which was enough time for Doc to calm down, but not completely.

A dishevelled Nikki escorted by a uniform was brought downstairs to the lobby where Doc sat on a bench. Sullivan handed Nikki her purse and belongings and had her sign for her stuff.

Her head bowed in contrition, Nikki smiled at Doc who gnashed his teeth with his mouth closed.

The, uniform checked with Sully who nodded she was free to leave but couldn't resist a last crack at Doc.

"You just fuck up everything you touch, don't you McKeowen?" He called from behind the desk.

By way of a response Doc walked back over to the desk and reached over to touch Sullivan on the arm then hesitated and pulled back his hand.

"Oh, too late." Doc stated. "Already done!" Doc pocketed the bail papers and breezed past Nikki and out through the double doors bumping into a civilian coming into the station house.

Doc's action compelled Nikki to realize that what she had done was more than just get caught with her hand in the cookie jar. To her credit she also realized that she was going to have to face the music. She took off after Doc.

"Doc! Doc wait!" Outside, shielding her eyes from the sun Nikki called after him as he bounded down the sidewalk. "Doc please!"

He stopped several yards away, in front of a brownstone but didn't turn to face her. "Doc I'm really sorry! I mean, I never intended-"

He stared off into the distance and spoke.

"Jimmy Kinecki!" He said.

"Who . . .?" She started as he stepped to within a foot of her and yelled to her face.

"Jimmy fucking Kinecki!" He repeated.

"Who's Jimmy Kinecki?"

"Jimmy Kinecki is a former cop buddy who IS DEAD! Redbone's young nephew is DEAD! My father, DEAD! THIS IS NOT A GAME! DO YOU GET THAT?!"

"Doc I –"

"You do understand the fact that death is not like love or life don't you? Death is FOREVER! This job is not a game. The reason people like Sullivan

182

are assholes is because they deal with death every day and that makes them scared. Scared of their own mortality and the fact that they are going to die."

"I thought Sullivan's assholedess was due to genetics." Doc didn't smile. "We're all gonna die! I —"

"Yes we are all gonna die, some day. But who the hell wants to fuckin' do it being shot by some lousy punk stickin' up a god damned pharmacy?!" He pushed harder to drive the point home. She nodded meekly. "You don't get that do ya! No of course not! You can't get it, you're a woman!"

"Really?" Nikki's face flushed beet red as she stood dead still for a few seconds, gritted her teeth and turned and stomped off past him.

"SHIT!" Doc declared realizing he had to chase after her. A couple of doors down he caught up to her and spun her around by the shoulders.

"Sorry about the crack, but what you don't get is, what you can't possibly get is, this is the wrong city, the wrong system and the wrong people to pull this self-righteous shit on. The kind of people we deal with don't give a shit about your feelings! This game doesn't operate on what any honest person understands as a moral basis."

"So we're all supposed to believe there's no right or wrong? That there's no rules and to hell with everything?!" Nikki snapped back, her anger no less dissipated.

"No, there's right and wrong, but it's got nothing to do with school girl morality! It's based on who thinks they can fuck who over."

"Language!"

"Oh sorry! FUCK OVER whomever they can and get away with. In this world, a man's world, the law only applies if it can be used against your opponent! Let me explain what you don't seem to get! That fat assed Sullivan would not hesitate for a micro second if he thought he could link that crime they're investigating to you and Louie and that's a whole world of shit you do not want! For people like him solving crimes is simply checking boxes, it's got nothing to do with nailing the people who actually did it! Most of the collars guys like him make are because the crook screwed up, somebody ratted him out or just dumb luck! There's very little Sherlock Holmes shit involved. And that truth and justice shit-"

"LANGUAGE!"

"STUFF! That 'justice' stuff is only in comics books!"

"So, in a world where everybody's guilty, the only crime is getting caught?!" She surmised. Doc drew back, smirked and slowly nodded.

"Hey! That's pretty good! For a girl I mean."

"Prick!" She cursed as she punched him hard in the chest and arm. Doc feigned being knocked out of breath.

"I'm sorry I butted my nose in on the case." She apologized. "Okay?"

"It's okay, just please, if you really wanna help. . . just ask. I got no problem with you helpin' out as long as it doesn't involve you getting killed."

There was a long pause. She calmed down, smiled and took him by the hand.

"Thanks, that means a lot!"

"I mean if you got killed I'd have to find somewhere else to keep my razor, move all my clothes back into the office -"

"Very funny wise guy!" She smacked him again then suddenly reached into her blouse and started digging around. "Maybe this will help." From under her bra Nikki produced a folded over piece of paper and passed it to Doc who opened it. It was a carbon copy of the police report on Benny's Joules' death.

"Did you know they only search you coming in, not when they let you go?" She coyly asked.

"His real name is Saul?" Doc asked as he perused the carbon up to the sun to read it. "Where'd you get this?"

"Apparently the NYPD didn't get the memo."

"What memo?!"

"Downtown at Naval Intel we always had to put carbons in the burn bags, never in the scrap baskets near our desks."

"I still don't get how the hell you . . .?" Doc puzzled as he read through the investigation report.

"They didn't have a matron over at the Ninth Precinct-"

"Nina gave her initial statement here at the Sixth."

"Correct! The Ninth is where they first took me but there was no matron to search me so, they brought me back over here to the Sixth. So, this morning in there, while they were out processing me the cop left the pad on the desk. I started quickly flipping through it when I came across the carbon copy of the report so . . ."

"So you decided to up your career status from novice felon to two time offender. You realize this is exactly why I refused that German girl the first time she showed up? Possession of stolen police property?"

"So I did bad?" She meekly mumbled.

"Did you get caught?"

"I'm out here aren't I?"

"Then you did good. But how did you . . . I mean, I still don't get where you . . .?" He asked brandishing the carbon.

"Not important but, as soon as we get home I'll need a shower. So, are we good?"

"We're good so long as I can get you to understand one thing. No more P.I. sh- stuff! I'm not emotionally equipped for anything to happen to you! Besides, you're not trained. That's all I'm asking. Bad enough I gotta babysit -!"

"LOUIE! Holy shit, you didn't bail Louie out!" Nikki realized.

"Oh yeah." Doc apathetically said.

"Aw come on Doc! You can't leave him in there until the arraignment!"

"It's only a week, two at the most. He'll be grateful for the break from Doris."

"DOC!"

"Alright, alright!" He acquiesced and glanced at his watch. "It's nearly ten, go around the corner to the bank and pull two and half yards out then go back and bail him out."

"It would mean a lot more to him if you did it." Nikki coaxed.

"Look, I **have** to forgive you, but I still have to calm down before I face him! This is not his first rodeo, he knows better! But when he gets fired up he can't keep his-" He trailed off.

"Can't keep his what?"

"His gun in his pants. . . his holster I mean."

"Oh. Okay."

"I'm heading back over the West Side. Retrieve Mancino and meet me back in the office in about an hour." He walked away then turned back. "And don't forget the pink copy of the bail papers!" He reminded as he kissed her and walked away.

"It's not my first rodeo." She meekly called after him as she watched McKeowen head down the block.

Three quarters of an hour later Cole and Mancino were walking back over to their Christopher Street office.

"Hey Nikki, I was thinking, you think it would be a good idea to have your driver's licence picture taken when you're drunk?" Mancino mused.

"Why?"

"You know, fer later in case you get stopped after you been drinking?"

"Louie do us all a favor for now, stop thinking!"

"Where's Doc?"

"Said he wanted to cruise by Benny's block. We're to meet him back in the office at eleven."

Louie leaned into Nikki and spoke.

"You know he's gonna take the case now, don't ya?"

"Yeah, I know." She grinned. Louie glanced at his wrist watch.

"Great! Twenty-five minutes, plenty of time to catch breakfast! There's a café around the corner on Houston." Louie offered.

"Okay, but we have to make it fast. I will not be late to the office! I'm in enough trouble with Doc!"

"You?! What about me?"

"YOU?!" She shook her head and grinned. "You're screwed like a cigarette machine in a cancer ward."

"I know."

"Like a soup sandwich in the rain brother!"

"Yeah."

"We're talking about screwed like a fat dog in a Korean restaurant!"

"Christ Cole! I get the picture already!!" Louie drew the line.

"Language Mister! Language!!"

The Majestic Apartments
115 Central Park West

At the same time Doc was going against his better judgement on the Twissleman case things were progressing Uptown for Frankie Costello now heading up Luciano's branch of the New York mob.

. .

The two well-dressed centurions Jimmy Dugan picked up in the marble laden lobby now stood motionless on either side of the drug running pilot as he suddenly felt like the elevator was far smaller than it should be.

Each easily stood a full foot taller and 60 pounds heavier than the nervous pilot. The fact that they made no effort to conceal their shoulder holsters added little comfort.

These two weren't anything like the goons Jimmy had initially dealt with when he was first let into the organization nearly two years ago, nor were they akin to the professional bone breaks he had been dealing with lately. These two were proper torpedoes. Trim, well-built polished. Not a word had been spoken to him since they frisked him on entering the building. They just nodded in the direction he was meant to go and he went.

There was an audible sigh of relief when the bell dinged and the doors slid open on the twenty-fifth floor of the north tower. The human monolith on his right nodded and he stepped out of the lift first.

Jimmy was there to meet the Prime Minister himself, Frankie Costello.

Costello inherited control of the New York families a year and a half ago when Charlie 'Lucky' Luciano was deported back to Italy. The Genovese gang reckoned they were the rightful heirs to the throne but when Vito got himself indicted for murdering a labor leader who had made enemies of the wrong politicians, they were rendered leaderless. So now, with the backing of Meyer Lansky, alias 'The Accountant', Frankie Costello a long time trusted friend of Luciano, inherited the reins of power. At least until it was time for the next ambitious Mafioso to make inroads into The Council at which time he would send his hired guns to install an extra hole or two in Mr. Costello.

A few weeks ago Jimmy Dugan casually let slip, accidently on purpose, that he had a good idea of how to better deliver the drugs he was flying into the U.S. Word filtered up to the top and an order was sent down that an audience would be granted.

As if in some futuristic sci-fi, a third taller automaton opened the door while the other two disappeared. He signalled hands up to Jimmy who complied and was patted down again.

The apartment's front door opened to reveal a ten foot by fifteen foot picture window on the far side of the expansive room.

Jimmy perused the spacious penthouse as he was again searched. He spotted Frank Costello reclining on a white fur couch sitting on the white fur rug, off to one side on the white mirrored wall. The wall lined with the white lamps, the couch white end tables. To add some variety there was an off-white ottoman in front of the white easy chairs guarding the couch.

Finished being frisked Jimmy mistakenly stepped forward and was immediately intercepted by a large opened palm to the chest.

"Shoes!"

"Sorry." He kicked of his two toned Nunn-Bush's and neatly set them off to the side. The guard motioned him in.

"Mr. Costello, your guest is here."

"Thank you Adonis." Costello stood and moved over to the ten seat mahogany table. Two servants had already begun ferrying food from the kitchen off to the left.

"Have a seat. We were just about to start lunch, you hungry?"

"Actually, yes I am Mr. Costello. Thank you." Jimmy took the seat indicated to Costello's right.

Only one of the three torpedoes took a chair sitting himself opposite Jimmy on Costello's left.

"So you're the daredevil fly boy that runs our product up from the Bahamas?" Frank asked.

"Anywhere you need sir."

"What's your brainstorm on this new drug delivery system you're proposing Dugan?"

Fighting the distraction of the two and half pound, fully dressed lobsters being set in front of them, Jimmy collected his thoughts.

"Well sir . . . I'm no Capo-"

"I know that. Eat! You can eat and talk at the same time can't' ya?" Costello went to work on his lobster.

"Yes sir." Jimmy manned his fish fork and dug into the split open lobster tail. "As to my take sir is this, anything this lucrative will, eventually, catch the eye of the government. And Truman, same as any other top politician is going to come at this with the same philosophy."

"Which is?"

"Which is if you can't stop it, get some money and votes out of it by controlling it."

"And if he can't control it?" Adonis pushed.

"I think you know the answer to that sir. Get as big a piece of the action as possible."

"You sayin' Truman's gonna start running drugs?" Costello asked.

"Maybe he'll go in with us on the next shipment?!" Adonis joked. They all laughed.

"No Mr. Costello, the president is not about to start running drugs. Point is," Jimmy continued. ". . . at the moment you're on top of the Feds, but, soon enough they will catch up."

"Soon enough?"

"Politicians are like entertainers sir, very little difference. Singers, actors etc . . . they're only worth as much as their last hit movie or record and given The Federal Bureau of Narcotics' recent expansion mixed with Anslinger's zealotry and the fact that the press has discovered they can sell more newspapers with increased PR about drug running, thus raising our profile, which we would like to avoid . . . I can see them pressing in on us happening sooner than later."

"What exactly do you see Mr. Dugan?" All ears perked up. Jimmy set his utensils aside and focused.

"Under the guise of the Harrison Act Anslinger is going to keep asking Congress for more money. He just got another million beginning of this year. And every time he makes a splash in the press . . . well, you get the idea."

Jimmy showed he was no dunce, remaining silent and allowing his last point to sink in.

"Keep talkin' Dugan." Adonis ordered.

"This Professor Lindesmith's report claiming Anslinger's wasting a lot of the tax payer's money is gonna kick up a stink in the press. Anslinger is gonna dig his heels in deeper, guys like him don't like to be second guessed. He's already called for a Congressional hearing for next month."

"So you're sayin' there's a big crack down coming, that it?" Adonis joined in.

Jimmy now knew he had Costello's attention and pushed his plate away then wiped his mouth with the linen napkin.

"Mr. Costello, sir, I'll answer that by asking you a question, okay?"

"Okay."

"How far would you go to protect your position in the organization?"

Adonis was the only one who laughed and even his chuckle immediately trailed off leaving silence in the room.

"A bunch a senators went over to Sicily after the war, to see what was what you know, politically speaking." Jimmy ventured. "Long after the senators concluded their detailed reports and inspections and went home, Lt. Colonel Nesbitt, the man in charge of distribution of food and supplies to the starving Sicilian population, realized that most of the U.S. Army and international aide being trucked into the area was being pilfered enroute. The colonel gave Don Calogero Vizzini the Sicilian crime boss, known throughout Sicily as Il-"

"Il Primo. We know who he is." Adonis interrupted.

"The Colonel gave Vizzini a choice; find the sons-of-bitches 's taking the food and medicine out of the people's mouths or he would reinstate marshal law. Twenty-four hours later the flow of supplies had been restored and a day after that a courier delivered a gift to Army Command H.Q. It was a beautiful signet ring and it was addressed to the Commanding Officer. The ring was still attached to the former owner's finger."

"I heard about that." Costello admitted before sipping his Vermentino di Galhur and sitting back.

"How far would I go to protect my position?" Frankie turned slightly and spoke to the whole table. "Adonis, tell the man how far I would go."

The biggest of the three torpedoes in the room smiled across at Jimmy and made direct eye contact.

"Personally I thought it should'a been his balls in that box, not just a finger. How far would Mr. Costello go? As far as is required. No limits." Adonis quietly answered as he opened his suit jacket to expose the Colt .45 tucked into his shoulder holster.

"So what's your point Dugan?" Frankie pushed.

"I appreciate your position Mr. Costello, but do any of you believe the guys in Washington would do any less?"

Costello took his unlit cigar from his mouth. The room fell silent again as Costello eyed his guest. Dugan knew it was the moment of truth.

"You're a pretty smart guy, ain't cha?"

"I read Mr. Costello. I read and I follow the news, current events and various politicians' careers. You can tell a lot about what people might do in the future by what they've done in the past and what they're saying in public now about what they're gonna do in future."

"Alright, Jimmy Dugan. Tell me about this 'revolutionary idea' that's gonna change the drug business."

"I never used the word 'revolutionary' Mr. Costello! But it has to do with aircraft."

Frankie offered Jimmy a cigar, which he had the political sense to take it even though he didn't smoke cigars.

Jimmy paused for a further response from Costello. All he got was a dead pan stare. Dugan readjusted his chair closer to the table before he spoke. Adonis interrupted.

"What about them small planes don't show up on radar?" Adonis threw out.

"Piper Cubs. Useless for our purposes. Max speed is eighty-five miles per hour with a ceiling of 12,000ft. The Feds'd out run them with a Plymouth!"

"What kind'a plane do you think would best suit what we're trying to accomplish?" Costello asked.

"Well, our biggest concern is getting through the new Coast Guard cordons. They're flying Pipers and Catalinas. Pipers are no challenge, but the Catalina has a max speed of 196 miles per hour."

"I ain't no pilot but that sounds kind'a slow for a plane." Frankie commented.

"Essentially it is but with a range of over 2,500 miles they can fly nearly across the country on one tank of fuel. Nothing short of a small bomber can out last them."

"So how do we get around them?"

"With a ceiling of only 15, 800 feet we get something that can out climb them."

"Okay so you're looking for something that can go faster and higher."

"And can carry the loads we require."

"What'a you recommending?"

"The De Havilland Mosquito. Up to 400 miles per hour topped out at altitude."

"How far can it go?"

"Depending on head winds a range of 1,355 miles but a ceiling of 37,000 feet. Nothing any of the feds have will be able to catch us."

"Except another Mosquito!" Adonis wryly quipped. Jimmy was prepared.

"Which is why we keep military markings on the plane and if challenged we tell we are ex-military enthusiasts."

"All this of course depends on the models out there that are still available."

"You came loaded or bear, didn't you Dugan?!" Costello half criticized half congratulated.

"Our big advantage Mr. Costello is that the CG aircraft are designed for search and rescue. Long distance performance and speed is not a consideration because when you're looking for a ship lost at sea speed's not an issue, as a matter of fact it's a disadvantage. You can't fly like a fighter jet and expect to see anything bobbing in thousands of square miles of ocean."

"Stands to reason. What else you got?"

"The reason I'm suggesting we spend the $10 to $20 thousand to buy a decommissioned Mosquito sir. In the Army, during the war, we often had to resupply troops in the field. Most times there was some kind'a landing strip, small airfield or we'd wait until the ground pounders captured one of the Gerry air fields. But when none of that was feasible and the troops needed beans and bullets in a hurry, we'd paradrop the stuff in."

"What the fuck is a parrot drop? Sounds like something in a bird cage." Costello laughed as did the others in the room. He set his cigar in the ashtray next to him.

"Parachute, Mr. Costello. If you know the weight of the freight you wanna drop and how fast you want it to hit the ground, there's a formula you can apply which will give you the recommended diameter of the canopy you need and your required aircraft speed for the drop. Plus it'll allow you to calculate, within a few yards, where the package will land. Cut the canopy to size, apply it to your package, put it in the aircraft and kick it out the door over the drop area. The ground crew retrieve it. And it's good night Irene! No more secret meetings, code words or worrying about losing two delivery teams if the score is compromised."

Jimmy jumped when the phone in the other room rang. Somebody answered it.

"Sounds complicated. All scientific like." Costello commented.

"Not really. It's pretty basic."

"And you can do all that stuff?"

"Given the tools, and materials, yes sir. I can."

"How many people you need?"

"None."

"NONE? What'a you a one man fuckin' army or what?"

"No Mr. Costello, it's not that involved. But what we do need is to have people on the ground that know what they're doing. Packers at the pick-up point and guys on the ground who can set up drop zone markers and be ready to get the hell out'a the area pronto."

"And where do you propose we find such guys?"

"Any unemployment line! There's plenty of ex-G.I.'s looking for work. We recruit them and I can teach them."

Frankie sat back, puffed on his Cabaña and appeared to seriously consider Jimmy Dugan's proposition.

"Properly managed sir, I could see possible drop zones all across the Eastern Seaboard. Maybe even the country."

"I doubt drug runnin' would ever get that big Dugan!" Adonic commented.

Jimmy shrugged and nodded,

"Theoretically how much product can you deliver at one time?" Adonis asked.

"The limits are down to the aircraft, sir. With a DC-3 we routinely dropped eight, eight and a half."

"Eight hundred pounds?!" Costello clarified.

"That's a lot'a product Boss!" Adonis exclaimed.

"Eight **thousand** pounds." Jimmy corrected. Adonis dropped the pencil he was playing with. No one spoke for a full minute.

"Dugan, how'd you like a raise?"

"Rita Hayworth got a nice ass Mr. Costello ?"

"We'll meet again in two weeks. I wanna know everything you can get me on the Feds interdiction ops specifically the air arm of the FBI, the FBN, if they have planes yet and the Coast Guard. Any questions Jimmy?"

"Just one Mr. Costello. Can I get a doggie bag?" He nodded over at the half eaten lobster plate.

"Get Mr. Dugan another lobster to go!" Costello ordered.

74 MacDougal Street
Greenwich Village
Benny Joules' Apartment

For the second time in as many days Doc arrived at Benny's apartment, only now with Louie in tow. The property had been downgraded and no longer designated a crime scene.

They watched as the landlord withdrew his pass key from the door and pushed it open. Doc turned to Mancino.

"Louie give the man a tenner."

"What?! Why me Doc? You're the one who wanted to come over here. Why should I give him a tenner?"

"You're right Louie. Give the man a twenty." Doc amended as he went in. Mancino, still in the dog house, got the message. The stubby little landlord brandished a broad smile and held out his hand.

Doc perused the layout. The front door led directly into the living room, straight ahead was the single bedroom and off to the right was a small galley kitchen. Save for the bedroom and toilet there were no doors, the apartment was open plan.

All of Benny's household possessions seemed to still be there. A collection of clothing was strewn about and on the coffee table in front of the couch were two very stale pieces of rye toast, a half cup of slime covered black coffee and an ashtray sat next to where his typewriter used to sit. Now in its case it had been dropped off back at Benny's place that morning by Nina at Doc's request.

"What'a ya think?" Mancino probed.

"Well it'd be helpful if we had more details."

"Ya want me to go call Nina?! I mean Miss Twissleman." Louie offered with far too much enthusiasm.

"No!" Doc shook his head.

Just then there was a knock at the door. It was Nikki accompanied by the blond German girl.

"I thought we talked about this?!" Doc chastised. Nikki smiled and shrugged.

"What?! All I did was bring her over here in case you had some questions." Nikki defended. "I mean you always say it's a good idea to have the witness at the scene, you know for questioning."

"Nice try!" McKeowen quipped.

"She may or may not make a good P.I. but she'd make a helluv'a lawyer!" Mancino whispered from behind Doc.

"Ya know Louie . . ." Doc dropped his head as he responded. ". . . it'd be a real shame if Abe Goldberg got a call not to show up at your arraignment hearing next week."

"Just sayin' Doc."

"And I'm just lettin' ya know you're still on thin ice mister."

Unseen, Louie gave a mock military salute behind Doc's back as Doc turned to the girls.

"Alright you two, let's get some prelim questions out'a the way. First some ground rules. Twissleman, any monkey business, any half-truths, facts that don't jive or any bullshitting and I hit the bricks! No second chances! We green?"

"Yes Mr. McKeowen, I understand. And thank you for taking my case."

"Uh huh." Doc grunted as he walked into the bedroom.

"He always this friendly?" Nina whispered to Nikki.

"Twissleman, get in here!" He yelled from the bedroom

"No. Sometimes he's really grumpy." Nikki whispered back.

"Okay, form the top." Doc prompted as the girls came in.

"Well, we first met-"

"No. From the night Mr. Joules died. Where were you?"

"Oh, uh . . . I was supposed to come over at around nine or ten but got hung up. I called him from a pay phone and he asked me to pick up some Chinese on the way in."

"What time was that?"

"Nine-fifteen, nine thirty."

"Why were you late?"

"I had a paper due the next morning and was late at the library. I had to return a book."

"Still in school at Columbia?"

"Yes! How'd you know?"

"Not important. Did the librarian stamp the return card on the book you brought back?"

"Yes, why?"

"Because now I can verify your story."

"Wait a minute! You think I-"

"What time'd you show up here?"

"Sometime after eleven. I brought the Chinese and we ate. He was trying to write when I showed up but was too distracted."

"He say why?"

"Like I told you at your office, he signed a movie deal with a Hollywood agent who sold the script to Warner Brothers who optioned it and less than two weeks later they reneged."

"I remember. You don't know if it was the agent or the studio?"

"No but it was the agent sent the telegram and since he stood to make a bundle on the deal I seriously doubt he had anything to do with cancelling it."

"Makes sense. So probably no skeletons in his closet. Anything that Benny might have been mixed up with? Anything could put a damper on a big financial deal that you know of?"

"Like I said, Benny was clean as a whistle. Didn't even have his first cigarette until he moved down here."

"Nothing you knew of that might bring bad P.R. down on the deal? Embarrass the agency or the studio?"

"Definitely not." She shook her head no.

"Any chance you know the name of the agent?"

"No but I'm sure he gave Benny a card or something. Also there were a couple of telegrams. At least two that I know of."

"Any idea where he kept them?"

"No but I spoke with his parents on the phone. There was nothing in the personal possession bag when the cops signed his stuff back over to them." She explained. "So it might be around here someplace." Nikki ventured.

"Naw! The cops would'a gone over this place pretty good. Standard procedure." Louie added.

"Maybe not. They seemed to be writing this off as simple suicide. Probably didn't even follow up on prints even if they bothered to dust for them." Doc pointed out as he closely perused the closet door and immediate area. "No traces of lycopodium dust. Nikki, Louie have a quick look around the place for black print dust. Don't disturb anything."

The two drifted out into the apartment and Doc turned to Nina.

"Did you spend the night?"

"He wanted me to but I couldn't I had to be in class at half eight in the morning. I had an exam."

"When did you discover that Benny was dead?"

"The next day. When he didn't show for our afternoon coffee I called and a policeman answered and asked who I was. As soon as he identified himself I knew Benny was in trouble, I came right over. That's when they told me."

"Did you at least bring the stolen police photos?" He challenged Twissleman.

Nina dug in her purse and presented Doc with the large manila envelope stamped NYPD in the corners.

He pulled the black & white glossies out and passed her back the envelope. "When you get home tonight burn that."

Doc instructed as he compared the photos orienting them to the room. The photos showed Benny died in the toilet adjacent to the bedroom.

"Who found him?"

"The landlord. He's the one called the cops. He came down to see Benny."

"Why'd he come down?"

"To tell Benny that the hot water was going to be out for the next few hours."

"Okay, Louie!" Doc called and Mancino appeared. "Go talk to Mr.-"

"Lesko. Sergei Lesko, he's Russian. He's up on the first floor, back apartment." Nina informed.

"Talk to Mr. Sergei Lesko see if you can find out anything of any significance." He glanced over at Nina. "Twissleman, go with him." He added.

"Why?"

"Two reasons. You might be able to add something to the conversation and because I said so."

Louie and Nina left.

Nikki who had been sitting quietly but paying attention, slid across the bed to Doc.

"Don't you think you're being a little rough on the girl?" Doc shot her a stern look. "I mean she did just lose her fiancé. To a suicide no less!" She half pleaded.

Doc readjusted his position and faced Nikki.

"Okay Nancy Drew. First rule of detective work; trust no one ever! Rule number two; EVERYONE is a suspect. Rule number three: Trust the facts, not your 'gut feeling' about the facts."

"Like what?"

"Anything strike you strange about this female?"

"How'd ya mean? She seems honest enough. Straight forward."

"Facts: Stolen NYPD photos which are material evidence in a possible homicide case carrying a minimum sentence of three to five. Yet she plays them off like stealing them is nothing."

"Okay, I give you that. What else?"

"As a woman you don't find it the least bit strange she hasn't shed so much as one tear the whole time we've been talking to her? Not even a crack in her voice as she, once again, sees these gruesome photos and is reminded of her loss. Loss of the guy she was supposedly going to spend the rest of her life with? Set up house, have kids?"

As Nikki sat silent Doc realized it was decision time. Whether or not to allow Nikki to work in the office and more importantly if so how to keep her safe, that is off the street and out of the investigation portion of the business. How and whether or not he would include Nikki would either help or adulterate the most important thing now in his life – their relationship. Just then Mancino and Twissleman came back.

"Well?" Doc asked.

"Niente, nada, bupkis Doc!" Mancino blurted out as he and Nina came through the door. "What's next?"

"Nina, give Nikki a number where we can reach you and we'll call you in a couple of days."

"But-"

"And get back to the library and get a hold of that index card from the back of that book you say you checked out."

"Yes sir!" Twisselman quietly snapped as she showed herself out.

"And don't steal the card!" He called after her. "Just check the book out like normal!"

"A thousand P.I.'s in New York City and I gotta get one with bad sense of humor!" Nina mumbled to herself.

CHAPTER X

Editing Room #3
Warner Studios

With not enough room to swing a cat, Editing Room 3 on lot D at the Warner studios was not much larger than your standard middle-class household toilet. Two people could sit side-by-side at the Steenbeck editing suite mounted along the back wall, but one of them would have to get up if the door had to be opened.

The editor and director now staring into the twelve inch square monitor, running and rerunning the disputed scene, had a diminutive, bespecled and noticeably fidgety representative from the Hays Office squeezed in between and standing behind them.

The Hays Office was the moral guardian of Hollywood. If they weren't happy with what you wanted to put up on the big screen you reshot, re-edited or rethought what you intended to release to the theaters. Of course it wasn't codified by state or federal law, you really didn't need the Hays Office stamp of approval at all. Unless you wanted distribution.

"Run it one more time." The director nudged.

They watched the action for the fourth time.

It was a bedroom scene were a young, curvy actress oozed out of a cheap hotel bathroom loosely draped in a silk, Japanese robe.

The handsome young man sitting on the single bed lit the pair of cigarettes dangling from his mouth, turned to make eye contact with her and smiled as she sat on the bed next to him.

"There! That's it!" The Hays rep declared. The director slapped his own forehead and looked up at the censor, a guy named Harold.

"C'mon Harold, ya got'a give me something here!" The director pleaded. "This ain't a Disney production! The story stinks, the acting is middle of the road and it's gonna be played against two A list productions! How are we supposed to sell this picture without any sexual allure?!"

"Look Marty, I got strict orders from Mr. Breen himself!"

The director dropped his head onto the table next to the Steenbeck and sighed. He spoke without lifting his head.

"Harold, can I talk to you for a minute?" The director sat up and looked over at the editor. "Alone." The editor glanced back at the director. "Doug here was just about to go out for a smoke, weren't you Doug?"

"But Mr. Kims, I don't-"

"Good man Doug! I'll be extra careful to mention to Jack how good an editor you are and the extra effort you put in on this project."

"Okay." Doug shrugged and vacated the room.

As soon as the door closed over the director addressed the rep.

"Okay, look. I seen you eyeing that little blond over in Make-up."

"The short one? With the blue eye?" Harold reaffirmed.

"Her name's Janeanne. Nice girl, from the mid-west. She's got a year of college, Poetry and Philosophy major which means she's a sure thing! You cut me some slack on this and I'll see she accepts your invite for dinner and a movie! Say, Friday night?" The Hays rep assumed an irritated expression.

"Kims, if you're bullshitting me your next three pictures will rot in a vault somewhere for the next ten years before they get an MPPA stamp!"

"Hand to God Harold! Friday, dinner."

"The best I can do for ya is I'll let you show them sitting on the bed together but the full shot of the broad in the kimono coming out of the bathroom has to go!"

"Okay, okay, I'll lose the broad in the kimono seg. But you're killing me here Harold! Killing me!"

"And at least one foot on the floor at all times for both of them when they're on the bed! Ya got it?" Harold iterated.

The director stood up, slid his chair away and allowed the rep from Joe Breen's office to leave.

After Harold exited and the editor returned he looked over at the director who smirked broadly.

"You got him to okay the bed sitting bit?!"

"Yup!"

Doug the editor pulled back, stared and smirked.

"You put that kimono bit in there just to get them on the bed together, didn't you?" The kid challenged. "You knew he'd never give you them on the bed together otherwise."

"There's a reason they call me The Weaver kid!"

The editor rendered a mock bow and whispered.

"Teach me all that you know oh great god of the industry!"

Originally formed as a sub-committee of the Judiciary, what eventually morphed into HUAC, the House un-American Activities Committee, was founded in 1918 at the end of WWI to look into Bolshevik/German political activities in the United States.

Twenty years later it had become a standing committee with permanent funding which had gone through nearly half a dozen iterations but by 1947 HUAC, now essentially a parasitic body, was scrambling and scrounging around for hosts to leech off.

Over time annual funding given to politicians with questionable motivations allowed the Committee to serve as a convenient stepping stone to any politician ambitious enough to employ what Doc McKeowen commonly referred to as 'The Magic Formula'.

J. Parnell Thomas a staunch New Jersey Republican, and John E. Rankin a life-long Mississippi Democrat, upon discovering that they could both benefit from a sacrificial lamb to offer to the gods of political righteousness, temporarily brushed political ideologies aside and decided to cooperate.

Their recipe for collusion simmered while moving through the self-serve line of the Rotunda commissary perusing the plates of green and orange Jell-O salad neatly aligned under the glass sneeze guard.

"First we need credible evidence, you know, to insure we don't wind up like we did back in '40." Thomas prompted Rankin "We have to be more cautious this time."

"What's your point?" Rankin asked.

"Now that HUAC is a permanent committee and there's funding, I had my secretary book me a suite for three days at the Biltmore out in L.A."

"Why L.A. and why the Biltmore?"

"Why not the Biltmore?" Thomas defended.

"I can just see the headlines in *The Times*: *Congressman on L.A. Holiday as Americans Fight Recession*!"

"I fly out on Thursday, back in on Monday. I got a plan!" Thomas countered.

"I should damn well hope you do!" Rankin countered. "You got people to interview lined up?"

"One or two."

They paid then made their way to a corner table.

"Must be some pretty big hitters if you're flying all the way across the country just to interview one or two people."

Thomas glanced over his shoulder then leaned in to Rankin.

"Jack Warner." He whispered. Rankin nearly dropped his forkful of tuna casserole.

"You're going after Jack Warner?! You crazy? He's pals with Truman! He's had dinner at the White House fer Christ sakes!"

"No need to go after him. He came to me!"

This time Rankin not only dropped his fork, but sat back and stared off into the distance.

"This could be big J. P. Really big!" Rankin uttered.

"Pearl Harbor big!" J. P. added

J. Parnell Thomas a hard-charging ambitious go-getter from arguably the most corrupt town in New Jersey, Jersey City, knew a prime political opportunity when he saw one. When the Dies Committee operation under the auspices of HUAC was given the green light by the Congress back in 1938 to chase suspected commies Thomas, whose real name was John Patrick Feeney Jr,, was fanatical about advancing his career.

A Mississippi democrat and racist to the core John Rankin made no bones about his political beliefs. One of the strongest supporters of the KKK, stating once that the Klan must not be made illegal because ". . . it was an old American institution", Rankin was as fanatical about protecting his version of the U.S. constitution as Thomas was about career aspirations.

Sparked by Wilkinson's timely article in *The Hollywood Reporter* and Jack Warner's ever increasing headaches with actors' and writers' union growing like weeds in the foundations of the studio system, J. Parnell smelled his sacrificial lambs.

While the avant-gardists such as Eisenstein and Pudovkin saw film as a means to inform the populace and individuals such as Walt Disney and Jack Warner saw the potential financial value in film, politicians like Thomas and Rankin were quick to realize the propaganda value of attacking the medium.

The propaganda coup they scored would, in quick order, lead to the investigation of millions of government workers, interrogation of thousands, nine days of hearings resulting in thousands of people losing their jobs and hundreds of honest, innocent artisans being blacklisted for life.

Medical Examiner's Lab
St. Vincent's Hospital
Greenwich Village

Watching from the side as the Coroner's assistant pulled the long body draw out and peeled back the sheet Doc and Louie got a look at what used to be Benny Joules.

His stunning youth, prominent even through the cyanotic pale blue of his flesh, took Louie off guard. The Coroner's Assistant seemed a little edgy as well.

"Make it snappy Doc, Donnie's up in the cafeteria on break. He'll have my balls if he knows you're here. I can't be caught down here with you so I'll be back in ten." The assistant said over his shoulder as he left. Put him away when you're done."

"Thanks." Doc nodded and started to peruse the corpse. "Was this kid left handed or right handed?"

"Beats me." Louie shot back as Doc moved to his hands and examined the palms and finger pads.

"Right handed. Signet ring tan line on his left ring finger and wrist watch tan line on his left."

"Okay, why?"

"Look at the right side of his neck what'a ya see?" Doc quizzed.

"Couple'a little scratch marks." Louie shrugged.

"If you were gonna strangle somebody and they weren't asleep, how would you attack them?"

"This another Italian thing?"

"Which way?"

"Same way you're supposed ta, from behind." Louie blurted.

"Exactly. Look here." He tilted Benny's head further to afford Louie a better look.

"A couple'a long, little scratch marks. So?"

"Which side they on?"

"The right."

"If this kid punched his own ticket why would he struggle to get the rope off?"

"How do you know he struggled?"

Doc grabbed a piece of rubber tourniquet from the exam table next them.

"Turn around." Louie complied and Doc stood behind him and wrapped the foot long tube around Mancino's neck. "Okay, I'm chocking you. What's your first impulse?"

"To turn my head and make sure it ain't Doris tryin' to kill me for something I probably didn't do!"

"Be serious asshole!"

"Okay I reach up and try to grab whatever it is around my neck. I try and get my fingers under it to stop it chocking me."

"Exactly." Doc affirmed.

"Maybe he realized what a dope he was being trying to off himself and tried bailing out at the last minute?" Louie countered. "He found out the rope was too tight and by then it was too late."

"Even if you had second thoughts about icing yourself at the last minute you'd use both hands. In addition you'd be kickin' like hell."

"Then there should be more scratch marks and probably at least one damaged nail." Louie caught up.

Doc held Benny's hand up to show Louie. "No damage."

"You thinkin' this kid was waxed on purpose?" Louie nodded.

"I think that's a safe bet."

The C.A. slipped back into the room and Doc indicated they were finished.

"Coroner made a call yet on probable cause?" Doc asked.

The C.A. crossed over to a file cabinet, pulled a manila jacket from the second drawer and perused the sheaf inside.

"Says here Asphyxiation through Strangulation: self-induced'."

"What's it say down the bottom, Line 18? Under 'Manner'?"

"Ah . . . just 'Suicide'" The C.A. closed up the body drawer, pulled off his lab coat and threw it on top of the filing cabinet then hurried towards the door.

"Ah just one more thing, sorry to keep you Jimmy." Doc pushed. "When was he admitted?"

"C'mon Doc! I got tickets to the Pennant game fer Christ's sake! Traffic out to the Bronx is gonna be murder!"

"Take ya one minute!" Doc coaxed him with a twenty dollar bill he pulled from his pocket. The C.A. snatched the note from Doc's hand and scurried back over to the filing cabinet and pulled the file.

"Says here 21:37."

"He was D.O.A., yes?"

"Yeah."

"So arrival time upstairs maybe fifteen twenty minutes earlier, I mean before they route him down here?"

"Yeah, maybe. I mean, I wasn't on that night but if it was a crazy night up in the E.R. he might'a gotten pushed aside for a little while. Doc I gotta go! My girl will have my nuts if we miss the first pitch! She's a baseball fanatic!"

"Okay, let's go Louie. Jimmy, thanks for ya help."

Upstairs Doc pushed further. "What'a you make of it?"

"We're in your league now Doc. You tell me." Louie answered.

"What did you take away from that?"

"Well, I don't know much about anorectics, but I definitely know that I would not want to be in Jimmy's shoes!"

"It's forensics. Why, too gory?"

"No! Trouble holding onto to his balls!"

It was well after lunch time when the guys came out of the hospital and Mancino's seemingly bottomless pit of a stomach was talking to him so they decided to find a place and eat.

Stopping at a corner newsstand Doc threw a nickel on the counter and grabbed a copy of *The New York Post* from the kiosk in the building's lobby on the way out.

The Italians had their pick of restaurants, the Jews usually brought their meals to work with them,

Paddy Kelly

but the Irish and the British locales were blessed with The Chinaman.

The Chinaman, no one could pronounce his name, along with his wife and sixteen kids owned and ran Chanze Chinese Chippy, which served the most authentic fish and chips in Ireland's western most county, New York City, located out on the East docklands.

Doc and Louie hopped out of a cab just before the lunch rush hour hit.

Louie laughed out loud as they came up to the restaurant.

"What?" Doc asked. Mancino nodded at Doc, shook his head and smiled as he glanced at the six stove pipes Chan had installed at different points on the roof and exterior walls.

The pipes served no structural purpose, but instead vented the smell of the fried fish dishes in various directions, and could be opened or shut individually so as to allow the aromas to waft in any given direction. The strategy of course, to this venting conspiracy, was to entice patrons who might otherwise waste their time eating more healthy lunches and suppers, or whatever their after-pub meal might be called.

They entered the eatery and took one of the red enamelled booths in the back. As always Doc sat facing the door.

An attractive Chinese girl with long, silky black hair and green eyes, one of Chan's sixteen offspring, approached the booth the minute they sat down. She looked to be in her late teens.

"You want I should bring youse menus, fellas?" She was born and raised in New York, and so spoke perfect English.

"Moo goo gai pan, steamed rice." Doc ordered.

"Same." As she began to walk away Louie called over. "And two, make it four egg rolls." Louie added.

"So, did'ja finally agree to take Doris to that new play?" Doc knowingly asked.

"Get serious!"

"Why not?"

"Who the hell wants to go see a play about a street car named after some broad named Desire?! Stupid name! Besides, we ain't even got no street cars no more!"

"They still got streetcars out in Frisco! Besides, it's by Tennessee Williams."

"So who's he when he's home? What's his dad's name? Nashville?" Louie laughed at his own joke.

"He's a rising playwright ya dunce!"

"Oh, rising huh? What's his name after he stood up? Shakespeare?!" He chuckled harder.

"You're a freakin' idiot, ya know that?" Doc admonished as he turned to the *Local News* section of his paper. Louie reached into his back pocket and pulled out the latest copy of *Amazing Stories* science fiction magazine.

"Hey Doc, what the hell's a com-puter anyways?"

"It's a person that computes large sets of numbers to find a solution. The military uses them to calculate trajectories for naval gunfire and artillery."

"I thought computers was to add things up?"

"That's an adding machine Einstein."

"Says here that one day they'll be able to build a machine that will add over a thousand numbers a minute!"

"No doubt they will because unlike you, machines have expanding capabilities. Soon enough they'll probably have a machine to replace most any job."

"You mean like, cops fer instance?"

"I suppose."

"Cops like Sullivan?"

"Wouldn't be surprised." Doc answered as he continued to peruse the political page of the paper.

"Really?!" Louie pushed. "They're working on a machine that fucks up cases, arrests the wrong guy and blames it on somebody else?!" Louie ventured.

"Nah. I reckon we'll always have cops like Sullivan for that."

The food arrived, they ate and as Mancino was flirting with the chocolate layer cake under the glass cover on the dessert counter Doc's mind was lost on Benny's case.

McKeowen was about to speak when Louie peered over at the article Doc had been reading.

"Whose these Thomas and Rankin guys you're reading about?"

"Just two more crooked politicians living off the American taxpayer. Rankin's a southern redneck and Thomas is a patsy for the New Jersey branch of the Mob. According to this editorial their paths have apparently colluded . . . I man collided, at the same time when the two of them were both sniffing around for their next prey."

"Doc, how's come you're always up on all this political shit? Nobody cares about that kind'a crap now that the war's over."

"And that's exactly why everybody's surprised when bad shit wars happens! You remember a guy named Chamberlain?"

"You mean the English guy Winston Chamberlin?" Doc hung his head. "Ya see Doc? I ain't so dumb, as I look!" Louie bragged.

"That's Churchill ya dope!"

"Then no, I guess I don't remember him."

"Back in '38 Chamberlin came back from the Munich Agreement and declared that there 'would be peace in our time'. What he neglected to mention was it would be a piece of Austria, a piece of Belgium, a piece of the Netherlands, a piece of France and then the rest of the world."

"You sayin' 100 million people died because nobody follows politics?!"

"That and bad politics mixed with poor leadership. Assholes like these two putting politics before leadership." He indicated the *Post* article. You know what I mean?"

"No but I got a bad feelin' you're gonna tell me."

"You're right Louie! You aren't as dumb as you look. I'm talkin' about the Magic Formula."

"I'm listening. Kind'a." Louie grumbled through a bite of egg roll.

"If you want to be painted as the 'good guy' and climb the next rung up the ladder but have nothing to offer all you need is a law degree and someone to paint as the bad guy. Then just crank up the rumour mill, posture yourself as the hero and when you think you have enough support, attack and let the press do the rest. Little or no evidence required. Just ask Bruno Hauptman or 'Big Bill' Haywood. The possibilities are endless."

"Whose those guys?"

"Not important. All that matters is The Formula is neat, clean and efficient. In the right hands. "

"Pretty slick trick."

"Yeah except for the innocent people it gets sprung on! Perjury is a prosecutor's handiest weapon, no real proof needed. It's all done with words, yours against his."

"And his word always wins!" Mancino reinforced.

"Exactly." Doc agreed.

"You figure somebody with connections in the Congress was after this kid?" Louie probed.

"Not likely. He probably just got in over his head with some scumbag drug dealer, owed some money he couldn't pay back and since mommy and daddy cut him off the drug pins sent a couple of gorillas after him."

"You figure they killed him for some drug money?'

"They've killed for a lot less! But more likely they just got carried away. Some of those goons enjoy their work a little too much." Doc refolded his newspaper.

The headlines read:

'HOUSE TO PROB H'WOOD STUDIOS'

"Jesus." McKeowen quietly declared.

"What is it?"

"Looks like the D.C. crowd are setting their sights on the movie execs." He nodded at the paper.

"Good luck with that witch hunt!" Mancino guffawed.

"What makes you say that?"

"Hollywood's all owned and run by Jews. Jews have lawyers."

"Most of the congress is lawyers." Doc countered.

"Yeah but not Jewish lawyers! As far as I know there ain't no Jews in congress. is there?"

"I think maybe one but your point is taken."

"No matter how you look at it, that fight is gonna get ugly. And no matter who wins, it's gonna be messy." Louie added.

Doc once again glanced over the front page article.

"Someday this post war hysteria's gonna be over Louie. And when it is, a lot'a people are gonna be askin' a lot'a serious questions!"

"Like what fer instance?"

"Like why aren't things what they're supposed to be in the halls of power? Like how'd we all of a sudden jump into a not-so-gradual, practically overnight conversion from you needed some kind of proof to accuse another politician of wrong doing to where you can just say shit to the Press and it somehow becomes truth? AA place where your opposition is guilty by accusation? Some of these politicians better get it together or they're gonna wake up one day and find out the people have had enough."

"You mean like in the Dead End Kids when Bugsy says, 'Wake up Satch! School's out!'"

"Yeah, sumthin' like that." Doc chuckled. "At least we'll never see what other countries have seen, Italy, Germany the Balkan states."

"What's that Doc?"

"An attempt at a coup."

They stood to leave.

"One thing's for sure though we need to see that script the kid was working on." Doc pointed out.

"You think there's something in it, maybe the kid knew something?"

"Not sure but if there's something in there, it'll help us get to the facts. At the very least it'll help us understand what he was thinking at the time."

"And if not?"

"Then we cross off another piece of the puzzle. Bottom line we won't know till we look, will we?"

"That's what she said!" Louie snapped.

"Louie?"

"Yeah Doc?"

"Do you sit up at night thinkin' up bad jokes?"

"Oh hell no! They just pop into my head. I should go on the Jack Benny Show huh?" Mancino, bathing in pride, leaned back and smirked. "They just come to me, on their own. Pure artistic respiration!"

"Let's get back to work. Leave a tip will ya? Ya cheap bastard!"

CHAPTER XI

That summer of '47 J. Parnell Thomas held clandestine hearings in the Biltmore Hotel in L.A. with a view towards starting his sham circus back in D.C. during the October session. In typical political tradition these meetings were held in secret. Secret meetings that turned out, in what would become typical political tradition, to be not so secret as they were 'leaked' to The Press even as they were being conducted. Who exactly leaked them was the subject of much speculation but no one could rule out the possibility that Thomas himself was the source.

Part #1 of the Magic Formula: paint yourself as the good guy. Part #two – crank up the rumor mill via the ever compliant Press.

Politicians had long ago learned the effective techniques of accusations without evidence then leaking those accusations to a scandal hungry press so as to allow the public to make the condemnation. This was a handy way to achieve your goal to satisfy Part #1 of Doc McKeowen's Magic Formula.

It worked. As word leaked out chills ran up the spine of Hollywood.

JPT had learned his lessons well following his humiliating defeat back in 1940 after being trounced by Al Smith and the movie producers he accused of disseminating communistic propaganda when he attacked the Hollywood producers with a list of over 100 films Noir productions none of which, it eventually came to light, he had actually seen.

"There will always be a threat to the American way of life," Thomas dramatically opined at the hearings. "And it is that ever present danger that the people of these United States have entrusted to us, the members of the House and Senate to guard them against." He preached.

By mid-1947 Thomas appeared to have learned his lesson about past failure to prosecute innocents. But not by much.

The U. S. Constitution specifically does not give The House prosecutorial powers. However led by a handful of zealots the H.U.A.C. representatives, with no challenges from the courts, were allowed to work from an imagined, largely fabricated mandate.

Given the humiliating defeat of the congressional attacks on film makers in 1940-41 during the Dies Committee hearings on the industry, now six years later, The House was out to win big against the Hollywood swells. To make an example of the movie moguls, some would argue, and show them who was really running the show.

Now regrouped and divested of the FDR socialism that plagued them with the shackles of free speech, life-long career politicians such as Thomas and Rankin leaped at their chance to slither to the front pages of America's newspapers.

Although they had no judicial powers and so were not a court of law it was to the credit of their ambitions that they didn't let such minor details stop them.

Unfortunately the American people had always been led to believe that because they had been, under the Constitution of the United States given freedom of speech, they were protected against being compelled to disclose their religion or political views to a hostile government appointed board of inquiry.

The people of the United States were about to be given a harsh lesson in the reality of domestic civics.

✝

Warner Brothers Studios
Jack Warner's Office

Sitting at his desk Jack Warner stared for a long time at the headlines on the front page of the latest issue of Wilkerson's *Hollywood Reporter* spread out in front of him.

'Film Dividends Dip to New Low'

It had been several weeks since the Hollywood Hills party at Hal Holstein's place when Warner got word of the writer's successful efforts to organize.

The decision finally made he reached for the oak framed intercom box.

"Agnes?"

Yes Mr. Warner?

"Track down the number to the main Congressional switchboard, find a number for a Congressman J. Parnell Thomas and get me in touch with him."

Yes Mr. Warner.

With the information gleaned from his Pinkerton agent who had the meeting in Coronado with the union socialist leader Harry Bridges and after reading a copy of William Wilkinson's *Hollywood Reporter* article, Warner put the wheels in motion to counter act the biggest current threat to his studio - the formation of the Screen Writers Guild.

When Jack Warner, through his Hollywood pipeline, found out that J. Parnell Thomas was heading out to La La Land he wasted no time to arrange a meet.

There's an old American saying, he who dies with the most toys wins. Jack Warner, senior stockholder at Warner Bothers studio probably more than any of his seven siblings, embraced this philosophy.

His Polish-Jewish family, eking out a living on a cobbler's wage, emigrated from Poland by way of Hamburg, Baltimore, Canada back to Baltimore and finally to Youngstown, Ohio to become permanent Americans in the early 20th Century.

With initial forays into Vaudeville combined with encouragement from his brother Sam his future in show business was assured leading him and his brothers permanently into the burgeoning film industry in1910.

That afternoon, having begged off a previous appointment so that he could meet with Senator Thomas, Warner sent his limo out to the Biltmore Hotel in downtown L.A. to bring Thomas out to his studio office.

Never failing to impress anyone, stars, directors, producers and politicians alike, the Warner Studios always served as an impactful incentive to inspire a sense of achievement and importance. A towering symbol of Warner's unbridled success, a lesson Jack Warner learned well in the early days of the fledgling studio enterprise. It was precisely for this reason that, using business as an excuse, he insisted on meeting Thomas at the Brother's head office.

After a short guided tour, conducted by Warner himself it was late that afternoon that the two high-powered execs rode in Warner's limo out to his Hollywood Hills home.

"Amelia will love this." Thomas thanked as he indicated the rolled up lobby poster of *Anna and the King of Siam* on the seat between them. "She's a big fan of Rex Harrison."

"Leave it with me if you like and I'll get Rex and Irene to sign it and have it sent out to you."

"That would be swell Mr. Warner!"

"Please senator! I voted Republican. It's Jack!"

"In that case call me J. Parnell!"

After struggling up through the jungle of the early studio system, fighting to introduce sound pictures on a large scale, constantly bargaining with established talent for cheaper contracts all while dealing with the deaths of his closest brother Sam and one of his salesmen being beaten to death by Nazi thugs, it was by 1947 that Jack Warner was not only adept at high stakes negotiations but hardened to the point where no one or anything was going to interfere with his latest goals or him enjoying the opulent life he had established for himself. Least of all a gang of talentless writers most of whom he could replace at the drop of a hat.

Of course now that those low level writers had government sanction to unionize, the gloves, he reckoned, would have to come off.

"You saw the article in *The Hollywood Reporter*?" Jack casually asked.

"No why?" Not wanting his image to be associated with *The Hollywood Reporter*, widely regarded as a gossip rag, Thomas instinctively lied about having already seen the article.

"Some interesting takes on the industry by a guy named Wilkinson. You might be interested. Show them to you later out at the house."

"Okay." Thomas nodded avoiding further comment.

Warner wanted to hold off on the main topic of conversation and so padded the remainder of the car ride out to The Hills with small talk.

"Did you read where Hoover balks at the theory that there's organized crime in America?" Warner threw out.

"That's because Hoover's probably on the take!" Thomas quickly shot back.

"You crazy?! Mr. Squeaky Clean on the take?" Warner feigned shock.

"Please! You ever notice how he's a little too adamant about denying there's no such thing as organized crime in this country?"

"Only natural!" Jack, who knew firsthand about The Mob's extortion racket against the industry's Hollywood electrician's union IATSE, as well as the inside scoop on Hoover's suspicious winning streaks at the race track just shrugged.

"Yeah? Then how come he has such a reputation for always winning at the track?" Thomas added.

"Lots'a folks play the ponies and lots'a folks know how to pick them!" Warner chided.

"At the same New York track? Always betting to win, almost never to place or show?" Thomas countered.

"Well, I actually never met the man."

"I'll tell you this, there is at least one thing that America's top cop is adamant about and that's all I'm interested in, Commie hunting." Thomas spewed.

Warner realized he was about to make the right play.

Twenty minutes after leaving the studios they were coming up Mulholland Drive and arrived at the house.

After dinner and light cocktails they retired to the balcony where Jack decided it was time to pounce.

"You know Senator Thomas-"

"J. Parnell. Please!"

"J. Parnell, now that the war's over and America is adjusting, the film industry landscape is changing with it."

"Especially with people buying those telee-vison boxes!"

"BAH! Idiot boxes more like!" Jack scoffed. "Black and white pictures, lousy reception and audio that sounds like there's a midget trapped in a crate! Take my word for it Senator, T.V.'s a fad that'll die out in a couple of years!"

Thomas cautiously refrained from mentioning that at that exact moment members of congress were actually negotiating with T.V. producers to broadcast their next set of congressional hearings live from the Capitol Building, an event that would give 'the idiot box' the first major spike of its career.

Additionally, although the next hearings had been announced in the press, he was particularly careful not to broach the subject that he was to be the chairman of the sub-committee at the upcoming HUAC hearings.

"I may have something for you." Warner relayed.

"Oh?"

Warner reached into his breast pocket and passed him an envelope.

"Do I want to see this?"

"I think you do." Warner coaxed.

Thomas opened it and removed the single typewritten sheet inside and took his time reading it.

"Who wrote this?"

"Eric Johnston, head of the MPAA."

It was a draft of a declaration to be agreed upon by members of the Motion Picture Association of

America disavowing any communist connections in Hollywood.

"What do you intend on doing with it?"

"I . . . we have a duty to protect the industry."

"That all? To protect the industry?" Thomas, a suspicious man by nature, smirked.

Warner knew his cards were on the table and decided to come clean.

"That and I have something of a situation with my writers." He confessed.

"Yes, they're wanting to unionize along the lines of something like the Actors Guild which means you'll have yet another union to contend with which means if the writers are successful and they lock arms with the Actors and electricians . . . you're fucked seven ways from Sunday."

"You're very well informed." Warner commended.

"Our job in the Congress is to keep an eye things." Thomas leisurely reached over and selected a cigar from the humidor on the table between them. "Most things. Everything actually." Thomas clarified.

"I can't afford to let this writer's thing get out of control like it did with the lighting union guys and Al Capone." Warner argued. "With a $600,000 weekly payroll and a $20 million annual gross last year alone I'm not about to let a mob of disgruntled 'so-called artists' muck things up!" Warner continued. "Hell, only reason they came out here was because the garbage cans froze over in Winter time and they couldn't find anything to eat, so they came out here and became writers!"

"You know. . ." Thomas removed the small ringed cigar label and examined it. ". . . I'm organizing hearings for some time during the Fall session." Thomas casually informed.

"I heard rumors."

"If it comes down to it . . . will you, or any of your guys in the MPAA come out and testify?"

Jack sat back in his chair and hesitated.

"Well, I can't speak for all . . ."

"I could subpoena you ya know." The senator clumsily nudged as he snipped the end from the cigar.

"That would look just dandy! You force me under threat of contempt to go to D.C and say what you want to hear. I refuse, my brigade of lawyers gets involved and this thing drags out for what? Weeks? A month? A year? Meanwhile Congress is hamstrung while you're tied up doing nothing for your constituency? No laws passed, no post-war infrastructure improvements. That'd go over real well in the papers. Not to mention the P.R. disaster for your party Senator." Jack sat back and carefully assessed Thomas' reaction. "What are you gonna do? Muzzle The Press?"

"It is our sworn duty as public officials to carefully monitor what information is being put out to the public regardless of the source."

Parnell, who was vehemently against FDR's politics and especially Roosevelt's New Deal 'communistic' ways, had every intention of playing the anti-commie angle for all it was worth.

"I'm gravely concerned that this communist thing seems to be creeping up on us." Thomas added before checking his emotions. "And, if I may discreetly enquire, what exactly is the price for this so called 'useful' information you might or might not produce?"

Warner was perfectly capable of recognizing a good rouse when he saw one.

"Look here Senator, let's put our guns on the table. We're both good solid Americans, men of integrity and have the best interest of the American public in mind. But that doesn't preclude us from pursuing our own goals like providing for our families and their future, whatever form that takes, now does it? I mean life, liberty and the pursuit of happiness, right?"

Warner had found Thomas' wavelength and took his cue as the senator leaned forward in his over-sized, Queen Anne chair.

"You steer your senate committee in another direction and away from pushing for regulation of the film industry and I'll see what I can do to sniffing out some people your committee might be interested in taking a look at."

"Mr. Warner, all the way back to Overman after the First War and up through the Fish committee and the Dies Committee we in the senate have sought to fulfill our function as a guardian of the people. However, if you ask me I blame the communist insurgency on a gradual loss of humanity spawned by an over exposure to violence in the press and the cinema."

"That's exactly why we have a $30 thousand dollar fine on any studio that dares to broadcast, display or distribute a film without the MPAA seal!" Warner now sought common ground.

"You understand we are anxious to head off the creeping coagulation of the economics of the American caste system aggravated by an over exposure to violence as well Senator Thomas?"

"Trust me Jack . . ." Thomas took his time teasing the cigar tip with the flame of his lighter. "What I got planned is gonna make the Lindbergh thing look like a sideshow!"

"Oh yeah?" Jack probed.

"Besides . . ." Thomas confidently added as he took the first puff of his cigar. "We ain't concerned with The Press anymore!"

Adjusting the cigar between his teeth, the Senator reached over, lifted the humidor and offered Warner one of his own cigars.

"I'll give it some consideration." Jack took one, snipped the end and allowed Thomas to light it.

Reading between the lines what Warner meant was, *I'll have to see which way the wind blows.*

They wrapped up the evening around ten that night as Warner called out for his personal assistant then saw Thomas to the door.

"Judy, have my car brought around. Tell my driver to take the senator back into town, to his hotel."

"Yes Mr. Warner." She left to fetch the driver.

238

"Parnell there is something I need your absolute word on."

"Anything Jack! What is it?"

"I'm worried that the WASPs in Congress will conflate Commies with the Jews."

"I wouldn't be concerned. I don't see that happening." Thomas assured. Not sensing much sincerity the Jew in Warner was less than comforted and so pushed the issue.

"What about John Rankin? He's well known for the proclivities of his racial attitudes."

"I'll handle Rankin. Trust me."

They shook and parted. But Warner didn't trust him.

No sooner had the limo pulled out of the driveway and Warner again summoned his P.A.

"Judy get me Billy Frank on the phone, he's a producer over at 20th Century. Tell him it's important."

"Yes sir."

Not trusting Thomas and his HUAC committee in Congress alone to accomplish what he wanted to happen, needed to happen, Warner decided the MPAA's Waldorf Agreement might be a good idea after all.

"Frank? Warner here. Can you get me the final details of this MPAA thing you mentioned to me at Hal Halstein's party in the Hills a couple of months back? No. all I have is a rough first draft. Good! Send it over in the morning by bike messenger will ya? Thanks Billy."

Jack, who already had a list of names drawn up he was willing to betray, was careful not to let on that he knew about Hoover's spy in Hollywood - Ronald Reagan.

✝

"Meet me under the CTA, at the *Kingfisher*. Wabash and East Cermak." Steadman spoke tersely but with respect. In return Brasi just grunted into the phone.

An hour later Jake Steadman was sitting at a back booth off to the side of the worn, purple curtain guarded by a pair of Jack LaLanne wanna-be bouncers which led to the back room.

Steadman sat until he began to get irritated when he was noticed fidgeting by the one of the barmen, who flagged a waitress, pointed at Steadman and nodded. The waitress nodded back and crossed the floor.

"Scuse me, you Steadman?"

"Who wants to know?"

"Some mug left this for ya." She handed Steadman a note scribbled across a bar napkin.

DOWN THE STREET AT BOB'S

Steadman cursed, threw a fiver on the table and left.

It had been over a decade since *Bayou Bob's Workingman's Tavern* on Wabash and East Cermak had been anything approaching a tavern.

Located just down the street in the predominantly black neighborhood it was a dive of a place, a strip joint-come-brothel posing as a late night restaurant just under the tracks on the south side of the street. Although at that time of night the menu was very limited.

Little Jimmy Carnelli, the six foot five, 275 pound Mafia manager leaning against the bar had no idea who Steadman was when he came through the front door but by virtue of the fact that he was the only one of three white guys in the crowded place, the bartender included, he knew he must be there to meet Brasi and so nodded towards the back where there was an improvised stage squeezed into the far corner.

Steadman made his way back past the bar and scanned the dimly lit back space.

Even before you met him Sollozo Brasi was exactly what you thought he might look like.

With the rough proportions of a fire hydrant his too-small head sunk down into his shoulders just enough to make you wonder if at some point during his childhood someone hadn't dropped an anvil on him.

Back during his school days his mother was compelled to sew extensions on his shirt collars and trim several inches from his trouser legs.

Facially speaking Brasi could be deceptive. Flawless skin and an olive complexion hid his only

241

scar; a three inch razor slice under his jaw. The razor's former owner was later found in the south river.

And in the alleyway outside Old St. Patrick's and in the East Side rail yards.

With the strength of a Sicilian bull, the temper of a young, pissed off Irishman and the I.Q. of a cumquat Sollozo Brasi naturally gravitated towards the one social niche that most suited him; hurting people.

Physically there was only one word to describe Sollozo Brasi; pugnacious. Mentally any number of unflattering adjectives could apply.

"Why do you come to these fuckin' places?!" Steadman challenged as he slid a bent back chair over to the small cabaret table, checked to see if the set was clean then sat.

"What's wrong with this place?!" Brasi defended.

"It's a shit hole! My toilets are cleaner, the booze is pissed down and the women are dogs!"

"There's some lookers!"

"Yeah, they make ya look alright. Look the other way! The place is fer Jigs!"

"Maybe I like Jigs!" Like a pit bull baring his teeth Brasi's slowly reddening face signaled for Steadman to back off. He did.

Sporadic, cursory applause follow the latest act off stage. A rough hole which had been hammered through the wall then covered by a blood red curtain served as a stage exit and entrance.

"How'd the Jew job go?" Steadman coaxed.

242

"You read the papers don't ja?"

Under the table Steadman passed Brasi an envelope which Brasi immediately cracked open the and quickly flipped through.

Although more or less always along the same lines of work during his short thirty-seven years, Sollozo had what most would describe as a checkered career and not much you'd put on a CV.

As an ex-fed sacked for screwing up several times he then tried his hand as a P.I. but on his third try at the state P.I. exam, gave up. Next he then fell into some part-time but well-paid work with The Mob. However, by virtue of his uncontrolled, Vesuviain temper, he really screwed that up when he broke the jaw of the son of a soon-to-be consigliore during a card game. Trading a hit job no one wanted to take on, Brasi was square with The Mob but was once again on the street and unemployed when he finally stumbled into casual construction work as a navvy on one of Steadman's crews.

That was a year or so back about the time Steadman was approached and struck a deal with a Chicago mob boss to use his main construction warehouse as a back-up drug drop point after Jimmy Dugan delivered his latest run.

Recently a wrinkle had developed; although Dugan's runs had become a primary source of product supply, other methods of supply had evolved at a quicker pace and from different source routes. Shipping was back up to and surpassing pre-war levels. The Canadian border patrol, although experimenting with a couple of helicopters without much success, was still patrolled largely on horseback by the RCMP and the U.S.-Mexican border was a virtual sieve where drug mules could be hired for pennies and paid in pesos.

This naturally increased pressure to find temporary storage space which turned the screws just a little tighter on guys like Steadman, just when he was looking for a way out.

"Was it clean?" Steadman asked.

"It's ruled a suicide. The cops'll get nowhere. And they're not gonna." Brasi hooted as a two hundred pound, scantily dressed Hispanic dancer took the stge. "But, his little Kike German girlfriend is sniffing around."

This took Steadman off guard but didn't put him off.

"So? We'll take care of her! I'll foot the bill."

"I ain't takin' the fall for no more dirty work."

"Little late to bow out now pal!"

"You threatening me?"

"Just stating a fact Big Man." Steadman shrugged.

As a tribute to his lack of good judgment Brasi momentarily considered diving across the table and attacking Jake. As a tribute to his yielding to reality he remembered that Little Jimmy had a sawed-off 12 gauge behind the bar and that the bar was a protected entity.

"I'll double the price."

"I ain't waitin' no month this time. I want half up front half on delivery of the body."

"What the hell am I gonna do with a body?!"

"How the fuck should I know?! Put it in one'a your warehouses like ya do with all that scag you stash!"

"A little louder asshole! I don't think the stripper heard ya!"

Steadman's mind immediately turned back to ways to get out of what he believed, what he was told was a limited contract whose fine print had no escape clause.

"Don't nobody here give a shit about no dead body."

"Put a sock in it, will ya!" Steadman snapped as he nervously looked around.

The connected gentlemen he signed with had a somewhat different interpretation of the phrase 'escape clause'.

"Now that's a body!" Brasi declared as he nodded up towards the 150 pound, forty-something bleached blond jiggling across the stage.

"You need fucking glasses!" Steadman cursed as he threw a tenner on the table or the beer he didn't get and left.

M&M Investigations
Friday Morning

"AAAGGGHHHH!!" Nikki's shrill scream blasted through and unnerved the entire office. Doc sprang from his desk and bolted through the door to find Shirley and Nikki smothering Mancino with hugs and kisses until they brought him to the floor.

"What the hell?" Doc demanded. "Nikki, you okay?"

She looked up from the fetal ball Louie had become as the two continued to maul him.

"Doris is pregnant!" She quietly squealed.

"We need to call and congratulate her!" Shirley threw out as she reached up for the phone on her desk.

"NO, NO, NO!" Mancino panicked and stayed her hand.

"Why not?" Nikki and Shirley climbed up off of Mancino.

"She finds out I spilled the beans and I'm toast!"

"Louie, how is it all of your metaphors are always food related?!" Doc challenged.

"They ain't!" He defended.

"Do you even know what a metaphor is?" Nikki playfully challenged as she climbed up off the floor and assisted Shirley.

"Yeah! Yeah as a matter of fact I do! It's for when ya measuring things! They use them in Europe. You know, like in the Olympics, the races and the Broad Jump and stuff. We got yards and they got metas! One hundred metas, two hundred metas! That's what they're for!"

"Louie your kid's gonna need one helluv'a lot of tutoring!" Doc commented as he headed back into his office.

"What's a metaphor?" Louie whispered over to Nikki. She took a moment to briefly explain.

Doc sat down behind his desk as an indignant Louie followed him in.

"Ten bucks says I can make a metaphor without using food!" He produced his wallet, fished out a tenner and slapped it on Doc's desk. Doc casually reciprocated.

"Okay, let's see you do it without a food reference."

"You kiddin'? Me doin' a metaphor is a piece of cake!"

"Chocolate layer or lemon cake?" Doc called after him neatly stuffing the twenty bucks in his wallet as Louie stomped out of the office.

"Like a walk in the park!" Mancino yelled back in from the outer office then smirked as he nodded over to Nikki.

"That's a simile." She quietly informed him.

"Okay, so we all got us a vocabulary lesson." Shirley broke in. "Now can I say it? Sounds like we need a party!" She half suggested half declared.

"Good idea! First we'll need to organize a shower!" Nikki added.

"We'll also need to-"

"Guys, we don't really need to schedule a party! I mean the time, expense. Besides -" Louie headed off.

"HOLD THE PHONE Cowboys and cowgirls!" From inside his office Doc slammed the brakes on the festivities. "They'll be no party planning on company time, no time off work for parties or any special considerations just because Mancino slipped one past the goalie!"

Nikki and Shirley instantly shifted into anger over drive.

"What are you talking about?!" Doc's girl moved to the office door. "And more importantly, why are you being such a Scrooge?!" She dove to the rescue.

"That's a simile! Right?" Mancino attempted.

"Let it go Louie!" Nikki tersely cut him off. "We're giving Doris a party with or without you!" She clarified to Doc.

Doc rose from his desk and with folded arms purposefully strode out to the main area.

"In that case, Miss Drama Queen, we'll have to schedule a proper party!" Doc declared looking over at Louie understood the reference.

Simultaneously they both yelled, "BAPTISM!"

"There's just one snag Louie."

"What's that Doc?"

"I'll have to clear it with the guys!" McKeowen threw out. "I mean we've never had a woman at a baptism before."

"What 'guys'? It's just you and Louie!" Nikki indignantly challenged.

"Well, maybe Harry will want to come up from the Front Page."

"And perhaps Redbone will want to drop by!" Mancino quickly added.

"Oh, okay." Nikki nodded as she methodically occupied herself with collecting her things. "In that case Doc, I just remembered, Kate's coming back from Upstate in a week, maybe it would be better if you slept at your place for the next week or so. You know just to let her get used to coming home and all."

"On second thought," Doc quickly added. "It's my office, my baptism and my whiskey. I don't think the guys will mind about a few girls."

"That's nice! I like those guys." Nikki smugly complimented setting her things back down on the desk.

It was around seven-thirty when a Sunshine cab pulled up on the corner of Christopher and Hudson outside Harry's *Front Page News*. Doris and Louie climbed out and made their way upstairs.

Doc and Nikki had stocked up with a bottle of Jameson's Irish, a bottle of red and bottle of white along with some light snacks. Doris bought two bottles of Cordon Negro and brought a tray of cannolis she baked that afternoon.

Louie tagged along behind her with an almost full case of Ballantine's beer. The two bottles missing went to the taxi driver after the hackie waved the cab fare and congratulated them on the baby.

'Baptisms' were occasional events which were staged at the office after hours, usually on a Friday. These events, held sometimes more occasionally than other times, initially served for Doc to clear his head and focus on a case, blow steam or just forget about life for a while.

When Mancino gradually shoehorned himself into Doc's life five years ago and Redbone, the building's resident caretaker, became a confident and part time look-out man for McKeowen also assimilated himself into the ritual over the last few years, he too took to showing up with a bottle. This was alright with Doc mainly because his Irish whiskey was safe. Redbone drank Southern Comfort.

It wasn't long before Harry, the one legged owner of the ground floor news stand which occupied 1929 ticked on that whenever he saw Doc coming through the front door after hours dutifully clutching a brown paper bag roughly twisted into the shape of a whiskey bottle, it was consultation time.

Unlike Nikki or Louie, Harry, a WWI vet who had seen action in the Ardennes, was a little older and acted as Doc's ersatz priest. Doc when stumbling onto some conundrum, would confess, Harry would faithfully listen, maybe ask a few short questions then give penance with which Doc could find absolution.

Redbone, a late seventy-something, Louisiana Cajun' would sit off to the side, sip his Southern Comfort from a coffee cup, nod and contribute by mumbling the occasional "Amen ta dat Brother!" or a "Got dat shit right!"

Redbone, the newest member to appear at the as-of-late, few and far between Baptisms, was welcomed into the fold only a couple of years back when Doc and Louie helped track down the thug that sold his young nephew Leon some bad heroin. A short week or so later the thug himself was found dead in a church alleyway, the fortunate victim of the same poisonous arm candy. It was Redbone himself who had administered the fatal dose.

Shirley, the office receptionist and Nikki's best friend had a standing invitation but always seem to have a hot date.

And so in just under five years Doc McKeowen's private, occasional, Friday night Baptism had swollen into a near block party and regular event, usually lasting till sun-up the next day.

In the words of Frank Capra, Doc came to realize that, 'No man is alone who has friends.' However, due to the growing reputation of M&M combined with the recent boom in business over the last year there had been little time for celebrations.

Less than an hour after the Mancinos arrived the consultation circle had formed. Doc, Nikki, Louie and Doris had rearranged some chairs into a rough circle after the cannolis vanished and the group was settling into a rhythm.

By nine o'clock everyone was oiled up well enough to let down their shields and several topics had been flipped through.

The topic of books had led to films which segued into movie stars and the topic at hand – Lana Turner.

"I will admit that just to hear that girl speak gives me an eargasm. But–" Louie started but was cut off by McKeowen.

"Mancino am I mistaken or do you not have a very pregnant wife sitting right next to you?"

"That's okay Louie, you go right ahead and dream about your little blond bombshell. Nobody's gonna blame you. She is a looker alright." Doris assured which, not really knowing Mancino's wife, shocked Nikki.

Doris picking up on Nikki's silent reaction quickly clarified her philosophy.

"I know what Louie feels for me is true love!"

"How?" Nikki asked.

"Because he still looks at me the way he looks at other women." She embarrassed Mancino as she leaned in and kissed him hard on the lips. "It's when your man stops looking that the woman has to worry!" She emphatically added.

"But . . ." Nikki jumped in.

"Stand-by Mancino, there's a 'but'!" Doc cautioned.

"**But** if Shirley or I ever even hear of you straying off the path . . . let's just say there's a reason God gave you two of them!"

"Two of what? What's she talkin' about Doc?" Doc patted Louie on the back as he handed him another Ballantine.

"Think about it champ. It'll come to you."

"You can't really blame us for looking! It's always easier for a woman to get a man's attention than the other way round!" Doc opined.

252

Just then harry limped through the front door brandishing a bottle and distributed several large bags of potato chips he pilfered from his newsstand stock.

"Sorry I'm late all. Late locking up the store."

Louie ripped open a bag, popped one in his mouth then immediately spit it out.

"CHRIST HARRY! How old are these things?! Pre D-Day landing?"

Nikki who had followed suite was too polite to spit hers out and so spit it into a napkin.

"Pre-Gallipoli landing more like!" She said. "You know there are health laws in this city Harry?! Seriously how old are these things?"

"I dunno! I just grabbed 'em off the rack. He cracked opened his bottle of Jameson's and poured a heavy shot. Harry had some catching up to do.

"I'll tell ya how to impress a man." Doris laughingly contributed. "Show up naked with beer."

"Not necessarily." Doc objected.

"True." Nikki stipulated. "In his case whiskey."

Doc lifted his glass then threw it back.

"Naked with whiskey! I like that." Louie smiled.

"Louie slide ya chair over a little." Doris requested. Louie complied and was immediately elbowed in the ribs.

"That ain't very Christian-like." Harry downed his drink.

"You guys gonna have your kid baptised?" Nikki asked.

"I think the important question is have you two really prepared yourselves for the patter of little feet around the house?" Doc challenged.

"Shit Doc, we talked about it but . . . I don't know if I'm ready for kids! You spend the first 2 years of their life teaching them to walk and talk. Then you spend the next sixteen years telling them to sit down and shut-up. At least that's the way it was in my house."

"He's **gonna be baptised!**" Doris put out in no uncertain terms.

"Your baby gets baptised you guys are gonna have to go to church all the time. It's in the rule book." Harry pointed out. Just before he threw back his third shot.

"Doris still goes on most Sundays." Louie weakly defended.

"Louie, you still go to church?" Nikki asked. Doris laughed.

"Louie goes to church the roof would fall in!"

"Hey! We got married in church!" Louie defended.

"Yeah, and about a minute after we stepped outside a thunderstorm kicked up!"

"Lemme tell ya something, going to church doesn't make you a Christian any more than standing in a garage makes you a car." Doc informed. "I think you two should wait and see how it goes!"

"That's good advice. Take what happens as it comes and with a grain of salt." Nikki reassured.

"I always take life with a grain of salt." Doris tagged. "And a slice of lime and a shot of tequila!"

"I. . . I got something to ask you guys." Harry spoke up. "Just give me a minute." Harry was catching up. They all sat quietly staring as the old guy who was focused on the floor in front of him. He stared and they waited some more. Finally Doc spoke up.

"That's a pretty long minute there Harry."

"How long a minute is depends on what side of the bathroom door you're on. Isn't that right ladies?" Louie earned another elbow.

"I remember now!" Harry triumphantly declared. "Speaking of politics . . . how come we choose forty-eight candidates for Miss America and only two for the White House?" He queried.

"Simple, Americans would rather look at 48 beautiful women for six hours then two ugly politicians for four years." Doc answered.

"Too bad we can't have two pretty politicians to look at for four years!" Louie successfully blocked the next elbow.

"If they were pretty they'd be in movies and wouldn't have to resort to bein' politicians." Nikki added.

"Good point."

"You guys see the latest polls in the papers?" Harry, tossed out. "They're sayin' Dewey by a landslide especially after he hit that triple header by fryin' all those gangsters!"

"How do mean?" Doris asked.

"Mendy Weiss, Louie Capone, and Louie Lepke all got the chair. Within minutes of each other!" Harry informed.

"Huh! Strange ain't it, Louie?" Doc probed.

"What's that Doc?"

"Louie Lepke. Louie Capone, Louie ..."

"That's not funny Doc!"

"C'mon Louie! What'a you got against bein' Italian anyway? There were lots'a great Italians all through history!" Nikki posed.

"Yeah! Politicians, actors ..." Doris joined in. "I'm always telling him he got nothin' to be ashamed of!"

"No presidents though! How come do you explain that?" Mancino countered.

"Can't run for office with a police record!" Doc remarked.

Louie was visibly insulted.

"Knock it off Doc!" Nikki chastised.

"Yeah Doc, don't be giving Mancino a hard time." Harry defended. "That ain't the reason there ain't been no Italian presidents. It's because all the silverware in the White House is counted!"

Harry and Doc shared a laugh.

"That's not very nice! It's funny, but not very nice." Doris half consoled.

"Ahh, Louie knows I'm just yankin' his chain." Doc added. "Besides I gotta ride him after he tried to kill me with his garbage truck."

"Doc you know that wasn't me driving!" Mancino defended. Doc passed him a bottle of beer.

"No hard feelings! You handled that Plymouth like a champ down in Florida that time!" Doc commended.

"You mean the time we both wound up in the Atlantic ocean and had to swim back to shore?" Mancino laughed.

"We wound up getting that bastard though didn't we?!"

"Yes sir we did! Yes we did!" Louie affirmed.

"Partners!" Doc offered his glass and they toasted.

"To partners!"

"My dad taught me how to swim at an early age." Harry broke in. "It came pretty easy to me too." He sipped his drink. "Once I got my hands untied and got my ass out'a that damn canvas bag I found it pretty easy." Harry mumbled to the floor

"Any of you guys notice they ain't making as many war films as they used to?" Louie threw out.

"People are tired of war and war movies. They've gone out of fashion. Besides they were kind of getting a bit unrealistic." Nikki added.

"Yeah you always know how they're going to end." Doris said.

"I don't see too many moving pictures," Harry piped in, ". . . but, I like crime dramas! That's the future of cinema. Crime dramas. Least ways I think so."

"I'll tell you the truth, the few crime dramas I've seen don't look very realistic either." Doc offered. "The cops, the laws et cetera. The police are all good guys, there's no crooked judges and all the bad guys are just misunderstood." Doc explained.

"That's because of Breen, the Hays Office and the codes. They're not allowed to show any crooked judges or politicians." Nikki informed.

"Which makes Breen and the Hayes Office and all those guys completely antithetical to the truth." McKeowen argued.

"Those film dramas always polish the truth." Nikki added. "When someone asks you what you thought about a movie, you don't launch into a deep analysis of the lighting and cinematography, sets and dialogue. You answer with a subjective response of how you felt."

"Exactly." Doc concurred.

"What's your point?" Doris asked.

"American trials are rarely decided on actual 'evidence', they are decided on feelings. Like movies." Doc explained.

"You can't really compare politics to Hollywood." Doris objected.

"Why not?" Nikki challenged. "They're both full of elitists, both living in an alternative universe in a land of make believe and-"

"And both located on a coast!"

"Thank you Louie!"

"You're welcome Nikki." Mancino nipped. Nikki continued. "After all when you get down to it, American politics is only a popularity contest anyway. No real qualifications are required just X number of signatures on a petition and a driver's licence for ID. And it is just like working in movies, plenty of people to tell you what to do, when and how to do it and you still get to act in front of a camera. Only this time, unlike the 'B' pictures you're in, you're guaranteed world-wide distribution, you get to write your own script material and you're not really bound by any contracts! Whether you previously signed them or not!"

"Speaking of movie scripts . . ." Louie threw out. All but Harry exchanged glances as the comment couched the room with an unexpected blanket of reality. "Doc and I were batting that around a few days ago at lunch."

"What exactly?" Doris enquired.

"We think there's something in the script that kid was working on that might give us a clue." Doc replied.

"You talk to Nina about getting a copy?" Nikki asked.

"That's the red flag. She says there was a copy in the apartment but neither any of us or the police found one."

"What about contacting the kid's agent out in L.A.?"

"She says he won't take her calls. Secretary keeps givin' her B.S. excuses." Louie filled in.

"Which is kind'a something I been meaning to bring up to you." Doc said to Nikki.

"You and Louie want to go out L.A. and talk with the agent?" Nikki nodded.

"I knew there was a reason I hitched my horse to your wagon." He kissed her on the forehead.

"I'd love to see L.A.!"

"Actually, with your office skills, I need you to stay here and mind the store. But-"

"Aw Doc! Come on! I've never been out west! And besides-" she pleaded.

"Nikki! I love you but we already talked about this. You want in here? You work for me, I call the shots and NO field work! Sorry, that's non-negotiable!"

Pouting, it was with folded arms that Nikki sank back in her chair.

Doris grunted and shot a stern look at Mancino.

"What?! You can't fly, you got bun in the oven!" Louie shot back. "Besides we goin' out there to sight see! It's business. Out there, poke around and straight back. One two days tops.

"But, as I was saying," Doc continued to Nikki. "I promise you, right after we close this case you, I and Kate will fly off to where ever you want for a week's vacation. God knows we all could use one."

"But-"

"A full week, anywhere you want! In the U.S.!"

"Okay, I suppose. But I want full pay and benefits!"

"You draw up a contract and . . ."

"And what?"

"And we'll fight about . . . I mean talk about it when I get back."

"Very funny!"

Minutes later, after Harry had left and as the sun began to seep through the windows, they rang for a cab and were downstairs seeing Louie and Doris off.

Without turning Nikki absent-mindedly stared down Christopher Street watching the taxi turn the corner.

"Doc?" She quietly spoke.

"Yeah Sweetie?" He lifted an arm to her shoulders.

"You do what you need to do to find out who killed that kid! I'll look after things here. Nina as well."

They tuned to face each other.

"I'm not careful I might just fall in love with you woman!"

"Got dat shit right!" Redbone mumbled as he shuffled passed them into the building's main entrance returning from an obvious all-nighter.

CHAPTER XII

Union Station
Los Angeles, CA
10:35 Tuesday Morning

We're in the Big Time now Doc!"

"Just don't forget, we're on a budget here Rockefeller!" McKeowen cautioned.

Spewing steam across the platform as the conductor deftly hopped down from the last of the passenger cars, The Pacific Flyer slowly rolled into Union Station.

Like a kid at his first trip to the zoo, fascinated by the star-studded flamboyance of being in L.A. Louie Mancino was glued to the widow trolling for movie stars as they coasted to a halt.

"What's the plan Doc?"

"Get off the train, find a taxi, locate the hotel, check in, track down this agent fella and, if there's enough time, make our way out to his lair."

"What about lunch?"

"Louie, it's not even eleven o'clock!"

As they carried their single bag each, Mancino's three times the size of McKeowen's, across the parking lot to the taxi port Louie scooted up closer to Doc.

"Hey Doc! Do ya suppose we could be in a movie?"

262

"I'd say they got enough P.I.'s and P.I. movies to fill their quota Louie."

"Oh, I wasn't quotin' nobody! I was just wonderin' what it'd be like, ya know?"

"No Louie. No movies."

From there all went according to plan, almost.

Temporarily forgetting they were no longer in Manhattan and that taxi cabs in L.A. weren't exactly a dime a dozen, they waited in the beating sun for half an hour at the designated taxi line outside the station before a lime green and bright orange cab arrived. At least they assumed it was a taxi. There were no discernable markings anywhere on the vehicle.

The Hispanic diver had halting English at best and, after agreeing on a price to their destination, there was no meter in the cab, they were finally off.

Thirty minutes later they pulled up in front of the Blue Swallow hotel on Gower Street where the desk clerk couldn't locate their reservation. As Doc was cursing his secretary/receptionist Shirley, the reservation card was located, they checked in and were shown to their adjoining rooms.

A short time later as he was unpacking his small suitcase McKeowen was suddenly startled as Mancino burst through the common door between rooms.

"Doc! We're in Hollywood!"

"Jesus Louie, you trying to give me a heart attack?! It's West Hollywood Louie! I told Shirley to keep it under twenty a night."

"You want a heart attack come and look at this view!"

Mancino scurried to the window and threw back the lime green curtain.

Doc moved to the double window to view a panoramic vista of the Hollywood Forever Cemetery, rolled his eyes then strolled back over to the bed and resumed unpacking his suitcase.

"Nice! Now in case I do have heart attack I won't have far to go."

McKeowen rang down to the desk, requested a long distance line and ten minutes later the operator rang him back.

Your call is through to New York sir. The operator reported just before Doc heard the line click over.

"Is this a Miss Nikki Cole?" He teased in a falsetto voice.

Is this the guy who runs off to Hollywood and leaves his best girl behind?

"You can't still be sore about that!"

I'm not, but we are taking a vacation this year come hell or high water!

"Word of honor Dollface! Anywhere you want."

So you guys made it out there alright I assume?

"It's a different planet out here."

So how is the Red Robin Hotel?

It's *The Blue Swallow* and we're finally here. I feel like I've been living on a train these last four and a half days."

Perhaps because you have.

264

"Plan here is to wrap it up in two or three days and head back."

What's the weather like?

"Exactly like it was this time last week. And this time last month and this time last year. Probably the same as it's going to be this time next week. Hot, sunny and humid."

I still don't see why Doris and I couldn't have come out with you! Nikki sulked.

"Sweetheart you have my solemn promise that the very next murder case involving a novice screen writer found hanged in his apartment-"

You mean strangled to death? She corrected. *I thought you weren't sure?*

"I'm not so sure any more. We'll talk about details when I get back."

Doc, watch yourself out there. Remember, they don't play by the same rules and you don't have any cop connections in L.A

"Yes dear."

Just under an hour later they were compelled to shield their eyes as they pushed through the revolving door of the hotel's front entrance.

From his jacket pocket Doc produced a pair of sunglasses and put them on. Louie stared.

"Where'd you get those?!"

McKeowen brandished a second pair and passed them to a surprised but grateful Mancino.

"Brought them with. If we're gonna be bouncing around out here we need to look like a couple of cool cats."

"How do I look?"

"Like a producer. C'mon, let's get our bearings then maybe find a way out to this guy's office in Melrose." Doc suggested.

Louie reached in his back pocket and came up with a folded up, one page map. It displayed colourful caricatures of mansions sprinkled along streets and residential boulevards around the heart of L.A.

"Where'd you get that?" Doc asked.

"From a little Mexican kid around back." Louie proudly brandished. "Two bucks. Maybe we'll get to see some stars while we're here!"

"Yeah maybe." Doc took the map and scanned it. "'*Homes of the Stars*? Louie this is a tourist map."

"WHAT'A YA MEAN?!"

"What do I mean?" Doc pointed out a caption. "'See the house of John Barrymore'? John Barrymore's been dead for five years!" With each successive chastisement Doc slapped the map with the back of his hand. "House of Fatty Arbuckle, heart attack on his first wedding anniversary, 1933. Rudolf Valentino died 1926–"

"Okay, okay I get it! The map's a little old"

"A little old?! This map's older than most of the buildings in this town! It's from 1921!" Doc crumpled it up and tossed it in a nearby garbage basket.

"So now what'a we gonna do for a map? We still got'a buy one!" Mancino challenged.

Doc reached into his back pocket and produced a color coded city map.

"Free from the concierge at the hotel." He informed. "Here's the number and address." He passed Mancino a piece of note paper. "There's a phone booth back inside the lobby, to the left. Go and call for directions to the agent's office,"

Louie perused the paper.

"Doc, this number don't look right."

"What'a mean? What's the matter with it?"

"It ain't got enough numbers."

"What'a you talking about? There's seven numbers."

"They got this new thing, it's called Area Code."

"What the hell's an area code?" Doc challenged.

"It's a code for an area! Hence the name, 'Area-Code'!"

"Clever. So what 'area' are we in and what's this secret code?"

"I dunno. One, two three I guess. Maybe it's on the map?"

Doc checked.

"So it is. Good eyes Louie."

"Gimme a nickel fer the phone." Louie held out his hand.

"Use one'a your own!"

Mancino went back inside, made the call and got directions to a downtown L.A office building on Olympic and Grand.

Twenty minutes later as they got out of the cab Louie stared up and perused the five floors of the seemingly new art deco structure.

"Office building?! My apartment's bigger than this!"

They started to the door.

"They can't build too high." Doc informed.

"Why not afraid of heights?"

"Earthquakes."

Mancino froze in place and looked around beneath his feet. Doc noticed.

"Don't worry. They normally announce on the radio."

Upstairs on the second floor they made their way to office number 209 where across the front door's glass panel the hand lettering read:

H. Sheinfort's
Guaranteed Talent Agents

§§§§§

'Affiliated with Wm. Morris'

"Hey Doc, what's it mean, 'affiliated with'? They got
another big office in New York?"

"Probably not, probably just using the name."

"Won't the New York guys get mad and sue?"

Doc rapped on the glass a few times and not eliciting an answer tuned the knob and went in. As they entered they perused the office.

One desk one chair one filing cabinet, a few odds and ends and one window looking down on the rear alleyway of the building behind and, in the far corner, one dead Areca palm. A framed and faded certificate of some description hung on the wall behind the desk.

"Probably not."

"Why not?"

"This look like a New York affiliate to you?"

"Can I help you gentlemen?" A voice from behind barked.

In the open doorway stood a short, thin and balding guy holding a large glass of water in one hand and a roll of toilet paper in the other. He noticed them noticing the toilet roll.

"Oh yeah, sorry. They don't always stock the men's room here like they should. What can I do for youse two?"

"We're looking for a Mr. Sheinfort?"

"What for, exactly?"

"We'd like some help straightening out an estate."

"In case you ain't noticed this is a talent agency not a lawyer's office." He informed as he dumped the glass of water on the dead plant. He invited them to sit but with the one chair they declined.

"We're looking into wrapping up the affairs of a Benny Joule. On behalf of the family."

"You guys cops or something? If you are you got'a tell me." He quizzed as he stowed the toilet roll in a bottom desk drawer.

"No, nothing like that. Friends of Benny's fiancée and the family. Asked us to take a trip out here and see if there's anything we, she, needs to take care of before the funeral."

"Funeral? Benny died days ago! Jews are supposed to be in the ground by sundown the next day."

"Normally yes, but being that the case is under investigation and all, I guess the authorities put the kybosh on that ritual." Doc shot back.

"Okay, how can I help?"

"Like I said, we just want to make sure there are no loose ends with this picture deal you got for him. Well done on nailing that movie contract by the way. I understand those deals are impossible to close."

As expected Harry took the flattery bait.

"Hey it's what I do." He shrugged.

"Why'd they pull out?"

"The movie was cancelled for one stupid reason or another. Happens all the time. For every project that gets the green light and makes it to first day of principle photography there's a couple of dozen that don't."

"But they already cut a check for the option fee? I understand it was a substantial sum they paid for the rights."

"A few grand to save a couple of million on a potential flop. It's all relative." Sheinfort explained.

"Interesting." Doc nodded.

"These people don't think like you and me. I didn't get your name?"

"Mike, this is a friend of mine, drives a garbage truck back east, Carmine."

"Hi Mike, Carmine." Thy shook hands.

Harry suddenly decided to unload all his recently pent up frustrations to them and proceeded to give them the skinny. "These guys, the movie people, live in what I call 'The Hollywood Bubble.'"

"Meaning?"

"They labor under the delusion of how they're all better than all us 'regular' Joes. How they've achieved something special that none of us, you and I, could ever achieve." Harry leaned in across his desk as if to take them into his confidence. "The reality of the situation is most of them either fell into it by birth, have some kind'a connection or are all pretty boys and girls who get to step in front of a camera by virtue of the fact that every yokel in the movie house will be fantasizing about them tonight while they're pumpin' away on their fat ugly husband or wife! Why the hell ya think most people turn the lights out when their bumpin' nasties?"

"Very graphic Harry." Doc commented.

"That, and the other obvious, magic key to get in the front door."

"Which is . . .?" Louie probed.

"Please! Are you fer real?"

"You lost us Harry." Doc added.

"You think Jack Warner's American? His mother's name was Eichelbaum. He's a Polak. Sam Goldwyn? Szemuel Gelbfisz. Paramount Pictures set up by Lansky and Zukor." Doc and Louie sat expressionless. Doc shrugged.

"What? I gotta draw you guys a picture?" Harry pushed.

"No, we get the picture Harry." Doc affirmed.

"In Technicolor." Louie added. "Just out of curiosity, any idea what the picture was about?" Louie probed.

"Yeah of course! I read the script didn't I? It was a gangster melodrama. Pretty good writing too. It's a shame it got flushed."

"Did it name any actual Mob guys? Politicians, cops anything like that?" Doc picked up.

"No, of course not! I wouldn't have signed off on it if it did. Besides not allowed under the code. Closest the story came was hintin' at one of these left wing, racist, anti-communist groups you sometimes read about in the papers."

"Was the group based in Chicago?"

"Yeah! How'd ya know?"

"I didn't really but when you said newspapers I remembered a story I read back East about a week ago about some crazies outside of Cicero. Some left wing group anti-something or other." Doc came by his vagueness honestly. He had read no such article but employed it as a tactic to further pump the agent.

"Don't remember exactly where Benny set these characters but it was defiantly in and around Chicago. He originally set it in New York but I suggested we had a better shot at the studios picking it up if it were set in Illinois."

"Why?"

"Better tax breaks, lower more liberal permit fees and cheaper union help with sparkies, chippers, drivers all those guys."

"Sparkies?" Louie inquired.

"Electricians." Harry clarified. "Ever since the Mob got the unions boxed in back in the days of Capone there's no movies without the unions and there's damn sure no unions without the Mob."

Neither Doc or Louie were shocked by this revelation.

"Harry tell us, you read people all the time. What kind'a guy was Benny? I mean how did he come off to you?" Doc probed. The agent got quiet, looked down and sighed.

"In a word gentlemen, he was a rube. Knew nothing about nothing. About the real world that is."

"Did you know his girl?"

"No, didn't know he had one. I didn't really know anything about his personal life. I only acted as his agent. His temporary agent that is."

"Well Mr, Sheinfort, if there's nothing we need to do here . . ." Doc signalled their sign-off.

"How long you guys in town for?" Harry asked as he stood to see them to the door.

"A day or two. Then back to The Big Apple."

"Sorry I couldn't'a been more help."

"You did all you could and we thank you for your candor."

They shook hands and left.

Sheinfort went out to the hallway and watched out the window, looking down at street level until he saw them exit the building and walk north. When he was satisfied they were clear of the place he returned to his desk, sat and dialled the phone. It rang twice before being picked up.

Yeah? A gruff voice grunted across the lines.

"It's Sheinfort. Let me talk with Vinnie."

What's it about?

"JUST GET VINNIE WILL YA!" The transceiver on the other end was heard to be laid on a table then picked up again.

What is it Harry? The distinctively East coast dialect impatiently queried.

"I just had two visitors might interest you."

Oh yeah, who?

"Two guys tried passing themselves off as friends of the writer's fiancée."

Nina, the cute little blond?

"Yeah. They were askin' about Joules, the script that kind'a stuff. I think they might'a been P.I.'s"

Shit! There was a loud click followed by a dial tone.

While Doc and Louie were striking out on the west side of L.A. further east in the city Eric Johnston, president of the MPAA, was in full organizational mode preparing to go to war.

Although the film industry had been warding off attacks from politicians and do-gooder organizations virtually since its inception, the political squall gathering on the horizon at the

Paddy Kelly

moment was clearly going to be the a knock-down, drag-out that would leave a Category 5 hurricane-like swath of destruction across the industry which threatened to linger for years to come.

Formally known as the MPPDA it was in line with a massive revamping, brought about by the post-war altered landscape of the motion picture industry itself, that the official title had been revamped as well. In fact it was the former four-time president of the U.S. Chamber of Commerce, Johnston himself who did the revamping two years ago when he was brought in to replace Hays who, after a quarter of a century at the helm, had stepped down.

A true politician, it was behind the scenes that Johnston was quietly revising the old Draconian film code. That effort had, only a week ago, been put on the back burner.

Now he had the present headache of loss of revenue due to the organization's banning of exporting movies to Britain in protest of the English tax on imported films.

Now that internal crisis had to be set aside to deal with the U.S. Senate's renewed attacks which were partially motivated by the upcoming elections.

Originally established in 1922 to ensure the viability of the fledgling industry the MPAA had now advanced to dominate film content and to a large degree, the behavior of film's practitioners.

Johnston had decided that an organized, unified front approach was the strategy called for and so was in the process of preparing to convene an abbreviated conference of the thirty or forty top players in the industry in an attempt to get everyone on the same sheet of music with which to protect the home front. The alternative was to allow the D.C. legislators un wild with new battery of regulations.

Fully cognizant that Hollywood had a very slim chance of winning against the D.C. horde, Johnston sought to avoid a prolonged war of attrition such as resulted from the Sherman Act, a fight still being fought since 1890.

However, being the bastard step child of both La La Land and the D.C. circus Johnston realized he held some advantages. Advantages such as his lingering political connections in the U.S. Chamber of Commerce coupled with the fact that by their own admission, most members of congress only drifted into a cinema house once or twice a year. In fact several hailed from one horse towns so small there were no movie theaters in them at all.

Although not committed to the film industry per se, Eric Johnston was whole-heartedly committed to the MPAA, but it was with bigger and better political ambitions in mind that Johnston had decided to convene a big boys' meeting to head off the latest D.C. attack.

Johnston had settled on the Waldorf Astoria Hotel in Manhattan for his meeting to negotiate handling of the D.C. wolf pack currently being led by Thomas, Rankin and the House on Un-American Activities Committee.

Sitting at his desk he consulted a yellow legal pad across which was scribbled a column of names and phone numbers.

He dialed the next number on the list.

"Mister Jack Warner's office, how may I help you?"

Afternoon Leslie, its Eric Johnston. Is he in?

"Yes sir. I'll put you right through."

"Hello, Warner here."

Jack, Eric here. I've worked something up I'd like your help on.

"You have my ear Eric."

Jack, I've reserved a conference room at the Waldorf in New York for the end of next month. Can you be there?

"For what exactly?"

I think we need to stay ahead of this brouhaha in D.C.

"I agree."

To that end I want to call a closed door meeting no press. We need to plan a strategy.

"You honestly believe you're gonna be able to keep such a meeting quiet from the press?"

This is not my first rodeo Jack. Pending the attendees' approval, and a final vote I intend a full press conference right after the congress releases their findings."

"What kind of resolution?"

I'll send copies of a statement to . . . no actually better if I hand them out at the meeting. But basically it will disavow any knowledge, complicity or collusion with any known communist members, sympathizers or activities by any of the major studios.

"Uh huh. Who have you got commitments from so far?"

Spyros Skouras, Balaban at Paramount, Sam Goldwyn, Billy Goestz.

"Except for Goldwyn I don't hear too many big names."

Warner's criticism stung but Johnston was too big a man and too experienced a politician to get snagged up on it.

That's why your name would lend a lot of weight to our cause Jack.

Warner on the other hand was too selfish a man and too inexperienced in big politics not to get hung up on the compliment.

"Eric I support what you're trying to do and will help where I can."

Can I count on you to show up and sign, give us your endorsement?

"I'll definitely consider it Eric. I'll have to see the resolution. That's the best I can do for you now."

Think about it Jack. Thanks for your time.

They hung up and both immediately placed another call.

Johnston to call Harry Cohn over at Columbia and Warner to ring someone with a little more weight.

White House switchboard. How may I direct your call?

"This is Mr. Jack Warner I'd like to speak to Rose please. Rose Conway."

Yes Mr. Warner, please hold.

Few had direct access to Harry Truman's personal secretary. Jack Warner was one of the chosen.

Rose Conway speaking.

"Rose, Jack Warner here. Is he in town next week?"

Yes he is Jack, why?

Any chance you could squeeze me in some time early next week? It's about this HUAC thing. Some of the guys out here are planning a meeting and I think the President ought to be aware of what's shaping up on this end of the country."

How much time do you need?

"At the outside, twenty minutes."

Jack give me until this afternoon and I'll get back to you, okay?

"Thanks Rose. I owe you one. Hi to the family."

I'll be back to you by end of business Jack.

That evening, having drawn a blank at the agent's office and not really knowing the town, the guys were now looking for a place to eat. They asked the girl at the front desk who, since they were tourists, recommended the Formosa out on Santa Monica as a good bet.

They walked from the hotel for while then, having not seen any taxis to flag down like you could back in New York, or even any buses, they came to a realization.

"Not much on public transport in this town are they?" Mancino observed.

"Town's too small to have a subway and not enough of a population to support a bunch of bus routes, with only a million or so people, most of which with cars . . ."

Not doing so well in the evening's heat and having walked twice as much as he ever remembered walking in New York Louie decided enough was enough and stepped out into the street as he spotted a taxi cruising on the opposite side of the road and waved it down.

The cab ride was a relatively short one but they were able to chat with the driver and get a good feel for the city's layout.

About fifteen minutes later they pulled up on the corner in front of the one story, red stucco building.

Powerful enough to tint the entire exterior, the green neon screaming 'Formosa' mounted across the building's façade also transformed Louie's yellow bowling shirt into an orange tinged apron.

Inside they were greeted by red walls, red-tinted table lamps and the red Chinese lantern, festooned ceiling.

McKeowen and Mancino exchanged glances.

"Needs more red!" Mancino critiqued.

Predictably when the waitress tried seating them in the main dining room Louie insisted on sitting in the red dining car, a makeover of a turn-of-the-century Union Pacific Pullman attached to the side of the eatery.

However, Louie's child-like behavior serendipitously gave them the break they were looking for.

After the meal they ordered dessert and Doc glanced over again at a customer who had caught his attention when they first came in. His thoughts were interrupted when the waitress re-appeared with the check.

"Can I get you boys anything else this evening?"

"No thank you, but even though it wasn't Italian that food was fantastic." Louie's backhanded compliment made her stare briefly.

"I'll pass that onto the chef. Maybe next time he can rustle you up a chow mein lasagna." She shot back with sincere sarcasm.

"Can he do that?" Louie sincerely queried.

"What' your name?" Doc casually asked the young waitress as she casually slid the check from McKeowen's place to Mancino's.

"Mary Kay, what's yours?"

"I'm Mike and this is Louie." Doc grabbed her hand as she extended it to shake Louie's hand just as Louie dug into his strawberry sorbet and whipped cream.

"No, no, no! Don't ever put your hand between the food and his mouth! Very dangerous!" Doc warned.

"Dat ain't funny Doc!" Louie mumbled around a mouthful of sorbet.

"Mary Kay, can I ask you something?"

"Sure! What's up Doc?!" She giggled. Doc sneered.

"Who's that guy across at the bar? The one in the rumpled suit slamming shots and washing them down with his mai tai?" He casually probed keeping a surreptitious eye on a guy at the bar.

"Not sure, never seen him in here before. I heard him bending Sam's ear though."

"Sam's the bartender?"

"Yeah. He was going on about how bad the studio system is in this town and how he had a fight with his boss or something."

"You suppose he's from across the street at the Sam Goldwyn lot?" McKeowen's wheels were turning as he quizzed the waitress.

"Like I said Doc, can't say. He looks like a producer type. Well dressed, well groomed and looks like he doesn't know squat about talent. But hell, you wanna find a producer in this town just throw a rock you'll hit one."

"Mary Kay, do me a fav. Tell the gentleman we'd like to buy him a drink." Doc threw another tenner on the table. "Put the change in your pocket."

"Thanks Doc! But who should I say it's from?"

"Tell him it's from Mancino Productions."

"You got it!" She squeaked back already halfway down the aisle, the tip folded over and tucked neatly into her bra strap.

Doc nodded over to the bar when the guy turned to observe his benefactors, then smiled and waved the pair over.

"Mancino, you don't speak English!" Doc ordered as they got up from the table.

"Sure I do! You hear me all the-" A sharp whack to the shoulder helped Louie to focus.

"Speak only Italian! In other words play dumb. That shouldn't be too hard."

"Got it."

At the bar introductions were made and by consensus they agreed to relocate from the bar to a back table.

After ordering another round Doc took control of the conversation. The producer guy wasn't as lit as he was attempting to be but he came off as relaxed and unassuming. The perfect mark.

"We're a small outfit out of New York working with Mr. Mancino's company back in Rome trying to break into the biz out here." Doc explained.

For the second time the stranger tried speaking to Mancino who just smiled and nodded.

"How is it he doesn't speak English?"

"He works out of the Rome office. I'm from the New York office. I gave our translator the day off. We're heading back day after tomorrow and she wanted to see the sights."

"Oh, so you've seen the traffic?" Producer guy joked.

"Kind'a hard to miss."

"Well, that leaves the studios and the zoo and you seen it all! Of course if you work in one of the studios there's not much difference than the zoo!"

"I can imagine. So Sam over at the bar says you had a hard time at your studio, Paramount isn't it?" Doc fished.

"Warner Brothers."

"Warner's, oh yeah. I hear they're a bitch to work for. Can't you go back to the big boss and square things up?"

"You don't get it Pal! In the movie game in this town, hell in the country, Jack Warner is . . . is . . ."

"A god?" Doc ventured.

"NO! Not a god. He's The God!"

"Como?" Louie asked to garnish the charade.

Il signor Jack Warner è Dio." Doc informed.

"Ahh capish! Il Dio."

"So what happened?" Doc pushed and signaled for another round.

"So I'm in the studio commissary, eatin' my tna casserole when Warner and his entourage stroll in, sit down and the son-of-a-bitch looks around the table, points at me and says; 'What's your name?!' I tell him and next thing I know a minute later he yells over at me, 'MARGOLD! I want you off the lot by close of business!'"

"That's it, no reason?" Doc supported.

"THAT'S IT! No warning, no reason nothing! Just hit the bricks! Yesterday's news. Foot note in the archives."

"I'm sure you'll find something else."

"Not now that I'm branded! I may as well move to Europe and look for work in Italian avante garde or fatalistic love stories in France!"

"You say you were at Warners, yeah?"

"Until week or so, yeah."

"Mind if I ask you, just out of curiosity, you ever come across a script titled *The Formula*?"

"*The Formula*?"

"Yeah, some first timer sent us a copy. Says there's an agent out here looking to get it made." Doc led.

"*The Formula*? Can't say as I have, no, not off the top of my head. You got a story line?"

"Basically from the pitch his agent gave us over the phone, what I got was it's basically a who-done-it centered around a reformed mobster wanting to break into politics."

"Huh! Plenty of material there!" Producer guy grunted as he looked down, knitted his brow and combed his rapidly blurring memory banks.

"It was tentatively gonna be set in Chicago." Doc added.

At the mention of the word Chicago producer guy looked up and nodded.

"We might be talking about two different projects because they're not that many projects that get the go ahead to shoot out there." Margold started. "But the story line rings a bell. From what I remember they changed the name. The studio called it *Lethal Deception* or some such nonsense. It was earlier this year. I wasn't in on that project but I think I heard they killed it before first day of principle."

"So they actually started it?"

"Far as I know they sent location scouts out there, hired a local building company for sets and everything. Couldn't tell ya why they pulled the plug, could be a hundred reasons, but usually if a deal is a stinker they won't spend the money to go that far."

"How would I find out the name of the set outfit in Chicago? You know if I wanted to hire them for a project?"

Doc nodded over at Louie who was already discreetly jotting down notes under the table.

"On out'a town projects we don't usually drag set companies along with us we hire local. The Chicago outfit wouldn't have been a set company per se." Producer guy finished off his third mai tai then continued. "More of just a building firm I'd guess. But in any case you'd have to look them up."

"What's the best way to do that?"

"Call this number tomorrow." He scribbled a note across a cocktail napkin and slid it over to Doc. "I'll do. . . do some askin' around."

"Would they have gotten a script?"

"Well yeah, if they went that far they would'a been given copy of the script."

"How about another round?" Doc offered.

"Only. . . only if you wanna carry. . . carry me home." The producer didn't have much luck standing but with Doc's help made it to his feet. McKeowen nodded at Louie to find a cab as he helped the producer to the door then put him in a cab.

"One thing fellas . . . call after twelve will ya?"

"Sure thing." Doc assured. Producer guy fell over on the seat and passed out. Doc dug in his jacket pocket, found some I.D. and gave the driver an address along with a twenty.

"Make sure he's okay will ya? That should cover it for you." Doc instructed the driver.

"Yes sir. Thank you."

They stood at the curb as the taxi pulled out.

"You suppose he'll talk to anybody?" Louie asked as the taxi faded down Santa Monica.

"Probably. But he won't remember any details other than two producers from out of town at a restaurant."

"Ya think?"

"Well he might remember that one of them spoke English the other looked like Lou Costello."

"Very funny!"

CHAPTER XIII

After a late night wandering the town it was the next afternoon that Doc and Louie were sitting in the Blue Swallow Cocktail Lounge on the first floor of the hotel working on their second round.

"God damn cab fare is gonna bankrupt us! This place is spread out like first century Rome!" Doc complained as he fished another twenty out of his pocket.

"Doc obviously we gotta go to a studio! And where else but Warner Brothers? They optioned the script. The used-to-be producer we got drunk worked there and besides, going to a studio might help round out the picture. Get it? Studio-picture? Round out? Huh, huh?"

"Louie?"

"Yeah Doc"

"Put a cork I it will ya?"

"Sorry Doc! Just tryin' to add some levitation to the situation."

McKeowen threw back the last of his whiskey.

"Besides, coming all the way out here and not seein' the studio?" Louie pushed. "That'd be like visiting Brooklyn and not seeing at least one sewer rat swimming in the East River or visiting the Bowery and not tripping over one drunken bum passed out in a doorway."

"You'd make a good travel agent Louie."

"Thanks Doc. I'm practicin' how to be more descriptive."

"I have every intention of getting us into the studios. I just haven't figured out how. We'd wait weeks for an appointment with a producer if not longer, any hint of who we are and we'd be permanently frozen out and we can't just waltz in the front gate past the security guards. Maniacal sociopaths inundate those studios all the time."

"I know what you mean. That and a lotta crazy people tryin' to get in too."

"Yeah, that too."

"Doc?"

"Yeah?"

"Why can't we just waltz in the front gate?"

"Louie, I'm trying to think here! Could you just-"

Doc broke off his protest as he turned to see Mancino brandishing a tourist brochure he pulled from a rack at the end of the bar. A tourist brochure with all the details of a one hour guided tour of the Warner Brothers Studios in Burbank north of the hotel.

An hour later, after Doc consulted the Yellow Pages at the front desk and they dressed the best they could to look like tourists, they were standing in front of Warner brothers Studio's Gate #4 where they were directed to the tourist entrance over on Riverside Drive. A short fifteen minutes later they were climbing into a twenty person articulated tram car. They purposely chose the very back of the last car.

"Twelve bucks each! This better be some tour!" Mancino complained as they took their seats in the very back of the last car. Doc leaned over and whispered.

"We're not here for a tour, so get your game face on!"

"I'm just sayin' twelve smackers to ride in a golf cart, ya know?"

"Yeah but . . . it's a really nice golf cart." Doc mocked.

Not quite full to capacity they pulled out and the female tour guide drove at a leisurely pace as she spoke into her overhead microphone pointing out locations of popular films and sets.

As they were all issued a three page fold out map of the studio grounds it was simple to plot the nearest bail point closest to the executive offices.

Unfortunately the maps were not to scale and the actual dimensions of the executive offices from the back lot where the majority of the tour occurred was several acres away from the Burbank lot where the main offices were located.

It was then that McKeowen saw their chance.

"As we approach our New York Street currently dressed for shooting *My Wild Irish Rose* starring Dennis Morgan and Arlene Dahl, if you look to the right . . ."

"Here!" Doc whispered and nudged Louie out.

The tram slowed to take the acute angle turn and the guys quickly and smoothly slid out of their seats and scurried across the street to hide behind the corner bank building until the tram was out of sight.

"Okay, the exec offices are in this direction." Doc instructed.

Twenty minutes later, tired and sweaty they reached the executive offices.

Quickly adjusting their neckties they composed themselves and entered.

"May I help you gentlemen?"

"Yes, we're here to speak with a Mister Marigold." Doc stated trying not to sound like a B movie actor.

"Margold, sir. It's Barry Margold." Louie astutely added further enhancing the charade.

"Margold, Barry Margold. We're from the Federal Communication Commission." They quickly flashed their P.I. shields. "We'd like to ask him a few questions about a script he's involved with."

"I'm sorry Mr. Margold is no longer with us." She informed.

"Then can you tell us who is currently producing the script with the title of *The Formula*?"

"I'm sorry sir, all script material is strictly confidential and-"

"Look lady, we don't want any trouble, but this investigation isn't going away and we have a job to do. So if you could just help us out here we'll be on our way."

At mention of the word 'investigation' the receptionist froze up then reached over for her intercom.

"John, can you come to the lobby please?" She gave the two a second look. "Hurry please!"

A minute later a short, casually dressed forty-something appeared.

"Christine, what's the problem?" She didn't speak but nodded and pointed at Doc and Louie who had moved to the plush couch on the left.

"I'm John Samuels, executive producer. What can I do for you guys?"

The two stood and again flashed their badges just brief enough to have the desired effect.

"We're from the FCC, L.A. office and we're presently investigating an FCC fraud case related to a production being handled by a Mr. Barry Margold which we believe may contain some classified government information."

"Barry Margold is no longer with Warner Brothers and I don't know anything about any classified information."

"Then perhaps you can help." Louie suggested.

"I don't see how!" The producer defended.

"We'd like to see a copy of the script. If there's nothing compromising in it then we'll be on our way and call it a dead end."

"You can't just waltz in here demanding to see scripts!"

"Why not?" Louie asked.

"For obvious trade considerations, they're confidential!"

"Mr. Samuels, we have an important investigation to wrap up, " Doc interjected. ". . and we're due back in D.C. by the weekend. Now as lovely as it is out here in La La Land we are going to obtain the evidence we need one way or the

292

other. Now we can either forward an official letter of recommendation to Jack Warner or a letter of subpoena for him to appear in court and explain to a California circuit court judge why you're hiding material evidence."

"Chrisy, call security!" The producer ordered but as she reached for her phone Doc quickly beat her to it.

"Won't be a second love. Then it's all yours." He leisurely dialed a number.

Despite the fact that McKeowen heard nothing but a dial tone on the other end, he spoke anyway.

"Gerry? Nick here. Yeah we're down at the Warner offices they're refusing to cooperate. Can you call Judge Dinkins and get a bench warrant for a search of the premises and have the FBI run it on over. We'll stick around in case they try anything. Name on the warrant? Make it out to a John Samuels. Middle name? Hold on." Doc turned to Samuels. "John, you got a middle name?"

The stunned producer just stared in return then flipped Doc his middle finger. "No Ger, no middle name. Thanks Ger." Doc hung up. "You don't mind if we wait, do you John? It'll be about an hour or so till the agents show up."

Samuels and the very nervous receptionist exchanged glances.

"Okay asshole! What's the title of the script?!"

"The Formula, John. We believe the title is The Formula. "

"Who wrote it?"

"Sorry we don't have the author's name. That's part of what we're here to verify." The producer stormed down the hall.

Minutes later Samuel returned and tossed a bound script at Doc.

"Feds or not, you two clowns aren't off the lot I ten minutes and I'm calling the L.A.P.D. and reporting a disturbance! Now get the fuck out!"

"Thank you for your cooperation John. It will be note din our final report."

Believing they were out of the woods, once outside, Doc and Louie halted in their tracks when they saw a pair of security guards in the front seat of a golf cart slowly cruising down the street. But that wasn't the worst of their problems. In the back seat was the female tour guide they had bailed on.

"That's them!" She yelled and pointed.

The driver quickly pulled on his Olive drab green security cap with 'W.B.' in orange embroidery on the front and steered the cart at full speed towards the two who were tearing up back between the exec offices and an adjoining building. Fortunately the golf cart was chasing behind at full speed. A full nine miles per hour.

Running flat out they were able to just clear the side exit gate startling the gate guard who fell back in his tilted chair as he sat in the small guard shack reading as they whizzed by.

They dodged the Wilshire Boulevard traffic and kept running until at least a block away.

"You okay?" Doc asked.

Louie puffed out a sporadic reply.

"I ain't run that fast since Doris' brother chased me from behind the bleachers at Saint Anne's gym."

"What were you doing under the bleachers?"

"Well . . . it was Doris' brother so . . . guess who I was with and . . . what we were doin'! I'll give you three guesses and . . . the first two don't count."

"Were you doing math homework?"

"No Mr. Wizard . . . biology!"

McKeowen slapped Louie on the back and they had a good laugh as they walked off with no idea of where they ere going.

"Doc you get the feeling somebody doesn't want us at this party?"

"That or maybe, just maybe we're sniffing a little too far up somebody's skirt."

"That or maybe we're in over our heads."

"Could be that too."

"You think we could pop over to Knott's Berry Farm or Ghost Town?! We're pretty close." Louie pushed as he scanned his map.

Doc's answer came in the form of a stare Mancino had grown to know well. It was McKeowen's 'Say one more word and my foot will be up your ass' look.

"Okay. Maybe next time we're out here." Mancino mumbled then clammed up.

The Californian Restaurant
Corso Umbert, Naples, Italy

The Broad in the Kimono

Noon, Friday, 15 August

At the same time Doc and Louie were cruising around in a string of golf carts and being chased by security guards 6,500 miles away in Naples a special messenger was arriving by private car at the restaurant owned by his boss Salvatore Lucania who still went by the name of Luciano, Charlie 'Lucky' Luciano.

Back in Italy only a matter of weeks now since his release from prison in America, Luciano, though not happy, had quickly settled back into the leisurely pace of Italy. A place he reasoned he was not well suited for.

Back in 1942 with the burning of the luxury liner *T.L.S. Normandy*, re-christened the *U.S.S. Lafayette* and the concurrent rise in fear of German saboteurs in the New York harbor area Luciano and his people were approached to supplement the woefully undermanned Naval Intelligence department and act as waterfront guard dogs.

Good for the Mafia, bad for the odd German occasionally kidnapped, killed and dumped into the river then reported to Commander Haffenden, head of *Operation Underworld,* as another 'dirty Gerry saboteur' taken care of.

Then in 1943 during the U.S. Navy's planning of *Operation Husky* for the invasion of Sicily it was realized there were no up-to-date naval surveys of Gela Bay, the Allies intended landing site. Luciano's people were once again sought to covertly put out the call to local Italians for photos, post cards or any other information of the southern shores of Sicily.

A notorious criminal sorely in need of jail time but too clever to get caught by the NYC prosecutors, Luciano was finally trapped when three-time presidential hopeful Thomas Dewey rounded up every prostitute in the greater New York area and threatened them all with jail time if they didn't testify against Luciano.

Imprisoned in 1936 with ten times the guideline recommended sentence but released and deported just eleven years later, press addicted politicians were still tripping over themselves to lambast Luciano and get their fix of newspaper headlines. Amongst them was Harry Anslinger, honcho of the newly formed Federal Bureau of Narcotics or FBN.

Anslinger, another politician who barley walked the line of legitimacy, banqueted on Luciano's name while, like a starving hyena following a scent, literally built a career out of chasing the Sicilian across the globe.

As Harry Anslinger was putting a fire under his agent's asses Lucky Luciano was enjoying the fruits of the labor Anslinger et al were struggling to keep him from.

The hundred seat eatery christened The Californian, and which overlooked the scenic port had been one of Charlie's investments shortly after being chased out of Rome by the local cops. A legit investment was necessary outside the capital city not because he was such a high profile gangster, but because the Roman cops had their own rackets going and didn't need a world-wise pro muscling in on their territory.

Lucky, sitting at his regular corner table, was relaxing with an afternoon espresso and a cannoli. His miniature pinscher Bambi in his lap.

Lucky's right hand man in the restaurant game was a late fifty-something named Gino Kinelli. Gino was never part of The Mob, in fact he had very few dealings with the 'wrong' side of the law, which was in part why Luciano choose to work with him. Gino had a good rep for being trustworthy. This however, did not mean that Signor Kinelli was not amenable to that old Neapolitan tradition, money laundering, which was why Lucky choose the restaurant business in which to invest. Lots of untraceable cash on a daily basis.

By four that afternoon the place was less than half full with only a couple of them being locals as the location also attracted a good many tourists. Gino came across the floor and took a seat next to Lucky who, as always, sat facing the dining room.

"What's the word Boss?" Gino set his cappuccino on the table.

"The little lady's out shopping, we had our afternoon walk and now I'm just sitting here reminiscing."

"About?"

"Same old, same old. New York, the old life." Lucky shrugged.

"You built a pretty good set up here." Gino commented as he casually sipped his coffee. "I mean, it ain't Angelo's, but then again this ain't Mulberry Street either."

Luciano smirked as he glanced through the front picture window out into the Mediterranean.

"I suppose I can't complain. This time last year I was coolin' my heels in the can. So, all things considered . . ." He let the thought hang as he fed bit of cannoli to Bambi.

A group of American sailors in their dress blues, a small gaggle of young Italian girls in tow, piled through the front door and scrambled over to the bar on the opposite side of the room.

As if to reinforce Luciano's melancholic nostalgia a smile crept across his face as he watched them.

He was snapped out of his stupor when he heard one of the sailors say his name. He looked up to see the half dozen swabbies drifting over to his table.

"Excuse me, Mr. Luciano."

"Yeah son, what can I do for you?" Lucky asked. The sailor extended his hand.

"My name is Petty Officer Cavallo. My mother lives in Manhattan now but she's originally from Palermo."

"Beautiful city Palermo. Lived there myself for a little while."

"Our ship's up in Rome but we came down here for a couple days R&R."

"You fellas see any action during the war?"

"Quite a bit sir. We were all stationed on board a tin can, I mean a destroyer during Normandy, all except Jojo here. He was hit at Anzio."

Lucky glanced over at the blond haired sailor barely out of his teens. The kid had a partially healed over scar across his right cheek and two rows of ribbons on his chest. Lucky smiled at the kid.

"Got a couple of those myself." Pointing to his own scar he jokingly boasted.

Luciano was comforted by the American accents and the chance to engage in conversation with guys from what he considered his real homeland.

"Mr. Luciano, can I ask you a question?"

"Call me Lucky, son. All my friends do."

"Can I get your autograph?"

Over the shoulder of one of the sailors Gino noticed a well-dressed stranger in a black fedora standing just inside the vestibule perusing the place. With his foot he tapped Luciano's and nodded towards the front door. Lucky looked over and responded with barely perceptible nod.

"Sure, why not? You got a pen?" Luciano asked. The sailor fished a pen out from under his black silk neckerchief and passed it to Lucky.

The stranger spotted Luciano and Gino and with his hands in plain sight slowly made his way over and took a seat off to the side.

Lucky grabbed several small beverage menus, signed them and passed them out to the navy men.

"You fellas will have to excuse me. I got some stuff to take care of."

"Sure thing Mr. Luci- Lucky!" They shook hands and left.

"Gino, buy the guys a drink on me, will ya?"

"Sure boss." Gino understood that Lucky wanted to be alone with the visitor.

The stranger, whose face Luciano had seen before but couldn't remember where, didn't move to the table but brushed by it and surreptitiously slid a sealed envelope across the table top to Luciano as he passed by.

He watched the stranger head for the door and leave then opened the envelope which contained a simple note.

'Hotel Nacional December'

Charlie smiled and waved to Gino who was now over at the bar. Gino scurried back to the table.

"Gino, I need a favor." He tucked the note back into the envelope and stashed it in his breast pocket.

"Si Charlie?"

"I need some papers, visas. I'll need them for Cuba, Mexico and see what other South American countries require papers to travel through."

"Sure, I'll drive over to the embassy first thing Monday morning."

"And get them in the name of Lucania, not Luciano."

"Si Capo!"

Before leaving New York Lucky had given instructions to Meyer Lansky to pick a location and arrange for a meeting. But not just a meeting for a cup of coffee and some chit chat. A meeting of all the North American bosses, their Cuban associates and anyone else deemed necessary to bring to life a dream he had hatched back in Dannemora prison a decade ago while counting the hours.

With Lansky having established a firm foothold in Cuba, and their current venture in Vegas, he had toyed with the idea of an international drugs and gambling racket to surpass all national efforts in the U.S.

Luciano had decided it was time to go international.

So just as he had helped unite the New York Families, he would now attempt to unite all the major U.S. families. But first he would have to secure the loyalty of all the capos.

Such a substantial operation would of course require a head man. A head capo of all the head men.

A Capo di tutti capi.

Meanwhile the Sicilian Capo di Tutti, Don Carlo Vizzini, now Mayor of the strategically located, central city of Villalba in Sicily had helped Luciano set up the back-up operation to his restaurant, right there in Naples.

The operation? Tomato canning. Their primary export destination? The United States. Only the tomato cans weren't all filled with tomatoes.

The shipments from Turkey and Afghanistan were flowing on a regular basis providing even enough excess revenue to pay the provincial governor and his staff more than did their state wages.

Having set up the preliminary steps for an international drug operation back 1944 only months after the Allies liberated Sicily, Luciano had plugged into Vizzini's enterprise, and now in conjunction with Luciano's was, four short years later, taking in just short of a half a million dollars a month. The poor chicken farmer from Villalba now ran or owned most of Sicily and his neighbor of three decades ago, Luciano, not only controlled powerful influence across the island and well up into Naples on the mainland, but across the sea to New York.

The Blue Swallow
Room 207

"Hey Doc, why's there all this wasted space on these pages? I mean you could write one'a these things with half the paper. Save money ya know?"

After narrowly escaping apprehension by the Warner Brothers security team Doc and Louie had headed straight back to the hotel room with Benny's script to see if they could try and decipher any clues or connections to Joules' death. A death they were by now convinced was not suicide.

Having arrived back in the room just after lunch time they read through the script halves, switched texts then read though again.

Louie lay comfortably on his bed while Doc sat at the one seated desk across the room, each perusing half of the script.

"The formatting has to be very specific. It's meant to make it easier to read for the actors as well as the director and support people. Plus everybody's got to have room to write their notes about how they want to change everything. Nobody ever takes movie scripts as written."

"Why not?'

"The movie business is all about egos so everybody's wants to inject their idea of the best way to do something."

"Which explains why it takes so long and costs so much to make movies?"

"Like I said Louie, those night courses are paying off."

After removing the binder pins Doc had given Louie the first fifty pages of the manuscript to peruse while he took the last half and casually read.

"We could write one'a these!" Mancino bragged.

"By 'we' you mean 'me'?"

"Well yeah, but-"

"Just read okay."

"Read, read, read! Now we're fucking librarians!" Mancino quietly complained as he rolled over and read.

A mere ten minutes later and Mancino was again distracted.

"Doc, how come all the pages have this blue tint to them?"

"Because they've been mimeographed." McKeowen answered with thinly restrained patience.

"Oh, yeah. I knew that." Louie boasted. "What's this little mark mean?"

Doc dropped his head on the desk. "What little mark?!"

"This little mark they make across the letter Z all the time."

"Lemme see that." Louie brought his pages over to Doc and pointed out the mark.

"That's not a mark. It's a chip in the middle of the typewriter key. It must have been an older typewriter the original script was written on. The mimeo picked it up when they ran the copies."

"That would be Benny's typewriter, no?"

"Yeah that's right."

"That's incontinent."

"What?!"

"Incontinent. You know like doesn't make any sense."

"Inconsistent ya dope! Didn't you ever go to school stupid?!"

"Yeah! And I came out the same way. But that still don't make no sense."

"How does what not make any sense?"

"Benny's typewriter was less than a year old, if his girl was giving us the straight skinny."

"Okay, explain." Doc's curiosity was aroused.

"Nina told us Benny bought his typing machine just after he quit NYU."

"Columbia."

"Yeah, Columbia, That's what I said. That was just last year which means his typewriter, a Capital I think."

"It was an Underwood." Doc again corrected.

"Yeah, an Underwood that was only about a year old. And given that he was in such an all fired fit about not being a lawyer and wanting to be a writer, my guess is he took care of that machine like I know Doris is gonna be a pain in my ass about when she drops our little mud skipper."

"Your what?!"

"Mud skipper. Drops our rug rat, pops out our crumb snatcher, our curtain climber. Ha un nostro bambino!" Louie shrugged. "I been reading up on babies."

"Oh. And I thought you had a limited vocabulary! You might have something to look into. Make a note for me to speak to Nina when we get back home to Christopher Street."

"Will do."

"Louie, take this pad and annotate the major characters, who they are and what they do."

"You mean write down who's who?"

"Exactly. I'll do the same and we'll compare."

"I gotta tell ya Doc, this story's pretty boring. There's no gun fights, to chase scene, no explosions. I don't see how they were gonna make a movie out'a this anybody'd wanna go see!"

"It's not meant to be an action movie. It's a critique of the post-war political landscape in America and the fractionalization of society."

"Ya mean like the price of war?"

"Very good. See, you were right." McKeowen encouraged.

"About what?"

306

Paddy Kelly

"You're not as dumb as you look."

"That ain't nice Doc!"

"Read."

By five o'clock they decided it was time to eat. By 'they' it's meant Louie, so they headed down to the restaurant, taking their notes with them.

By the end of dinner they had deduced a synopsis from the perspective of their murder case.

Essentially the storyline dealt with an ideological fanatic who forms a not so secret-public patriotic, pro-democracy organization which in reality is a front for an anti-Semitic hate group.

An honest senator, who just happens to be a Jew, discovers a plot to frame, through false testimony, a prominent Jewish leader due to arrive in the U S. to make a speech at the U.N.

This group's leader hopes that by discrediting the Jewish leader, funding for the new Jewish state, currently up for a vote in the United Nations, the money will evaporate and the proposed state of Israel will never come into existence.

"You remember a few months back a Gramercy area business man jumped out a window because of money problems?" Doc threw out. "Wasn't he Jewish?"

"I think so yeah. Epstein I think. Money problems."

"But it wasn't money problems. They later found out and reported that it was because he thought he was in trouble with the Federal Bureau of Narcotics."

"So we got a scandal." Mancino mumbled around a mouthful of breadstick. "Benny was a Jew. If this guy Epstein was Jew and he was murdered there could be a connection." Louie proposed. Doc sat back and stared.

"You think there's a doubt that a guy named Saul Epstein was a Jew?" McKeowen challenged.

"I don't know! Maybe he converted from something."

"You can't convert from what you're born! You can't change you're heritage!"

"I dunno, I bet there's a politician somewhere that'd try to lie about their heritage if they thought they'd get something out of it!"

"You're probably right, but, let's stay on track. So, we've got a potential scandal and let's assume Epstein's a factor. We still need a bad guy, an organization and an M.O. if we think there's a connection to the script."

"So are we now going on the premise that Benny's script had something to do with his death?"

"I don't know. Let's finish building a picture and we'll see."

"So what's next Chief?"

"Well, we already hit the agent and-"

"Tits on a bull!" Louie opined.

"Exactly. We got the script and given that the kid never really ever came out here I don't see that there's a whole helluv'a lot more that we can discover here."

"Okay, agreed. So what's next?"

308

"We get a good night's sleep and tomorrow we up stakes and head east."

"Thank God! Hollywood's a great place to visit but I miss New York."

"We're not going to New York we're going to Chicago."

"Aw DOC! I don't wanna go to Chicago!"

"Why not?"

"It's cold, it's windy, the pizza is shit!"

"What's wrong with the pizza?"

"The slices are a foot thick, the crust looks like somebody bent a small water pipe into a circle and the sauce tastes like ketchup!"

"That all? You ever actually been to Chicago?"

"Well no but . . ."

"Okay, here's your chance. I'm going down to the desk and get us a train schedule. We leave first thing in the morning."

"I'll come with."

Down stairs at the hotel reception desk Doc and Louie waited while the concierge referenced a time schedule from Southern Pacific.

"Mr. McKeowen, there are two trains a day leaving from Union Station. One at six in the morning and one at five-thirty in the evening. Both offer free dinner on the day of departure."

"When do we arrive in Chicago?"

"If you depart here in the morning you are scheduled to arrive at Union Station on Canal Street at seven a.m. on Wednesday."

"Monday at six a.m. until Wednesday at around six p.m.! Sixty hours?! Jesus!" Doc declared.

"Not counting stop overs. Yes sir." He confirmed.

"It's faster than when we come here Doc."

"Well sir, there's an express train the Zephyr Flyer. It's a little more expensive but-." The man offered.

"How long's that take?" Doc pushed.

"Only forty-eight hours!" He beamed.

"Why-in-the-hell did I take this freakin' case?!" McKeowen moaned as he drifted away from the desk and plopped down in an overstuffed lounge chair.

"There is one other alternative Mr. McKeowen."

"What grow wings and fly?"

"Not exactly sir. You could take the new plane service offered by Pan Am. There are three flights a day, it's the same cost as the Union Pacific Flyer and they get you there in six to seven hours."

"WOW, six hours!" Mancino exclaimed. "Not bad, hey Doc?" Louie tapped Doc on the back who was no bent over with his in is hands.

"Planes? I dunno Louie."

"He don't like flying!" Louie informed the clerk. "Do they serve whiskey?" Mancino inquired.

"Drinks are available on all cross country flights sir." She answered.

"Hear that Doc?! Drinks are available on all cross country flights!"

Doc slowly fell back in the big, overstuffed chair and looked up at Louie and the desk clerk.

"Then I guess we're going up in an airplane." McKeowen reluctantly acknowledged.

Ten the next morning found the guys at the check-out desk of the hotel.

"What's the best way to the airport?" Doc asked the elderly male clerk.

"Depends on which airport ya want, You want THE airport or one'a the airfields? We got half a dozen of 'em."

"The L.A. airport."

"Ain't the L.A. Airport no more. Got a new name now!" He answered with all the pride of someone who built the place himself. "Called L.A.X., now!"

"What's the 'X' stand for?" Louie ventured.

"Got me son. Maybe somebody thought it was kind'a mode-ern."

"Okay, what's the best way to the L.A.X. airport?" Doc pushed.

"Southeast along Echo Park to Chinatown pick up the 110 though south of the city to the 105 then straight west."

"We're not driving. How long by bus to the L.A.X. airport?" Mancino asked.

"Pending on traffic, about thirty-five to forty-five minutes."

"What's traffic like this time of day?" Doc asked.

"Same as it is most other times of day." The clerk dryly answered. "Shit."

"Good to know."

Thirty minutes later they were aboard the city shuttle heading south.

For the second time in three blocks Louie glanced around and peered out the rear window. Three cars back the late model car was still there and quickly swerved back into the right hand lane in an apparent attempt to duck out of sight.

"Hey Doc, ain't that that Plymouth was in the Hotel parking lot when we left?"

"Two guys, black sedan dark suits, one in a light grey fedora?" Doc replied without turning around.

"Yeah. Who ya suppose they are?"

"Not a clue my cuisine challenged partner but we're gonna find out. Come on, we're getting off. Don't look back"

"I don't like the sound of this. Couldn't we just lose them instead?"

"I'm not as interested in losing them as I am in finding out who the hell they are."

McKeowen headed for the front of the bus with Louie close behind. "Make like you're sick." He quietly instructed over his shoulder. Louie ticked on, grabbed his stomach and began to quietly moan.

"Driver, I need you to pull over to the nearest phone booth."

"Sorry Mac, I'm not supposed to stop."

"We have an emergency."

Mancino stepped up the moaning and fell back into a side seat.

"What's the matter, he drink too much?" The driver probed.

312

"We're from back east. Too many burritos and beans for breakfast. Unless you want the floor of your bus redecorated I suggest you let us off."

"There's a drug store with a phone just after the cross-over. I'll let you off there."

"Thank you.

The driver pulled over and as he did the sedan was forced to change lanes and navigate around the bus. Doc surreptitiously watched as the car drove off.

"I didn't know any better I'd swear that was a government car." McKeowen observed.

The driver deposited the two with their bags outside a row of stores.

"Why would the Feds be tailing us?" Louie asked.

"Maybe just coincidence. Your guess is as good as mine brother. Mistaken identity, maybe connected to the people who wasted Joules. Maybe they're just a couple of bored cops. Let's go." Doc led the way across the street and under the highway.

"Where to?"

"Chinatown's just a few blocks over, we'll lay low over there for a little while, with any luck they won't realize we got off until they reach the airport.

As they rounded the corner and came off Broadway, passed under the decorative Chinese arch and onto Central Plaza the acrid-sweet aroma of ginseng immediately permeated the air.

Unlike the Chinatown of New York, the largest in the country comprising over half the combined total of the top ten such enclaves in the United

States, the Chinatown district of L.A. is marked by wide open, sunlit streets and is in direct contrast to the pedestrian packed, winding, narrow streets of Manhattan.

They walked for a short bit heading for the narrow streets and alleys off the main thoroughfare to maintain as low a profile as possible.

"You suppose they got one of these in China?" Louie asked gazing around.

"There's probably no Chinatown in Peking. But there are a bunch of them all over the world. There's even one in Deadwood, South Dakota."

"Huh, Deadwood. Must be where they make all the chopsticks!"

"You're damaged."

Doc ducked into a small souvenir shop off the plaza to buy a local map while Louie wandered across the road to the Seven Star Cavern Wishing Well across from the forbidden palace Restaurant.

When Doc emerged a few minutes later and headed across to his partner he happened to look up and spotted two suspicious guys in dark suits, about one hundred yards away casually walking towards him and Louie. He nudged Mancino.

"You ever heard of any tourists that go sightseeing dressed in three piece suits, neck ties and hats in ninety-five degree heat?"

As Louie glanced over the two men slowed their pace and meandered off to window browse.

"Well, I'd say we can rule out coincidence!" Mancino observed.

314

"Give a ten count then follow me back into that little shop. There's a back door. Maybe we can turn the tables on these Hoovers."

Doc went back over and into the shop, Louie followed.

Inside Doc gestured Mancino forward through the narrow, over packed aisles to the back door leading to the cramped stock room.

"Now what?" Louie blurted. The fire door to the back alley was chained over.

Back in the front of the shop the two suits burst through the front door.

Louie listened intently from the back room as Doc searched for a way out.

"Where's those two guys just came in here a minute ago?!" The big one demanded. The young guy behind the counter in the black cheongsam smiled and nodded.

"Most welcome to shop! How can help preese?!"

"Where's those two guys just came in here a minute ago?!" Thug #1 repeated.

"So sorry, no speakie English." The young traditionally dressed guy politely spewed. He plucked a small imitation Ming vase from a shelf. "You ryke? You rykie maybe? Buy girlfriend! She rykie bery much!"

At the same time Doc was helping Louie up an iron ladder and through the access hatch to the roof.

"Well we're not in Kansas anymore Dorothy!" Doc declared looking around.

"We're not gonna get far here on these roofs!" Mancino added.

They scanned around and unlike the flat-roofed tenements buildings of New York City, all the roofs there were heavily decorated pagoda style.

Downstairs the two heavies, after one look at the crate strewn stock room, had neglected to search it. Fortunately that meant they also hadn't seen the two small suitcases buried under the boxes of collapsible lanterns and paper figurines in the corner.

"Fuck this! Let's go. You check around back I'll go this way." The two suits split up.

Peering over the roof's ledge Doc watched as they lit off in different directions.

After the suits vacated his shop the young guy replaced the souvenir vase and stepped across the aisle.

"Okay guys, Coast is clear! The assholes are gone!" He yelled back into the stock room. "Guys?! Asshole-free zone!" There was no answer.

The young Asian smiled as a twenty dollar bill found its way into his wallet. "Uncle Wan always thinks he knows everything?! Well, he doesn't have to know about this!"

"Thank God that's over! That was a little close!" Louie declared as they made their way down via a rear fire escape which let out into the rear alley behind College Street.

"Not as close as it's gonna be!"

"Shit!" Mancino quietly declared as he realized it wasn't over.

"C'mon!" McKeowen ordered as he ran back out to the main street just in time to see the big suit, up the street on his left, rounding the corner and vanishing out onto the street.

"If we get separated, meet me back at the wishing well in thirty minutes! You got that?"

"If this is gonna become a foot race after that guy we're already separated!" Louie confessed. "I'll go back and get the bags, see you in half an hour."

Doc ran flat out until he reached the corner where the suit had turned and was able to see the stranger casually walking down the sidewalk, apparently having given up the hunt.

Dodging traffic he dashed across the street, flagged a taxi and hopped in.

"Where to?" the driver asked.

"I'm a cop, I'm following a guy. I need your help."

"No free lunches here Pal! Money talks."

"Drive." Doc ordered passing him a tenner.

"Where?"

"This is College Street yes?"

"Yeah, that's Yale. Next one over is Cleveland, leads down to Alpine."

"Okay, go over to Cleveland, make a left and head south."

Doc's hunch paid off. The suit had just reached the corner and ducked into a store.

Doc hopped out of the cab. The driver called after him.

"I know that store. There's no back way out. Ya got him corned. But watch out for Chun's wife!" The cabbie warned before driving off.

Doc entered the store with caution and spotted the big suit in the back at the soft drinks cooler.

"Hey, asshole!" He called. The suit slowly turned and McKeowen realized the man had a full foot over him. In height and width.

"You must be the one they call Doc!" He smirked.

"That's Mister Doc to you, Numbnuts! Who the hell are you and what'a want?!"

"What'a your connection with Steadman?"

"Never heard of him!"

"Don't bullshit me, Doc!"

"I told you Dickhead, my name is-"

Just as Doc moved towards him both men's attention were distracted by the cocking of a gun off to their side.

They turned to see a short middle-aged Asian woman with a double barreled Remington leveled at them.

"You two gwai lo, go now!"

"As Doc smiled, hands raised and looked down at the weapon the suit slammed into him punching him in the jaw and into a pile of canned soups and made a dash for the front door disappearing out onto the street.

McKeowen looked up from the pile of soup on the floor at the woman shaking her head, profusely cursing in Mandarin as she walked away.

Fifteen minutes later he met back up with Louie.

"You catch up to him?"

"Yeah, yeah I did."

"What'd you find out?"

318

"He fights like a J. Edgar!" He said wiping a drizzle of blood from his lip.

"How's that?"

"Like a pussy! Hits like a girl and runs when he's chased." Doc replied.

"C'mon, we can still catch the afternoon flight to O'Hare." They set out to find a taxi or bus stop.

"Hey Doc, the next plane ain't for nearly four hours. Ya think we could-"

Doc stopped and stared at Louie staring at Wong's Lucky Mu Shu Palace on the other side of the street.

"Alright let's go!" They headed into the restaurant. "But you're payin'!"

"Could be worse."

"How ya figure that?"

"They could'a been Treasury Agents."

"So who the hell exactly are these Sons of Liberty guys?"

"A group of do-gooders up in Chicago. They flavor people with Red sauce then feed 'em to Congress."

"Nice guys."

"A few guys with the same mentality tried it back in '39 and again in '40 and went after the movie moguls through the big producers."

"What happened?"

"Jack Warner got Al Smith for a defense council and between them, they made the Boys on the Hill look pretty stupid."

"You think they're gonna try and pull something like that again?"

"Not sure, but if the Boys on The Hill do, they sure as hell won't make the same mistake twice."

CHAPTER XIV

Doc glanced down at his watch as he and Louie stepped off the Pan Am DC3 onto the air stairs and into a breezy but not cold Chicago evening. It was six fifteen.

"Doc I'm still pretty concerned about those two thugs back in L.A."

"Relax, that was in L.A. We shouldn't have any trouble here. We'll find this guy Steadman or one of the construction companies Margold mentioned to us and take it from there."

"Steadman who is . . . ?"

"No idea. That's the name Asshole #1 threw at me back in that store. If we can find him we ask him if knows anything about Benny."

"Probably not."

"No, probably not."

"Then what?" Louie pushed.

"Then we go home."

"I like the sound of that!"

They walked across the tarmac into the terminal and waited at the baggage claim.

"Once we get into the city you go over to the Proxy and check us in."

"Where you going?"

"See if I can find a listing in the Yellow Pages for a Steadman or anything on a construction company that might do movie contracts. Then I'll have a walk around get the lay of the city. I'll meet you at the hotel by eight or nine the latest."

They hopped a cab and made their way south into the city.

The Proxy Arms on West Adams, was one of the many themed hotels that had popped up during the war and was located a couple of miles west of the downtown area less than an hour away from the airport with traffic and so following dinner and a few more drinks they left a nine o'clock wake-up call and headed out again the next morning.

"Well where to start?" Louie probed as they stepped through the revolving door into the glare of the humid morning.

"The library. Business Directory."

An hour later, construction company list and hotel map in hand they had flagged down a taxi outside the Carnegie Library on Washington Boulevard.

"Where to fellas?" The driver finally asked.

"We're in from Hollywood and we're looking for a construction company to do some sets for a film."

"Movie men huh?! Any parts for a moderately good looking, semi-middle-aged taxi driver?" The driver joked brushing back what little of his salt and pepper hair remained.

"Ya never know pal! What's your name?" Doc asked.

"Jimmy, Jimmy Balduci." Over the seat they shook hands.

"Glad to meet you Jimmy. Mr. Smith and this is Mr. Ravioli."

"Really? Ravioli! I bet you get a good ribbing about that, hey?" Jimmy laughed. Mancino curtly nodded.

"All the construction companies are down on the south side or west of here." Jimmy informed.

A block away he pulled over to a bright yellow, road side phone box planted around the city for those cabs not yet equipped with the new two-way radio the police had had since the beginning of the war, He dialed up the dispatch office.

"Rose, its Jimmy. Do me a favor love, ring Spiro and ask him where was that construction company he was shuttling them Hollywood producers back and forth from a few months ago when they was in town to make that movie. Yeah that's the one. I'll hold"

There was a short pause and the dispatcher came back on the line.

"You sure? Okay Doll! Thanks." Jimmy happily signed off and climbed back into the cab.

"Got it boys! It's United Engineering and Construction out in Oak Park. About a twenty minutes from here."

As they entered the neighborhood Jimmy was again prone to commentary.

"This guy must have some serious contracts!"

"Why's that Jimmy?" Doc asked.

"Rents out here ain't in the Connecticut Avenue and Vermont neighborhoods. More like Boardwalk and Park Place!"

Doc and Louie exchanged glances.

Jimmy slowed the taxi as they approached the small cluster of buildings. The central structure, an oversized Quonset hut styled affair, was prominently labeled:

United Engineering & Const.
J. Steadman Pres.

"Youse want me to wait?"

"Yeah Jimmy, wait but don't drop us at the door. Drive around the back and wait there. We shouldn't be too long." Doc passed him a twenty as he stepped out of the cab.

"You got it Mr. Smith! Take your time, I'll turn the meter off."

Around the corner walking towards the main office entrance Louie couldn't contain himself.

"Seriously? Mr. Ravioli?! That's what you come up with?"

"Hey, it was short notice. Next time you get to lie to people about who we're not. Deal?"

"Deal!"

As they stepped through the front door the rough unfinished exterior below the twenty foot sign board betrayed the stunning eloquence of the interior of the main office and reception area.

A fashionably dressed, dedicated receptionist was seated behind a black walnut and Canadian maple, Art Deco desk which led to similar décor throughout the wide office area partitioned off by a waist high, long service counter and ten feet behind that a floor-to-ceiling plasterboard wall finished with an over-sized mural of the building of the 1869 Chicago Water Tower separated the office area from the warehouse proper.

Doc inadvertently stared at the professionally rendered, full length wall mural.

The half dozen office workers, all well-dressed women, busily scurried, typed or filed away as the two P.I.'s entered and were cordially greeted.

"Good morning gentlemen! How may I be of assistance today?" The pert little brunette offered.

"We're here to speak with a Mr. J. Steadman."

"Please have a seat while I buzz him. May I offer you a cappuccino, espresso or a latte while you wait?"

"A latte?" Louie queried. "What's a latte?"

"It's a coffee made with espresso and steamed milk sir."

"That sounds lovely! I'll have one of those." Louie complimented.

"For you sir?"

"Uh, nothing thank you." McKeowen declined.

The girl bounced from her desk and disappeared behind the other end of the counter.

Doc frowned at his partner.

"I never heard of a late tea! It sounds good!" Louie defended.

"Get your game face on!" Doc quietly admonished.

Suddenly the young girl reappeared.

"I almost forgot. Who shall I say is calling?"

"Mr. Smith and Mr. Tagliatelli of Republic Pictures."

She again vanished. Louie leaned over to Doc.

"It still ain't funny Doc!" Louie whispered back.

Minutes later yet another well-dressed employee appeared, this one a thirty-something man who apparently just stepped off the cover of a Charles Atlas magazine ad.

"The Director will see you now." As they made their way off to the right towards the office door Doc was compelled to ask.

"Is that an original Diego Rivera?" McKeowen barley suppressed his shock at seeing the signature at the base of the large oil painting.

"What do you think Mr. Smith?" Steadman's assistant proudly boasted.

One of the women behind the counter made eye contact with Doc and shook her head no.

In the middle of a meticulously arranged and appointed office complete with imitation busts, paintings and antique artifacts sat a dark oak, Brobdingnagian desk behind which sat Joshua Steadman. He stood as they entered.

"What can I do for you two gentlemen today?"

"May I introduce ourselves? I am Mr. Smith and this is my boss a Mr. Tagliatelli. He speaks very little English." Doc quickly added. Louie nodded and smiled. "We represent Republic Pictures."

"Howard Hughes' set up?" Steadman coyly confirmed.

"That's right. We understand that you are available for movie set construction?"

326

"Well that all depends." Steadman replied.

"On what exactly?"

"On exactly how big the pay check is. I mean the story requirements of course." Steadman laughed as he gestured for them to sit.

"Oh budget's not a concern Mr. Steadman. Mr. Hughes is adamant that this picture be first class all the way. Some big names lined up to appear in this one."

"Like who?" Jake pushed.

Just then Brasi Sollozo stepped out from the rear of the warehouse into the front area wiping his hands with a cloth when, through the office window he noticed the pow wow in the office and drifted in.

"We have it through the grapevine that you were in line to do a low budget feature a few months back and got bumped form the project."

"I wouldn't call ten million a low budget and we didn't get bumped. Warner Brothers pulled the plug on the whole thing. At least that's the story they gave us."

"Just pulled it?! Did they give you a reason at least?"

"Said one of the producers had some personal issues."

"That's too bad. It could have gone a long way to promote your business."

"It was a tough break but my business is doing very well."

To keep up appearances Doc spoke a few cursory words in Italian to Louie. Though not as fluent as Mancino Doc did a convincing job.

Neither of the two detectives could know Jake Steadman's drug sideline was what he meant by his business doing very well.

With the war contracts a thing of the past a mild economic depression had set in across the country and construction in Chicago, though not halted, had slowed significantly.

"So what is the title of your project and what sort of budget are we talking Mr. Smith?"

Louie's latte arrived and the receptionist set it on the table between the two cops.

"It's called *The Thin Man in Chicago*, a police drama. But that's a temporary title. The budget currently stands at seven million but these things inevitably run over so . . ."

"So sometimes there's a few extra perks?" Steadman nodded knowingly.

"Your words J.S., not mine, your words!" Doc laughed along with Steadman. Louie played it well pretending to be lost.

Just then Brasi let himself into the office and quietly stood off to the side.

"Lui capisce, lui capisce!" Doc explained queuing Mancino to laugh.

"What is your studio's schedule for this project Mr. Smith.?"

"A release date hasn't been set yet but we're tentatively hoping for late spring of '48. Principle photography to start in three to four months."

"I'm pretty sure we can accommodate your requirements."

Doc stood and offered his hand. Louie followed suite.

"Pleasure meeting you Mr. Steadman. I'll have the studio deliver you a copy of the script so you can work out a budget and when you're ready you can contact me through the studios. Meanwhile I'll set up a meeting with your man and my second unit producer."

The same male assistant led them back out to the front door and thanked them for coming.

Back in the office Brasi spoke first.

"You buy them being movie producers?"

Steadman folded his arms as he sat back on the edge of his desk.

"Get serious and think white! I was born during the day but it wasn't yesterday. That ass hat must think we don't have newspapers up here!"

"What'a ya mean?" Brasi asked.

"If they're big shot movie producers how come he didn't give me a card? And what's with all the Italian bullshit?! No picture company in the world would travel halfway across the country and pay to build sets. They use what they call 'availables'."

"Sounds like you learned something from them Warner Brother guys when they was here."

"Yeah, maybe." Steadman went back around behind his desk.

"So who are they?"

"Come on! They try to dress like regular guys, the one doing all the talking speaks with a West Side accent and they just happen to pick **my** company to show up at? And that little guy couldn't look any more like a fucking torpedo if he tried!"

"I still don't follow Jake."

"They speak Italian that's not a hint to you?!"

"So?"

"They're from the New York mob!"

"Shit!"

"Those are the two bozos that hit that grifter from L.A back a few years ago over on the south side, I'll bet money on it!"

"I remember that. Was in all the papers. You don't think they're here about Epstein?"

"Nah! The NYPD closed that off as a suicide. They're poking around after something else."

"Like what?"

"Don't know but if they're from New York those fucks the Manganos must have sent them in."

"You think?"

"They're getting ready to pull something! I can feel it!"

"What'a ya wanna do? Ya want me to take care of them?"

"Yeah! That's all we need to do, start a fucking war between the Manganos in Chicago and New York! No asshole, just follow them and get back to me."

"Okay."

"Don't go near them! You got that?"

Yeah, yeah. How?"

"Take the Indian and tail them, find out where they're staying and if possible how long they'll be in town."

"I'll call you soon as I find out." Sollozo said as he headed out back of the warehouse.

He caught them just as they reached Jimmy's cab and got in. He waited as they seemed to have a short chat in the taxi then mounted the motorcycle and slowly pulled out the back gate after them.

Out in the taxi the guys conferred.

"What'a you think?" Doc asked Louie.

"One word. Class, with a capital K!"

"If he's dirty he puts up a good front."

"You trust his story about the movie contract?" Louie queried.

"Yeah, yeah I trust him. About as far as I can throw him."

"If you guys are talking about Jake Steadman I'd tread cautiously." Jimmy the cabbie warned.

"How do you mean?" Doc asked.

"Word has it Steadman's connected and I don't mean he's got extra phone extensions in his house!"

"Appreciate the heads up Jimmy."

"What'a ya make of the gorilla listening in?" Louie asked Doc.

"Don't know who he is, maybe Italian, but whoever he is he was listening in a little too intently."

"He's Corsican." Louie stated.

"How do you know?" Doc probed.

"I can smell him."

"The thing that smells fishy to me is Steadman never bothered to introduce the guy."

"And he didn't introduce himself." Mancino added.

With Sollozo at a discrete distance behind they took the cab back to the city and looked for a diner.

Shortly after McKeowen and Mancino's taxi pulled away from the back of the warehouse with Brasi tailing them a couple of pugnacious individuals appeared from a repair garage across the street and made their way over to Steadman's office.

They breezed past the receptionist who mounted no protest but they politely knocked on Steadman's office door before letting themselves in. The visit was obviously unexpected.

"Jack, long time no see!" The smaller of the two greeted. Steadman took the man's animated salutation as a warning and was momentarily on his back foot but decided best to play it cool.

"Hello John."

"Word has it Jake you had some visitors."

John took a seat directly in front of the desk. The big guy took up station across the room in front of the door and stood there holding a tan leather briefcase.

"Jealous I'm seeing other people John Boy?"

"Don't get smart ya prick!"

"Relax, couple of movie producers wanting to talk about us building some sets, that's all."

"Wow, movies! Big bread there, no?"

"You know my philosophy John, there ain't no money until there's money."

"Good spiritual philosophy Jake. Speaking of which, that's what I'm here about. More money."

Steadman suddenly grew angry.

332

"This recession ain't my fault and I ain't about to lower my take!"

"Relax Action Jackson! Relax!" John produced a small pocket knife and proceeded to methodically clean his nails. "What's with all the bad vibes? I'm talking about more money for you brother!"

From experience Steadman greeted the words with a healthy dose of suspicion.

"And?" Jake pushed to terminate the conversation as soon as possible. He John had history and it wasn't good.

"The situation is this: the Big Guys have come into a bit of a new transport and delivery system."

"What's that got'a do with me?"

"Well, with this new system we're able to bring in ten times the amount of product previous. We simply need you to store and move a bit more product."

"Move?! I don't move nothing! Your mules drop it here, I store it and your delivery boys come and get it. That's it, nice and simple. I'm in the construction business, not the delivery service. And I'm damn sure not interested in moving any scag for anybody!"

"Jakey Baby! Isn't that what relationships are all about? You do for us we do for you?"

Steadman sat forward in his seat and leaned on his desk.

"John, let me be clear. We're are not a married couple, we are not lovers and we are not a couple of high school kids dating. You had a body you had to make disappear. That body is now and forever more acting as concrete aggregate in the foundation of a south side car dealership. Now for few grand a week I hold some packages for you. That's it. An arrangement that started off as a one-time deal which is now going on since the end of the war."

"Not enough bread Jakey Baby, that what all the negative energy is about?"

"The money's –" Steadman was cut short as John signaled his large sidekick who stepped forward and tossed the tan leather satchel on the desk. Two dozen bank sealed stacks of hundreds spilled out. Steadman's mouth closed up. The two thugs exchanged smiles.

"If this is turning into a going concern I want my share of product as well!" Steadman softly said.

"As far as those decisions are concerned brother, it's not up to the Manganos. New York is bringing it in. That's where the big Daddies are!"

"Glad to see our ying is in synch with your yang, brother." John stood, he and his torpedo made for the door.

"What the hell you talking about?"

"Our karma is once again in coordination Daddy-O! Don't you feel better? I do." He and the heavy stepped to the door. "First delivery is due in next week. They'll be no call ahead but expect a truck from Ajax Lumber. Love to the wife and kid."

Steadman assumed an uneasy smile as he stared down at the $240,000 splashed across his desk.

With more mixed emotions then he felt the day he lost his virginity, he re-bagged the cash and reached for his intercom.

"Jan, book me a round trip flight to New York and a hotel room for next week."

How many nights Mr. Steadman?

"One or two. I shouldn't be down there too long."

Will do sir.

Sitting at a Woolworth's lunch counter down town on Pacific Avenue Doc and Louie were just finishing off a couple of hamburgers.

"Why you smiling? We didn't get squat out'a that guy!" Mancino challenged.

"Actually we did detective Mancino, we did."

"Like what?" Mancino asked as he took the full plate of French fries and placed it on top of the empty plate he had just finished off.

"When I tell you, drop your spoon and when you bend over to pick it up look across the street into that pharmacy window."

Louie purposely dropped his spoon and glanced straight across the street. He spotted Brasi drinking a glass of beer and trying not to be too obvious as he was obviously and intermittently stealing a glance over at the restaurant.

"We got the fact that we made him as a suspect." Doc smiled.

The Broad in the Kimono

Office of the Editor-in-Chief
The Hollywood Reporter
Wilshire Boulevard, L.A.

Wilkinson collected his hat and coat and headed out.

"Betty, I'll be out for the rest of the day. I'll call ya before five to collect my messages." Wilkinson instructed as he breezed through the reception area where Betty, his secretary, was chatting with the receptionist as she was sorting through the morning mail. He was out the door before they could look up.

"Got'a catch that 11:30 race!" Betty whispered to her co-worker.

"How can people drink and gamble so early in the day?" The young receptionist inquired. The lithe young blond was the third in two weeks.

"Compensation for something!" Betty quipped.

"Like what?"

"Never mind! I'll be leaving after lunch as well. You gonna be okay on your own?"

"But what if Mr. Wilkinson calls in and asks for you?"

"He has no intention of 'calling in'! He'll get his messages tomorrow. He just pulls that malarkey to try to keep me here till five." Betty explained as she headed back to her desk down the hall.

"But what do I do if there's an emergency?"

"Simple! If there's a fire call the fire department, grab your stuff and get out. If it's a hold up give

336

them your typewriter and the petty cash jar and if it's the cops just tell them you don't know nuthin'!"

Wilkinson not only made it out to Santa Anita race track for the 11:30 post time but also for the 12:15, the 1:10, the 2:40 and the 3:20 post times as well.

By 3:30 that afternoon William R. Wilkinson was up by more than $5,000 cash and figured it was time to go home.

The elderly Negro steward out in the betting area stopped sweeping and leaned forward on his push broom.

"Good day Mr. Wilkinson?"

"Good doesn't even begin to describe it James!" Billy passed the man a fiver as he swept by on his way out to the parking lot.

"Thank you suh!" The janitor snapped the bill between his hands.

"You're most welcome James, most welcome!"

With the Vegas property soon to be under clear contract, building already underway and no bumps in the immediate road ahead, Billy congratulated himself on his newly discovered winning streak.

He had no pressing business in L.A. for the next few days so he decided to turn back northeast and take a weekend drive out to monitor progress on the Vegas building site.

On the way north along State Route 91 he stopped by Tony's Diner outside San Bernardino to get a burger and called into the office to tell Betty he wouldn't be in tomorrow and then he made himself a reservation at the Apache, a local landmark hotel, on Fremont Street.

The four and a half hour drive out through the desert was tedious and radio reception was sketchy but he occupied his mind with improving the plans for his grand casino.

Taking the time off for business was just a cover story, so flimsy a cover story in fact that he knew he'd need a cover story to cover the cover story. That's where his uncontrolled gambling addiction came in. His passion for the ponies worked out well to disguise his real motive; to drive out and see his dream casino now under construction in the middle of the Nevada desert near a town no one ever heard of.

A one-horse town called Las Vegas.

Billy Wilkinson pulled into the dusty little town around nine that night and reckoned he was too tired to go out to the site. Besides, it was too dark. A few drinks at the bar turned into a few more when he started to make some friends and just as he realized he was talking a bit too much he decided one more then went up to his room and fell into bed.

Next morning, after breakfast, which consisted of a fist full of Bayor aspirin washed down with a Brioschi, he drove the three miles out to the site and was pleased to see a hundred workmen crawling all over the large framed structure. Others were unloading lumber and roofing materials from a pair of open bed trucks and a handful of others were going in and out of the portable trailer serving as the on-site office.

Billy was headed to the office to check in with the foreman but was distracted by the three men out by the road erecting the 'Opening Soon' sign.

He walked out to the road about 300 yards away from the main building site and paused and turned back to look up at the 40 foot banner the workmen were nailing to the sturdy wooden frame facing the main road.

The Flamingo
New Luxury Casino!
Coming soon!

He could picture the finished interior. The grand lobby opening into the expansive gaming room. The poker and blackjack tables to one side divided by the double row of slot machines all garnished with tall slender models posing as serving girls bringing free drinks to the patrons.

But most of all he pictured the piles and piles of cash he was on the verge of rolling in.

"Mr. Wilkinson?"

His fantasies slowly evaporated when he turned to see a burly workman in clean work clothes standing next to him. It was the site foreman.

"Mr. Wilkinson?"

"Yeah Nick, what is it?"

"Mr. Wilkinson, can we talk?"

"Sure Nick!" Nick was the type of guy who only asked if he could talk with you when it wasn't the kind of news you were going to smile about after he talked to you about it.

"I got a call from Carson City this morning. At this rate sir . . . well sir to put it bluntly, unless there's a substantial transfer to the company's account by the end of next week, I'll have to lay the men off. I do that and they'll scatter to the four winds to find work elsewhere. We may wind up having to scrounge up a whole new crew and there's no telling how long that would take."

"SHIT!" Billy was immediately embarrassed by his overt display of temper. "Sorry Nick!" He patted the big man on the shoulder. Thanks, thanks for the update. I'll get it straightened out."

"Okay. Sorry about that Mr. Wilkinson."

"It's alright Nick, it's alright."

The sign hangers now gone he looked up at the banner again.

He noticed the upper left hand corner of the banner had come loose from the frame and was flapping in the breeze.

On the drive back to the hotel he wrestled with the offer Rothman had made back in June.

Rothman who had one toe in the big rackets on and off, seemingly since he was a teenager, had offered to set Wilkinson up with some backers. Billy had initially refused. But now the scenario had changed.

Billy had just decided to climb in bed with the big boys.

†

Paddy Kelly

Tail o' the Pup
La Cienega Boulevard, L.A.

Not wanting anyone to know what he was about to do, by even his trusted secretary, he waited until she was out of the office on an errand, closed over his office door and picked up his desk phone then dialed.

There were times when Wilkinson harbored doubts about what he was about to do even as he did it. Unfortunately for him this was not one of those times.

It was answered on the fourth ring.

"Abe it's Billy. You free for lunch?"

For you Billy boy, always. What's cookin'?

"Not on the phone. There's one of those new novelty places over on North La Cienega, in and about the three hundred block."

Name?

"Tail o' the Pup."

What's it a Korean joint? They serve dog?

"Only dogs are the gals you hang around with! Hot dogs ya dolt! Ya can't miss it. Be there at three."

Tail-O-The Pup was hard to miss. It was an actual enormous hot dog in a bun with a fast food kitchen carved out of it.

Wilkinson's choice of the small, out of the way Mimetic structure was reinforced by the fact that there were less than half a dozen tables scattered around the tiny hot dog stand but more than adequate parking so they took their order and retreated back to the cone of silence Wilkinson's car afforded.

"You remember back in July you offered to set me up with some people?"

"Yeah, I remember. You told me to fuck off!"

"Don't get dramatic! I said I'd call if I'm interested."

"So?"

"I'm interested."

"Now suddenly you're interested?"

"I'm not playing *Truth or Consequences*! Yes or no?!"

"Yeah, yeah. I can set something goin'. A meet at least. But I ain't guaranteein' nuthin!"

"I'm not askin' you for any guarantees. Just do what you can."

Rothman's façade of coyness was strategic. After securing Wilkinson's interest he was now free to negotiate terms from his mysterious backers. That is to say his guaranteed percentage of whatever deal the two parties agreed to with Rothman's cut coming out of both party's pockets. Only the money the 'other' party would fork over to Rothman as a 'finder's fee' would be added onto Wilkinson's percentage interest.

Known as the 'juice' Wilkinson would have no way to find out anything about the hidden fee and Rothman his 'friend', wasn't about to ever bring the matter up.

CHAPTER XV

FBO Studios were set up in 1928 by Joseph Kennedy Senior father of future president JFK, who partnered with the notorious gangster Frank 'The Enforcer' Nitti. This small studio would be parlayed into what became RKO, a brief but major player and was but a seed of the mobster-movie merger forest that continues to grow and flourish in the business to this day.

In the United States the time honred blend of mobsters and moguls forge d through manipulation and muscle may have its roots in the late Twenties when it comes to the movie industry with capos like Capone and Bugsy Siegel but it was in the Second World War years that it finally reached the White House.

FDR himself is known to have made several visits to Hot Springs, Arkansas ostensibly for bath treatments to ease his polio crippled legs but few knew The Springs was also a hot bed meeting please for the heavy hitters of crime such as Arnold Rothstein, Charlie Lucky Luciano, Meyer Lansky and others.

Negotiations between politicians and gangsters there-in did occur.

Realizing that he had to hedge his bets before the upcoming Congressional hearings scheduled to begin sometime in October, Jack Warner had begged off a party for Ronnie Regan who had just been elected President of the Screen Actors Guild. He bowed out of the soirée to fly to D.C. to meet with the president to discuss the state of the film industry but really about another major issue – the pending accusations of communism in Hollywood. More specifically, the possibility that the HUAC subcommittee, now headed by Thomas, might point the finger at him. Even after their prophylactic chat Warner knew better than to trust a politician, particularly a Jersey City Republican.

During the war FDR ordered that Warner be given the rank of a field grade officer in the army after Jack joined the movement to make anti-Nazi pictures, help the war bond drive and allow his theater venues to be used for rallies and drives.

"Loved your Bogart movie Mr. Warner, *Marked Woman*!" The President's secretary greeted Jack to the Oval Office. "It really captured the mood. I've seen it three times!"

"Thank you Rose I'll tell Bette and Bogart you said so. I'll have the studio mail you a signed lobby poster if you like."

"You certainly know how to score points, don't you?" Her desk intercom light blinked on. "He's ready for you now." They exchanged nods. "And Jack, twenty minutes!" She reminded.

"Yes Rose. Thank you Rose." He rendered a mock salute as he pushed through the door and discreetly slid the friendship ring he wore on his left hand before entering the Oval Office.

The friendship ring given him by a member of the Genovese crime family a few years back when he was dealing with the Mob over labor relations about the same time Bugsy Siegel was getting involved in picture business.

Warner spied the small stack of dailies piled on Truman's desk. 'DEWEY LIKELY TO CAPTURE 30 STATES' the top headline proclaimed.

"Jack, good to see you again." Truman came out from behind his desk and they shook.

"Same here Mr. President. Bess is well I trust?" By way of an answer the president reached over to his desk and lifted a brown bag. "Twenty-eight years, still packs me my lunch when I'm in town!"

"That's one helluv'a relationship you've got there Mr. President, I don't mind telling you."

"Going on three decades she's never even wavered." Never having done business with Truman Warner could read the underlying stress in the president's tone. Here was a man who was harried.

With the extremely popular New York governor Thomas Dewey expected to be the Republican presidential nominee next year and the GOP controlling both the House and the Senate, the Dems were buying Pepto Bismol by the crate.

Truman caught Warner eying the newspapers as they sat.

"Third time's a charm hey?" Truman joked of Dewey's last stab at the White House , a twinge of nervousness in the comment.

"I wouldn't be too concerned Mr. President, you're the incumbent and your record speaks for itself. Dewey's biggest claim to fame is convicting

Charlie Luciano only to later sign his release papers."

"You know I don't approve of the way Dewey won that trial, don't you? Don't get me wrong, Luciano needed to go away, but Dewey threatening witnesses was no way to try a case. We do that, makes us no better than the folks we're trying to put in jail!" Truman declared.

"I couldn't agree more sir. But Mr. President, I know you're time is valuable so I'll get to the point. This HUAC thing's got people out on the coast pretty keyed up sir."

"Communism should have everyone keyed up Jack! It's a dangerous road to put a country on!"

"Yes, I listened to your speech before the joint session a while ago. 'The Truman Doctrine', I like it, has a nice ring to it. And this –"

"Yes Acheson came up with it."

"Sir, I support rooting out the communist presence one hundred per cent but I'm concerned over the net effect this latest HUAC action may have on the industry."

"Jack, HUAC isn't out to destroy the pictures!"

"That's not what I'm getting at sir."

"So?"

"The Jewish angle could very well come up and . . . it could go either way."

"How do you mean?"

"Mr. President, we're less than two years off the bloodiest war this planet has ever seen. A war no small amount blame on the Jewish people. A war which started as the virtual world-wide purge of

Jews, the Holocaust, and now the with the Brits pulling out of the Jewish territories and five Arab nations preparing to invade which will no doubt be in the headlines for the rest of the year . . ."

"We're considering all our Mid-East options. What has that got to do with the moving pictures?" Truman protested.

"Everything sir. I lost one of my number one overseas producers before the war. Kicked and beaten to death by a bunch of Nazi thugs. Why? Because he was Jewish."

"Are you asking me to stop the HUAC investigations to protect the Jews in this country? You know I can't do that!"

"No sir, I'm not asking you to do that. But I am asking you to consider the fact that more than half the producers and others in Hollywood are Jews. You know from experience how the public react when something like this hits the headlines. Especially the way the Press twists things for the sake of sales and sensationalism! They'll write anything for a headline. Not to mention the more unsavory political elements who are only too happy to conflate the association of people they don't like with something the public are led to hate."

"What are you getting at Jack?"

"I'm asking you to not let this turn into a Jewish witch hunt."

Warner produced a folded over sheet of paper from his breast pocket and slid it across the desk. Truman opened it and read. It was a list of names.

"Just to help you and the committee to focus your work Mr. President."

The President quietly perused the list.

"Some of these people are quite well known!" Truman involuntarily declared. "You have evidence of the communistic activities of these people?"

"Well no, I don't have photos of them attending meetings or anything but they are quite loose with their talk sometimes."

While using his plea for protection of Jews, which was no doubt genuine, Warner gladly seized the opportunity to possibly eliminate a few of the 'troublemakers' in his studio. Since he couldn't do it by contract he'd root them out using the government. It was an old gangster ploy, let the authorities do your dirty work for you.

The meeting now over, mission accomplished, Warner flew up to New York where he had reserved a room to spend a few days before returning to L.A. Not knowing what to expect at the Waldorf meeting and knowing he could not fight a senate subpoena should one come, he was no longer concerned with the outcome of Eric Johnston's efforts. He had played his hand and positioned himself ahead of the curve come what may.

Thus the most miserable period in some people's lives, people such as John Garfield, Dalton Trumbo and many others had begun.

†

Paddy Kelly

Lobby of the Apache Hotel
Three miles from the
Flamingo Construction Site
Las Vegas, Nevada

Contrary to popular myth, Paradise, Las Vegas, Nevada wasn't just a desert wasteland.

The Hoover Dam project which employed up to twenty thousand workers from 1931 to 1936, all of whom descended on the desert town of Paradise, population five thousand, at the time, were instantly drawn to the local hot spot which was and remains the Apache Hotel and Casino.

Established in 1932 during the massive dam project when the town was flooded with thousands of workers, it was one of the cement contractors who shifted his profits into the hospitality trade to accommodate the sudden increase in human influx. It was the right call. He did quite well with it. The workers and most of the fly-by-night dance halls and bars are now all gone but The Apache remains.

With the first elevator in the territory and being the first fully carpeted hotel and casino in Vegas word spread quickly. From the day of opening the three story, eighty-one room hotel, the casino and bar had never wanted for business.

Not heading to his room Billy diverted to the desk to ask for an outside line than headed to the small bar room across the lobby.

By his second drink, only minutes later, a phone was brought to his table, plugged into the wall jack by his table and he placed his call.

"I'm out at the Apache."

Nice place. Billy, if this deal goes through what'a you offering? Rothman pushed from the other end.

"What'a ya want?" Fighting hard to maintain an artificial air of detachment Billy asked into the phone.

I'm not interested in money right now, I'm doing okay but I got'a think about my future, a time when I get-

"After we open I'll cut you in for two per cent for the first year, your own table and an extended credit limit when you're out there."

Straight five points off the back end once you open, expense paid weekend four times a year and extended credit limit.

"Three points off the back end once we open, expense paid weekend two times a year, extendable to guests plus extended credit limit. If your man comes through!"

He'll come through!

By three o'clock that afternoon articles had been agreed upon.

Although he marked the conversation down as another coup, Wilkinson didn't realize Rothman's man was Meyer Lansky, alias 'The Account', the money man for the New York mob. Someone who's reputation everyone, himself included, knew all too well.

And so it came to pass that Rothman, who always had one foot on the wrong side of the fence, sent word down the pike to New York, that there was a prime investment opportunity out in Vegas.

Preliminary inquiries were made and it was agreed that an emissary would be sent out to hold a meet. A date was set.

A week later Meyer 'The Accountant' Lansky smiled and nodded as he stepped out onto the Airstairs from the DC-3 which had just landed at the Los Angeles Municipal Airport. From across the tarmac standing outside a hired limo Benjamin 'Bugsy' Siegel smiled back.

"Hey Boss, I think our guests are here." Nick the foreman, who had been seated at the large plans table, nodded to the window. Wilkinson jumped off the love seat and parted the flimsy curtains.

A black Cadillac limo pulled up beside the trailer office and two men climbed out. The driver held the door for the older man. Both passengers wore light linen suits and fedoras.

Wilkinson burst out of the trailer and stood at the foot of the small stairs. He stepped forward to greet them.

"Mr. Lansky, first it's a real privilege to meet you and may I say I really appreciate your taking the trouble to come all the way out here and view my operation." They shook hands. Lansky nodded and smiled as he shook Wilkinson's hand.

The younger man with Lansky stood with his hands folded in front of him, crystal blue eyes staring past his greeter, ignoring Wilkinson's hand. Meyer Lansky spoke first.

"This is Mr. Benjamin Siegel. He has business experience plus connections in Hollywood. I hope you don't mind I asked him to come out."

"No, no! No problem at all."

"I'm sure, Mr. Wilkinson, you would never consider such a substantial investment without personally visiting the operation, seeing for yourself where your money, or the money of those who trust you is going to wind up?"

"No, no of course not! You're absolutely right Mr. Lansky. I wouldn't. I never did, I mean when I opened all those clubs along the Strip back in L.A.-"

"I understand you only invested in two clubs. You really didn't open anything yourself. That right?" It was the young man with the sleepy, crystal blue eyes that finally spoke.

"Well . . . no but it's the backing! The backing that matters. You know like in a film."

"How so?" Siegel pushed.

"Well, without the script there's no film, no story so the project can't go ahead." Siegel responded with a barely audible grunt. "Why don't I give you the tour and we can adjourn back to the Apache for lunch and discuss business?"

They started to make their way from the trailer over to the building site.

"I thought we'd have a walkthrough of the site then head over to the Apache Hotel and talk particulars." Wilkinson proposed.

"Actually Mr. Wilkinson-" Siegel added.

"Call me William please! My friends call me Billy!"

"Mr. Wilkinson," Lansky raised a hand to quiet Benny Siegel be taking over the conversation. "The fact that I came all the way out here is no guarantee we are willing to invest in your project. This is sort of a recognizance mission if you will. Although the mainstream media sells millions of papers flaunting my name as 'The Account', I have people I have to answer to just as you do. Do we understand each other?"

"Yes Mr. Lansky. Perfectly."

Lansky tuned to face the wooden skeleton of the building that stood 100 yards out form where they stood and stared for an uncomfortably long time before speaking.

"Okay. Why way out here in the middle of the desert? Why not in L.A. where people have access?"

"With a project of this size, a project unrivalled in magnitude and therefore potential return, I feel it's critical to look to the long term future of the project. Once we're up and running-"

"What's you projected grand opening date?" Meyer pushed.

"How soon you expect to see money coming in?" Siegel tagged.

"With your organization's help we think a December date is not unrealistic." Lansky nodded in apparent approval, Billy continued.

"I foresee, down the road, that once we start making a real return the town fathers, city fathers in the event we tried this in L.A., would pass more and more regulations to find ways to eat into our profits." Wilkinson focused on 'speaking their language' while offering comparisons they would identify with. "I mean, Cuba has been very profitable for anyone with the foresight to invest in operations down there."

"And Batista always had his hand out!" Siegel interjected. "How do you think he can afford to stay in the Waldorf whenever he comes to New York?"

"Precisely!" Wilkinson agreed. "Additionally, with all the revolutionary activity down in that part of the world just now, is it such a bad idea to have a fall back location?"

"Good point Mr. Wilkinson. Good point." Meyer confirmed.

The tour went on for another thirty minutes. They never made it to the hotel and with the excuse that they had a four o'clock flight to catch, Lansky concluded the meet.

"I think I might be able to sell it to the council. I'll be in touch." Were his parting words to Wilkinson as they shook hands. Benny Siegel left without any further comment.

Wilkinson watched the limo drive off down the dusty road and into the sunset.

Perhaps it was his craving for adventure, a propensity to walk on the wild side or maybe it was just his gambler's mentality kicking in, but whatever the motivation, Billy had just unknowingly and significantly raised the stakes in and on his life.

CHAPTER XVI

Meanwhile, Doc McKeowen and Louie Mancino were not the only ones working away and making progress.

Comfortably cruising at 15,000 feet and having maintained a westerly heading for the last forty-five minutes Jimmy Dugan was now approaching the Jersey-Pennsylvania state line. Hoping to fool anyone following him on radar he planned to let them establish his westerly course and dip down to a couple of hundred feet, below radar, before turning 90 degrees left and heading south. From there he would fly NOE, nap of the earth, for as long as possible.

Just over a year ago when he started flying drug loads for the Mob Jimmy had told himself it was a temporary stint, something to tide him over until he could score a proper commercial gig. Now into his second year and the country facing a nation-wide recession combined with the fact that he would earn more in one run then he did in two years of combat duty in the military, even with hazardous duty pay thrown in, he was reconsidering his strategy.

Unable to make the 1,300 mile plus run from New York to Miami in one leg Jimmy would have to refuel at least twice in route. Given that the feds somehow were on to him in New York, he would have to use any one of the small private airports, some of them merely flat grass strips in the countryside, in route to land and refuel.

Shortly after crossing the Delaware Water Gap Dugan took a bearing off the factories of Allentown he estimated at about thirty miles off to his ten o'clock and executed a slow wide turn to the left, pulled back on the stick, and completing his turn, rechecked his azimuth. With his passenger snoozing quietly in the seat next to him settled in for the long haul.

A short time later, as he approached south Jersey, a strange feeling came over him, a sensation he hadn't felt since his patrol days flying over the front lines during the war. A creeping sensation that something was wrong.

Dugan gently pulled back on the yoke and climbed a couple of hundred feet and did a partial roll to port, a standard manoeuvre in a small aircraft when the pilot wanted to see behind him.

"Shit!" He was not happy about what he saw behind him. There was a white PBY-5 Catalina about five to six miles back and off to his right.

Suddenly Jimmy's future came close to being decided for him when a short burst off bullets, marked by red tracers, ripped past his side window.

"Shit!" His middle-aged, well-dressed passenger was startled awake by Jimmy's expletive, sat up and watched wide-eyed as a second stream of little red dashes streaked alongside the aircraft.

"Was that bullets?!" The passenger demanded as he squirmed around in his seat his face pressed up against the small side window.

On this trip, as was sometimes usual, Jimmy was saddled with a passenger, Moses Steinway, a bean counter who normally worked out of Meyer Lansky's office in New York but who was needed down at the Miami racetracks for the week.

"Yeah Mo, Yeah it was."

"Who the hell is tryin' to shoot us down way up here?!"

"Nobody, those were just warning shots. Probably the Coast Guard." Jimmy informed in a controlled but not altogether calm voice.

"COAST GUARD? We're a hundred miles inland, there's no coast to guard around here!"

"Could be they came out'a The New York station." Jimmy calmly rationalized.

"New York's over a hundred miles east of here!"

A second burst flew past the aircraft as Jimmy veered right then left in an effort to see more clearly behind the plane and judge distance. The Catalina was creeping up on them.

"Could be from the Jersey station, Toms River maybe." Dugan speculated.

"Tom's River's **two hundred** miles away!"

"Well Moe, where ever the fuck they're from they're here now!"

Unfortunately for Dugan the two feds who had chased him back at Battery Park some weeks ago in New York City were able to get his tail number then get the word out.

Alert aircraft from several stations along the north east coast were put on stand-by and on of then had now been launched. One of the stations got lucky when the APB the Feds put out was picked up by an amateur flyer in New Jersey who intercepted the transmission and reported seeing Dugan's plane. A PBY crew from Lakehurst Naval Air Station drew the lucky card.

Jimmy's 'Shit!' was not because it was the Heat on his tail or that he was carrying over 100 pounds of uncut heroin and if captured he would be out of a job and in jail for up to twenty years, all that was incidental. But of primary concern his De Havilland Beaver was out matched by the PBY now in pursuit.

Only one bunch of guys flew PBY's, the U.S. military. And only one branch of the military flew PBY's painted white: U.S. Coast Guard. Jimmy was in a chase, a 'cat and mouse' situation and Dugan immediately realized he was the mouse. More disturbing was something he also instantly realized; the USCG were upping their game.

"Can't we out run them?!" Moe's cracked as he spat the question.

"He's flying a PBY-5. They top out at around 200 miles per hour with a range of over 2,500 nautical miles. With a full tank they could make it from New York to Reno non-stop, land at any airfield along the way and have local cops waiting to nail us."

As he spoke, reminding himself of exactly how much shit he was in, Dugan' brain raced.

Jimmy's De Havilland was good for 455 nautical miles tops with a maximum speed of 158 knots flat out and had already been airborne for nearly an hour. Jimmy knew he was out gunned.

More disturbing was something he also didn't miss; by arming their planes, something they never did before the war, the USCG were sending the clear signal that they also had learned from their years chasing bootleggers and were now tired of being humiliated.

"Fucking Anslinger!" Jimmy quietly cursed.

Essentially all the PBY crew had to do, since Dugan couldn't out run or out last them, was loiter behind him until he ran low on fuel and was forced to set down somewhere. Any town large enough to have an airfield would have some kind of local cop shop which the Coastie's were no doubt in radio contact with, so it appeared only a matter of time for Jimmy, Moe and their cargo.

Another short burst zipped past the left side of the fuselage.

"DUGAN WHAT THE HELL ARE WE GONNA DO?!"

"I'm working on it Moe, I'm working on it!"

"Well please work a little faster! I hate my wife but I'd like to see her again and not through a set of bars at Leavenworth!"

"Our only advantage is that their PBY is designed for search and rescue, long distance performance is the primary consideration, not speed because when you're looking for a tiny life raft speed's a disadvantage. You can't fly like a fighter jet and expect to see anything a thousand feet below."

Jimmy's latest run was never intended to make it to his final destination, southern Florida, in one hop, he had planned at least two legs but the closest leg and his first pit stop was a small airstrip outside of Richmond, Virginia, over a hundred miles away. Jimmy estimated he had less than 100 miles to play with.

Suddenly having stopped off to see that hot little blond in Brooklyn seemed like it had been a real bad idea.

"Dugan . . . what'a we gonna . . . d-do?!"

"You're gonna buckle up, shut up and I'm gonna find us a way out'a this!"

Jimmy's mind kicked into overdrive. As it did the PBY drifted up alongside them and he looked out the port window. Waved and smiled at the uniformed co-pilot signalling for him to drop altitude and land. Moe dropped down in his seat and hid his face with his briefcase.

The co-pilot held up a chalkboard with a radio frequency neatly written on it in yellow chalk.

Jimmy gave the thumbs up then pretended to adjust his radio and held the mike up to his mouth.

The PBY shotgun spoke into his mike and Jimmy followed suite.

"You don't have the radio on!" Moe astutely observed.

"No shit! I told you to buckle up! Now shut up and hold on!" He ordered.

This little radio charade went on for the better part of ten minutes when Jimmy threw up his hands, signalled for the PBY to wait one then rummaged around for a piece of cardboard and a marker. He scribbled a message then held the sign he had just improvised up to the window. It read: 'FUCK OFF!'

The PBY gave up on attempting conventional commo and dropped back behind Jimmy's plane.

Without warning, tossing the sign aside, Jimmy pulled over hard right on the yoke and shot the nose up at nearly 90 degrees over into a small cloud bank. The pissed off Catalina pilot followed suit but his less maneuvrable craft, having to make a much wider arch, quickly fell over two miles behind. In the cloud Jimmy slowed the plane to near stall speed and altered course.

"Look in that glove box. There's a book of air charts, a compass and a note pad with a pencil get all that shit out." Steinway did as instructed, dropping half the contents as Jimmy desperately scanned the sky for another, larger cloud bank, Moses gathered the gear and handed it over to Dugan.

"Not me, you dumb shit, you! Open the chart, find the Pennsylvania-Virginia border."

"I don't know how to read aeronautical charts! I'm an accountant!"

"You read English don't ya?! I just promoted you! Now you're a navigator."

Moses fumbled a bit. "Open to the index in the back."

"Got it."

"Find the page with the Sectional Chart for Washington."

"There's two listed."

"Try the page labeled 'D.C.'!" *Fucking desk jockey!* Jimmy's internal dialogue jumped in. "Now scan the page for a small airfields."

"There's loads'a airports.'

"No airports. Look between the airports, little ed airplanes stamped on the page.

"How about here near Suffolk?"

"Show me." Moses passed the chart book to Jimmy.

"Nah! Too close to all the military bases. Find me something further west, some place with a small airfield, a strip anything where we can set down."

Not able to spot any appreciable cumulus cloud masses and realizing the Feds had fallen back and were now lined up probably somewhere on his six o'clock, Dugan's concern meter had just jumped a notch.

"Franklin?" Steinway pointed out.

"Franklin? Show me." Jimmy looked again as Moses gave a running commentary.

"It's inland away from the naval bases, no major highways for the cops to get there in a hurry and this little symbol next to the air strip means gas pump', don't it?" Moses innocently asked. Jimmy gave a quick glance and nodded.

"You're not as dumb as you look Moses. Well done, you get an atta-boy! Now use the protractor and get me a distance from this road junction to the airfield."

"What's an atta-boy?"

"Not important Moses. Measure!" Beaming with pride Moses plotted the distance.

Suddenly they ran out of cloud cover and found the PBY was not only behind them but catching up fast.

"Eighty miles give or take a mile."

A second burst of machine gun fire ripped across Dugan's side of the plane.

"Stow that gear and hold on, time to run these backwards ass country fucks!"

"What'a you gonna do?"

"That pilot looked to me to be too young to have been in the war."

"Meaning what?"

"Meaning he probably goes to bed each night wondering if he would'a had the balls to do what he needed to do when the time came."

"I don't follow you?"

"I'm gonna do him the biggest favor in his life!"

"Which is?"

"I'm gonna test how big his balls are."

With that Dugan pulled back hard on the yoke and took the DeHavilland straight up at 90 degrees. With essentially the same ceiling but a rate of climb only about twenty feet per minute more than the Catalina, Dugan quickly formulated a three step plan.

"Our ceilings are close to the same but I think we can out climb him. It's gonna get cold in here, get your jacket on."

Although both aircrafts' upper ceilings were right around 18,000 feet, rate of climb and maneuverability were where Jimmy thought his best bet lie.

"We can climb a little faster, the best that PBY jock can hope for is 610 feet per minute, about half our output."

The details were lost on Moses as he gripped his seat with both hands and tried not to scream like a girl.

Of course out climbing the CG guys didn't mean they were home free. They would have to come down at some point. Plus, thanks to his Army issue radio interceptor and the fact that he now had the frequency the CG's were using, Jimmy knew they were keeping regular contact with ground control which included giving updates on their position.

At around 14,000 feet frost gradually began to creep up the windows and across the windshield which meant the wings were next which in turn meant gradual loss of pitch and taw control if it went too far.

By 17,500 he had long ago lost sight of his pursuers but knew from their radio traffic there were others flocking to what the Feds no doubt considered a turkey shoot of an aerial fox hunt.

He decided to take advantage of the thinner air, level off to try and lose the ice then push for speed. Betting they would not expect him to maintain his heading he did, temporarily.

Minutes later spotting the ocean off to the left and oriented to his whereabouts, Jimmy was able to turn sharply into a cloud bank, slow his plane to just above stall speed and temporarily again become invisible. He heard the Catalina below him still traveling at speed.

Ten minutes later hearing nothing, he dropped out of the clouds and chanced a recon of the area below him where he was able to locate a string of inland water way islands just off the coast of the cape.

"Moses, you're shakin' like a dog in a Korean restaurant! There's a thermos of coffee in my bag there."

Steinway's trembling hands found the coffee, poured some and cuddled the hot cup in both hands.

"I'll say . . . this for ya . . . Dugan-" Moses' sentence was interrupted by another burst of machine gun fire that scrapped along the starboard side of the plane.

"Bastards!" Jimmy swore, banked slightly left then looked behind him. A Catalina was tailing him but not the same one. This one was steel blue. He didn't need to see the marking to it was a navy plane. He checked his fuel. The needle hovered just above empty.

Pulling back and banking hard right he half looped into a nose dive and headed straight at the PBY from its two o'clock.

Aboard the Catalina the pilots were taken off guard. The petty officer in the passenger seat tapped the pilot.

"Lieutenant, you seein' what I'm seein?" The lieutenant looked over to see the red DeHavilland coming at them.

"That asshole is crazy!"

"That asshole appears to be shooting at us!"

"Bullshit! It's a bush plane!"

"You look, tell me what you see!"

The co-pilot squinted, manned his binos and from his two o'clock high starboard quarter, about five miles out, he saw Dugan's DeHavilland diving down at them, a gun barrel flashing in short bursts as the small plane quickly closed the distance.

"A fucking DeHavilland with a machine gun?!" The petty officer declared.

"To hell with this!" The L.T. banked hard left and dove for the hard deck steering towards the sea. "I didn't live through all them Japs in the Pacific to get shot down by a god damned DeHavilland Beaver!"

Jimmy flew flat out over the PBY, half looped back and headed straight west and back up into the early afternoon clouds.

Dugan howled like a coyote as he tossed the industrial flashlight aside he used to send the flashes of light at the PBY simulating distant Machine gun fire.

"What'a ya think Moses? How's it feel getting out of the office?" Moss gave no response. Jimmy reached over and shook him. As Moses slumped forward Jimmy spotted the blood stained bullet hole in the back of his seat matching the one in the middle of Steinway's back.

"Scratch one accountant." He mumbled.

With no sign of the two chase aircraft Dugan did a quick functions check of his controls, took time to get his bearings and focused on his fuel situation.

Ten minutes later he was coasting down a countryside road towards a gas station he had spotted from the air.

Jimmy propped Moses up, leaned him over to the side folded his arms over and covered his face with his baseball cap as if he was sleeping.

"At least I'll have someone to talk to until we get to Miami!" Jimmy said to the corpse before tapping him on the head and climbing out of the plane.

The gas station was little more than a wooden shack with two gas pumps outside. An old man hobbled out the door.

"Howdy." He greeted.

"Afternoon Old Timer! How ya doin'?"

"Better than your friend there!" The old fella teased as he spied Steinway's head leaned over on the passenger's door.

"Yeah, late night last night, a little too much booze."

'Hope it was unleaded!"

"No, I think there was bit of led in it! You got anything besides ethyl?"

"Like what?"

"Pure kerosene or liquefied natural gas?"

"Got a tank of kerosene around back." He led Dugan around in back of the station to a small tank mounted on low stilts. "Folks around here use it for heatin'."

"Is it unleaded?"

'How much ya'll looking for cowboy?"

"About a thousand pounds."

"Pounds? What's that in plain speak young fella?"

"About a hundred or so gallons ought'a do me."

"That's a good bit!"

Jimmy climbed back up into the plane and returned with stack of twenties. He waved them in front of the old man.

"Hell Son, back her up to the tank! Looks like I'm going home early today!"

Flamingo Construction Site
Las Vegas, Nevada

It was well into the third month of construction at the Flamingo when Wilkinson made the decision to make a surprise visit out to the construction site.

It was a bad decision.

In the interim since they had signed a deal whereby the Commission, with the support of Luciano and Lansky, had agreed to round out financing for the Flamingo project Bugsy Siegel, who was tasked with babysitting the project, had metamorphosed himself into a Capo.

There were two bumps in the road on the way to completion of the big project; the first of which beginning to manifest itself, was that Siegel, although a stylish guy and a snappy dresser, knew less than nothing about construction, layout and the practicalities of interior design or the intricacies of

369

accounting. The two million dollar budget seemed to him to be a bottomless well from which he drank much too often.

The second smaller bump was that William Wilkinson, as he happily made the four hour drive west out to check progress on the site, was under the impression that the Flamingo was still his baby.

He was about to discover the child had been abducted.

Aside from wanting to check building progress Billy had also done some quick math before taking to the open road. The well was running dry, well ahead of schedule.

As he entered what would be the main entrance Wilkinson was greeted with the sight of two workers tearing out all the brand new wallpaper along the entire warren of hallways into what was scheduled to be the main gambling parlor.

As he pulled up to the font of the now closed in main building he was shocked at what he saw.

"JIMMY! WHAT THE FUCK ARE YOU DOING? That paper cost $13.50 a yard!"

"Mr. Siegel said to tear it all out and put the new wallpaper in!"

With the New York Mobsters involved in his operation Wilkinson had become that much more attentive to the budget.

"WHAT NEW WALLPAPER?!"

"The silvery stuff over there." The worker nodded and Billy glanced over to see a dozen large boxes marked: '100 Rolls Silver Jubilee'

Reluctant to make waves with his investors, Billy carefully contemplated how he would broach the fact that, according to his accountant, the current rate of expenditure would bankrupt the Flamingo project in the next two to three months, long before it was ready to open much less had time to realize a profit.

With a sample roll of the wallpaper in his hand Billy made his way through the building site until he tracked Siegel down out back, jacket off, sleeves of his white shirt rolled up and Colt .45 holstered and hanging from his left side. Benny was supervising the installation of an oversized gazebo which was not on the original plans.

Siegel shouted orders as the twenty-five foot diameter, ornate structure was slowly being lowered by crane.

"Benny can we talk a minute?"

"Yeah sure Wilkinson." Siegel immediately turned away and yelled at the banksman directing the crane operator via hand signals. "A LITTLE MORE TO THE LEFT FRANK! BETTER! RIGHT THERE, SET HER DOWN!" Siegel yelled. "Yeah Billy, what is it?"

"We're redoing the lounge area?"

"Yeah, so what?!"

"This is the third time in as many weeks. Each time is another ten grand plus, in labor and materials."

"Your decorator was shit. Place was looking like a fucking whorehouse instead of a high class casino."

"Wait, wait . . . what do mean my decorator 'was' shit? What happened?"

"I sent him packing! Fucking L. A. fruitcake!"

"Benny! You may represent my investors but this is still my project! My baby! I hire and fire here. I'm in charge!"

Some men are slow to rage, allowing their anger to gradually simmer and percolate to the surface before allowing it to boil over. Siegel wasn't one of those men.

There was no shortage of rumors that he once shot a man for calling him 'Bugsy' as a term of familiarity. Bugsy took it literally - bugs in the head – insane.

On Siegel's second step towards Wilkinson Billy knew enough to step back.

"Oh yeah?! That so Mr. big L.A. strip night club owner who don't really own any night clubs for himself?! You're in charge?!" Siegel unsnapped his holster, drew his .45 and pulled back on the slide to chamber a round.

"Who is in charge here?" Siegel softly asked.

The single roll of Silver Jubilee Billy had been holding unraveled across the back veranda coming to a halt several yards away in the bushes. Billy however didn't stop until he reached the front parking area.

As Siegel looked through the half closed in building the 200 yards out to the front, he smiled as he watched Wilkinson's car throwing dust and gravel back across the building, head for the open road and screech right and vanish.

"I guess that settles who's in fucking charge?!" Benny clearly stated for all the workers, poised like living statues across the work area to hear. "I'M IN CHARGE, GOD DAMN IT! That's who's fuckin' in charge! I'm in charge, that's who!"

He stepped back into the unfinished lounge area.

"I'M IN FUCKIN' CHARGE HERE FUCKERS!!" The workers all ducked for cover as Siegel let off several rounds in the air and screamed out into the work space.

"I'm in charge. That's who's in charge. I'm in charge." Benny walked off, .45 dangling in hand while mumbling.

After Wilkinson did a Jesse Owens to his car and an Alberto Ascari all the way back to L.A. he was not seen nor heard on the Flamingo building site ever again.

Not only was Willy Wilkinson never again seen on the Flamingo building site, for the most part he was never again seen in the state of Nevada. At least not until over a year later.

Deciding the four hours between Vegas and L.A. were not enough Billy had temporarily relocated to Paris France.

It may have been five and a half thousand miles from home, but at least gambling was legal.

By early October buzz in the Press had been building over the last few months regarding the theoretical communist infiltration of American society. Hardly a newspaper, magazine, radio report or, now television news report, failed to highlight the imagined threat. It was as if a deadly viral outbreak had been let loose on the U.S.

While Willy Wilkinson was dancing a jig around Mafia killers Jack Warner was waltzing around with the murderers who were the big wigs of Hollywood.

Neither entrepreneur had any way of knowing when the music would stop but both realized that when it finally did their lives would be inextricably altered.

The primary difference between Warner and Wilkinson was that one had some control over his future and the other only thought he had.

At the same time general public perception of the Big Five Hollywood studio heads sticking together through thick and thin to form an impenetrable shield against outsiders prevailed.

However this was a purely mythical supposition.

The first time a cash worthy talent, a saleable script or a promising producer reared its ugly head, all bets were off.

The Hollywood hunting grounds were a shooting gallery of a high stakes soap opera where in lieu of somebody's husband or wife stealing away to cheat on their spouse the friction arose from one studio head locking horns with another over market share. One head banging against another just to get that little bit ahead. After all, Hollywood might have been birthed by Jews in the incubator of American culture but it was clearly fathered by Wall Street where there are no rules except those set by the government. And even those are for sale. But, all-in-all the Hollywood business bubble was relatively safe from political invasion.

Until now.

All of that changed the day a group of obscure congressmen decided that they could move from the limelight to the spotlight by whipping up a scare.

In essence to apply 'The Formula'.

But what to use as a vehicle became the question.

Horror films always worked best when the big scary monster was never seen at least until the third act. From failed efforts in the late Thirties these congressmen had learned that there is one big scary monster that could work well, if applied with the right amount of rhetoric, innuendo and bullying, and that was the C' word. No, not cancer, but the other C word - Communism. And, as The Medieval rules of guilt by accusation had never really been abandoned by the American legal system, it was in the autumn of 1947 that these senators realized they were onto a win-win situation.

The fact that the House of Representatives had no legal power under the U.S. Constitution to try accused defendants was a minor snag easily ignored. After all who was going to challenge the Congress?

However, to absolutely hedge their bets the Congressmen would rig the rules.

Defendants would not be allowed copies of the 'charges' beforehand, defendants would not be allowed to have legal representation and most importantly defendants would not be allowed to speak on their own behalf, they would only speak when spoken to and respond with direct answers to questions, no matter how outlandish or vague the question.

To cement the deal, the HUAC Committee took the additional precaution of not announcing the rules.

So by publically labeling what they were doing as 'hearings' the House could call and 'try' anyone they deemed necessary.

This established a pattern of illegal behavior that would be carried well into the future.

What would follow would be one of the most overt attempts at a power grab accompanied by career enhancements since Woodrow Wilson had Eugene Debbs imprisoned to keep him out of the 1912 race.

Although they were far better at such maneuvers, Congress was not the only one hedging its bets.

Jack Warner hadn't exactly called the impromptu meeting he now attended but he was clearly there to attempt to take control and assert himself.

The topic of discussion that afternoon in the Executive board room of the L.A. Biltmore was the exact details of how the MPAA would respond to the Congressional hearings scheduled to start in three days on Monday morning out in Washington.

Like Doc McKeowen's well-educated prediction, Warner too realized people would see jail time. The writing on the wall for Warner was the increasing manipulation of the all too complacent press allowing itself to be manipulated by the congressmen.

As subpoenas had already been served to several writers and directors and more were sure to follow, the MPAA advised its members to brace themselves. Many had already registered as 'voluntary' witnesses cleverly labeled as 'friendly' witnesses by the Committee when their names were released to the press.

Congressman Thomas and Rankin, in a further effort to build a frenzy of media attention and sway public opinion, had granted unprecedented access to the press and went out of their way to 'announce', in reality 'leak' every little detail of what was to come. Kind of like the hype before a championship wrestling event.

To top it all off and ensure maximum coverage television cameras for the first time ever would be permitted to broadcast the whole show live as the action unfolded.

NBC and its affiliates as well as RCA's TV manufacturing division were delighted.

The primary reason for the informal MPAA meeting was to hedge their bets before the storm. Unbeknownst to any Jack had already taken that precaution last week when he suddenly flew off to Washington and met with Truman.

Present at the last minute gathering in the Biltmore were about a dozen reps of the top guns of the five major studios, MGM, Universal, Columbia, Paramount and Warner Brothers. Eric Johnston

President of the MPAA was out of town but sent an emissary to take notes and report back.

Now, an hour into the meeting the MPAA rep currently held the floor.

"Mr. Johnston has asked me to pass along to you that he will be testifying as a friendly witness."

"'Friendly' witness! Cute anachronism for cooperative!" Someone called out.

"It's not his term. It's what the congressmen are calling it."

"Does he intend to point fingers and name names?" Louie Mayer's Associate Executive demanded.

"I have no insight as to what Mr. Johnston intends to testify to."

"Let's not forget this whole circus is gonna be televised!" The Columbia rep added.

"Television is a passing fad and people won't pay one bit of attention!" Warner jumped in. "There's not even a couple thousand people's even got one of those idiot boxes!" He argued.

"Try more like nearly fifty thousand!" Dore Schary countered.

"What are you an encyclopedia or something?" Louis Mayer challenged.

"My sister-in-law lives in Jersey. She works for RCA."

Dore Schary, a producer at MGM was at odds with Louis Mayer largely because he was appointed by the parent company Loews MGM in NYC. Louis B. saw this as the Wall Street Boys once again

378

poking their noses in where they didn't belong. He wasn't alone in his beliefs.

The fact was that, of the five majors only Warner, having weathered the Great Depression, WWI and WWII without going hat in and to the banks had no one to answer to back on Wall Street. Every one of the others did.

"None of which still helps us with what anybody's gonna say once they get us in front of those bastards!" Warner bravely barked.

Warner's big fight was with his talent, particularly his on screen folks and their writers. At odds with his talent pool since before the war he now found himself in a fight he hadn't expected, didn't want and had no idea how to defend against. Thanks largely to the War the world had changed forever and was moving on. Jack Warner, still stuck in the 'Studio System's' way of dealing with talent, had been slow on the uptake to grasp this fact.

He stood to deliver his lecture.

"This is a great industry. A great industry in a great country where anybody with a little brains and a lot'a hard work and elbow grease can not only get ahead but make something of himself."

The dramatic pause was purposely timed. "But sometimes, after a man has established himself and made his mark, some low life bunch of mugs comes along want'a to take it all away."

"What's your point Jack?" Schary called over.

"The studio system is coming apart. We all realize that by this time next year most big stars will have broken away from the studio contract system.

The war has pushed them more and more into using independent producers to diversify and pursue personal projects and increase output by producing pictures faster. The writers have received the okay from Washington to organize. If they break off like the actors and are able to name their demands than we become just a bunch of suits kow-towing to a bunch of, so called 'artists'!"

Fully cognizant of Jack Warner's penchant for long winded speeches and lecturing people, the MPAA rep jumped in.

"If there is nothing else . . ."

"What can we expect from Johnston's office in the event this gets really ugly?" Someone asked.

"The MPAA office expects that, if called, you will all be truthful, speak in defense of the industry we have all worked so long and had to build and testify according to your conscience."

"In other words we're on our own!" Warner opined.

"We have no idea how long this thing is going to drag on for, so-"

"As long as the sons-of-bitches can milk it!" Jack angrily spouted.

"We have no idea how long this thing is going to go on for however, there will be a meeting called as soon as the Congress announces its findings at which time we will meet again to form a consensus reaction, formulate a response and decide when to make an announcement which will be transmitted to the general public through the press."

CHAPTER XVII

80th U. S. Congress
Washington D. C.
October 20th, 1947

And so once again, like a disgruntled housewife the fickle nature of American politics reared its ugly head. The 80th Congress which had convened that January broke for summer recess and now had reconvened for the autumn session.

The most prominent congressional committee that year, one which would dominate the headlines for the next six to seven years, was the House on un-American Activities Committee, or HUAC which to hundreds of artists and workers would become more than just another four letter word.

Although tracing its roots back to the Overman Committee in 1918 it wasn't until 1940 that the House un-American Activities Committee first became what was essentially an elaborate, tax payer funded publicity stunt.

By 1947 in post-war Washington it had evolved into a full blown circus, some say freak side show.

By this time elements of the dishonest press, in conjunction with certain publicity seeking politicians, had whipped public interest in communist infiltration into a virtual frenzy in fear of the 'Red Hoards' looking to take over the country.

By October of that year 'Red Baiting' had truly become congress' second favorite indoor sport.

In light of the humiliating defeat of the congressional attack on film makers back in 1940-41 before The War, it was now six years later that those same members of Congress were out to stage a second assault and this time win against the film industry and make an example of the movie moguls and show them who was really running the show.

As the House prepared to convene that morning Doc and Louie were thirty thousand feet over Illinois sharing a flight while heading south back to New York.

Louie popped the last bite of his tuna sandwich into his mouth, folded over the Chicago Sun Times and nudged a-none-too-happy Doc awake.

"What?!" Doc fought the sudden transition back into the real world.

"Doc, I got a question."

"In the back on the left! Ask the Stew, she'll give you the key!" He slumped back down.

"Doc, what's your take on this whole commie thing goin' on down in D.C.?" Mancino indicated the article he had just read. "

"You woke me up to talk about commies?"

"Not just. We can talk about anything you like."

McKeowen stared at him.

"How about we talk about me going back to sleep!?"

"C'mon! You know more about all this political bullshit than I do! Give me your take."

Maybe it was a mistake to ask or perhaps being fully aware of Doc's opinions on politics, Louie just wanted to make conversation to pass the time.

"I mean, all these movie stars can't be commies, can they?"

"Get me some whiskey!" McKeowen demanded as he shook the last tatters of sleep off himself. Louie leaned over his seat rest, leaned out into the aisle and signaled the stewardess who, having served Doc several whiskeys prior to take off, nodded knowingly.

"My take? Here's my take. Politicians and newspaper people have been debating about when the exact moment was that we as a country lost our innocence. Most people you talk to agree it was just after the war when we found out about the atrocities of the Japs and Nazis and what they did to all those people. Others argue it was a long time before, maybe during the Great War –"

"Which don't seem so great now!" Mancino interjected."

"Good point." Doc confirmed. "Point is if the decline of a country can be calculated to have started at the deterioration of its political structure, as happened with the Greeks, the Babylonians and the Romans, then the communist witch hunts of '47, as they will become to known, will have set a political behavioral pattern that I don't doubt will be followed many times in the years to come and be recorded as the appearance of the first real cracks in our political foundation."

"So these congressional hearings are a big show trial?"

"First off, the House of Representatives doesn't have the legal power to try anybody, even if someone is a real commie. Which by the way is also not illegal. It might be stupid and a waste of a good vote but it ain't against the law. The C.P.U.S.A. might be a bunch of misled idiots but they've been around since before the First War and they're still legal."

"Then how can a couple of congressmen put them on trial?"

"Who's gonna stop them? The people put them in office."

"And the people can vote them out!" Louie countered.

"Yes but not for four years. The Nazi's started their little traveling road show in 1940 it wasn't until 1944 that we had our guys knocking on their door and shut them down. You can do a helluv'a lot'a damage in four years brother!"

"In between we lost millions and the body count still ain't in!" Mancino confirmed. "But that's not what I'm talking about. I'm reading here in the paper about this congressman who says there's millions of commies amassing on the Mexican border ready to invade the U.S. right now!"

"Where'd you read that?"

"Here." He brandished the paper he had been reading. "On the political page."

At that Doc pulled back in his seat and stared at Louie's uncharacteristic revelation.

"WHAT?!" Louie defended. "Can't a guy make no attempt to immolate himself?"

A smile slowly crept across Doc face not as a result of Louie's mistake, but out of pride at Mancino's attempt at self-improvement.

"A-MELI-OR-ATE himself, can't a guy ameliorate himself?! Means to improve. And yes you certainly can. Well done Louie and keep it up! You're on fire all right!"

"Thank you." He humbly accepted.

"You're welcome. Now, about commies on the border, is the story on the front page?"

"No, like I said it's in the back on the political page."

"This congressional idiot give any evidence of this wild claim?"

"If he did it's not in the paper."

"Don't worry, he's not gonna offer any proof because there is none. If there was any military build-up on the border don't you think the Mexicans would have picked up the phone and given Truman a courtesy call?"

"Okay, okay!" Mancino, unexpectedly injected with a shot of enthusiasm, sat up and faced Doc. "Therefore we can conclude two things: politicians and newspapers are subject to lying!"

"Not only subject to being untruthful but worse, oft times are not held accountable for their lies."

The lesson hitting home Mancino leaned back in his seat, pursed his lips and nodded.

"I should read more." Louie contemplated.

"Everyone should. You remember back when we got that mob guy convicted of killing his wife?" Doc posited.

"Yeah, then we found out he didn't do it?" Louie confirmed.

"After they fried him!"

"Yeah, I remember! Can't take that screw-up back!"

"Exactly but my point is trials are not decided on evidence they're decided on emotions! Emotions which come largely from testimony."

"I know what you mean. I remember that forensics guy on the stand, his testimony about them plants in Central Park. He didn't know nothing about that guy but he **wanted** that guy to be guilty."

"And the jury picked up on it like a hungry dog picking up on the scent of raw meat!"

"So what's your point?"

"This commie thing's been going on since the end of the war. Plenty of time for everyone to form an opinion one way or the other. So, if there are many Americans who realize that these hearings are largely bullshit, being staged to enhance political careers by putting Thomas, Rankin and those other Bozos in front of the TV cameras, which are for the first time, don't forget few people are speaking out about it! Including the so-called Free Press!"

"Well, you can't blame the Walter Winchell wanna-be's! They gotta sell newspapers."

"Exactly and these trials are the biggest thing since VJ Day so they're gonna help keep them going as long as possible."

"You saying you think there's gonna be more witch hunts? Thomas and his mob are gonna keep lookin' for commies?"

"That too, but I'm talking in the long run, down the pyke. It's all part of *The Formula*. Create an enemy, in this case the threat of communists, the opposite party whatever, then convince the people that you're the best solution to fight those demons whoever they are. If you can lie, cheat and steal your way through that you've got yourself a pay check, a limo and a roof over your head for the rest of your life."

"I guess there's a reason they're all lawyers before they go into politics!"

"Of course, they have to do their apprenticeship first. Where's my whiskey?"

The first of the HUAC's 'hearings' began that morning where they had left off last week which was with a debate to formalize Executive Order 9835 also entitled the Loyalty Act which was an attempt by the president to quell the right wingers in Congress and make it look like he, Truman, was not being too soft on communists while allowing the White House to limit the unbridled aggressiveness of Hoover's FBI and the questionable tactics of others.

The fact that over three million government employees and untold numbers of other Americans were still investigated is a testament to Order 9835's failure in that regard.

Now regrouped and divested of the FDR socialism that plagued them with the shackles of free speech, life-long career politicians such as Thomas and Rankin leaped at their chance to slither onto the front pages of America's newspapers.

Although they had no judicial powers and so were not a court of law it was to the credit of their ambitions that they didn't let such minor details such as legality stand in their way.

Unfortunately the American people had always been led to believe that because they had been, under the Constitution of the United States, given freedom of speech, they were protected against being compelled to disclose their religion or political views to a government appointed board of inquiry.

The people of the United States were about to be given a harsh lesson in the reality of domestic civics.

By mid-morning back in the Congressional chambers the opening formalities had been run through and there was not even standing room in the packed congressional hall meant to hold a couple of hundred but, by ten o'clock was jammed with twice that number.

A half dozen movie cameras on tripods stood off to the left of the twenty foot long dais behind which sat the five members of the HUAC sub-committee Richard Nixon, Richard Vail, John Wood and John McDowell, all headed by J. Parnell Thomas.

Cameras were rolling, boom mikes dangled and the press box, the size of a standard jury booth, also to the left of the committee was dribbling reporters over the railing.

Jack Warner had taken the stand to be cross examined but was permitted to make an opening statement.

Amongst studio heads he was in his element. But a fish out of water doesn't even begin to describe Jack Warner once he was called on to testify.

"Ideological termites have burrowed into many American industries, organizations, and societies. Wherever they may be, I say let us dig them out and get rid of them! My brothers and I will be happy to subscribe generously to a pest-removal fund. We are willing to establish such a fund to ship to Russia the people who don't like our American system of government and prefer the communistic system to ours. That's how strongly we feel about the subversives who want to overthrow our free American system. If there are Communists in our industry, or any other industry, organization, or society who seek to undermine our free institutions, let's find out about it and know who they are. Let the record be spread clear, for all to read and judge. The public is entitled to know the facts. And the motion-picture industry is entitled to have the public know the facts."

Murmurs rippled through the crowd.

"To this end I have given to the Committee a list of about a dozen people I strongly believe may have communist ties." Warner also knew how to play to the cameras.

"Yes the Committee has your list Mr. Warner. We thank you for your cooperation." Thomas brandished a piece of paper for the TV and movie cameras. "About these two brothers the Epsteins, Julius and Philip. Do they still work for you?"

"No Senator they do not."

"Did you release them due to their communistic activities?"

"Among other reasons, yes sir."

The 'other reasons' were in reality the Epsteins were fired from Warner studios due to a personal dispute with Jack. They resented having to punch a clock like common factory workers every day and one day when Warner asked them to take a script over the weekend they agreed. However Monday morning when it wasn't ready he went off on them. They didn't shut up and take it like he thought they should've and they were fired. But they had no communist ties.

"And this writer, Howard Koch? Also a communist?"

"I believe so Senator, yes."

"He wrote your company's picture *Mission to Moscow* did he not Mr. Warner?"

"Yes he did."

HUAC initially accused Warner of producing New Deal propaganda in support of the Democrats New Deal political agenda, a pre-ear solution to the ravages of the Great Depression and something Thomas and his cronies were dead set against.

This question was a curveball Warner didn't expect so he put on his dancing shoes.

"Our company is keenly aware of its responsibilities to keep its product free from subversive poisons. With all the vision at my command, I scrutinize the planning and production of our motion pictures. It is my firm belief that there is not a Warner Bros. picture that can fairly be judged to be hostile to our country, or communistic in tone or purpose. Many charges, including the fantasy of "White House pressure" have been leveled at our wartime production. *Mission to Moscow*. In my previous appearance before members of this committee, I explained the origin and purposes of Mission to Moscow. That picture was made when our country was fighting for its existence, with Russia as one of our allies. It was made to fulfill the same wartime purpose for which we made such other pictures as *Air Force, This Is the Army, Objective Burma, Destination Tokyo, Action in the North Atlantic*, and a great many more. If making *Mission to Moscow* in 1942 was a subversive activity, then the American Liberty ships which carried food and guns to Russian allies and the American naval vessels which convoyed them were likewise engaged in subversive activities. The picture was made only to help a desperate war effort and not for posterity."

"Well, is it your opinion now, Mr. Warner, that *Mission to Moscow* was a factually correct picture, and you made it as such?"

"I can't remember."

"Would you consider it a propaganda picture?"

"A propaganda picture?" Warner was taken aback.

"Yes."

"In what sense?"

"In the sense that it portrayed Russia and communism in an entirely different light from what it actually was?"

"I am on record about 40 times or more that I have never been in Russia. I don't know what Russia was like in 1937 or 1944 or 1947, so how can I tell you if it was right or wrong?"

"Don't you think you were on dangerous ground to produce as a factually correct picture one which portrayed Russia –"

"No! We were not on dangerous ground in 1942, when we produced it. There was a war on. The world was at stake."

"In other words –" Thomas tried to interject.

"We made the film to aid in the war effort, which I believe I have already stated." Warner fought back his anger.

"Whether it was true or not?"

"As far as I was concerned, I considered it true to the extent as written in Mr. Davies' book."

"Well, do you suppose that your picture influenced the people who saw it in this country, the **millions** of people who saw it in this country?"

"In my opinion, I can't see how it would influence anyone. We were in a war and when you are in a fight you don't ask who the fellow is who is helping you."

"Well, due to the present conditions in the international situation, don't you think it was rather dangerous to write about such disillusionment as was sought in that picture?"

"I can't understand why you ask me that question, as to the present conditions. How did I, you, or anyone else know in 1942 what the conditions were going to be in 1947?! I stated in my testimony our reason for making the picture, which was to aid the war effort."

"I don't see that this is aiding the war effort, Mr. Warner, with the cooperation of Mr. Davies or with the approval of the Government to make a picture which is a fraud in fact."

Shocked that Thomas, someone Warner may have mistakenly considered a non-threat, had just given Jack Warner an abject lesson in American politics quickly sank in. The lesson? American politicians, particularly lawyer-politicians, have no friends, only temporary clients.

"I want to correct you, very vehemently! There was no cooperation of the Government!"

"You stated there was."

"I never stated the Government cooperated in the making of it. If I did, I stand corrected. And I know I didn't."

"Do you want me to read that part, Mr. Thomas?"

"No; I think we have gone into this *Mission to Moscow* at some length. . ."

After rambling on at length, as if he were back in his studios executive dining room Jack was excused from the stand.

Warner left the congressional chamber soaked in sweat and shaking with anger. Not anger directed at the committee but at himself for the unsolicited and unnecessary level of cooperation he bowed to the senators.

A standard tactic when you have nothing solid to prosecute on, is to probe at random until you inadvertently unearth some scrap you think you can exploit into an issue to muddy the waters in order to create as much doubt about the truth as possible. It's sometimes referred to as a 'perjury trap'. This technique is particularly useful when aided by the added pressure of microphones, TV cameras and assorted press coverage.

Although Warner did not allow himself to be caught in a perjury trap, he would never forgive himself for giving up names.

Eric Allen Johnston a dyed-in-the-wool Republican, who along with J. Thomas Parnell, Rankin and that crowd, hated FDR's New Deal policies, had just become the president of the Motion Picture Producers Association the year before.

By virtue of the fact that Johnston was the former President of the U.S. Chamber of Commerce and would later go on to be appointed special emissary to the Soviet Union by President Eisenhower, he was well acquainted with both political parties and so had more D.C. connections then Bell Telephone.

Johnston, presently responsible for re-establishing American films abroad following their virtual obliteration by the Nazis during the war and as president of the MPAA was the man that all of Hollywood now looked to to solve the problems caused by J. Parnell Thomas and his sub-committee's attacks. Later in the week Johnston was called to testify. When his time came to testify he dove right in.

"Would you please state your name for the record!" Congressman Thomas directed as Johnston took a seat.

"Eric Allen Johnston and I'm not here to try to whitewash Hollywood, and I'm not here to help sling a tar brush at it, either. I want to stick to the facts as I see them.

I have had a number of close looks at Hollywood in the last two years and I have looked at it through the eyes of an average businessman. I recognize that as the world's capital of show business, there is bound to be a lot of show business in Hollywood. There is no business, Mr. Chairman, like show business. But underneath there is the solid foundation of patriotic, hardworking, decent citizens. Making motion pictures is hard work. You just don't dash off a motion picture between social engagements.

I wind up my first point with a request of this committee."

The dramatic pause was as much to collect his thoughts as it was to play the cameras. This wasn't Johnston's first rodeo either.

"The damaging impression about Hollywood should be corrected. I urge your committee to do so in these public hearings.

My second point includes another request of the committee. The report of your subcommittee stated that you had a list of all pictures produced in Hollywood in the last eight years which contained Communist propaganda. Your committee **has not** made this list public. Until the list is made public the industry stands condemned by unsupported generalizations, and we are denied the opportunity to refute these charges publicly.

Gentlemen, I maintain that preservation of the rights of the individual is a proper duty for this Committee on Un-American Activities. This country's entire tradition is based on the principle that the individual is a higher power than the state; that the state owes its authority to the individual, and must treat him accordingly!"

For not the first nor the last time Thomas lost control of the chambers as spontaneous applause rose to erupt into an explosive crescendo drowning out the conversation and pinning the little red arrows of the volume meters on the T.V. mikes across the gallery.

"SILENCE IN THE GALLERY! SILENCE IN THE GALLERY!" Thomas scolded like a disgruntled father as he banged away to nearly fracture his gavel.

The ensuing standing ovation lasted the better part of five full minutes before order was restored.

The TV people had finagled the rights to the hearings in the hopes of catching some drama. The boys at NBC were not disappointed.

Reality T.V. was born and television sales spiked that year as sales surpassed 250,000 up from 44,000 just the year before.

But there was more to come.

After Albert Maltz, a successful screenwriter and several others were called to testify and refused to disclose their political beliefs, J. Parnell Thomas addressed the House and included some ludicrous statements typical of any lawyer arguing a case with little or no evidence.

Thomas' charade had ensued for two full weeks and he concluded that day by claiming that:

"Most of these later witnesses are writers-writers who receive $100,000 to $150,000 a year and who have written scripts for hundreds of movies which you have seen from time to time." He claimed with completely false authority.

This of course implies that about 18 writers, (as he only subpoenaed about 40 witnesses, in two weeks, twenty per week), were paid hundreds of thousands per year for many years as they have written 'hundreds of movies.'

For yet again not the first or the last time a member of the House of Representatives lied outright to their public. Neither Thomas or any of the other senators bothered to do any actual research.

All their accusations were based on total speculation secure in the belief that no one would challenge them, no one would actually check the facts and that the intimidation of a gaggle of high powered politicians sitting a full three feet above you aggressively pelting you with pointed questions would intimidate anyone fool enough to challenge the committee.

As in most big cases in the American legal system, especially criminal cases, the number one guideline is to never let the facts get in the way of a good case, particularly if you can create a crisis then exploit said crisis.

The fact that the three major studios produced less than 100 films each in 1946 and, thanks to the first mass production of televisions, did not much better in 1947 was conveniently omitted. As in most big cases in the American legal system it's not what you tell the people, it's what you don't tell them that counts.

In reality the screen writers' wages were the lowest of the studio feeding chain. 10% of the studio writers earned over $10,000 while over 50% earned less than $4,000 per year and 30% earned $2,000 annually. This is why they wanted and needed the Screen Writers Guild.

As facts are essentially kryptonite to individuals like Parnell Thomas and others of his ilk, the vast majority of what he had stated, was an outright lie.

Eventually, following two weeks of melodrama, false accusations and Constitutional abuse, so as not to embarrass themselves, the hysterical House Committee had to show something for their weeks of efforts and tens of thousands of taxpayer's money squandered.

So in a time before criminals like "Tail Gunner" Joe McCarthy went crazy a few years later, pointing fingers at everyone as he plied a completely compliant press with free alcohol and tax funded junkets around the country, indictments were drawn up, announced and handed down.

At the same time the D. C. Congressional Circus was winding down Pan Am flight 101 with Doc and Louie aboard was preparing to land at La Guardia Airfield in New York.

"You reckon people will go to jail?" Residual thoughts of politics still drifted around in Louie's head as they gathered their things.

"Louie, there's three things in this life that are for certain; death, taxes and nobody from the deep dark recesses of Washington D.C. ever sees the inside of a prison cell! You can take that to the bank." Doc opined.

"That's a given, but-"

"But in answer to your question, HUAC would look pretty stupid if they didn't lock somebody up. And since this whole fiasco is about image and looking good, yes some people will go to jail."

"Who do you think?"

"The ones with the cheapest lawyers."

Ladies and gentlemen on behalf of the captain, the crew an myself Pan Am would like to welcome you to La Guardia Airfield. You may now disembark the aircraft and thank you for flying Pan Am!

That evening J. Parnell burst into his office after the latest session, blew past his secretary and headed straight for his desk. He was in an obvious hurry.

Helen rose from her desk stepped to his office door and mustered her strength.

"Parnell . . . we need to talk." She meekly blurted out as he fussed at his desk. She couldn't discern if he was ignoring her or didn't hear.

"Parnell we need to talk!"

He looked back over his shoulder as he lifted his Mackintosh from the corner coat rack.

"Helen, I'm really late! Can't it wait?"

"No, not anymore." His suspicions grew.

"Alright then, what is it?" He sat his briefcase on top of his coat on the desk.

In the years he and Helen Campbell had been together Thomas had seen her agitated but this time she seemed extra edgy. Time to pull out the magic.

"It's about this thing with Myra & Arnette –"

"Oh Helen! Helen, Helen!" With each iteration he stepped closer. "We've been over this. I told you it's just until the end of this session and all this communist stuff has settled down."

"I don't feel good about it! What if somebody finds out?"

"Who's gonna find out?" He cajoled.

"I'm getting really uncomfortable with all this publicity in the press, radio and now on TV! They're here every day! In the morning when I come to work, at night when I go home! I had to start bringing my lunch and eat in here, I'm even afraid to go to the commissary!"

"This has nothing to do with you!" Thomas nimbly donned his spin meister hat.

The hand is quicker than the eye.

He took her by the shoulders and kissed her on the cheek then moved to collect his things. At the front door he bade her good-bye.

"Have I ever lied to you?" He smiled his crooked smile and vanished.

Helen spent the night at home drinking and debating whether or not to telephone her sister which she eventually did.

Two weeks later the junior FBI agent was visibly nervous as he stood just outside the congressman's office door. He looked down at the court order in his hand than over to his middle-aged partner.

"Relax kid." His partner encouraged. "You got **any idea** how many Americans would pay good money to be in our shoes right now? Serving a subpoena to a big time politician!"

The two agents stood just outside the Congressional office of J. Parnell Thomas.

What Doc McKeowen had no way of knowing when he told Louie that, 'nobody in D.C. goes to jail', was that not everyone remained silent about the HUAC atrocities, in particular the committee's domineering bully Parnell Thomas.

Rumors of Parnell's corrupt nature had long been whispered about but would finally come to light via one of his closest confidants.

It was only a week ago that, after looking around to see who might have left the large manila envelope on his desk marked 'Special Delivery', Jack Anderson perused the office again to reassure himself he was alone before taking a seat at his desk. A desk located at the syndicated offices of the United Press International.

Anderson, who has been branded the 'Father of Investigative Journalism' was the first to reveal evidence that the Mafia was a nation-wide operation, this much to the endless aggravation of J. Edgar Hoover who consistently denied as much since 1919 when he started at what would become the FBI.

Hoover did this because, largely under the recommendation of Meyer Lansky applying rule Number One of the covert Mafia code, he was being bribed. Rule Number one of course dictated that if bribery was necessary start at the top, don't waste time working your way up the chain of command.

Few ever openly questioned Hoover's unusual good luck at the race tracks. Race tracks largely influenced and controlled by Organized Crime syndicates.

Jack Anderson who was proficient enough at his job to have been later targeted for assassination by the CIA, was a writer for the column called *The Merry-go-Round* which focused on D.C. corruption and gossip with a view towards exposing wrongdoing. Anderson took his work very seriously.

Helen Campbell, Parnell Thomas' secretary, Campbell's niece Myra Midkiff & Arnette Minor, Campbell's maid were fraudulently being carried on the government payroll as Senator Thomas' clerks.

This illegal activity had been on going from January the 1st 1940.

The scheme allowed Thomas to steal thousands in taxpayer money and avoid taxes by requiring the women to kick back money to himself, in Midkiff's case her entire salary.

A staunch opponent of HUAC's tactics and long following Thomas and his pugnacious ways, Anderson verified the information Helen Campbell had left in the envelope and then went to work.

In his August 4th column the reporter penned an article detailing Thomas' fraudulent 'clerk' scheme and thereby exposed the career politician.

Thomas and his secretary were subpoenaed to a grand jury and faced with the charges. Campbell cooperated but Thomas arrogantly pleaded Fifth Amendment, the same as his victims had in the witch hunt trials and so refused to answer questions.

He was found guilty and the front page news resulted in him having to resign from Congress, being fined and being sent to prison for eighteen months. Ironically right alongside Lester Cole and Ring Lardner Jr. two of the famous 'Hollywood Ten' he had falsely prosecuted during his show trials. His career would never recover.

When Doc read the article he had one extra drink that night.

CHAPTER XVIII

M&M Investigations
Christopher Street
Greenwich Village
N.Y.C., N.Y.

It was just before noon when Doc and Louie hopped out of the Sunshine cab in front of their Christopher Street office and ducked in through Harry's Front Page News.

"You two finally back from your gallivanting there Dick Tracy?" Harry chided from behind the counter.

"Nice to see you too again Harry. You still missing a leg?" Doc returned as he dropped his bag and grabbed a *New York Daily News* from the shelf in front of the counter.

"Fuck you Doc! That'll be five cents!" Harry barked as he reached over for his prosthetic leg then retook his permanent perch, the stool set just behind the long counter with the three foot square space surrounded by cigars, cigarettes, chocolate bars and gum.

"Put it on my tab." Doc answered.

"Cheap bastard!" Harry grumbled. "Hey Louie." Harry greeted.

"Hey Harry."

Harry's Front Page, everyone called it "The News Stand", occupied the entire ground level of

The Broad in the Kimono

1929 Christopher Street. The corner entrance and small display window were capped by a hand lettered, green enamel sign which hadn't seen a fresh coat of paint since the WWI Armistice.

Packed with black wire, twirly racks, stacked with post cards that never sold, (come to think of it, nothing ever really sold except newspapers and an occasional stale candy bar), you'd be hard pressed to squeeze four people in there at any one time. That included Harry.

Harry's life had long ago settled into a permanent station on a high backed stool behind the counter, framed by racks of candy bars and potato chips. He was rarely seen to venture out from behind the counter.

From a clandestine location somewhere in the store radio constantly played in the background as he read all day long. To his credit, other than newspapers he read only the classics: Captain Marvel, The Shadow and The Phantom. These were by far the best, for it was common sense that they were the most realistic. Every time Superman or Batman got in a fix, they would come up with some wild gizmo they just happened to have nearby or hanging on a belt and escape certain death. Ridiculous.

Who ever heard of yellow kryptonite anyway?

Harry lost a leg in the last war, and in between warm sodas and cold coffees the old man would give Doc tips on horse racing, despite the fact Doc had never been to the track a day in his life.

Doc respected Harry because he was one of those old people who could tell you what he had for breakfast on any given day, six months ago, and he seldom ate the same thing every day. This made Harry the perfect lobby watch-dog.

Harry never advertised the fact that he had done time for counterfeiting. After the First War when Woodrow Wilson and the government reneged on the money they promised the soldiers who made I through the war, Harry and couple of vet buddies decided they were owed. They set up a counterfeiting operation to see them through the bad times and got pretty good at it. Until they encroached on Al Capone's territory and a phone call got them turned into the Feds.

Doc knew this side of Harry and so never had to ask how it was that after five years in the Federal pen Harry was able to pay cash-on-the-nail in full to buy the *Front Page News*.

"So Harry, what'a ya know?" Louie asked grabbing a Hershey's bar and tossing a nickel on the counter's rubber mat.

"Life's a bitch and then you die, that's all I know."

"The girls upstairs Harry?" McKeowen asked as he perused the headlines.

"Nikki came in this morning, didn't see Shirley. You two gum shoes find out anything about that kid's murder?"

"What makes you say he was murdered?" Doc asked.

"I hear things. I got sources." Harry shot back.

"Sources like a cute auburn haired, blue-eyed female goes by the name of Nikki Cole?" Doc remarked.

"Nikki and I were bouncing a few theories around, yeah."

"Like what fer instance?" Doc pushed as he read.

"Like fer instance who ever done that kid-"

"'Benny', Harry, his name was Benny." Doc informed as he perused the front page of the tabloid. "Son-of-a-bitch! Hey Louie look at this." He beckoned and Louie wandered over to where Doc stood with the wide opened newspaper. "That nut job Howard Hughes got the Spruce Goose off the ground!"

"No kidding?!" Louie leaned in to scan the full page, centrefold black and white photo spread of the behemoth, eight engine aircraft skimming the waters of Longbeach Harbor. "That thing sure looks like it could hold five hundred troops!"

"Seven hundred!" Doc corrected. "I'm telling you, we live in amazing times fellas!" McKeowen declared.

"AS I WAS SAYIN'!" Harry shouted catching their attention and tearing them away from the newspaper article.

"Sorry Harry. Didn't mean to get your blood pressure up. Please continue."

"Like fer instance who ever done that kid might just have erased a few other people because-"

"What makes you think that?" Louie cut him off.

"If you two knuckleheads'll quit interruptin' me!"

"Sorry Harry." Doc motioned Louie to let Harry speak.

"Well you two was away some young fella over in Brooklyn off'ed himself."

"There's half a dozen suicides a day in this city." Doc countered.

"Yeah, but how many of 'em are Jews? Jews got laws against suicide! Their book tells 'em if they off themselves they go to Hell!"

"That's Catholics Harry, Jews don't have Hell." Doc corrected.

"Oh yeah? You ever heard of Mabel Klugman?!"

"Who's Mabel Klugman?"

"A girl I almost married back during the First War. She was a Jew and that bitch was hell!"

"Harry, your point? How'd this guy die?" Doc prodded.

"Sorry Doc. The Brooklyn kid was a Jew found hanged in his backyard. At first the coppers ruled it a suicide but three days later the Coroner ruled it a homicide! A Jew killed by hanging made to look like a suicide?" Neither Doc or Louie responded. "What, I gotta draw you two a picture?" Harry pushed.

"Nice connect Harry but it's still a bit thin. How'd you come by this little tid bit?"

"What the hell you think I do sitting around here all day long, six days a week besides using my ass as a seat warmer?! I got access to every paper in The City fer cryin' out loud!" He gestured down to the two dozen different newspapers stacked along the underside of the front counter. "I read!"

409

"Okay, which paper did you see this little item in?"

"How the hell should I know?! It was all the way back in May, or June. Could'a been July maybe." Harry searched the recesses of his seventy-nine year old brain. "It was buried back on the obits page. Probably not deemed very news worthy with all this HUAC investigation nonsense going on."

"What'a ya think Doc?" Louie asked.

"I think it's worth looking into. C'mon, let's get up to the office." Doc signalled and they headed through the side door and upstairs. "Thanks Harry. Appreciate your input. You think of which paper let us know will ya?"

"Sure thing Doc." Harry slid off his stool and tested that his prosthetic leg was seated correctly. "Hey Doc!"

"Yeah Harry?"

"Welcome back."

"Thanks."

Back when McKeowen quit the force and his wife ran off, 1929 Christopher Street was the first place he found that suited his newly found ambitions of setting up shop as a P.I. *Harry's Front Page News* had already occupied the ground floor since just after the Great War.

Doc and Harry hit it off and eventually came to an arrangement. Harry's newsagent was conveniently located with windows both on the street front side and to the left of the counter with a large window looking out into the building's vestibule, elevator and staircase. Harry would keep an eye on comings and goings for Doc and in return McKeowen would slip him a fifty at the end of a month. Plus Harry had a standing invite to Doc's semi-regular 'Baptisms', known in lay speak as drink ups.

As McKeowen and Mancino entered the office Nikki emerged from Doc's office, smiled and hurried across to Doc with a big hug and several kisses.

"Missed you!" She gleefully greeted.

"Missed you too gorgeous!" There was more kissing than Mancino thought necessary.

"Get a room!" He called out from his office just adjacent to Doc's.

Prying himself away from Nikki Doc dug in his bag and produced a small box and a cardboard poster tube. Nikki, having followed him back into his office pointed to what were obviously a pair of gifts.

"And what are those?" She asked with feigned innocence.

"That's for you and this one . . . is for Kate. It's an autographed movie poster autographed by Simone Simon."

"She'll love it! Is it authentic?"

"Probably not, nothing I saw out there was."

"Can I open it?" She brandished the small box.

"If you like."

"Louie, when you get a minute come in here, will ya?." He called next door to Louie's office where Mancino was on the phone to his wife.

"In a sec Doc." Mancino was on the phone with his wife Doris.

"Oh my god! Doc they're gorgeous!" Nikki complimented as she stepped over to the door mirror and held the pair of emerald ear rings up to her eras.

"Found them in a little shop off the strip in L.A. They're handmade."

Louie popped in.

"How's Doris?" Nikki asked.

"Good, she's doin' good. Big dinner planned tonight!"

"Good." Doc offered. "Louie, after you get settled in here get over to the Brooklyn Coroner's office. Check out Harry's story, get all the details and see if they have a suspect."

"Aw Doc! I was hoping for some break time with Doris! Can't I run this down in the morning? I mean we been away the better apart of two weeks!"

"I see your point. Break time with Doris is pretty important now with her being pregnant and all huh?"

"See Doc, I knew you'd understand!" Louie smiled and lightly punched Doc in the shoulder.

"I do understand Louie. I understand that the two or three hours you're going to spend taking the train over to Brooklyn and talking to the coroner's office is not going to make any difference about when your baby is gonna come, whether it's gonna be a boy or girl or whether or not it's gonna look like you or be a beautiful good looking, successful, well-respected child. Now, get over to the Sheridan

Street station, hop on the N Train and go talk to the Brooklyn coroner's office. "

"Then I gotta come all the way back here and tell you what I found?! I won't get home till five or six!"

Nikki looked at Doc and, on Mancino's behalf, gave Doc a sympathetic glance.

"Okay you can let me know what you found out tomorrow after lunch when you come in." Doc relented.

Mancino spent just enough time in his office to grab his hat and coat before he dashed out the door. Nikki laughed. She moved back into Doc and threw her arms around his neck and kissed him again.

"So, Mr. traveling P.I., now that we're all alone, what are we gonna do in this very big, very empty office all by ourselves?"

"Well, I thought a lot about that in the cab on the way in this morning." He held her closer and kissed her lightly on the lips.

"And . . . what did you think about doing?" She prodded.

"And . . . we could lock up the office, go over to my nice, big flat desk and . . ." He gave her a peck on the lips between each beat. "Or, I thought we'd have a nice early dinner at Mario's near your place then instead of my desk we could use that nice big soft bed in your place and enjoy each other's company for the rest of the night."

"Okay, if the desk is too risqué for you I have a better idea. We go straight back to my place, shag each other's brains out, stay in bed, order delivery from Mario's, eat in bed and share a bottle of wine?"

"Yeah? Then what?"

"Wash, rinse, repeat!" She moved in for another kiss. "I'll get my coat and purse!"

To Nikki's surprise, once downstairs they both turned in opposite directions.

"C'mon, we'll just cut up Seventh Avenue." Doc informed.

"Seventh Avenue? But my place is this way!"

"I know, but just a quick stop over at St. Vincent's."

"For what?!" She demanded.

"The morgue."

"To visit all the other dead stiffs?" She pouted.

"I just need to ask Jimmy a few questions."

"Seriously McKeowen, can you not stop being a detective for just five minutes?!"

"Sweetheart, you badgered me about letting you get involved in the office. Now you're involved in the office. Which reminds me, where the hell was Shirley?"

Nikki became noticeably disarmed

"Well?" McKeowen pushed.

"I . . . I kind of gave her the afternoon off."

"For what?!"

"She has a new boyfriend."

"What's that the fifth one this year?!"

"Fourth Doc, it's only her fourth." Nikki defended.

"Oh well, I guess that's okay then." He sarcastically jeered.

"Give her a break Doc. She's not good with men."

"NOT GOOD?! Any better she'd be hauled in for being a hooker!"

"I'm working on her Doc. I'm working on her! She just needs to learn to not come off as so opinionated all the time. It turns guys off."

"Uh huh."

"Okay, forget about it. I'll stop trying to help her out!"

"On the subject of forgetting, let us not also forget that it was you who harangued me into taking this case! Remember I didn't want it."

"I guess I'm going to hear about that for the rest of my life?"

"Probably, but there is one way you redeem yourself." Doc offered.

"Jesus it's cold out here!" She pulled her coat tighter around herself as they walked. "Yeah how's that? She asks with no small amount of trepidation!"

"By putting all those years of research skills to some good use by first thing in the morning finding out everything you can about a crowd calling themselves the Sons of Liberty. They're up Chicago."

"You think there's a connection with Benny?"

"Don't know for sure but you're gonna tell us. And after that you' gonna get to a hold of the client-"

"Nina Twisselman."

"Yeah, Twisselman, and find out where Benny's typewriter is, and if she knows if he ever used it to correspond with anybody, you know wrote them letters or anything like that then double check if she's sure there was no suicide note."

The four block, fifteen minute walk up to the hospital was cold but brief. Doc and Nikki went straight to the rear of the long corridor.

"Jimmy downstairs?" He asked the receptionist.

"No he's off. But Donnie is." Doc nodded and headed for the stairs. "I wouldn't go down there if I were you." She called after him.

Down in the morgue Doc spotted Donnie in his office at his desk filling out a form.

"Hi Donnie." He greeted in a neutral tone as he stepped through the doorway. By way of reply Donnie reached for the phone on his desk and pressed for an in-house line.

"Hello Mabel could you please send security-" McKeowen was across the room with his finger on the hook cutting Donnie's request off before he could finish it. Donnie hung up and made eye contact with Doc.

"You got some set'a balls using Jimmy for-" Doc put a finger to his lips and nodded over his shoulder at Nikki who stood in the doorway leaning against the door jamb.

"Lady present!" Doc pointed out. Nikki smiled and waved across the room. Donnie nodded back.

"You got some set'a balls showing your face around here!" He whispered to Doc.

"C'mon Donnie! You had a suicide case come through here back in May. I just need to know what happened to the personals afterwards."

"You do understand that this is my god-damned job you're playin' around with?!"

"Lady present!" Doc reiterated. "And all I'm asking is for you to do your job! If this kid was murdered isn't it your job to help catch the bastards?"

"That still don't give you the right to go off on your own fucking . . . screwing around with a police investigation!"

"Remember that Mob guy was given the chair for killing his wife a few years back? The one they - "

"Yeah the one they later found out didn't do it." Donnie quietly acknowledged.

"The one who was convicted on your lab findings!"

"That lab report was 100% and independently verified!" Donnie defended.

"'Yeah, yeah it was. It was an honest mistake. But you think anybody is gonna give a damn, especially his mob buddies if they were to find out it was you did the lab report? That they'd give a damn that it was an honest mistake?"

Shocked at the veiled threat it dawned on Donnie that maybe he didn't know McKeowen as well as he thought he did. He broke eye contact with Doc first, cleared his throat and took a breath

"A suicide case back in May you say?"

"Yes, May."

"Which one?"

"How many suicides did you have in May fer cryin' out loud?!"

Donnie rose from his desk and went to the top drawer of the filing cabinet. He pulled a file and read aloud.

"Six came through here." He said reading the record he held.

"Try Joules."

"Joules, B.?"

"That's the one." Doc winked over at Nikki.

"After the Coroner's testimony we handed all the personal possessions back over to the police who presumably gave them to the next of kin once the case was closed."

"What's the name under the NOK?"

"Doc that's classified!"

"Yeah, yeah I know. Line 17, bottom of the page where it says 'Next of Kin'. Name?"

"Joules, Emma Jean Joules."

"That Mrs. Joules the mother?"

"That's the name listed under 'mother'."

"She show up alone or the cops send somebody?"

"Don't know, wasn't here I was off that day."

"Well do me one more favor will ya? Check who signed for the stuff."

"You just about used up all your favors in this neighborhood McKeowen!"

"Thanks Donnie. Just this then I'll leave you alone for the rest of the year, word of honor!"

"What a sport!" Donnie flipped a page and read. "Name here is a Rochford, Finnis T. Rochford."

"Finnis T. Rochford? Is that a person or an insect spray? Who the hell is that?!" Doc queried.

"Dunno, maybe her lawyer. He signed it, 'for Mrs. Emma J. Joules'."

"Must be her lawyer. Many items on the list?"

"You really don't know when to quit, do you McKeowen?"

"No he doesn't!" Nikki called over from the doorway.

"Here asshole!" Donnie gave a sarcastic smile and nodded a cursory apology at Nikki as he passed the file to Doc who opened at the page marked 'Itemization of Personal Possessions'. McKeowen scanned the list.

"Thirty-seven dollars and fifteen cents, one Bulova watch, alligator strap, one alligator wallet. Guy liked alligator. Various personal photos, Beth Israel membership card, one Jerusalem Shekel and . . ." Doc suddenly clammed up.

"What is it Doc?" Nikki asked.

"I just remembered something." He handed the file back to Donnie and went to leave.

"You're welcomed McKeowen!" Donnie threw one last jab.

On their way out Nikki turned back.

"Donnie, about your profanity?" She called back into the room.

"Yeah?"

"I used to work for the Navy. I heard a lot fuckin' worse!"

On the way upstairs Nikki questioned Doc.

"So is that how you get your leads? Threatening people with going to the Mob?"

"No I get them through deduction, leg work and psychology."

"Would you really have given the Mob his name?"

"I never threatened him. I only made him think I was threatening him."

Up in the main corridor Nikki stopped Doc.

"What did you see on that list?"

"Something Twissleman told us didn't exist."

"Like what"

"A suicide note!"

"Maybe she just didn't know!" Nikki reasoned.

"Maybe, but we're gonna find out!"

Nikki stopped dead in her tracks, clamped her hands on hips and pursed her lips. Doc read her body language.

"Okay, okay! I've seen that 'you're sleeping on the couch tonight' look before! We'll find out, tomorrow." He relented.

They went to dinner where several glasses of Cordon Negro brut cava ensured he didn't have to sleep on the couch that night.

✝

CHAPTER XIX

Next morning Doc hit the ground running showing up at the office at half past seven and drawing up an airtight attack plan involving the whole crew, Nikki Cole included.

With an impromptu huddle in his office he handed out assignments.

He got Nikki to call the D.A.'s office and confirm their current policy on handling of personal possessions of the deceased, whether by homicide or suicide. At first the D.A.'s secretary was stand-offish and resistant but on remembering an Assistant D.A. Nikki knew from her years Downtown in the Woolworth Building at the Office of Naval Intelligence during the war working for Commander Haffenden during *Operation Underworld*, she not only got what she needed but was able to cajole the Assistant D.A. into dictating to her the complete list in the D.A.'s file.

The D.A. confirmed that with the exception of ongoing or ancillary, connected crime cases all possessions were returned to the next of kin or their legal representation, as soon as that particular case was declared closed.

The D.A.'s list matched the Coroner's records with one exception - no suicide note.

Louie had showed up on time, almost, and related what he found from the Brooklyn Coroner, which wasn't much. They wouldn't release any details of that suicide due to the fact that it was still under investigation. However they did confirm there was a suicide of a young man back in the May time frame.

"Okay Louie, good work, we put that case aside for now. You remember that Bozo we talked to in Chicago, the guy with the construction business?"

"Steadman?"

"Yeah. Dig up all the info you can remember on him from your notes, contact details et cetra, and get it to Nikki. Don't forget about that creepy little gorilla who popped his head into the meeting when we were taking to Steadman."

Louie who had been furiously scribbling notes in his trusty little note book flipped back several pages and found the name.

"Sollozo is what Steadman called him when we were standing there." Mancino informed Doc.

"Sollozo great, see if we can find his full name and anything else about him."

"Gotcha!" Louie snapped and vanished back into his office pausing at the door.

"What'a ya want me to do after that Doc?"

"Get the train out to Queens and talk with Benny's parents, mom whichever one is home. Have Nikki call first. We need three things from her, what items were returned, was there a note and can we borrow Benny's typewriter?"

"That'll take me rest of the day."

"I know. Scratch out some detailed notes on the train back into The City and fill me in on what you got in the morning when you come in. On time!"

"Sorry Doc! Doris was kind'a glad to see me last night. Maybe we could go away again sometime?"

"Get out'a here, pervert!" He laughed at Louie.

Doc's energy being contagious, Louie dashed into his office and went to work.

"And Louie!" Doc called after him.

"Yeah Doc?"

"When you talk with the mother, be sensitive."

"Count on me Doc!" Mancino called back out. "I'll be completely pathetic!"

"Good Louie." Doc looked over at Nikki who mouthed 'empathic' and smiled. Doc nodded back and shrugged.

"At least he's trying." Nikki encouraged.

Nikki snapped to attention and rendered a mock salute. "Okay General, what are my orders?"

"You, Private Cole-"

"PRIVATE?!"

"Okay, Lance Corporal Cole."

'That's better! What's a lance corporal?"

"Somebody who's real important! Now start a file on this guy." Doc scribbled Steadman's name on a piece of note paper and passed it to her. "First name Jake. Set it up in two parts, one professional and one private. Everything you can find out about him and his business. Trace him back as far as you can through the Chicago business community and that civic action organization he's mixed up with, the Sons of Liberty."

"What about the papers?" Nikki asked.

"What about them?"

"The newspapers will almost certainly have covered all the suicides. By scouring the microfiche files we might get a leg up on some detail we've missed. An inconsistency, an address who knows?"

"Good idea, glad I thought of it!" He teased. "Right after you get with Louie take a taxi up to the Bryant Park branch and comb through *The Daily News* and *The Post*."

"What about *the Times*?"

"Only check the *Times* if you find nothing in the tabloids and then go straight to the Obits section. Start with the first week in May. On second thought I think I remember that that guy Epstein was some kind of a high up muckity-muck in business circles so you might find something in *The Times*."

"I'll check the Business, Society and Obits pages."

"Good thinking Batman!" He gave her a quick kiss on the lips. "See you back at the apartment tonight."

"Where you going?"

"I got a couple of things to track down then some errands to run. I'll meet you around six for dinner."

Mancino made it over to Bayside in Queens an hour later and had no trouble locating the Joules' residence just off Bell Boulevard.

As she opened the front door the stress of the last weeks was clearly etched on the face of Mrs. Joules but didn't deter her from a stoic cordiality. She poured Mancino a coffee from the silver engraved, Revere coffee pot and kick started the exchange.

"What exactly is your interest in my son's death Mr. Mancino?" She took a seat in the Hepplewhite at the dining table across from where Louie sat.

"Ma'am my agency has been engaged by a good friend of your son's to have a closer look at why his script was rejected." Louie lied.

"Well, it was his first attempt and with no real background in that area . . . You know, he was supposed to go to law school."

"It probably wasn't his writing. If it makes a difference, people in the trade were complimentary about his writing." Louie was pleased to see a brief hint of a smile cross her face. "My client is particularly interested in why Benny's script was first accepted then suddenly, a short time later, rejected. We find that suspicious."

"And I don't suppose you're prepared to tell me the name of this client who is so interested in my son's death?"

"I'm sorry Mrs. Joules, it's about the script, it really is. Besides, we were made to sign a NBA."

"An 'NBA'?"

"Yeah, a contract that says we can't talk about it."

"Do you mean an NDA?"

"Yeah, that's it! NDA. We can't reveal any details about who's paying us."

"Glad we got that cleared up." Mancino dismissed the sarcasm.

"Mrs. Joules, may I ask who represented you in your son's case?"

"Our family lawyer, Mr. Rochfort."

"Is he also Jewish?"

She excused herself but returned immediately with her purse, rummaged through it and handed Louie a business card. "Yes he's orthodox. We've used him since Benny was bar mitzvahed." She reinforced.

Mancino read the raised gold printing on the heavy black stock. 'Finnis T. Rochfort, Esq.' The name was accompanied by a mid-town address.

"Were Benny's personal items retuned directly to you after his death?"

"Yes. Well not directly, Mr. Rochfort collected them on the way to the funeral and gave then to my husband afterwards."

"May I ask what those items were?"

"The usual personal items any young man would carry around. His wallet, his watch, a small amount of money his commemorative Jerusalem shekel and all the writing they found in his apartment."

"What about his typewriter?"

"His typewriter?"

"Yes ma'am. He had a typewriter, a relatively new Underwood?"

"Oh, that thing!" Her obvious distain caught Mancino's attention. Although visibly uncomfortable discussing it she continued. "His father's idea. A reward I suppose for quitting law school!"

"I take it you didn't agree with Benny leaving school?"

"His name is Benjamin and I most certainly did not! What person in his right mind would want to be a writer?! Of movies no less! Benjamin was not meant to be a writer. He was destined to be a respectable member of society!"

"One more thing Mrs. Joules, then I'll leave you alone. Are you and Mr. Joules still together?"

"I don't see what that has to do with anything Mr. Casino!"

"Mancino, Ma'am. I see. Thank you for your time Mrs. Joules."

Louie decided to take it on himself to visit Rochfort's office in Upper Manhattan on the way back and inquire about the personal items list.

Forty-five minutes later Rochfort was eating a late lunch at his desk and was none too pleased at an unscheduled visitor just dropping in on him but with Mancino's ignorance of upper middle class behavioral standards and procedures, tempered by Rochfort not wanting to have to deal with this nosy detective later, he gave Mancino five minutes face time. Which was all Mancino needed. A few cursory questions allowed Louie to form an opinion.

Something aroused Mancino's suspicions during the brief encounter and so he made a brief stop in to the New York Bar Association office in Midtown on the way back down to The Village.

Late that afternoon Louie practically tripped through the front door of the M&M office, buzzed by the reception desk where Nikki was typing away and, without knocking burst through Doc's door.

"Forget which office is yours?" Doc looked up from his desk and challenged.

"Okay, okay, okay! So I'm talking to the old bat, right?!" Louie blurted out.

"Presumably you mean Mrs. Joules?"

"No, Rochfort!"

"Joule's lawyer?"

"YEAH! He-"

"What the hell you talking to the lawyer about?"

"I'm coming to that! She gave me his card."

"Mrs. Joules?"

"Yeah! His half eaten lunch was on his desk. He was eating a roast beef sandwich on rye with brown mustard and . . . drinking milk!" Louie dramatically delivered.

"So?" Doc challenged as Nikki wandered in and stood in the door.

"The old woman-"

"Mrs. Joules!"

"Mrs. Joules!" They said simultaneously. "Told me this guy Rochfort's orthodox! She told me when she gave me his card!"

"And your point is?"

"Mrs. Joules old me he was orthodox!"

"You already said that!"

"Louie's right Doc. Somebody's lying. Probably the lawyer!"

"What? Did everybody stop by the pub after lunch and have a few?" Doc quipped.

"The Kashrut forbids Jews combining meat and dairy when they eat."

"I know about the meat and milk thing! You were a research librarian for the Third Naval District." He said to Nikki. Then he turned back to Mancino. "But how in the hell did **you** know about what's in the Kashrut?"

"Our neighbor Mr. Levitz is orthodox. Doris cooked for him for a while after his wife died. He told us."

"What do you think you're some kind of detective or something?" Doc teased.

"Maybe, Louie he's not orthodox?" Nikki offered.

"Mrs. Joules told me he was orthodox. Besides he told me he eats oysters and Jews ain't supposed to eat shellfish!"

"So what? The guy just blurted out, 'I eat oysters'?" Doc again challenged.

"No, no, no! I baited him, just like you taught me!" To attain maximum delivery impact Mancino pulled a chair up to the front of the desk, twirled it round backwards and sat with his arms draped over the beck rail. "I made like I was having indigestion from eating linguine and clams for lunch, see? So I says to him, 'do you like linguini and clams? And what'a think he says to me?"

"No idea Louie but the suspense is killing me."

"He says, 'no! I like oysters!' OYSTERS no less!" Mancino smiled broadly and nodded his head to acknowledge his own victory. "How about them apples Doc?!"

"Hmm. Maybe Joules was wrong about him being orthodox?"

"That's what I thought just as I was getting ready to leave the bar Association's office Uptown then I went back and found this!" Louie opened his note book and brandished it to Doc who took it and read the scribbled notes aloud.

"Honored donator to the FNG and the GAB!" Doc fell back in his chair and smiled up at Louie.

"All I'm saying is it's a little suspicious if the guy is supposed to be orthodox, that's all I'm sayin', ya know?!" Louie added.

"Mancino I never thought I'd say this, but I'm impressed."

"Guys! Who the heck are the FNG and the GAB?" Nikki insisted.

"*Friends of New Germany* and the *German American Bund.*"

"NAZI's?!" She exclaimed.

Louie held his pocket comb under his nose and gave the Nazi salute. "Nazi's!" He barked with a mock German accent.

Waldorf Astoria Hotel
New York City
Wednesday, December 3rd

The HUAC investigations continued on through late November until the committee decided they had found their scapegoats and the results were released to the public

Congressional citations were announced through the headlines of the major news publications on Monday November the 24th.

The MPAA wasted little time building fences and nailing their colors to the mast to protect the organization.

In spite of the hundreds of times the studios had preached to America over the last three decades, with morally infused scripts clearly delineating who was the good guy and who was the bad guy, the Big Five studios through the MPAA clearly left their high ground ethics on the big screen when it came to endangering their economic bottom line. It was decided by the powers that be, that what became known as The Hollywood Ten were not important enough to defend, a fact no doubt taken into consideration by the HUAC Committee,

A mere week later on Wednesday, December 3rd Eric Johnston, as promised, held a press conference at the Waldorf Astoria in New York where the MPAA had held their closed door meeting of the top forty Hollywood movie executives to discuss how to handle the powder keg which had exploded all over them.

The controversy sparked by Willy Wilkinson's fabricated *Hollywood Reporter* article contained in his widely read *Tradeviews* column entitled "A Vote for Joe Stalin", in which he falsely reported of heavy communist infiltration of Hollywood and published in July of 1946 had finally sparked the political hatred seething below the surface since the end of the war and now gave gravitas to the infamous Hollywood Blacklist.

A list that didn't really exist. But really did.

It was to a standing room only mob that Eric Johnston held the press conference and publicly announced *The Waldorf Agreement*.

Johnston moved with deliberation as he stepped in front of the collapsible podium the hotel staff had just finished carefully placing in front of the large twin oak doors to the entrance of the Executive Conference Room.

He adjusted a thin sheaf of papers and perused the mob of press herded in front of him. Several uniformed NYPD stood between himself, the stringers and correspondents.

Behind him stood Mendel Silberberg lawyer for the MPAA and as if to emphasis the gravity of the statement, the well-known James F. Byrnes former Secretary of State.

"Gentlemen, thank you for coming. As you are aware the Congress has issued ten citations to ten members of the motion picture industry. To this end a recent meeting of forty or more members of the MPPA have agreed on the following statement."

He adjusted himself and read form the prepared statement.

"Members of the Association of Motion Picture Producers deplore the action of the ten Hollywood men who have been cited for contempt by the House of Representatives.

We do not desire to prejudge their legal rights, but their actions have been a disservice to their employers and have impaired their usefulness to the industry.

We will forthwith discharge or suspend without compensation those in our employ, and we will not re-employ any of The Ten until such time as he is acquitted or has purged himself of contempt and declares under oath that he is not a communist.

On the broader issue of alleged subversive and disloyal elements in Hollywood, our members are likewise prepared to take positive action.

We will not knowingly employ a Communist or a member of any party or group which advocates the overthrow of the government of the United States by force or by any illegal or unconstitutional methods.

In pursuing this policy, we are not going to be swayed by hysteria or intimidation from any source. We are frank to recognize that such a policy involves danger and risks.

There is the danger of hurting innocent people. There is the risk of creating an atmosphere of fear. Creative work at its best cannot be carried on in an atmosphere of fear. We will guard against this danger, this risk, this fear. To this end we will invite the Hollywood talent guilds to work with us to eliminate any subversives: to protect the innocent; and to safeguard free speech and a free screen wherever threatened.

The absence of a national policy, established by Congress, with respect to the employment of

Communists in private industry makes our task difficult. Ours is a nation of laws. We request Congress to enact legislation to assist American industry to rid itself of subversive, disloyal elements. Nothing subversive or un-American has appeared on the screen, nor can any number of Hollywood investigations obscure the patriotic services of the 30,000 loyal Americans employed in Hollywood who have given our government invaluable aid to war and peace."

He gathered his papers.

"Copies of the aforementioned statement will be carried by the *Daily Variety* as well as the *Motion Picture Herald*. We will now take any questions."

CHAPTER XX

Given recent developments Doc had formulated a plan of attack.

"Nina, thank you for coming. Let's go into my office. Nikki grab Louie and you guys step in here too." Nikki complied and the huddle commenced.

"Miss Cole says you have some news for me?" Twisselman started.

"Yes, no . . . maybe. On a suggestion from an informant we traced suicides in the New York area at around the time of Benny's death." At the first real positive turn of events Twisselman hung on every word. "We found three that were similar."

"You think we're dealing with a serial killer?!"

"I wouldn't go that far but there are similarities in at least two cases."

"You mean death by hanging?"

"'Apparent' suicides by unlikely candidates, all three involving Jewish men all between May and July of this year. We're still tracing the third but we know it was a hanging and Benny's and a businessman named Epstein have a strong connect in that they both left suicide notes that are questionable."

"But I told you, Benny left no note!"

"We think he did. Or at least there was a note of some kind."

"But-"

"We've contacted Epstein's next of kin, his wife. She tells us that the cops returned all her husband's personal belongings including the typewriter to her through her lawyer. When the lawyer went to return the machine she told him dispose of it. She didn't want it or his suicide note around the house. We're banking on the fact that her lawyer still has them or at least knows where they are. We're confident he'll work with us. But for what I have in mind I need both machines and both notes. You have Benny's Underwood?"

"Yes, at home, in my room."

"I need that typewriter! Bring it with you when you come back on Tuesday."

"Exams start in a week. I have classes on Tuesday."

"Not this Tuesday you don't. Louie we're gonna need a doctor's note!"

"One doctor's note coming right up!"

"What's so special about a dead guy's typewriter?" Nina asked.

"Two dead guys' typewriters and we're not sure but, the lawyer for Benny's family acted very strange when my partner here, Detective Mancino dropped by his office earlier in the week." Louie seized the opportunity to nod and smile at Nina who returned the gesture.

Louie here was only allowed in the outer office but was able to peer into Rochfort's inner sanctum."

"Finnis Rochfort?" Nina questioned.

"You know him?"

"Yeah I called him up once after Benny died to ask a question. Guy acted like a real prick! Pardon my language."

"Trust me, not an issue!" Nikki assured.

"But he's never seen you?" Doc reaffirmed.

"Not that I know of, no."

"He wasn't at the funeral?"

"I have no way of knowing, I've never seen him."

"Right, here's what's going to happen. I need you to wear something slinky."

"How slinky?"

"The slinkier the better."

"Where am I going?"

"You're both going." Nikki looked surprised but didn't object. "Nikki you're the bereaved but stoic aunt on a mission to get the final will details sorted for the family. Nina, you're the bereaved but barley-able-to-hold-it together fiancé. You have the critical mission! I need a mental picture of every detail of that office particularly if there's a safe and where it is in the room. Got it?"

"What are you gonna do?" Nina pushed.

"**We're** going to find out if the lawyer's only lying about his religion or about other things!"

"AHHHGGHH! SHIT!" Louie jumped and cursed as he inadvertently coated his left hand with hot coffee missing the cup in his right when Nina

Twisselman stepped through the front door of the office.

With her hair up, dressed in a tight black, knee-high, satin cocktail dress, charcoal stockings and five inch black heels Nina strutted into the office. Nikki looked over from where Louie was nursing his hand, shook her head then widened her eyes at the blond bombshell standing before her.

It was mid-morning that Tuesday when Nina showed up at the office to bring Benny's typewriter and be briefed by Doc on the next step in his plan.

As Louie had only been allowed just outside of Rochfort's office in the reception area he wasn't able to peruse the office space well enough to fill McKeowen in on the layout of the lawyer's work area. A layout Doc would need to know more about if his mission were to succeed.

"Well?" Nina executed a slow spin to show Nikki.

"Maybe a little . . ." Cole reservedly commented.

"PERFECT!" Louie exclaimed.

"Much!" Nikki finished.

Doc called them all into his office and the mission briefing started.

"The single most important thing I need is probably the most difficult." He made eye contact with Nina as he spoke to her from across his desk. Mancino stood in the doorway next to Nikki.

"What's that?" Nina asked.

"After you're confident you have the location of the front and rear doors, and any alarm mechanisms you can see . . ." Doc again indicated the catalogue photos of window tape and door jamb contacts he had already briefed Nikki on. "I need the location of his office safe. If you can't see one while you're sitting at his desk, look for any large paintings on the wall, throw rugs on the floor or any clear spots on the floor bigger than a foot to eighteen inches square."

"How will I know if there's a floor safe under there?"

"You won't but if the space or a small rug is in a common traffic pattern it's a good bet there's a safe under it, okay?"

"Got it!"

"Louie researched the city archives yesterday and the building was put up just before the First War which means the pre-1921building codes apply which in turn means the floor joists are eighteen to twenty-four inches apart, plenty of room for a small floor safe."

"Thank you Louie." Nina flashed a smile at Mancino who quickly stood upright and smiled back at her. "Does this mean you forgive me for lying to you at the hotel?" She added.

"What hotel?" Doc blurted.

"I'll explain later." Nikki rode to Mancino's rescue.

"Miss Twisselman, you understand you're risking jail time, hefty court costs and possible retaliation if this thing is as big as we think it might be?" Doc warned.

"Nice pep talk Doc!" Nikki admonished.

"Just giving the girl a reality check, Miss Cole!"

439

"Detective McKeowen," Nina jumped in. "I can't tell you how much I appreciate what you and your crew are doing for me. But as I told you when I first came here, I'm going see Benny's killer caught! Whatever it takes!" She stood and offered the typewriter case to Doc.

"Maybe I better go with her, you know . . . just in case!" Louie offered.

"Detective Mancino, take Benny's Underwood into your office and match the key patterns to a couple of the script pages we brought back from the studio."

"Yes Doc." Mancino pouted.

"That's very sweet of you Louie but, it'll be alright besides, just knowing that you care is encouraging enough!" She leaned in and kissed him on the cheek. Mancino bumped into the door frame on the way out.

"You got the number I sent you for?"

"Oh yaeh! Here." He passed Doc a slip of paper.

"And fill out an affidavit statement to the effect that the keys match the pages!"

"Yes Doc!" Louie skulked back into his office.

"Nikki?"

"Yeah Doc?"

"What time's her appointment at Rochfort's?"

"Two this afternoon, we've plenty of time." Nikki informed.

"Okay, she'll need somebody there if things do somehow go south. I can't be seen in the area but I will be a block away on 116th and Morningside, near the park. Memorize this number. There's a pay

440

phone on the corner, if things look bad or if you think he's on to you, ask to use his phone, call me and say you heard from the hospital and have to run. Make any excuse to get out of there. In either case meet me at the deli over on 115th, we green?"

"Gotch'a boss man!" Nikki teased.

"Stop that!" Doc scolded.

All went as planned and surprisingly by two forty-five the girls proudly strode into Angie's Deli on 115th Street.

"How'd it go?" Doc asked as they took seats at his small table.

"Smooth as a baby's bottom!" Nikki bragged. "This detective's stuff's easy!"

"Don't get cocky!" Doc warned. "Now why don't you two sleuthettes fill me n on what you found?"

"We will but first, I think this calls for a drink! We can fill you in on the way." Nina proposed.

"Then why don't we blow this popsicle stand and catch a cab down to O'Malley's in the village?" Doc proposed. You two can fill me in on the way downtown."

In the taxi they all sat in the rear with Doc taking the passenger's jump seat. As soon as they pulled out and headed south Nina passed Doc a sheet of paper.

"What's this?" Doc asked.

"She made believe she was taking notes while I asked questions and he was talking." Nikki answered.

"Weren't you afraid he'd see you?"

"Read it." Nikki instructed. He looked at it.

"I can't!" Doc declared. And he couldn't.

"It's in Hebrew." Nikki boasted as if she took the notes in square script herself.

"I thought this guy was orthodox?! Surely he knows how to read Abjad!" McKeowen challenged.

"He's not, he doesn't and he can't." Nina assured as she took back the paper and dictated.

"Halfway through I asked to go to the ladies'. The safe is in the toilet under a fake counter on the left as you enter. It's old, a Something-Whitfield model by the label on the door. I couldn't see it all the label was damaged and worn. There's alarm contacts on the front door and his office door. I couldn't get to the back door."

"Anything else?"

"Light switch is on the right as you enter the office and there's a catch under the bathroom counter to open the fake cabinet door and access the safe just to the right of the sink."

"That it?"

"He's a neat freak, probably has OCD, measures the distance between pictures on his wall." Nikki informed. "So I'd be careful to not move anything around."

Fifteen minutes later they were lifting mid-afternoon glasses in a back booth in O'Malley's Irish Pub on MacDougal Street.

While the three were celebrating their little coup, back in hi office, Rochfort was dialing a phone number. A phone number with a Chicago exchange.

"Lemme talk with Steadman." Rochfort demanded.

He's in New York.

"SHIT!"

You want the number to his private service?

"I have it. I'll leave him a message. If I miss him tell him I had a couple of visitors."

Cops?

"The blond."

The Jew kid's bitch? What the hell'd she want?

"I don't know but she had a snoop with her pretending to be a relative."

You didn't buy her as a relative?

"No!"

Who then?

"I dunno! Maybe a gumshoe."

A female P.I.? Don't be stupid.

"I'm not playing Twenty Questions here! I'm telling you what happened!"

Alright, alright, I'll tell Steadman.

"Yeah, you do that! And remind him, I only agreed to donate money, not to get mixed up with cops! I'm a fucking lawyer fer Christ's sake! People expect me to at least look honest." Rochfort slammed the phone down.

✝

443

"Nikki, you make up that file on Steadman?"

"Sure did boss man. You want to run through it?"

"Please. In here." Nikki grabbed a file from her desk and followed Doc into his office.

"Okay, the Chicago report." She started. "Joshua 'Jake' Steadman, married one kid, is the owner operator of United Engineering & Construction, the third largest building company in the greater Chicago area."

"Third largest?"

"Uh huh, three hundred and fifty to four hundred staff and crew at any given time presently running sixteen projects of various sizes spread over three states. Apparently they specialize in office buildings and hotels."

"How'd he make his money? Father?"

"No, built it up from scratch back in around '32, just after The Depression hit."

"There's a story you don't hear every day, somebody getting rich **during** The Depression."

"Kind'a fishy if you ask me." Nikki quipped.

"Yeah, I agree. What about his crew, his staff, that Neanderthal he drags around called Brasi?"

"His permanent office staff all work out of the HQ building, the one you and Louie dropped in on, and they number around a dozen not counting Brasi."

"Where's his lair?"

"Don't know. Couldn't find him listed anywhere on the company records and he doesn't appear to

444

have an official title of any sort like the other twelve."

"The Twelve Apostles. No illegal activity from anybody?"

"Two of them were picked up for drunk and disorderly New Year's Eve last and one was run in for possession of two marijuana cigarettes."

"And?"

"Twenty dollar fines for the drunk and disorderly and case dismissed on the pot charge."

"A dismissal on a narcotics charge?! That's normally five years. Somebody must have connections."

"Connections that go pretty deep. Evidence disappeared from the evidence room hence the dismissal." She recited.

"Wonder which young cop had a good time that night? That all?"

"Pretty much. Oh, the warehouse was raided once on a tip-off."

"Raided for what?"

"Drugs."

"DRUGS! I KNEW IT!" Doc slapped the desk. "I said it to Mancino, 'This guy is dirty!'"

"What'd Louie think?"

"The same. What happened on the raid?!"

"Found nothing. Steadman's lawyers brought suit against the CPD, and they settled out of court."

"I refuse to believe that in one of the most crooked states in the Union in the crookedist city in the state that all those people are good honest law-abiding citizens!"

"You think Chicago and Illinois are crooked?"

"They're run by the Democrats aren't they?" Doc snapped back.

"I typed up a list of all the addresses and phone numbers I collected so you can reference them later if need be." Nikki passed the list to Doc.

"Pretty good job there Miss Cole." He plopped back into his chair. "Remind me to speak to your boss about a raise."

"A RAISE?! How about a salary first? I'd make more money at one pull of the slots in Vegas then I do here! By the way, 'crookedist' isn't a word."

"Thank you Mrs. Webster. How'd you get all that info anyhow?"

"Told them I was a FBN rep calling from D.C. I talked with the desk sergeant of the local Oak Park precinct and told him I was assigned to do a routine background check on Steadman. Once I told him I was federal Bureau of Narcotics he opened up like a fire hydrant. I don't think the local cops like our man very much."

"You know posing as a federal agent in punishable by $10,000 fine and up to five years in the pen?"

"Oh, as if you never lied about who you are! The Treasury case back in '42, the feds at the Miami race track and Hollywood producers? Please! Who on earth would buy that?"

"The Hollywood producer at Warner Brothers bought it."

"There was one more potential lead." She added.

"Talk to me."

"When I spoke with Steadman's secretary she told me, girl-to-girl, she thinks he's got a girlfriend in every city he travels to."

"Girl in every port, huh? If infidelity were a crime half America would be behind bars!"

"You wanna hear about Brasi?"

"Yeah, yeah please. Sorry forgot about Brasi."

"I couldn't find much on any of the others but Brasi Sollozo has what most would describe as a checkered career, not much of which you'd put on a résumé."

"Big surprise." Doc quipped.

"As an ex-fed, he was an inspector for the Department of Agriculture but was sacked for screwing up several times including taking bribes."

"Nice, those are the personality traits I'm looking for."

"He then tried his hand at, ready for this? Being a P.I."

"Huh figures! Last refuge of losers!" Doc declared.

"However on his third try at the state P.I. exam he gave up. Next he then fell into some part-time but apparently well-paid work with the local Mob. However, by virtue of his uncontrolled, Vesuviain temper, he really screwed that up when he broke the jaw of a soon-to-be consigliore during a card game, somebody's nephew apparently. Trading a hit job no one wanted to take the commission on, Brasi squared himself with The Mob but was once again on the streets and unemployed when he finally stumbled into casual construction work as a navvy on one of Steadman's crews. Steadman apparently saw Brasi's potential as a torpedo and body guard, they've lived happily ever after and that brings us up to date."

"That must have been a year or so back about the time Steadman was approached and struck a deal with one of the Chicago mob bosses to use his main construction warehouse as a back-up for hot merchandise or drug drop point."

"You think that's what's going on with him? Drugs?"

"I'm very suspicious of that warehouse operation. Why have the entire rear eighty percent of the space blocked off by a drop curtain and no windows with the back shutter doors pulled down in this heat?"

"I'm getting the picture."

""Now we find out he built his fortune during the depression? Who besides politicians and other criminals makes money when the rest of the country is going broke?"

"Not research librarians, I can tell you that from experience!"

"Nikki just for the hell of it, call this alternate number up in Chicago, see who answers and ask for Mr. Steadman."

"And if he comes to the phone?"

"Say you're selling subscriptions to *Ladies Home Journal*, working your way through secretarial school."

"Why can't I be working my way through university selling *Engineering Quarterly*?"

"Working your way as what?"

"An engineer!" She boasted.

"Because when he asks you the tinsel strength of the flanges on a ten inch, steel I-beam, what'a you gonna say?" Nikki sat silent. "He owns one of the city's largest building firms. He's an engineer."

She rose and walked back to her desk.

"I guess I'm gonna say – 'Good morning sir, would you like to purchase a subscription to *Ladies Home Journal*?'" she muttered.

"Then get Twisselman on the phone, tell her we need to see her in here tomorrow."

"Yes sir!" She barked. *Nobody likes a smart ass McKeowen!* She mumbled on the way out.

"And Nikki?"

"WHAT?!" She called back from the reception area.

"You did good, thank you."

"Mr. McKeowen?"

"Yes Miss Cole?"

"You're buying me dinner tonight!"

The day after Nina and Nikki informed Doc of what they had seen and found in Rochfort's office things began to pick up pace.

When Nikki rang the Chicago number she discovered that Steadman was not only away for the next few days but actually in New York.

That afternoon after visiting a couple of locksmith's on Canal Street and buying a catalogue on the pretext of needing to buy a safe for his office, Doc met Harry that evening at the Front Page News.

Harry locked up and led Doc through the curtain into the back room where there was an old kitchen table and a pair of chairs next to an old cupboard.

"That's the closest to the safe in his office." Doc showed Harry the page he had torn out of the catalogue. "Same company, slightly different model, but looked a little older she told me."

"That there is an old Frederic Whitfield, an English safe." Harry expertly grumbled. "Three tumblers. Very easy to crack."

Harry reached under the table and came up with a one foot square mock-up of a safe door complete with lock. The door lock mechanism with a combination lock obviously came from a full sized safe door. It clanged as he dropped it down it down the table.

"You just happened to have demonstration safe locks hanging around in the back room?"

"Called in a favor yesterday when you asked me for help. Fella over in Bensonhurst has a scrap metal yard, gets a lotta safe, strong arm boxes and such in now that everybody's remolding their homes and businesses."

Doc retrieved the lock and examined it.

"Is this the same as a Frederic Whitfield?"

"No. This set up has four tumbles which makes it a little trickier but that's better for you. You master

450

this one and the lawyer's safe ought'a be a bit faster for you."

"Makes sense."

"Easiest way to crack a safe is to drill out the bolt and or tumblers, but that ain't exactly an option in your case. Best way to crack this one is to use manipulation, your hands and ears."

"Okay."

"Every lock has its own personality. If you listen it'll talk to you and tell you, 'you ain't coming in here brother!' But you gotta look straight back in the eye at that little bastard and say back, 'Yeah I am!' Ya get me?"

"If it talks to me, why can't I just ask it the combination? You know, maybe offer to introduce it to a nice French armoire lock?"

"God damn it Doc you gonna take this seriously or not?!"

"Sorry Harry."

"Now, sometimes you'll get a safe that's not gonna cooperate no matter how much you sweet talk it, but ninety-five percent of the time you can crack them with just a little manipulation."

"What about the other five percent?"

"That five percent is why God made B-3 plastic explosive. But we ain't got none'a that cause it's illegal and you don't wanna break the law now do ya?"

"No."

Harry lifted the mock-up and slowly turned the dial.

"Hear that? That's the drive wheel going over the tumblers. That black thing right there, that's the drive wheel. Each tumbler has a notch in it and the idea is to line up each with this post here. That's what you're listening for when you manipulate the dial. Never spin it! Always feel it. The post is called the fence. When you feel the first little click note the number on the dial. Repeat in the opposite direction, note the number and back again to the next click and that's your third number. Turn the dial right slowly and you should feel the tumbler notches lock into the post. Turn the dial a little more and that will retract the bolt and you're in."

"Doesn't seem too hard."

"Remember to note the exact number the dial is on before you start!"

"Why, what's the difference after I'm in?"

"He's a lawyer so he's probably a shyster but not stupid. If he's got anything in there that's worth a damn something he's not supposed to have, which is highly likely since he's a lawyer, he'll likely leave his safe on a given number when he closes up for the night. That way he can tell if the safe has been tampered with during the night. If he's careless it's possible the number he left the dial on might be your last number."

"You sure you don't wanna tag along? Should be an easy job. First floor, single bolt lock on the back door, no intruder alarm system on the doors or window." Doc offered. "All I'd need ya for is to drive. I don't wanna chance a taxi at that time of night."

"'Should be an easy job' Exact same words one of the fellas uttered just before we got pinched by the Feds. No thanks Doc. Besides that scam we pulled on them Feds during the crooked Treasury agent's case back in '42 was all the excitement I needed for a while."

"Well I appreciate you helping out!"

"Not a bother Doc. Just keep your head low and stay out'a the light! You need an alibi, let me know."

"I need an alibi I screwed up bad enough that an alibi probably won't help."

"Doc McKeowen, ever the realist!" Harry grumbled.

The next night just before midnight, Doc stepped off the subway at the 116TH Street station in Morningside Heights and walked east crosstown to Rochfort's Law Office near the corner of Amsterdam and 116th Street. After cruising by Rochfort's office earlier that day to survey the layout in daylight, McKeowen had returned.

The four story imitation Dutch style structure was fronted by a red brick staircase but had a side and rear entrance as well. Under the ambient light of the corner street lamp Doc slipped up the left side where there was a narrow one man alley where he scanned the overhang of the eaves along the roof's edge until he saw what he was looking for. The red ten inch gong of the alarm bell tucked just under the roof's ledge.

Adjusting the U.S. Army messenger's bag he had slung over his shoulder and bracing his back against the opposite building with his feet against the Dutch building he shimmed up the space in a mountain climber's 'chimney climb' technique until he was at eye level with the alarm box.

From his messenger's bag he produced an aerosol can of door foam used to insulate small wall spaces or seal off mouse holes in houses. Attaching the five inch spray tube he threaded the end between the building and the top of the gong and filled the alarm gong with foam until it dripped from the sides. He then used the remainder of the foam to fill the mechanism box just below the gong.

Waiting a moment to check that the foam had hardened, Doc made his way back down.

Once back on the ground he went to work on the side door. The simple deadbolt lock was easily defeated and he readjusted the messenger's bag and dug out a small flashlight being careful to keep the light beam aimed at the floor as he moved cautiously up stairs.

Rochfort's was the only office on the first floor and Doc came upon his name plastered across the glass door panel just as Nina described it.

Using the flashlight he carefully traced the mull post that the door closed into until he found the connect point of the ADT alarm high up on the jamb.

Paddy Kelly

Knowing that he had less than thirty seconds until the alarm went off, and not knowing if he might have missed a second alarm bell somewhere, he prepped everything before breeching the door.

He worked quickly but carefully and above all methodically.

Setting his bag on the floor he fished out a pack of Wrigley's Spearmint gum, a roll of industrial masking tape, a ten foot roll of copper wire and a small pair of wire snips.

Removing one stick of the gum he unwrapped it and popped it in his mouth then proceeded to tear the silver foil wrapper in half and fold the two pieces into squares just larger than the standard alarm contacts.

Next he peeled off two one inch pieces of masking tape and temporarily stuck them to the plate glass. Finally he snipped off a four foot long piece of the copper wire.

Wrapping the length of wire over his neck he took one end and placed it centered on one piece of the tape then stuck a foil square over that. He repeated the process with the other end of the wire.

Packing everything back into his bag then donning a pair of rubber surgical gloves he had swiped from Donnie's morgue he proceeded to tackle the single dead bolt lock.

Thirty seconds later he was carefully pushing open the door as he firmly pressed one end of the taped wire over the door contact and the other end over the contact buried in the door jamb

455

maintaining the integrity of the alarm's contacts while allowing a four foot gap.

Doc quickly slid a heavy office chair over to stabilize the door and keep it from closing over before he headed into the ladies room to locate the safe.

It was there under the false counter door that he spotted a second alarm contact point.

"Clever bastard!" Doc whispered.

There wasn't much he could do as he had already swung open the false cabinet door and broke the contact so he went straight to work on the safe. He was at least relived to not hear a second alarm bell ring on the outside of the building.

The safe lock on the other hand wasn't being as cooperative as the door locks. In the silence of the dark office he heard the first two tumblers fall into place as Harry had briefed him but the last one wasn't happening. Each miss required another go around and time was dragging on. He had already been on premises for near ten minutes.

"C'mon ya bastard!" Finally It was on the third go around that McKeowen was able to hear the last tumbler fall into place. "Gotcha!"

There were many items in the safe but he rummaged around until he found the prize. An envelope with Epstein scribbled across it. He cracked it open and slid the single sheet out.

"And the handsome gentleman in the back has Bingo!" He whispered. With no wasted movement he moved to the desk, laid Epstein's suicide note on a white sheet of typing paper.

He then produced a small, standard SLR Stamax 127 from the messenger's bag. The Stamax was favored by the military for its durability, ease of operation and relatively quiet shutter response.

He took several photos from different angles and distances.

Returning to the safe he replaced everything as it had been but hesitated at a stack of fifty dollar bills rubber banded together.

"Ah, what the hell?" He shrugged. He took the money justifying it by reasoning it would make it appear more like a cat burglar hit the place for the money but left all the contracts and paper work.

Closing the safe, the cabinet door and scurrying to the front door, where he dismantled his make-shift by-pass.

Doc and all his toys were heading down stairs when he hit the ground floor landing it was that the reality of his situation hit him. There were two green and white units outside on the street.

The police had obviously been alerted by a silent alarm.

Backlit by the headlights of the police cars Doc could see the silhouettes of two cops bouncing up the front porch guns drawn.

Doc considered his options.

Front door's a big no.

Alley way – too narrow also can't chance it's not covered.

Back door!

He took the stairs down to the basement two at a time and made it to the back door just in time to hear two more cops talking.

"Two thirteen, Frank and I have the back covered. No one here." One cop yelled up the alley way.

Doc quickly but quietly headed back upstairs where they were shining bright flashlights through the side lights of the front door forcing him to dance around the light beams.

When the lights moved away he kept going up and hoped there was a fire escape.

Through the back office window he saw there wasn't.

Last hope the roof! He headed up to the attic.

By the time he made it onto the roof through the narrow access hatch he could hear the downstairs was crawling with cops.

"Jesus!" He thought to himself. "An entire precinct for one lawyer's office?! This asshole must have some serious connections!"

He moved over to the other side of the roof to check the proximity of the adjoining building. The distance was a mere four to five feet but the adjoining ledge was walled up to about the four foot mark making a jump across very risky.

He looked down to see one fat cop trying in vain to squeeze into the alley way.

Over the back roof he saw the cops he heard earlier along with a cacophony of dogs all up and down the row of back yards.

"What the hell is this? The Uptown dog pound?!"

He strolled to the front and peered over the roof's edge where he watched several more Ford Deluxe Coupe, green and white units pulling up outside on Amsterdam Avenue, their red roof lights flashing off the apartment buildings.

"Shoot Sarge! Looks like them damn Injuns got us surrounded!" Doc quietly quipped to himself.

It was then Doc decided the most obvious solution.

He spent the next half hour laying low on the roof and when it got too cold and the hub bub had died down he deemed it safe to slip down into the attic where it was a bit warmer.

He was grateful when, four hours later, he saw sunlight seeping through cracks in the eaves.

After having spent the night in the attic, he finally heard someone downstairs.

After quietly dropping down through the attic's trap door he started down the stairs when a secretary exiting the third floor ladies room with a coffee urn in her hand coming from fetching water, stopped dead and stared up the stairs at Doc.

With flashlight in hand he pretended to be following the overhead wiring over the stairs. He looked down at her standing mannequin-like on the landing.

"Morning!" He cheerfully greeted.

"Good morning." She uttered back. He continued down to her.

"Yeah, tell your boss we'll have an estimate on the re-wiring by Friday."

"Ah . . . okay." She uttered.

Doc breezed past her and onto the second floor flight of stairs.

"How about those Yankees, huh?" He asked as he passed by her.

She gave no response as he casually continued on down and out the front door to Amsterdam Avenue where he caught a cab back downtown.

†

"Where were you all night?" Nikki questioned.

"In cold storage at Rochfort's!"

She notice hi shivering.

"You're freezing!"

"I know."

"Did you get anything?"

'Yeah, the son-of-a-bitch has the note."

"Great! Can I see . . . wait . . . what do you mean 'has the note'? Where is it?" Nikki pushed.

"Still in the safe."

"What?!Why didn't you take it?!"

"If it matches then it's material evidence and he needs to be nailed with. He's a lawyer, without getting caught red handed he'll worm his way out no problem. As it is, when they nail him he'll no doubt say he was holding it for his client."

"Will that stand up?"

"Don't know but I got pictures." He waved the camera over his head as he brushed past Louie sitting at the reception desk on his way to the coffee pot. "Stopped by an all-night Rexall's on the way in this morning and dropped the film off. Should be ready day after tomorrow."

He poured some hot coffee to warm up.

"Plus I got something better!" Doc tossed a brochure with a membership form on his desk. Nikki picked it up and read. She stared for an inordinate period of time.

"WOW! Doc I mean WOW!" The brochure was an information pamphlet on the Sons of Liberty. Additionally the application form stub had been filed out.

"Are we sure Rochfort filled this out?"

"It's got his name on it." Louie argued.

"What if he denies filling it out?" Nikki, now in full P.I. mode, pushed.

"Louie, anything else in that envelope?" Mancino opened it wide and fished out a folded over 8 ½ by 11inch letter with embossed heading. It was a hand written letter to a client. Doc passed it to Nikki.

"I swiped it off his desk. It's a letter to a client informing them the settlement for their case has been filled in the district court."

"What's that got to do with Benny's case?"

"Nothing but it's written in Rochfort's handwriting."

CHAPTER XXI

M&M INVESTIGATIONS

Doc looked again at the B&W, 8X10 glossies then passed the blown-up photos of Epstein's suicide note to Louie and headed into his office. Louie grabbed a magnifying glass from Nikki's desk drawer and perused them more closely.

"Son-of-a-bitch!" Was all he could manage. He sprang from his chair and followed Doc into his office where McKeowen was placing a call.

"Doc I can't believe you picked up on that little mark like that!"

"No partner, you're the guy that found that little mark. Detective Mancino." He congratulated as he finished dialing the phone.

"Yeah I did, didn't I!" Louie beamed.

"Hello Nina? It's McKeowen. When can you come down to the office? I . . . we think we've got something."

I'll be there inside of an hour.

Just as Doc theorized out in L.A. the 'Z' key on Benny's Underwood was chipped across the center stroke making any document typed on Benny's machine clearly identifiable. The copy of the movie script the guys had brought back from Hollywood had clearly been produced on the same Underwood as was Benny's missing suicide note. The question remained why was Epstein's suicide note also typed on Benny's machine?

Nina arrived just over thirty minutes later and Doc presented her with what they had found.

"The 'Z' in both notes and the whole script we brought back from L.A. do not match the 'Z' on Epstein's Capitol typing machine, but they do match on Benny's Underwood."

"I . . . I don't understand what that means." Nina's head reeled with the possibilities. "Are you saying that Benny was somehow mixed up with mobsters?"

"No! Epstein's suicide note was not written on his own machine. It was written before hand on Benny's machine." Nikki calmly explained.

"Why would Benny write Epstein's suicide note? They didn't even know each other?! You think Benny had something to do with Epstein's suicide?" Nina gradually shaking voice betrayed her mounting emotions.

"I'm telling you there's a zero chance Epstein committed suicide. Whoever wanted him dead made it look like a suicide by planting this note in his typewriter. The police never fingerprinted it because they assumed Epstein wrote it and treated it as an open and shut case." Louie explained.

"If Epstein's death was not by his own hand then neither was Benny's. The note wasn't written by Benny, it was written days before by whoever 'suicided' Benny and probably Epstein." McKeowen explained.

"Kill Benny then use the typewriter sitting right there out on the table?! Wow! But . . . Saul Epstein died weeks before Benny!" Nina suspiciously pointed out.

"Which is why we're pretty certain the same guy committed both murders. He couldn't very well have typed the letter with Benny there unless Benny wasn't home or was already dead. Since we know Epstein died first it means the guy we think did it broke into Benny's place, probably to punch Benny's ticket . . ." Louie was sharply cut off as Doc slapped him in back of the head.

"OW! What'd I say?!" Louie protested.

"'Punch his ticket!?'" Doc chided. "How old are you?! What my partner means is he came there to murder Benny, but found Benny not home. He already had Epstein marked, saw Benny's machine out on the table and took five minutes to type out the notes. You all saw how easy it was to break into Benny's place."

"With one of the killings here in the Village precinct and the other in the Uptown Precinct, there was no reason to connect the two . . ." Nikki added.

"Add to that the hundred to one hundred and fifty deaths streaming into the dozens of city morgues every day well, there's every reason for Brasi to think he'd get away with it."

"Wait a minute! Back the truck up!" Twisselman demanded. "Who's Brasi?!"

"We're pretty sure he's the goon who did this. He's a thug, complete muscle for hire." Doc revealed.

"That would explain why the wording in Benny's note is so awkward." She observed. "No writer would ever write 'thine by mine own hand'! What the hell does that even mean?" Nina challenged.

Sensing Nina's emotional struggles to take in all the news Nikki wet out to the coffee pot and fixed Nina a cup of strong tea.

"That also means whoever wrote that knew Benny was a writer and thought he was educated enough to sound like a writer." Doc formulated.

"He wasn't! So what do we do now?" Nina posited.

"Well I need to bring this to the cops, but first I want to be sure about Steadman. Nikki, you still got Steadman's home phone the one you got from the Chicago PD?" Doc asked.

"It's in the file I gave you." Doc opened his middle desk drawer and retrieved the file handing it to Nikki.

"And didn't you say something about him having girlfriends everywhere?"

"Yeah, guy must think he's a sailor. Girl in every port."

"Call Steadman's wife, Steadman should be at work."

"And say what?"

"Here, sit down." He drew the chair around side of his desk and slid the phone over. "When she answers ask for Jack. NO, Jackie Boy, ask for Jackie Boy!"

"And then what?"

"She'll ask who it is and you hang up."

"You're a dirty . . ." Nikki commented.

"What? I'm a dirty what?" Doc coaxed.

"Something not nice. Everybody be quiet!" She instructed as she dialed. It rang three times.

Hello?

"Hi whose this?!" Louie had to cover his mouth and step out of the room so amused was he by the sweet, girly voice Nikki used.

This is Mrs. Steadman, who the hell is this?!

"It's Candy! Is Jackie Boy there?"

'JACKIE BOY?!' WHO THE FUCK IS THIS? IF I FIND OUT WHO YOU ARE YOU F-

Nikki quickly hung up.

"JEESE! Somebody get some ice for my ears will ya?" She said as she rubbed her ear. "Talk about mad!" Louie couldn't control his laughter, Nina was trying to figure the plan but Nikki was quietly waiting. After about two minutes Doc took the phone and dialed.

"HELLO!" He yelled into the transceiver.

WHAT?! WHO IS THIS?!

"Who is this?!" Doc demanded. "Who are you?"

This is MRS STEADMAN! WHO ARE YOU AND WHAT'A YA WANT?!

"Oh, okay. Did you just get a call from my sixteen year old daughter Candy?"

There was an extended silence on the other end.

YOU GOTTA BE SHITTIN' ME! SIXTEEN?

"Yeah, what about it?" At that point he heard the phone drop and various noises which sounded suspiciously like pots and pans being flung around the kitchen. He covered the mouth piece and spoke to Louie and the girls. "Sounds like she's got a new decoration scheme for the kitchen. Or maybe she's looking for something."

"Probably a gun!" Nikki whispered. Presently she came back on the phone.

I don't know who you are mister but if you got dealings with my husband you better get them over with because when he gets back from New York-

"NEW YORK?! I live in New York! I'm speaking to you from Manhattan!"

Manhattan you say? Well what a coincidence! Her audible change in attitude signaled she suddenly saw an opportunity. *Mr. Steadman just happens to be at the Crestwood Arms in Manhattan for the next day or so.*

"The Crestwood Arms? Sounds kind'a swanky? Then you don't mind if I pay him a visit?"

Fifth floor, room 507! And while you're at it have a visit to that little slut out in Brooklyn where he buys his pot! He thinks I don't know about her skinny little ass and their narcotics parties!

"What a coincidence Mrs. Steadman! My brother lives in Brooklyn!"

She's on Flatbush Avenue. The last address he had in his journal for her was 1492.

"I'll see what I can work out Mrs. Steadman." He assured as he scribbled all the info on a note pad.

I didn't get your name sir?

"Neff, Walter Neff. It's been real educational Mrs. Steadman. Thank you!"

The Broad in the Kimono

If you're going to see my husband Mr. Neff, could you do me one ittsy-bitsy, teeny-weenie little favor?

"What's that Mr. Steadman?"

BRING A FUCKING GUN! Doc heard the phone slam down hard.

"That's how you do detective shit!" Mancino stood with crossed arms as he bragged for Doc.

"Nikki get us an address on the Crestwood Arms, sounds like an Uptown establishment. Louie I'm heading over to Brooklyn you want to come?"

"Try and stop me!"

"Nina, we'll need to keep Benny's stuff here."

"Okay."

"One last thing Nina. Did Benny ever let anybody else use his typing machine. Loaned it out to anyone?"

"No he guarded it with his life. From the day he left college it never left the apartment. Until the police took it."

"Okay, thanks."

"What'll I do?" Nina asked.

"You're welcome to hang around here until your next class." Nikki offered.

"Thanks Nikki, classes are finished. I'd like that. I don't like going home and being alone."

"In that case I know the perfect little café just around the corner." Cole proposed.

As Doc and Louie set out they were barley through the door when two grey suited men suddenly stood blocking the way out.

"You Mack Key O'wyn?" The big one grunted.

"Depends who's asking Big Guy!" Doc quipped. The tall man reached into his breast pocket and produced a Federal Bureau of Narcotics badge.

"In that case yes I am Mike McKeowen. What can I do for you two diligent representatives of the Federal government?"

"Questions wise ass! And I hope for your sake you got answers!"

†

Majestic Apartments
115 Central Park West
New York City

An hour or so after Doc and Louie had landed in La Guardia Jake Steadman's flight was touching down on the same runway.

With only a carry-on he headed straight through the terminal, hopped a cab from the rank outside and headed into Flatbush in Brooklyn to meet his local girlfriend at her apartment.

She wasn't home but he had only ducked in to drop his bag and change into his only Armani.

Before leaving he scribbled a quick, cursory note and left it on the kitchen table.

By mid-morning he was siting happily in a Sunshine cab making his way uptown.

He ran through events in his head as he saw them unfolding once he reached The Majestic on Central Park West.

The Broad in the Kimono

As a child Jake Steadman always remembered the wooden plaque his father had above his desk in his office.

"A man's only limitations are those
which he sets upon himself."

Unfortunately for Jake's father he never knew about Frankie Costello's bodyguards and the limitations they could set upon a man.

Blinded by his obsession with parlaying the Sons of Liberty into a viable political entity, of which he would naturally be the head, Steadman was about to initiate the second step in his grand scheme.

Further bolstered by the fact that many of America's political leaders, the Huey Longs, the Boss Tweeds and the Kennedys for example, built their family's political dynasties on a foundation of crime, Jake had decided to bypass the Chicago family he was involved with, the Manganos, and go straight to the top.

By securing backing from the top Mob guys, especially Frankie Costello, Jake reasoned he could build the solid foundation for the S.O.L. he was having difficulties with in Chicago. The potential political backing was there but only partially accessible and worse yet far too slow to garner.

He reasoned that it would be a simple matter to slowly shed the drug connections later once he rose to stardom.

Little could the hapless Steadman know that, like syphilis, involvement with the Mafia is forever.

Frank Costello's address wasn't hard to track down. Reporters like Walter Winchell had made the upscale Majestic Apartments between 71st and 72nd Streets well-known when Charlie Luciano had an apartment there. In fact Winchell himself had an apartment at the famous towers.

Full of hope, aspirations and desire Steadman hopped out of the taxi across from Central Park and headed in through the front door.

The six foot four, two hundred and forty-five pound receptionist with the Colt .45 tucked under his arm greeted the Chicagoan by stepping in front of him.

"Can I help you sir?"

"I'm here to see Mr. Costello."

"Is he expecting you?"

"It'll only need a minute."

"Who exactly are you?" The second torpedo stepped over closer and stood between Steadman and the exit.

"Steadman, Jake Steadman, from Chicago! Here to see Mr. Costello. I have a proposition for him!"

"He know you're coming?!"

"I'm not expected, no. But I have important business to discuss with him and I think once Mr. Costello-"

"Who you with?" The confrontational tone was the first red flag but, Jake chose to remain color blind.

"I work with the Manganos!"

"Never heard of them!" The first goon gently but firmly herded the indignant Steadman towards the doors. The second guard politely held it open as a well-dressed elderly couple, the woman holding the leash of a miniature Pomeranian, entered.

"Thank you young man!"

"You're quite welcomed Mrs. Abernathy." He replied.

"Look just-" Steadman insisted at which point he was manhandled and seconds later found himself back out on the street, his grey fedora floating down beside him.

"You're not in Kansas anymore Dorothy!" The thug called out to him with no sign of amusement.

"Why don't you try The Dakota!" The other one yelled out.

Steadman's humiliation quickly turned to anger. He decided to take their suggestion.

Down the block, by passing the doorman who was preoccupied helping a woman load her luggage into a taxi Steadman made his way to the main desk and grabbed the employees' lobby phone sitting up on the reception desk and began to dial.

"Excuse me sir." A receptionist interrupted. Clouded by his anger he didn't respond. "Sir?!" She repeated.

"WHAT!?" He snapped back as he continued to dial.

"Are you a resident here!?"

"No! How much is a room?"

"Sir our prices are confidential and to be negotiated with management. Shall I make you an appointment?"

Steadman was shocked and hung up.

"APPOINMENT?! What the hell kind'a hotel is this you need an appointment to rent a room?"

"Sir, this is **The Dakota**. We are not a hotel we are an apartment building, one of the most exclusive in The City!"

"Oh, I see." Even a thug like Steadman wasn't above embarrassment. "Then okay if I just duck into the bar and get a drink. I'm kind'a having a bad day."

"I'm sorry sir, the saloon is not open to the public."

Yet again Steadman was at an impasse. He forcefully exhaled while tapping his fingers on the counter.

"Young lady, I apologise for my abhorrent behaviour." He calmly explained. "I'm just off a long flight, they lost my luggage at the airport, my hotel room wasn't ready! You know how it is." He lied as he slipped a folded over fifty across the counter. She looked around, smiled and nodded.

"Yes I understand perfectly." The fifty vanished into the side pocket of her dark blue blazer. In return she slid him a guest pass cross the marble counter top.

"Tell them you're the guest of the resident in apartment 82 and ask for the courtesy phone." Steadman smiled back.

"Thank you for your assistance young lady."

"You're quite welcomed sir."

He cozied up closer to the service desk and leaned in.

"Maybe later, after you get off work you and I could-"

"Nothing personal Mack, but you're not exactly my type."

"Well what is your type Doll?"

"The type without a penis."

"What?!"

"You like women?" She asked.

"Yeah! Don't everybody?!"

"Well, so do I!"

"What?!"

"I prefer the company of women."

"You mean the company of women like . . ." Steadman slid his index finger through the looped fingers of his left hand. "Company like that kind'a company?!"

"You catch on quick, for a man. Enjoy you're drink."

Steadman, after being rejected twice in the last half hour, had come to the obtuse decision that if he were to prove himself to Costello he could gain an audience, selling his idea and get the New York family to back him there-by bypassing the Manganos altogether.

In the bar he placed a call to Brasi who, pending the outcome of the Costello meeting which hadn't occurred, was hanging around in a cheap dive motel over on the other side of the river in New Jersey.

"*How'd it go, you talk to the Big Guy?* Brasi excitedly asked.

"No! We need to prove ourselves. You still got the address them two clowns tried to pose as producers?"

Yeah, why?

"Get on the train and get over to Manhattan find out where they are and waste one of them. We need to send a message."

Doc led the two FNB agents into the office past a stunned Nikki and Nina into his office.

"Nikki take Nina around to the café would ya? Louie, wait here."

Once inside Doc took a seat behind his desk, one agent sat while the other closed the door but remained standing in front of it.

Doc addressed the sitting agent.

"So, since you're the senior agent on this case, what are your questions at this time?" McKeowen shot back as he crossed his feet up on his desk and leaned his chair back.

"What's your connection with Jake Steadman?" The senior guy blurted out.

"I ain't never hoid'a da bum!" Doc's comical assumption of a movie thug's voice was not amusing to the two Feds.

"Don't play games with us McKeowen! You and your dumpy little partner were seen in Chi Town less than a week ago!"

"We know you were in Chicago and it wasn't to see the
fire museum." The other one finally spoke.

"We were visiting a friend."

"A little yellow friend perhaps?"

'What are you talking about?"

"We understand you liked Chinatown."

Doc let his chair fall forward and leaned in on his desk.

"That was you guys?!" He fought back a smirk, barely.
"Seriously, that was you guys?!"

"Quit the shit McKeowen! What's you connection to Steadman?"

"There's no connection. We were hired by a client to
look into the possibility that someone might have stolen a movie script. Apparently the story was set in Chicago and we were led to believe Steadman's company was supposed to do the sets."

"And?"

"Turns out it was all bullshit. The guy's all smoke and
mirrors. He's a hard hat with a desk that's all."

"That all you can tell us McKeowen, or is that all you want to tell us?"

Doc tore the note paper from the pad on his desk and passed to the FNB agent who read it aloud.

"1492? What'a you gonna give me a history lesson?"

476

"Right before you two made such a grand and eloquent entrance I just got off the phone with Steadman's wife in Chicago."

"Go on."

"Seems she's none too happy about Jackie Boy screwin' around on her. She told me that was the address of one of his honeys. That's the address she gave me. It's out in the Bronx."

"Bronx is a big piece of real estate. What neighborhood? What street?"

"What'a ya want? An egg in your beer? How should I know? You're the Feds! When you find out let me know so I can close out this freakin' case it's draining all my resources here!"

"What can you tell us about a thug named Brasi?"

"Nothing. When we met with Steadman about halfway through the meeting this pugnacious little guy pops his head in the door and just starts hanging around for no good reason. Never says a word, just stands there and stares. What do I know about Brasi? I know he looks like the kind of guys that pulled the wings off of flies when he was a little kid."

"Anything else?"

"Yeah, he's someone I wouldn't want to meet in a dark alley."

The two agents traded glances.

"I think we're through here. Let's go." The head agent grumbled.

"Hey! How about throwing a little something my way?" Doc coaxed.

"Like what?"

"I got another case, a different client. Guy named Saul Epstein. Ring any bells?"

"Yeah. Old fella, business man. Punched his own ticket after a big investment in some political start-up group went south."

"Political start-up group huh?" Doc immediately connected that to the S.O.L "Ya know guys, I'm willing to bet dollars to donuts that if you mugs plug into that new FBI criminal filing system Hoover spent a million bucks on, Brasi Sollozo, or Sollozo Brasi is likely to get you a hit."

"We'll take it under advisement, 'Doc'!"

Louie cast a mock smile broader than necessary at the two agents as they left the office.

✝

Now the race was on.

"Doc what'd you find out? What'd they want?" Louie pushed as Doc exited his office and made straight for Nikki's desk.

"What do FBN guys always want? Somebody to crucify!" Doc opined. "Listen hang out here till Nikki gets back and-"

"Aw c'mon Doc, I wanna be in on the interview!"

"What for? We only need one man-"

"C'mon! I'm the guy who found the key that matched the note! I'm the one who brought you the case so I'm just as invested in this as you are in this thing!"

"Alright, let's go!" He signaled Mancino as he grabbed his brown leather bomber jacket and Negro League baseball cap off the coat rack then scribbled a quick note to Nikki.

'Off to Brooklyn. Call later. See you tonight!'

On the train over Doc filled Louie in.

"Young Joules was killed because he accidently wrote a script that was a little too close to real life."

"About what exactly?"

"Nikki was complaining about the light on my night stand last night so I only got through half through my re-read of the script but it deals with a right wing industrialist who fancies himself some kind of leader and so starts up a club which he wants to parlay into a political party. The story shows the guy to be an anti-Semite and willing to go to any lengths to achieve his goals."

"That could be any one of half a dozen guys."

"Yeah, but there's only one that matters!"

"And Epstein?"

"Apparently Epstein was approached as a possible backer for the S.O.L. probably agreed initially but pulled out after he somehow found out Steadman was involved with the Mob."

"And we strongly suspect Brasi was the trigger man or rope man as it were?" Louie Chided.

"Bingo partner!"

"What are we gonna do about the Feds?"

"Nothing. I sent them out to the Bronx. They'll waste a day or so out there and by that time I expect we'll have this thing wrapped up, located Steadman and the Feds in Chicago can deal with Brasi."

Thirty-five minutes after leaving the office the guys were strolling up Flatbush Avenue and found the address. It was a three story walk-up and of the six mail boxes set into the wall in the vestibule, one stood out.

"Take a look at this." Dos pointed to one of the small boxes. Louie leaned in. The box was labeled 'Steadman, Gina A.'

"Son-of-a-bitch is paying her rent!" Louie deduced.

"A bottle of Jameson's says that's not all he's paying for."

Doc pressed her apartment intercom button and a girl's voice answered. On the premise that they said they were NYPD, she buzzed them in.

As expected the twenty-something was an attractive young girl, with impeccably done up brunette hair. She worked at a local beauty salon. Doc observed the apartment was tastefully though sparsely decorated indicating she hadn't yet learned the tricks of the trade of being a mistress. *We all gotta start somewhere.* His internal dialogue said.

Gina A. was concerned but cordial and openly admitted she knew Jake was married but was in the dark when they got around to explaining Steadman's Mob connections and drug dealings but she took it in stride.

However, when Doc got to the part of why they were there, the murders, she grew skittish.

"Additionally, the Sons of Liberty and your boyfriend in particular, were and some still are members of several pro-German, pro-Nazi groups, such as the GAB." Doc informed. Louie started to explain further.

"That's the German Ameri-"

"I KNOW WHO THE FUCK THE G.A.B. ARE IS!"

She loudly burst out, sprang from the couch and started pacing erratically around the parlor.

Doc waited a minute until she started to calm down. He spotted the small bar table over between the two front windows.

"You alright? You want me to fix you a drink?" He offered.

"No." She lit a cigarette as she paced. "Yeah. Scotch, straight. No make it a Seven and Seven." She ordered. Doc nodded over to Louie who sprang to the table and poured her a Seagram's and Seven-up.

"We believe he's connected to this murder and possibly at least one other." McKeowen pushed.

On seeing Benny's morgue picture the girl stared for a longer time then necessary. Louie passed her the drink. She took several good sips and took a seat in the overstuffed chair opposite the couch.

"What'a wanna know?" She quietly muttered.

Over the next twenty minutes Gina relayed what she knew about her illegitimate part-time, sugar daddy/lover. That she suspected he was somehow mixed up with the Mob, was married and that he had other women in other cities.

By the time the guys left Gina was on her third scotch.

✝

"Slightly out of character wasn't it?" Doc later suggested as they made their way down tairs.

"Doc I'm Catholic and I know we believe in some weird shit which I have my doubts about, but there's one thing I truly believe in now!"

"What's that?"

"Possession! That girl became possessed right in front of our eyes! I mean she did a full-on Dr. Jekyll and Mrs. Hyde! I was reaching for my piece at one point!"

"You brought a gun out to this interview?"

"Yes." He defiantly answered.

"Why?"

"Why? It's Brooklyn why'd ya think?!"

"For what? It's an interview for cryin' out loud. What did you think was gonna happen?"

Even during his two years on the force McKeowen was never comfortable carrying a gun. He never had occasion to fire his service revolver, he was prepared to use it if need be, but it remained an unresolved oddity to him that as a New York City cop he never had to even draw his weapon but since becoming a P.I. he was already responsible for having taken the lives of four or five men in self-defense.

Just as they stepped through the front door out onto Flatbush Avenue Doc heard the screech of tires and out of reflex turned to look.

Three shots rang out in quick succession shattering the entrance door glass and biting two chunks of masonry from the brick façade.

Doc looked up from behind the parked car where he sheltered to see a '44 dark maroon Plymouth speeding north up Flatbush Avenue. A rifle barrel was being pulled in from the driver's side rear window as they sped away narrowly avoiding a collision with a city cab.

McKeowen ran out into the street to try and see a license plate but they were too far up the road to discern anything except that it was a maroon, late model Plymouth sedan.

Back near the front door Mancino lay half on the sidewalk half against the front of the building crunched against the low step to the entrance.

"LOUIE!" Doc ran to hm. He wasn't moving. "SHIT! SHIT! SHIT!"

Blood slowly flowed from his left temple as Doc adjusted the body so that Mancino was lying flat on his back. "Speak to me Louie! Speak to me asshole!"

There was no response.

Doc frantically threw back Mancino's jacket, lowered the collar of his green and orange bowling shirt and felt for but couldn't find a carotid pulse.

Doc made an improvised bandage from his and Louie's handkerchiefs pressing one folded up over the wound and securing it in place with the other.

Several bystanders scurried over and Doc yelled orders.

"Get across to that dry cleaners and call an ambulance! MOVE!" He shouted at a young man who complied. Doc quickly checked Louie for any other wounds and found none. But he did find Mancino's shoulder holster and grabbed his S&W, snub nosed .38.

Banking on a guess that they wouldn't want to attract attention by speeding up the avenue Doc calculated he could catch them, providing he ignored the speed limit.

But first he'd need a vehicle.

He glanced down one last time at Mancino's face and started running up the avenue dodging traffic until he saw what he wanted. He raised the pistol and side stepped into the outside lane.

"YOU OUT'A YOUR FUCKING MIND MAN!?!"

The burly leather clad man called to Doc as he brandished the pistol in front of the motorcyclist forcing him to skid to stop. Doc continued to point the gun as he spoke.

"Sorry about this brother, but I need your bike!"

"Yeah, and people in hell need ice water! Too bad tough guy, you want my bike you're gonna havt'a shoot me and take your chances with John Bull!" He saw McKeowen looking over the brand

484

new Indian motorcycle. "You even know how to drive a suicide shift, you dopey bastard?!"

Doc quickly scanned the bike and noted, sticking straight up out of the motor on the left hand side of the green and tan gas tank, was the shift stick.

"Look some assholes in a Plymouth just did a drive-by and they hit my partner. If I don't catch them now I'll never-"

"You a cop?!" There was no misunderstanding the animosity in the biker's voice.

"No a P.I."

"Get on!" The big guy ordered. "Just keep that heater pointed away from me!" Doc instantly complied. They did a 'U' turn and headed back north passing a screaming ambulance racing south.

About a half mile later, at the Prospect Park convergence of Flatbush Avenue and Ocean, just inside the park off to the left, they spotted a pair of cars pulled over to the side, one behind the other. The one in font was a maroon Plymouth. Three men were unloading some boxes and a rifle into the Chevy behind the Plymouth.

"That your man?" The biker yelled back.

"Yeah, don't stop, turn here onto Empire and pull over."

From about fifty yards away Doc recognized Brasi but not the other two who took their time climbing into the Plymouth while Brasi made his way around to the Chevy. Doc dismounted the bike.

"Thanks for the lift!" He slapped the biker on the back as he crouched and ran off. "Sorry about the gun thing."

"Forget it. Just get the bastard!" The biker disappeared up Empire Boulevard.

Keeping a tight profile to the few buildings along his right Doc doglegged right, cut through the trees to quickly close the distance focusing intently on Brasi. Just as the Plymouth pulled away McKeowen came out directly across from where Brasi was, noted the license number on the maroon sedan as Brasi was climbing into the Chevy to follow the Plymouth.

In the driver's seat Brasi dove for the floor as two rounds impacted through the passenger's window. He lifted his head, only just barley as he heard someone yelling from across the street.

"KNOCK, KNOCK ASSHOLE!"

Maintaining a bead on the car as several bystanders screamed and ran for cover McKeowen slowly crossed the road and moved in on Brasi.

Brasi, unarmed, slid out of the car and quickly low crawled across the path to vanish into the bushes.

By the time Doc reached the car he found it empty but seconds later he heard a man through the trees yelling obscenities, cursing someone who apparently knocked him over. Doc charged through the bushes in time to see a panicked Brasi dashing across a baseball diamond heading for the pavilion further up the park.

Worried that he could easily lose his prey in the endless warren of paths criss-crossing the park, Doc tried to think.

The nearest place to blend in and take cover was only 200 yards away, the zoo's pavilion.

By the time Doc reached the Deco-Revivalist pavilion dominating the lush plaza he could see there was some kind of function going on, a wedding. He tucked the gun in his belt, covered it by pulling his shirt out of his belt and carefully but casually perused the party goers. He made his way through the noisy melee of celebrants all the time scanning.

He stopped a waiter with a tray full of empty champagne glasses.

"Is there a rear exit here?"

"Yes sir straight through the main doors, through the hall and straight out."

"Is there a fence back there?"

"No sir, it opens directly out onto the street."

"Thanks."

No fence was bad news for McKeowen. He hurried into the building but quickly realized it was primarily offices inside and so, save for the small bar, there were very few people or open spaces.

Out back he made his way the hundred yards out to the edge of the park, through the well-manicured shrubbery and onto the street.

"SHIT!" Doc cursed having lost Brasi

After a minute or so, on the other side of park, down the side street directly in front of him he suddenly noticed half a dozen patrons hurriedly pouring out of a bar.

He hurried down the street to the gritty, neighborhood black bar and made his way inside.

With his eyes slowly adjusting to the dark interior Doc quickly scanned the premises.

The place was narrow but deep with its long bar on the right nearly reaching the rear and tables and booths lining the left. The far left corner housed the toilets which now seemed to be the center of the disturbance.

"What's going on?" Doc asked the bartender who stood motionless at the near end of the bar. Because he asked with such authority, was white in a black bar and was unknown to the locals, the tender automatically assumed he was a cop.

"I didn't see nuthin'!" The older tender blurted out.

Doc shook his head and pushed past the few patrons remaining and on into the men's room.

Again brandishing Louie's pistol but pointing it down he surveyed the two stall toilet.

Two negroes stood, one either side of a profusely bleeding Brasi who lay propped up against the back wall under a dirty mirror. He casually held both hands over a sizeable, gaping stomach wound. The smaller black man leaned against the second stall while the other, six foot three easy, held a bloody switch blade.

"Tell me what happened." Doc demanded.

"It was self-defense!" The small guy spat out.

"Man this honky muther-fucker comes bustin'in here talkin' bout, 'move over nigga!' like he own the place or something! Next thing he wanna fight!"

"Yeah he never was real bright." Doc conceded as he looked down at the now gasping Brasi.

"You know this cat?" The smaller one asked.

"In a manner of speaking." McKeowen nodded.

Doc put the gun away and, being careful to avoid the puddle of blood creeping across the floor under Brasi, crouched down to Brasi who wasn't breathing too good.

"Brasi, Brasi look at me." A pale face slowly turned to look at Doc. Why'd you try and kill me?" The two black men exchanged glances. "Who sent you?" Doc knew the clock was ticking for the dying thug. Two glassy, dark eyes locked onto McKeowen and a broad smile crept across Sollozo's face. Low chuckling interrupted by sporadic coughing ensued.

"What are you laughing at?"

"Jake . . . don't know!" He choked out.

"Know what?"

"Dumb son-of-a-bitch . . . has no idea!"

"No idea about what?"

"She's a god damn. . . cough . . . a kike. . . cough . . ."

"Who you talking about? Brasi why'd you try and kill me? Who wants me dead?!"

"Jake . . . Jake's girlfriend, Gina's a Jew!"

"Bubba, what's a 'kike'?" The big man elbowed his smaller buddy.

"I don't know, must be a white boy thing." Bubba answered.

"Brasi I'll get you an ambulance, just tell me-" Doc watched as Brasi's head slumped to the side and the pupils of his empty black eyes suddenly open to full to stare off into eternity.

"Brasi talk to me! Brasi-"

"That white boy dun bought the farm Mista'!" The smaller man said.

Doc sighed in exasperation and sat back on one knee.

"Now listen to me, here's how it's gonna be!" He instructed as he started to search Steadman's ex-associate's pockets.

"Who the hell is you? Just another white boy comin' here-" He was cut off when his friend backhanded him across the chest.

"T.J. you'd bess listen to this man!" His friend coaxed.

"WHY?! Cause he got a Negro League baseball cap on?!"

"Cause I got a feelin' dis da guy gonna keep our black asses out'a jail!"

"Unless you think you'll like jail?" Doc added as he gazed up at the two while still frisking Brasi's corpse. "While you're waiting for the electric chair that is." Doc stared at them. In silence they stared back. "Wash your hands, clean your knife and dump it where the police have no possibility of finding it. Preferably in the East River. Next," He turned towards the smaller guy as he continued to search the body and came up with a plane ticket. "You two trust the bartender?"

"Yeah, he's cool."

"Then as soon as I leave coordinate your story with him. Keep it simple, don't get creative! They probably won't even take the trouble to check, but if you left prints anywhere start wiping. Don't use the bathroom towel, use toilet paper then flush it. Don't forget the toilet handle and door."

Doc's search yielded a couple of hundred in cash, a handful of coins, a wallet with several forms of I.D. and a small set of keys.

From Brasi's back pocket Doc came up with a plane ticket dated for that afternoon leaving LaGuardia bound for O'Hare at 17:20. He checked his watch; *Three fifteen, Roughly two hours to go!*

"Okay, whoever discovered the body when they walked in here is the one the cops will question the most. Decide who that is and then nobody else saw anything! Green?"

"Why can't we say nobody saw nuthin'?!" The big man pushed.

"Because there is zero chance the cops are gonna buy that. I'll make sure they know who this guy was. When they realize that, trust me they'll back off and stop looking." Doc handed them the money

"Hey man, why you helpin' us?"

"Just tryin' to improve race relations brother!"

"Bullshit!"

"And tryin' to catch the asshole this asshole worked for."

"Who is he?"

"Somebody you don't wanna know."

"What'a we say about you?"

"I was never here but if anybody mentions me, I just came in to use the phone, speaking of which I need a phone."

"Who you gonna call?" Little Bubba was always suspicious.

"I need a taxi."

The little one produced a handkerchief, used it to pull open the toilet door and stepped out into the bar room.

"Pops!" He called across the last man sitting quietly at the end of the bar nodding off and over to the bar tender. "Call your brother-in-law. Tell him we needs him."

Five minutes later Doc's taxi was at the front door of the bar with instructions to ferry McKeowen anywhere he needed to go.

"LaGuardia." The middle-aged, partially greying driver nodded back then pulled out.

Doc desperately tried to organize himself as he wrestled with what he would say to Doris when the time came. Despite the amount of blood he saw oozing from the side of Mancino's head he kept telling himself there was a possibility . . .

Just north of the park he snapped out of his mental wandering, glanced under the dashboard and noticed the taxi was radio equipped.

"Is that radio full duplex?" Two way radios were considerably more expensive and not all taxis had them.

"Sure is! RCA-200! Set me back twenty-five bucks, installation included!"

Doc reached in his pocket and came up with a twenty.

"What's your name?"

"Julius."

"Julius I need to get a message to my girl." He passed the driver the twenty and with a broad smile the driver manned the mike.

"Agnes, Agnes you there girl?"

Sure am Julie Baby!

"This ain't the time woman! I'm gonna put you onto a man with an emergency. He needs you to make a phone call for him."

Anything you say Sugar! He handed the mike to Doc.

"Agnes I need you to make a call for me, can you do that?"

What's the message?

"You're gonna call my office and talk to Nikki, Nikki Cole."

Got it.

"Tell her to call the Federal Bureau of Narcotics agents who came to the office. Their business card is on my desk. Tell them they were probably right about his connections and that Steadman's man Brasi, that's B-R-A-S-I, Brasi is behind the Joules murder and that Epstein's death probably wasn't suicide. You got all that?"

Nikki Cole, FBN agents, Steadman and somethin' about some murders.

"Tell her to tell them Steadman's out at LaGuardia for a flight back to Chicago as we speak. I'm heading out there now. Be there in –"

"Twenty-five minutes." Julius informed.

"Twenty-five minutes."

That all?

"Tell her I'll see her tonight." He looked out the front window at the traffic. "Maybe."

Nikki Cole, Steadman. FBN agents, LaGuardia! You work for the government or something? Agnes asked.

"I can't qualify for government work Agnes. My parents were married."

Speeding up the still-under-construction highway 278 it was as they crossed Newtown Creek approaching Woodside that the radio crackled to life.

Julius you out there? Agnes' voice chirped.

Julius unclipped and passed the mike to McKeowen.

"Go ahead Agnes."

I called your office and spoke with Miss Cole. She called the Feds, and they've alerted their agents at the airport.

"Anything else?"

She says to tell you your friend Louis was taken to King's County hospital in Brooklyn. They took him into surgery a half hour ago.

"Thank you Agnes. You've been very helpful."

Suddenly they came up on a construction site in the road.

"Shit!" Doc cursed.

"What's wrong?"

"I need to know we're not wasting our time! I need to know if the guy I'm chasing is actually out there, he's supposed to fly out just after five which means we're pressed for time, now this!"

"What does this guy look like?"

"Blond hair, blue eyes. Tall about six foot two, well built. Probably dressed in an expensive suit and carrying little luggage, one maybe two bags."

"Sounds like you describing a movie star!"

"He thinks he is!"

Julius again reached over and manned the radio.

"Stymie, Stymie you out there? Where you at?"

Stymie here Julius! What can I do for you my brother?

"Where you located man?"

Out to the airport why?

"How many taxi's in the line?"

Man it is slow like molasses in winter slow! Ain't nobody travelin' today. Must all be at the game! They's only about six cabs here.

"Lookie here man, I got this cat here on a mission and need some help." Julius proceeded to pass on the description Doc had given him.

Okay. What's you want me to do?

"Ask him if he can duck into the terminal and have quick look around."

"You know that might mean he has to give up his place in line? He not goin' to be too happy about that?!" Julius informed.

"On a good day how much would he make working the airport?" Doc pushed.

"Thirty, forty bucks. Maybe fifty on a really good day." Julius relayed. "Why what's you figuring?"

"That terminal's not that big, it's a bit chilly today so he wouldn't be outside plus there's over an hour till flight time. If he's already there he should be easy to spot. He knows me. He sees me he'll run. Doc motioned for the mike.

"Stymie, you find my guy and there's a reward of $100 cash in it for you!"

A hundred dollas?!

"That's right!"

Get your money ready Baby! If that cat is here I'll find him!

Almost instantly another voice broke in.

Hey Julius!

"Who's this?" Julius asked.

Red Dog Johnston. I'm headin' over to LaGuardia myself. That reward offer good for anybody?

Julius looked over at Doc who nodded.

"My man here says yes." The driver reported.

Over the next ten minutes nearly half a dozen other cabbies turned Julius' cab into a mobile dispatch station as they called in to him to ask about the hundred dollars.

Thirty minutes after leaving Flatbush the green and gold taxi slowly cruised the giant circular road that curved in front of the terminal.

"You chasing this cat 'cause he did your partner?" Julius ventured.

"Yeah."

"Why you don't just let the cops handle it man?" Julius proposed.

"You're black, you trust the law in this city?"

"Hell no!"

"I'm white so imagine how bad it is if I don't trust them!"

"Point taken brother!"

Ten minutes later Doc's taxi was making its way around the giant circular approach road that led up LaGuardia's single terminal.

The taxi dropped Doc off and he entered New York's "Air Age Gateway", the large Art Deco terminal of the recently renamed Marine Air Terminal, or MAT, which some referred to as the New York Municipal Airport which had recently been renamed again, La Guardia Airport.

He did a quick perusal of the main circular lobby area but saw no signs of Steadman.

The circular, Carrera marble-faced information desk in the center of the lobby, dominating the central floor space like a giant black donut, was crowned by a 360 degree, colorful, air travel mural fully spanning the overhead wall.

Doc made his way to the ticket counter in the center of the vast room and double checked the flight time for the plane to O'Hare.

"Pan Am flight 107 is due to start boarding at five minutes before five, and barring any unforeseen problems will be taking off at seventeen-twenty." The well quaffed young lady in the dark blue uniform confirmed.

"What time will you lift the gate and let the passengers go out to the airfield to board?"

"As I said, five minutes before the hour sir."

"Thank you miss." Doc checked his watch, it was approaching four-forty.

Doc made his way across to the only café in the terminal where he took the corner table and faced the main entrance. He ordered a coffee, tucked in and sat to wait.

No sooner had the waitress brought Doc's coffee when he watched two guys in cheap, off the rack grey suits, dark ties and black highly polished Corfams enter through the main entrance. In other words they had 'Fed' written all over them.

"Ah! The sheriff's boys are here to meet Black Bart!" He quietly mumbled. But not quite quietly enough.

"Excuse me sir, did you say something" The waitress who appeared out of nowhere spoke over his shoulder.

"No, no. Just like people watching ya know?"

"I know what you mean." She agreed.

"Hey Doll."

"Yeah?"

"What's down that hallway on the left?"

"Toilets, offices."

"Is there an exit back there?"

"No. just the main entrance and the gates out to the airfield."

"Thanks love."

"You're welcome." She smiled.

He casually watched as the two suits repeated his movements scanning the large open lobby, going to the central ticket counter and asking questions then, following a short discussion they headed straight for the café.

In the lightly encroaching November shadows he had to strain to make out their faces. Doc surreptitiously turned away as they took their seats practically right in front of him partially blocking his view of the main entrance but he could now see they weren't the two who dropped in to his office earlier.

Remaining conspicuously inconspicuous they sat one table away from Doc and declined anything when the waitress cam to their table.

McKeowen glanced up at the giant wall clock over the gates. Four fifty-five. No Steadman.

Five after five and still no Steadman. Doc began to second guess his hunch that Jake would show.

Finally at ten minutes after five Steadman entered the terminal and went straight to the check-in desk. With his small handbag he hurriedly crossed the lobby to the toilets, waving back out to the drop-off area outside as he did.

This alerted Doc and he glanced over his shoulder and out into the drop-off zone. Two men were climbing into a '44 maroon Plymouth.

As Doc and the Feds watched Steadman ducked into the hallway leading to the toilets. One Fed tapped the other.

"That's our man, let's go!"

"Be careful, he's no light weight and probably armed." Doc called after them.

"Who the hell are you?!" One demanded.

"McKeowen, Mike McKeowen. I'm the P.I. that's been tailing this guy all over the City and alerted you guys."

"Thanks for your help 'Mike', but how about you stick to snoopin around on divorce cases and leave the heavy lifting to us!"

Doc wasn't exactly expecting a medal but he was put off if not surprised by the agents' callousness.

He mumbled to himself.

"Yes 'Sa, yes 'Sa Mista Boss man! I's just gonna go back to my biziness and keeps my big mouf shut!" He mock bowed and scraped as he turned to finish off his coffee while the Feds disappeared around the corner and down the hallway.

Happy that both Steadman and Brasi were now taken care of, Doc decided to relax and enjoy the rest of his coffee.

A long minute later a volley of three shots in rapid succession rang out from the direction of the toilets. They were shortly followed by a second report of two shots.

McKeowen drew his wheel gun and watched Steadman spring from the hallway and dash out onto the main lobby as the ticket girls ducked behind their counters and travellers screamed and scattered in all directions.

Crouching slightly McKeowen drew a bead on Steadman who turned towards Doc. The tall man smiled, their eyes met and both immediately realized that McKeowen, because of so many potential back targets, couldn't fire. But Steadman could and did. A slight hesitation before two casually aimed shots gave Doc just enough time to tackle the waitress in front of him as the rounds impacted through the glass of the deli counter behind them.

Steadman darted for the airfield.

"You okay?" Doc asked while they were still on the floor.

"Yeah, yeah I think so." She hesitantly replied.

Civilians who had already lined up at the gate and had begun shuffling through out to the airfield were now scattered around taking cover where ever they could as Steadman headed straight for the center gate and out onto the tarmac.

Doc dashed across the lobby around the giant circular desk to make for the boarding gate but glanced down the hallway as he passed. One of the agents was struggling to his feet, holding his left, lower arm and moaning in pain but was giving chase. The other was not to be seen.

A plain clothes cop who had come in from outside was also headed to the gates and he, the FBN agent and Doc all converged at the same time.

The narcotics agent arrived first and dashed past the female attendant.

"Federal Bureau Narcotics!" He shouted gun out and flashing his badge, as he reached the exit so she could lift the bar on the passenger gate in time.

Directly behind was the plain cloths cop who flashed his badge and shouted "NYPD!" She lifted the bar for him.

"M&M Investigations!" Doc yelled as he produced his P.I. badge and ducked through behind the cop.

Breaking through the gate out onto the sprawling airfield the two cops ran the hundred yards out to the remnants of the crowd waiting to board flight

107, and not seeing Steadman among them, pushed their way up the airstairs and into the plane.

Doc who intentionally hadn't made it out to the roller stairs, hesitated just outside the door as he watched Steadman feign to the far tarmac but at the last minute duck left and casually walk under the adjoining aircraft to double back and blend in with the crowd gathered at the next plane crowded around the roller stairs at the adjoining gate.

From behind a luggage trolley he watched as Steadman skirted the second boarding ladder then followed him down the tarmac along the terminal.

Suddenly from behind Doc heard the command;

"DROP YOUR GUN! HANDS UP! GET ON YOUR KNEES!"

He was quickly surrounded, handcuffed and walked back inside, the whole time trying to watch where Steadman was heading. He lost sight of his target once back inside the terminal.

By the time he was able to explain who he was, produce his I.D., badge and concealed carry permit and explain the general situation all he could do was watch as the maroon Plymouth calmly drove off, Steadman sitting comfortably in the back seat.

An APB was put out and Steadman was seen in Mid-town Manhattan an hour later but the Feds lost him in the crowd at Grand Central Terminal.

CHAPTER XXII

King's County Hospital
Brooklyn

oris Mancino was a wreck. She was already on her second box of Kleenex hadn't stopped moving for the last two and a half hours and was shaking so bad she couldn't drink any of the three cups of coffee Nikki had bought her since they showed up.

By the time the ambulance arrived at the ER of King's County the staff had notified Nikki when they found an M&M business card in Louie's wallet.

Nikki nearly passed out when she got the call and it was the better part of a half an hour until it sank in and she could muster the courage to call Doris at home.

Now holding each other and pacing in circles around the row of chairs like a couple of thoroughbreds on a race track both Doris and Nikki ran to Doc as he came in through the ramp entrance.

"What's his status?" McKeowen spoke first.

"They're not telling us anything! They took him into surgery as soon as they got him here."

"Doc he's been in there almost three hours! three hours Doc! What's that mean?!" Doris' quivering voice was almost too much for McKeowen.

"Doc! What happened?!" Nikki asked.

"Three hours is a good sign Doris!" He held her but glanced over at Nikki. "It means they haven't given up and they've likely got everything under control."

"Doc! What happened?!" Nikki repeated.

"It was a drive by. That Brasi asshole you researched, Steadman's man."

"Did he get away? Do we know where he is?"

"Yeah! He's down stairs."

'HE'S HERE! In the hospital!" Nikki shouted, turning heads.

"Down stairs in the morgue."

Just then a voice called out from over by the nurse's station.

"Doris Mancino!" It was doctor dressed in green scrubs. McKeowen waved him over to where he and the girls were.

"Mrs. Mancino?"

"Yes, how is he?"

"Well. I don't know how but he's alive."

"So he's gonna make it?" Doc pushed.

"We've stopped the bleeding, and left the wound open for drainage. There's a lot of fluid on the brain."

"Is he going to make it?!" She demanded.

"We'll know by morning."

"Doc can you give her something to help her calm down a little?" Nikki asked.

"How far along are you in your pregnancy Ma'am?"

"My last trimester the late sixth early seventh week."

"From the looks of you I'm guessing you've no intention of going home anytime soon?"

"NO!"

"In that case I'll arrange a bed for you and give you a mild sedative. But I'm gonna insist you spend the night here in case anything happens."

"We'll stay as well Sweetheart!" Nikki reassured as she took her hand.

The Doctor left to attend to the arrangements.

"Look at this way Doris, from now on when he screws up he's got an excuse."

"What'a ya mean Doc?" Doris asked.

"Now he really does have a hole in his head!"

Tears again began to well in Doris' eyes.

"I love you guys!" She hugged them both.

✝

A couple of days later with Louie still in the hospital recovering, as he promised Nina, Doc had Nikki type up a complete report of events and took Benny's suicide note as evidence to the 17th precinct on East 51st Street to speak with the homicide detectives who were originally assigned Epstein's case.

He was allowed up to the Homicide desk where he explained the evidence he had uncovered. They listened patiently before responding.

"Sorry Mack, that case is closed. If somebody wants it re-opened they're gonna have to get a lawyer and drag it through the courts."

"But it was closed out as a suicide! It's not a suicide anymore! There's new exculpatory evidence that it was clearly a murder!"

"Sorry detective McKeowen it sounds like you did real good here but, right or wrong the law's the law. If your client wants to hire a lawyer and apply for a review of the case . . ."

"Thanks for your time!" He cursed as he made his way back downstairs. "Make ya wonder what side the law is on!"

Doc left the precinct more pissed-off then he had been in a long time. Worse yet how was he going to break the bad news to Nina?

Later that afternoon, at the office, when Nina attempted to write McKeowen a last payment check he refused it.

"What am I gonna do Doc?"

"I don't know Sweetheart, I really don't know."

"Shit Doc! Is he gonna walk free? After all this?"

From across his desk Doc took Nina's hand.

"Unfortunately Nina . . . the good guys don't always win." The rejection on her face compelled him to have to say something. "But things have a way of working out. Trust me!"

"Yeah, things have a way of working out'! Exactly what my grandfather said. Right before he had a massive coronary!" Nina scowled.

The Back Room of

Paddy Kelly

The Oakwood Bar & Lounge,
Cicero, Chicago

The back room at the Oakwood, originally for storage, had since the days of Capone and prohibition had been 'acquired' by Chicago mobsters.

The room was unknown to the general public, could only be accessed from a back door in the alley behind the bar and was conveniently separated from the bar area by a phony wall. A wall with a small sliding panel.

Vic DiMaggio was the man responsible for the door guards in the lobby of the Majestic Apartments on Central Park West. Vic got word through the underground grapevine that there was guy in town looking to set something up with Frankie Costello. The guy was a complete stranger, unknown to anyone in Manhattan, but was not exactly keeping a low profile.

Putting this together with the incident where some guy tried to barge in to the Majestic to speak with Mr. Costello, Vic DiMaggio decided to make a phone call.

"Call for you Mr. Pantelli." The bar tender slid the small wall panel open, stuck his face through the opening and made an announcement to the four men at the card table currently redistributing their cash over a game of seven card stud.

One of the men went to the wall phone aside the back door.

"Pantelli speaking."

"Jimmy? It's Vic down in New York."

"Hey Vic, how'a they hanagin'?"

"Low and to the left brother! Hey Jimmy, quick question."

"Shoot."

"You or any your crew got a line on a clown named Steadman? Claims he's from up your way and that he's connected."

"Steadman, Jake Steadman? Tallish, pot belly, girly blond hair? Looks like a tall, blond Howdy Doody?"

"Bingo! You got his number."

"Yeah I know him, he handles merchandise for us sometimes. Why?"

"He came by for a visit a little while back."

"Steadman's in New York?!"

"Apparently. Couple of my guys stopped him tryin' to get into the Majestic."

"Frankie Costello lives at the Majestic!"

"Bingo!"

"What'd he want?"

"Not sure but, he shows up at the Majestic, no permission from you guys, no invite no appointment and wantin' to talk with the Big Guy? If you ask me, I'd say looks like your boy is lookin' to strike out on his own, what's it sound like to you?"

"Sounds like we need to have a little pow wow with our Mr. Steadman. Jimmy, thanks for the heads up." As soon as they hung up Jimmy turned to his crew.

"JJ?"

"Yeah Jimmy?"

"JJ get a hold of that jerk-off Steadman, here's his office number." Jimmy scribbled across a piece of note paper. "He's in New York so find out where he's staying." Jimmy scribbled across a slip of paper.

"You got it boss. Then what?"

"Tell him you're calling as a representative of Mr. Frank Costello, he wants to discuss Mr. Steadman's earlier proposal. Be apologetic, explain why the door guards didn't let him in."

"Gotch ya."

"Tell him to bring details of his ideas and let him pick the meeting place."

"He'll likely pick someplace in New York."

"If he's suspicious yes." Jimmy conceded.

"I'm gonna duck around to the bar for a beer and a sandwich. Let me know how ya make out."

JJ traced Steadman back to his Manhattan hotel where he re-registered and that he was registered for two to three more days. Steadman was thrilled at the news and with the Feds on his trail was now confident, after a deal was made, he could seek shelter with the heavy hitters of organized crime.

Jimmy returned from lunch and questioned his man JJ.

"Did he go for it?"

"Like a dog with a sirloin!"

"He pick a place?"

"Yeah, he wants to meet at some Italian restaurant, Il Vento's over in Jersey City."

"Jersey City?"

"Yeah, said it's safer to meet outside New York. There's too much heat on right now in Manhattan."

"Very kind of him to let us know about that. Okay you take Little Paulie with you. You'd better get going. It's a twenty hour train ride and-"

"Train?! What'a you still in the 1800's? La Guardia's only two hours by plane! We could be there by supper time!" JJ argued.

"Oh yeah? And who's gonna spring for the extra cabbage for two round trip plane tickets?" Jimmy countered.

JJ looked over at the cards on the table and smiled.

"Tell ya what Rockefeller, I'll cut ya for it!" JJ challenged. "I win we go by plane. You win we go by train." The room fell silent.

Jimmy accepted by reaching for the deck. He gave the cards a prolonged shuffle then set the deck face down in the center of the poker table.

The rules according to Hoyle dictate that the challenged goes first. Jimmy went and drew the Jack of hearts and smiled broadly.

JJ melted Jimmy's smile with the Ace of spades.

"BASTARD!" Jimmy tossed his card across the table.

"Double or nothing!" JJ offered. "I win we fly first class!"

"Don't push it you!" Jimmy warned. JJ knew his limits and so threw up his hands and stood to leave.

"Any trophies or pictures?" He asked before going. Jimmy considered the question for a moment before replying.

"Nah. Just make it clean. No need to send a message on this one."

"See ya in a couple of days Boss!" JJ signed off as h left to go pack.

"Fuck you!"

†

Early the following afternoon JJ and Little Paulie took the precaution of driving their rental car up West Side Avenue past Il Vento's Restaurant in Jersey City before returning to their cheap motel room on Route 9 where they were careful to ask for a back room on the ground floor, preferably with no one on either side of their room. The young clerk knew better than to ask any questions but with it being the winter season, half the place was empty so there was no problem there.

"You wanna go in?" Little Paulie asked later as they sat outside the restaurant.

"Fer what?" JJ challenged.

"To size the place up!"

"To get some lunch is what ya mean?" JJ knowing his colleague challenged.

Little Paulie stood six foot three and weighed in at 280 pounds and could put away a large pizza for an appetizer, a bowl of linguini and clams for a main, along with bread and wine all topped off with a large plate of tiramisu.

"You just wanna eat!" JJ accused.

"Yeah so what?! We peruse the premises, plan the hit and eat lunch! All on Jimmy's dime. We got til six before we gotta come here!"

"You gonna be able to eat dinner in six or seven hours after eating now?"

"What'a you think?" Little Paulie asked.

They parked around back and were pleased to see there was no establishment to the left of the restaurant. Instead the building adjoined the wide open Holy Name Cemetery which stretched for several acres.

Inside there was no 'lunch crowd' per se only a total of three customers, a young couple and a businessman who was in a hurry.

Il Vento's was a classic, Italian-American eatery styled in décor aimed at the middle class dinner crowd. There were no red and white checkered table clothes with candles jammed into Mateus wine bottles for faux atmosphere.

They were served right away, ate and kept to light conversation when dealing with the wait staff. Big spender that he was JJ left a five dollar tip and embarrassed the big man into throwing in a fiver as well.

An hour later, satisfied with

their reconnaissance, JJ and Paulie were back in their motel room listening to the radio.

Steadman suggested they meet at the restaurant at half past six to avoid the daily dinner rush. The plan was to hit him in the parking lot in back of the restaurant.

JJ noted the time on his watch, three fifteen and rolled off his bed when there was knock on the door

"Who is it?'

"Housekeeping." A high pitched voice responded.

"Paulie get that will ya." JJ directed as headed into the toilet to piss.

Quietly grumbling Paulie pushed off from the desk and lumbered to the door.

Paulie's ears heard the dull, muffled crack before his brain registered that he had been shot in the middle of the chest. A rapid follow-on shot to the forehead as he grabbed his chest and gasped finished the job.

On hearing the thud through the partially open toilet door, JJ peered across the two single beds to the outline of the stranger in the doorway. His eyes went straight to the pistol. He turned but by that time he realized his situation he had left a stream of piss over the floor and across the toilet doorway as he fell backwards into the tub taking the shower curtain, rod and all, with him.

"Next time you go out'a town to do a hit don't leave ten dollar tips at places that only charge three bucks for a pizza!" Unscrewing the silencer from the .38 Jake Steadman pulled the front door closed. "Stupid WOP bastards!"

Steadman climbed back into the '44 maroon Plymouth and casually drove off.

CHAPTER XXIII

A day later, with the Benny Joules case closed out, there was one loose end that McKeowen couldn't let go.

"I'm going out." Doc tersely announced as he kissed Nikki on the cheek and donned his brown leather bomber jacket.

"Where to?"

"I've got an errand to run. Be back in an hour or so."

"The show starts at nine sharp! Don't be late, you still have to change!" She prompted.

"The theatre's just over on Eighth. There's plenty of time."

"I just don't want to miss the short before the movie, Shirl says it's funny."

"What time is it now?"

"Five fifteen."

"Starts at nine huh, four hours? Then if you don't want to be late you'd better start getting ready now!"

"Very funny you!"

Doc walked down to the corner subway kitchen, descended and caught the train over to Brooklyn and headed to Wolcott Street in the Red Hook district of Brooklyn.

The dull flash of red neon sporadically painted the dimly lit neighborhood tavern overlooking the harbor as he approached.

Doc took a stool at the sparsely occupied place and ordered a Jameson's.

He was there to meet an ex-fed he knew who could set him up with a meet with a runner for the Genovese Family.

Doc didn't notice him but the man he was there to meet saw him come in and rose from his corner seat but ducked into the toilet as Doc ordered his drink.

A few minutes later the man emerged from the toilet and headed straight for the exit.

As Doc looked around to notice him, he nodded to a short, stocky, longshoreman type back in the corner.

The seated man drained his beer, wiped his mouth and ambled over to take the stool next to Doc's.

"Nick!" He set his Yankees baseball cap on the bar and called to get the bartender's attention. "Two more." Nick nodded back and poured the drinks.

"I'm told you have some information."

"Possibly. Who are you, exactly?"

"I'm the guy you asked to see. Who are you?"

"I'm a P.I."

"I know. You work outta the Village. Got a partner named Mancino. Neither of youse is connected. Which is why we're havin' this friendly chat and sharin' a drink all cozy like." Nick brought the drinks. Doc pushed a fiver across the bar. The barkeep pushed it back and walked away.

Before opening his mouth Doc glanced over at the bartender.

"Don't worry about Nick, he's awright."

"I just wrapped up a case but there's a loose end. I don't like loose ends."

"No smart man does."

"I have no connections in Chicago."

"What makes you think I do?" The man countered. Doc ignored the empty rhetoric and continued.

"A little bird told me. A little federal bird. I have some information. It has to do with the current whereabouts of a Jack 'Jake' Steadman."

"Who's this Jake guy to you?"

"Nobody. Just your every day, average pond scum. Hates Jews, negroes and Asians, is a neo-Nazi, runs drugs and is behind a couple of murders that were unwarranted. Other than that I'm sure his mother loves him."

"So what makes you think me and my friends would be interested in this Jake guy?"

"Because I know that your friends don't like competition and I know that they have a specialized group of people who take care of unwanted competitors. A special group of people who happen to be mostly Jews.

"Keep talkin'"

"I have it on good authority that certain Chicago mobsters associated with the Manganos would pay nicely for this information. On top of which there's probably a good supply of junk out in his Oak Park warehouse that he's been quietly skimming from the people that trusted him with it."

"If this skinny is worth so much how's come you don't go up there and sell it yourself?"

"I got a bad back, can't travel. My girl don't like me going out after dark. I'm afraid of trains. It's too cold up there, you know how it is."

"I see. What's your cut?"

"Nothing."

"Nothing?!" He pulled back in suspicion.

"Keep me on the books. I might need something someday." The contact sized Doc up and decided he was legit.

They tapped glasses and threw back their shots.

"I like the way you do business Mr. McKeowen."

They shook hands.

"You know who I am, what should I call you?"

"Gino, Gino Mangano."

Doc smiled at having made the right call.

"There's one more thing Mr. Mangano." Doc scribbled something on a bar napkin and slid it over to Mangano. This is the address of a secret apartment he sometimes uses to bring chippies around where no one will notice. If you can't find him at home or at his business up in Chicago he'll likely be hiding out there."

Mangano looked down at the number 1492 on the cocktail napkin.

"Where's this?"

"Right here in Brooklyn. Flatbush Avenue."

CHAPTER XXIV

Flamingo Hotel and Casino
Friday, December 19th

It was just after half past two in the afternoon when the taxi from the newly opened McCarran airfield dropped the four of them off at the car port of the main entrance to the ranch-styled hotel.

The three story building sat at the point of what was a large diameter ovoid of about a dozen, various use, one and two story structures including another outdoor bar, a changing room for the hundred yard swimming pool and a sauna equipped spa room.

"I don't know what you were afraid of! That plane ride was fine!" Nikki, now at a point in their relationship where she could, admonished Doc.

"Yeah Doc! They say planes are safer than cars." Louie added.

"Plane rides are safer until they crash. What'a the odds of you dying when a car crashes versus when a plane crashes? Planes are safer than cars is like saying swimming is safer than walking because most people die when they're walking or driving somewhere. How many times you heard," Doc assumed a comical voice. "'Oh gee, if only he was swimming to the office he would still be alive today! I bought him that life vest for his briefcase but he never used it!'"

"But that's what the airlines say, that it's safer." Doris piled on.

"'The airlines say'. Gentlemen of the jury I rest my case." He countered.

The four made their way over to the check-in desk.

"Why would they open such a luxurious hotel out here in the middle of the desert?" Doris asked as she perused the massive overhead crystal chandelier.

"Beats me!" Louie answered. "I heard they had some trouble getting it open but it's up and running now and getting some pretty good reviews." He added.

Nikki pulled Doc closer and whispered to him as they traversed the spacious hotel lobby.

"Jeese Doc! Can we afford this place?"

"Sweetheart I promised you a vacation you'd never forget and this is it! Besides, after five years without a vacation and the year we've had at the office . . . we could live here for a month and still be okay!" She pulled in closer, looked around and again whispered.

"Doc! Do you think we'll see any gangsters?"

"I sure hope not, at least not for a long, long time!"

"You won't see Bugsy Siegel, that's a safe bet!" Louie poked his head in.

Nikki stopped in the middle of the lobby and stepped face-to-face- with Doc.

"Thank you for this vacation! You're a good provider Mr. McKeowen. I love you." She delivered him a passionate kiss on the lips. Doc dropped the bags and responded in kind. Across the lobby near the desk Mancino glanced over.

"Jeessus people! Get a room!" Louie called over as he approached the desk.

Behind Nikki's back Doc saw Louie flip him the finger.

"That's exactly why we're here!" McKeowen commented. "You must be some kind of detective."

"I can't believe we're at the Flamingo casino!" Nikki gushed.

"Why don't you have a look round? I'll check us in." Doc took his place in the short line.

"Look at that huge casino room! It's so dark in there! When do they turn on the lights?" Nikki asked.

"I think the lights are on." He chuckled. "They're low so the suckers can't see how long they've been losing. Go! Go take Doris and have a look around so you can tell me later where everything is."

She took the very pregnant Doris by the arm and wandered off while Doc and Louie paid the deposit, filled out the guest cards and finished checking in.

Minutes later Nikki burst back into the lobby with the excitement of a child at Christmas.

"Doc you gotta come out back and look at this pool! It's three times the size of the Clarkson Street pool over on the West Side!"

"Sweetheart, let me finish checking in here and I promise we'll lounge out by the pool all afternoon if you want,"

"And drink Manhattans?" She prodded hanging on his arm.

"And drink whatever your little heart desires!"

"Okay." She gave him a peck on the cheek and turned to walk away but spotted a row of three slot machines just inside the entrance to the bar room and scurried back. "Doc gimme some nickels will ya?"

"What for?" He asked fishing through his pocket for change.

"I wanna play the one-armed-bandits!"

"Slot machines?! Nikki you know those things are fixed! You've got a better chance at talking fiscal logic to a Democrat than you do getting any money out'a those things! Why do you think they put them near the bar? They're tourist traps!"

"We'll I'm a tourist and a couple of nickels are not gonna break me."

"Which is why you're using my nickels, you socialist!" He sorted through a fist full of coins and came up with three or four five cent pieces then dutifully handed them over and turned back to the desk to finish filling in their breakfast menus.

"Miss, could we have a couple of blank breakfast menu requests." Doc asked the desk clerk.

As he did he heard a disturbance in the inning room. He also notice that Mancino had disappeared.

"Excuse me." He stepped away to allow the next guest in and walked over to the dining room.

There was a s mall group of guests laughing and joking.

Louie Mancino was on the floor, on his knees and was repeatedly bowing to the elaborate, twenty-five foot long buffet table decked out with enough food to feed all of Appalachia.

A pair of Japanese tourists were snapping pictures.

Doc shook his head and walked away.

Not five minutes later an alarm was loudly ringing, security were scrambling across the lobby and everyone swung around to see what was happening.

Doc immediately realized they were all running towards Nikki just inside the bar room entranceway. He followed suite.

"What happened?" He pushed through the still swelling crowd and asked her above the din of the constantly clanging bell.

"WHAT DID YOU DO?!" He questioned a visibly shocked Cole.

"I DIDN'T DO ANYTHIG!" Nikki loudly declared. "ALL I DID WAS PUT A COUPLE OF NICKLES IN AND PULL THE LITTLE ARM!"

Flanked by two uniformed officers the Head of Security scanned the crowd which had gathered and called out.

"Who was playing this machine?"

"We were!" Doc called back and stepped over to the guards.

"We're gonna have to ask you to come with us."

"Where to and why?" Doc made no effort to disguise the challenge in his tone.

"To the front office. We'll need you to sign the release forms." The head guy informed.

"What release forms?"

"The release forms for your ten thousand dollars you just won."

Neither of them had ever gambled in a casino before much less played a slot machine. Nikki felt weak legged and had to lean on Doc as they followed the guards to the front office surrounded by raucous applause, shouts and cheers.

That evening the mood had altered significantly as Doc stood at the foot of the bed and Nikki lay back against the head board reading.

"Nikki, Sweetheart, come on, be reasonable!"

"Sorry Doc, the answer's still no."

"We came all the way across country, spent half a day getting here, over five hundred dollars to stay here . . ."

"Sorry Doc. I'm not leaving the room."

Eight hours after arrival the holiday mood had turned to frustration.

On the first night of their first vacation together Nikki Cole sat on the bed reading *Pride and Prejudice*, for the second time, a paper claim ticket on the night stand next to her side of the bed and $10,000 cash in the hotel safe.

Despite Doc's desperate pleas she refused to leave the room for fear of spending any of her money.

"You can stay hold up here for seven days like some kind of monk!"

"Watch me." She politely answered.

Doc paced another round of the room.

"Let's go see a show! You like shows! I'll pay for everything!" She shook her head. "They got a show right here in the hotel! I'll buy you a Manhattan! Two Manhattans, you don't have to bring any money."

"Why don't you go? Bring Doris and Louie."

"Is there nothing that's gonna get you out'a this room?"

"Yeah!"

"What?"

"The taxi to the airport to take us home!"

"Son-of-a-bitch!" He stomped his foot.

"Language Mister, language!"

"I'll be down at the bar!"

The two couples had booked adjoining rooms which sported a lockable door between the two.

It was near two in the morning on the third night of the vacation, after a fun night of eating and drinking, mostly inside the rooms as even though her $10,000 in cash was safely locked in the hotel safe, Cole still refused to leave their room, that Doc and Nikki were awakened by a low rumble peppered by some sporadic conversation emanating from the Mancino's room. The low disturbance was followed by a long silence.

Doc and Nikki rolled back over.

Suddenly the adjoining door erupted with a loud banging followed by the panic stricken screaming of Louie's voice.

"IT'S TIME, IT'S TIME! HOLY SHIT, IT'S TIME!"

Jumping from the bed in his boxers Doc reached over and grabbed his Makarov 9mm from his holster and scurried to and threw open the partition door.

"Louie?! LOUIE, YOU GUYS OKAY?!"

Doc and Nikki were greeted with Louie running in circles dragging an empty suitcase behind him and shouting.

"HOLY SHIT! HOLY SHIT! HOLY SHIT!!"

A calm Doris, in her night gown lay in a wet puddle in the middle of the bed holding her stomach in moderate pain. She smiled over at Doc and Nikki and shrugged.

"I think it might be time." She quietly said.

"Louie! LOUIE." Doc grabbed his partner by the shoulders and made eye contact. "MANCINO! Calm the hell down!"

"Doc, call down to the desk tell them to call an ambulance." Nikki announced.

"Nearest hospital's five miles away. On these roads a taxi'll be faster. There's always one right outside. Help her get ready." He instructed Nikki.

"Louie get dressed and get Doris' things down stairs quick as you can. I'll get the taxi to radio the hospital."

An hour and a half later . , ,

"Six pounds 16 ounces! Almost seven pounds!" Mancino bragged to Doc and Nikki after talking to the doctor.

"Almost Louie, almost."

Doris and Louie would go home with a happy new addition to the Mancino clan. A little addition who would definitely be baptized and whose name was still being fought over on the plane all the way back to New York.

Nikki Cole would fly home $10,000 richer and secure in the knowledge that hers and Doc's relationship was just that much more firm than it had been this time last year.

And Doc? Doc would go home knowing that the unknown businessman who fancied himself a big shot businessman and who had ordered the murder of a young Benny Joules, a kid he had never met, never known and who had never crossed Steadman, would be dealt with.

And dealt with much more efficiently than the broken American legal system could ever deal with him! Doc pondered.

Paddy Kelly

Two weeks later Nina Twisselman returned to her desk from getting some coffee and picked up the small packet of mail the mail boy had just dropped there.

She smiled with curiosity as she selected a hand lettered envelope with a New York postal stamp but no return address. Inside was only an article torn from last week's *Daily News*.

```
"The body of well-known Chicago
businessman Jake Steadman was found
last night in a Brooklyn apartment.
The victim, who is reported to have
been in New York on business, had
apparently been strangled with a
garrote.
     The owner of the apartment has
not yet been able to be reached for
comment and police are not
releasing the renter's name."
```

Along the bottom margin of the brief article there was a hand written message:

"I told you things have a way of working out!"

Twisselman smiled, folded the note over, fished her wallet from her purse and stuffed the note in behind a picture of her and Benny in Central Park eating hot dogs.

THE END